MIDNIGHT
COMES
AT NOON

BY THE SAME AUTHOR

FICTION

The Last Assassin
The Seventh Sanctuary
The Ninth Buddha
Brotherhood of the Tomb
Night of the Seventh Darkness
Name of the Beast
The Judas Testament
Day of Wrath
The Final Judgement
K
Incarnation
The Jaguar Mask

NON-FICTION

New Jerusalems: Reflections on Islam,
Fundamentalism and the Rushdie Affair

AS JONATHAN AYCLIFFE

Naomi's Room
Whispers in the Dark
The Vanishment
The Matrix
The Lost
A Shadow on the Wall
The Talisman

MIDNIGHT COMES AT NOON

DANIEL EASTERMAN

HarperCollins*Publishers*

This novel is entirely a work of fiction.
The names, characters and incidents portrayed in it are
the work of the author's imagination. Any resemblance to
actual persons, living or dead, events or localities is
entirely coincidental.

HarperCollins*Publishers*
77–85 Fulham Palace Road,
Hammersmith, London W6 8JB

www.fireandwater.com

Published by HarperCollins*Publishers* 2001
1 3 5 7 9 8 6 4 2

Copyright © Daniel Easterman 2001

Daniel Easterman asserts the moral right
to be identified as the author of this work

A catalogue record of this book
is available from the British Library

ISBN 0 00 710348 4
ISBN 0 00 710349 2 (trade pbk)

Typeset in Sabon by Palimpsest Book Production Limited,
Polmont, Stirlingshire

Printed and bound in Great Britain by
Omnia Books Limited, Glasgow

To Beth, as always.
Twenty-five years, and more in love
than ever.

In memory of my mother-in-law,
Nancy Lewis (1910–2000)
who died aged ninety years and one day.

ACKNOWLEDGEMENTS

Thanks to everyone who helped behind the scenes: Patricia Parkin, my caring editor, for her judgement; Georgina Hawtrey-Woore, for masterminding the copy editing; and my Audrey Hepburn lookalike, Beth, for visual, aural and intellectual stimulation.

Prologue
1

Middlewick
nr Kielderhead Pike
Northumberland
August 2001

It was a scene of perfect tranquillity. Even the northern weather bowed to the inevitable and lent sunshine and a gentle breeze to the occasion. It was late summer, and the grass had the consistency of dried straw, and everywhere men were dreaming that the unaccustomed heat would pass away and let them continue with their lives and loves. Wherever you went these days, you'd see them in clumps, inert and dreaming: old men, young boys, and a scattering of men who should have been at work but weren't. Why stay in the office when you could be out here in the country becoming one with nature? It was a day for picnics, for leaning back against the crusty bark of an ancient oak, staring into space, reflecting on life or on nothing whatsoever.

Little bits of cloud drifted in the sky like teased out pieces of cotton wool. Far out in the distance, just above the US base, long lines of vapour trail spread out in even patterns, knitting sky and land together at the horizon's perfect commissure. The planes were so far up, you couldn't hear a sound. Just once in a while, a fresh one would lift off from the airfield, several miles away, its tail throwing out hot flames until it rose into that other world above this one.

*   *   *

1

The little girl's name was Polly. Her hair was curled and bright, her eyes were as green as the hedge beneath which she was sitting, and her new dress was stained with blackberry juice and grass. She was five years old, no more no less, for today was her birthday, and she'd just come down to Hoggart's Field to play with her dolls before the party started. She wasn't sure about the party. All the kids would be there, except the big ones, of course. There'd be a lot she didn't know, and that made her nervous, especially the boys from Holmeford, whom she'd seen chasing the girls from third form on Thursday afternoons.

Nestling beside her in the shadow of the hedge were the coarse yellow flowers of late summer: goat's beard and lady's finger, tall thickets of ragwort, the various hawkbits. The sun shone down on them through a dissolving mist. And the tall stalks of corn rustled in the breeze and made her half invisible.

Her attention was caught by a movement low in the sky, on the far side of the cornfield. She stood up to see more clearly. A little yellow plane with funny, swept-back wings had come out of nowhere and was beating back and forwards across the fields like her mother doing the hoovering. She thought it might be from the air base, which was only six miles up the road, and which she'd visited once, a year ago, when there'd been an airshow, and everybody from the village was invited.

She waved her arms and shouted, and, as it turned to face her, the little plane wiggled its wings as if in answer.

'Never seen one of them before.'

'What's that?'

'Them,' said Jeff Moulden, pointing through the front left window of the Percival Arms. His drinking companion, Malcolm Greenup, sipped his pint of Newcastle Brown and squinted in the direction Jeff's finger indicated.

'What the fuck is that?'

'Looks like nothing I ever seen.'

'Nooah, I'll tell you what it looks like. Looks like a fucking tricycle. On wings.'

'You divvn't think we're being alien abducted, do you, Malcolm?'

2

'What? Like *X-Files*? Dinna be so daft, you great bugger. He's just spraying the fields.'

If you looked hard enough, you could just make out the fine spray falling from beneath the outspread wings. Then the plane would turn, and light would engulf the bottom half of the little plane as if it had taken fire.

'That's just stupid, that is. All the fields that side of village are ready for harvesting. The rest were sprayed only a week or two ago. Whatever stupid bugger he is, he shouldn't be there. D'you think we should tell Bob Longstaff?'

'Aye, he should be told. Let me have my pint and a tab first, then we can go over.'

Dorothy Boustead steadied herself on the threshold of the church, then took the shiny knob in her arthritic hand and turned. The ancient wooden door creaked open, admitting her to the silent world it guarded so stubbornly, and had guarded for some seven hundred years. St John the Baptist itself was older than that, in its original founding. The first church on this site had been built in the days of the Venerable Bede, and named after St John, whose stone head still graced a low granite pedestal in the churchyard. It had gone the way of its sister foundations following the Viking invasions, only to reappear in the twelfth century, a small church without pretension but to serve its tiny parish, a duty it performed to the present day.

Dorothy blinked, letting her old eyes adjust to the dim light inside the nave. She did not believe in wasting God's electricity (installed in 1924, currently available at a variety of economy, super-economy, and off-peak rates), not unless the dark days of winter necessitated it. Slowly, what had seemed quite murky grew brighter and more like the abode of angels.

What met her gaze now was bank upon bank of gorgeous flowers, supplied from the gardens of twenty and more parishioners. There were eighty of them in all, children included, these being every man, woman and child in the village. Except for Dan Hedgecock, who considered himself a freethinker and worse. But even old Dan would attend the Christmas and Easter services regularly, and belt out the better hymns in his old but curiously beautiful voice.

3

The flowers stood in tin vases alongside huge corn wreaths and huge loafs baked in the shape of sheaves. These latter were the work of the Women's Institute, who, having kneaded and plaited and shaped their giant loaves, brought them every year to be baked by the nearest professional baker, Mr Hardwick in Botham, just ten miles down the road.

It was Dorothy's annual task to take the heap of flowers, vegetables, fruit, and other crops and turn them into seemly ornaments for the fabric of the church, some to decorate the pulpit, some the pews, some the chancel, and the altar in particular. And not a star-fruit or lychee among the lot. This was all local produce, destined for a nearby orphanage once the church had done with it.

Making the arrangements would take her all day, but she insisted, as she did every year, on being left to do the job alone. It was the great satisfaction in a life largely devoid of satisfaction in any form, for her to come first to church on Harvest Thanksgiving, then watch as her fellow-parishioners filed in, their dead faces lighting up as they caught sight of their church transformed. She shivered in anticipation: Sunday was tomorrow.

Just then, she made out a curious sound, like some kind of flying machine. Sometimes helicopters would stray down this way from the airfield. For the most part, the airmen were confined to base, but once in a while a few pious souls would get permission from their chaplain to come down to Middlewick to attend a service in a 'real old English church'. She wondered if any would come tomorrow.

The helicopter rushed past again, and this time she was sure it went right over the roof of the church, and very low. The Reverend Hunsley would have to be told about this. What if they started doing it regularly? It could damage the fabric of the roof or even destabilize the tower.

'Where's Polly?'

'I don't know. You were looking after her.'

Mrs Bridges raised her eyes to the sky. She was surrounded by cakes and jellies, trifles and custards, and was wondering what could possibly possess a normal human being to open up their home and lay on a spread for the worst riffraff of Middlewick's

4

child population. Now her husband was saying he didn't know where their younger daughter was, the daughter who was to be the star of the party.

'She's too young to be left alone outside. I've told you often enough.'

'I'm sorry, Jenny. But this isn't Newcastle or one of those places. There's nobody out here would want to harm a bairn.'

'There's somebody everywhere. We'll have to mount a search. You're in charge. I'll ask Sally to join in. By the way, did you ask anyone to come in to spray Hoggart's?'

His face changed colour.

'Hoggart's?'

'There's been someone out there the past twenty minutes, if you hadn't noticed. Where were you anyway?'

'Down at Max Henderson's picking up some Roundup. But what's this about someone spraying Hoggart's? There's no need to touch Hoggart's, nor any of the fields near it. They all had a good spraying last week.'

She ushered him out of the kitchen and pointed skywards.

'There,' she said. 'Now, what do you make of that?'

He squinted in the sun, then made out the profile of the little plane as it flew fast towards the east, catching the sun's rays and throwing them back towards the farm.

'It's an ultralight,' he said, lifting his hand to his eyes to help him see more clearly. 'A Cosmos trike, by the look of it. They're lovely machines. Martin was thinking of getting one.'

'Do you think that's Martin up there?'

'Could be, but why the hell would he be spraying when I haven't asked for any work to be done?'

'Maybe it's a free spray, to get you into the habit of using his new plane.'

'That's possible. I'll ring down to his yard, see what's up.'

'You'll come with me now and find Polly. She seldom stays away this long.'

It was Margaret Ingram in the post office who first noticed the thing with the traffic. Day after day, week after week, she sat, bun-haired

5

and principled, behind her glass-fronted counter, dispensing stamps (regular and special issue) and pensions, postal orders and post office savings books to her small but steady stream of customers, all the time staring out through the shop's one window, her one line of sight onto the passing world. For about an hour, she'd been unsettled without knowing exactly why. Now, it seemed obvious.

'Mr Powrie,' she said to the young man who'd just bought a book of first-class stamps and a clutch of blue ballpens from her. 'Would you mind just popping your head round the door to have look at what's become of the traffic?'

Middlewick lay right on the B6318, one of a string of villages marking out the ancient line of Hadrian's Wall. The bulk of the traffic between Carlisle and Newcastle went by the newer road, the A69, a more direct route that was dangerous in places, and often slow. Many cars left it to join the B6318. And most local traffic found the old road quieter and better suited to its purposes. In consequence, the B road was normally filled by a steady stream of cars and lorries, and the very occasional bus. It was rarely closed, the traffic seldom diverted.

Purchases in hand, Gordon Powrie went to the door. He was a journalist whose seasonal descriptions of the English countryside went down well with the readers of *Horse & Hound* and *The Countryman*.

He stepped out and looked up and down the road for a few moments. Seeing nothing obvious, he walked into the centre of the road and strained his eyes, trying to see signs of activity at either end. Still nothing. His eyes suddenly felt raw and stinging, as though something in the air had affected them. Then he felt the tickle in his chest that became something terrible in his throat within seconds. He started coughing, and once started he could not stop. Moments later, he was on his hands and knees, and blood had started to pour from his mouth. He tried to rip his collar open, but his hand had only gone halfway when it fell back lifeless.

'Polly, don't be so silly. It's time to come out. Your party will be starting any minute now.'

They were both feeling desperate, knowing that, if she'd been in

6

the field when it had been sprayed, she could be in a coma or worse by now. The ultralight was still buzzing away at the far end of the village, but the Bridges had all they could handle in their search for their daughter.

It was beginning to seem more likely that they'd find her in the village somewhere. Jenny was about to call off the hunt inside the field, when she spotted something bright and yellow about fifty yards away. They hurried to the spot, knowing the splash of bright crocus yellow could only be Polly's cardigan. The child was sprawled next to the hedgerow like a bird nesting. Jenny, still wearing the white filter mask that kept out any traces of pesticide that might still be around, knelt beside her and lifted her head.

'Oh, God,' she cried to her husband, 'I think she's dead.'

But he didn't answer, and when she looked round, she saw him on his knees. He'd was choking on his own vomit, and as he did so, his cheeks were turning purple. On the ground where he'd dropped it in a desperate attempt to get it off his mouth, lay his filter.

At 4.00 p.m. precisely three large black vans entered Middlewick from the west. One went to the far end of the village, the second parked dead centre, and the third stayed at the back. They were Fiat 55-13 armoured buses, with antennae and small satellite dishes on top, vehicles normally used to transport troops or police into riot situations. But there was no riot in Middlewick, just an arid silence.

Men (or it might have been women) disembarked from the vehicles, wearing loose white overalls and integral helmets with visors. They pulled out stretchers from the backs of the vans, then, forming into pairs, they spread out across the road and pavement that made up the bulk of Middlewick. There were bodies practically everywhere, frozen in little clumps, a family here, a couple of friends there, odd individuals where they had fallen by themselves.

Half an hour earlier, the ultralight had made a run over the village and its surroundings using thermal imaging to build up a picture of where the bodies lay. They were losing their heat quickly, but enough residual warmth remained to activate an image that could be placed on an ordnance survey map.

They started by bringing about twenty corpses to the oblong

of houses that marked the centre of the village. Meanwhile, an open-top lorry arrived and parked in the same place. More figures in white suits appeared and started to load the bodies onto the lorry.

Another Fiat bus arrived, bringing twenty more white-suited figures. These spread out and began to enter the houses in a search for bodies still indoors, and possible survivors.

In St John the Baptist's, Dorothy Boustead surveyed her finished display of harvest flowers and other offerings. She reckoned it the finest show of her long career, flickering with life for tomorrow morning's service.

She knew something was wrong, of course. She'd looked out once or twice and seen people lying on the road, not moving, and she'd guessed that something dropped by the plane had either killed them or rendered them unconscious. Whatever it was, it must not have been able to penetrate the seal of stone and glass that made the church a sort of diving bell.

Now, someone had come to sort things out. The army or the police, she could not tell. She just sat tight, waiting for them to take her out of here to safety.

The door opened, and heavy feet came marching inside. Two people wearing extraordinary white coveralls and plastic helmets came up the main aisle. She stood and waved unsteadily at them, feeling an immense sense of relief pass over her.

The first figure stopped about ten yards from her, reached into a pocket and took out what looked like a mobile phone. He punched in a number, then returned the phone to his pocket. She watched him speaking as if to himself, into a little microphone attached to the helmet. He spoke only briefly, then reached into his other pocket and took out a gun.

She tried to say something, to protest about how her life had been invaded by all this. The man raised his gun and pointed it right at her, then fired a simple double tap, knocking her back, stone dead before her body crashed onto the aisle floor.

There were more gunshots by the time the new team finished and left. Once the last body had been accounted for and crossed off

8

against the master list for Middlewick, it was time to dispose of the village's 114 dead. This was carried out with the help of a bank of industrial grinders which reduced flesh and bone to a bloody mash. The product was taken to a large pig farm nearby, and within a few days there was no evidence that anyone had ever lived in Middlewick.

The last act came before dark, when the ultralight returned and started to spray everything again. By the time it was finished, a visitor could have licked the pavements and walked away without so much as the least trace of damage.

Once it was dark, the buses and vans pulled away. Minutes later, the first of Middlewick's new inhabitants arrived. By midnight they were fast asleep in their beds.

Prologue
2

Summer continued to its end. The harvest was brought in, sheaf upon sheaf of ripe corn, truckload upon truckload of fat barley. The air was sweet to breathe, not a trace was left of the substance that had killed the village off. In those places where the survivors had been shot, the blood had been cleaned away meticulously. In the tiny village school, the voices of children rang out as before, and when it was time for lessons, the teacher would address her pupils with the names of those who had gone before them.

It was the same throughout the village. Each of the dead had been replicated by one of the new arrivals, each family reproduced uncannily: mummy, daddy, Barry and Bobby. There was a new vicar, a new sub-post office manageress, a new Polly complete with family, a new Mrs Boustead, who tended the church as she always had done. On the Sunday morning after the wipe-out, there had been a harvest festival as usual, and a collection of £97.10 had been taken up and handed to the surrogate Reverend Hunsley, who had kept £50 against weekly expenses and sent the remainder to the diocesan office as he always did.

On the Monday morning, the post van from Hexham rolled up in front of the post office. Jack Hazeldene, white-haired now and slower in his movements, had driven this route almost from the day he'd entered public service. He walked in carrying a small sack which contained any letters or parcels destined for the folk of Middlewick. In his other hand he held a file containing the shop's weekly stock of stamps and licences and postal orders. For reasons no-one had ever explained properly, sub-post offices like Middlewick were allowed only strictly rationed numbers of items like these. It was generally considered a waste of time to ask for stamps on a Friday or Saturday morning.

Seeing no-one serving behind the counter, Jack whistled, as he often had to, to alert Mrs Ingram to his presence. He'd have been happy enough to take his time, but ever since the new regulations were introduced, he was like a man pursued, he complained that he had twice the work to fit into half the time, there was no longer room to pass the time of day, not a moment to share a cup of tea or a mug of coffee.

The door to the rear of the shop opened. The woman who came through was not Margaret Ingram. All they had in common was their age, their bouffant hairstyle, and their pink cardigans.

'Ah, you must be Mr Hazeldene. I'm sorry you had no warning about this. I'm afraid Margaret's sister's been taken ill. The one down in Devon.'

'Patricia?'

'That's the one. Patricia.'

'I'm sorry to hear that. Is she very ill?'

'I think so. Margaret went down yesterday. I'm ringing her tonight, just to see if everything is well.'

'Well, let me know. I'd send a card if I had an address.'

'I don't have that myself. But I'll be sure to get it for you by next week. My name's Elizabeth, by the way. Elizabeth Benyon. Don't worry, I know the ropes. I had my own sub-office till a few years ago. I'll take those, by the way.'

She came round to the side and opened the little door that kept front separated from back. Jack handed her the sack and the file, and made as though to go. It was pressure of work, she'd know he wasn't being unfriendly.

'Mr Hazeldene, I know you're busy, but before you leave – I understand Margaret's sister's condition is very . . . unstable. She can't be sure what may happen one day to the next. It may be a day or two, and then it may not. She doesn't know what to do. If she comes back before it's over . . .'

'What are you trying to say, Mrs Benyon?'

'Just that I'd like to keep on doing things here in her name, if you understand me.'

'Oh, yes, that'd be the right thing, that'd be the proper thing to do. Just keep it like that, Mrs Benyon, and I'll say a word to no-one. There's no need. The office here runs itself like clockwork. No need for anyone to interfere, filling in endless forms and whatnot, and her about to come back any minute.'

It began like that in most cases. A simple denial, a shrug, a smile. Nobody thought to enquire again. This family had sold up and moved – come back next week, and I'll try to find their address. So-and-so had fallen badly ill, and they'd been forced to transfer him to a hospital in London – come back when you can and I'll see if I can remember the name.

No-one ever got the whole picture. All anyone really knew was that the person or family they asked after had gone, which may have been puzzling, but was hardly cause to call the police or set off a national alarm. The people who'd taken the place of Middlewick's original villagers looked much as any casual visitor might have expected them to look. Middlewick was hardly a much visited place in the first place, which was partly why it had been chosen.

Nothing was left to chance. Excuses were made for absences, visitors were invited in for tea and left with an impression of geniality and simple human caring, such that they would never have believed a harsh word about those sweet people in Middlewick. Letters were written wherever appropriate, to relatives and old friends, and replies received. They were mostly typewritten ('I hurt my right hand fixing the car/tractor/television last week – the Reverend Hunsley lent me his typewriter') and the content was taken from earlier letters that had been intercepted and later scanned into a computer. A few were prepared using advanced computer techniques, taking handwritten words from a glossary prepared by scanning whatever was available.

During the weeks of their tiresome wait, none of the new population of Middlewick came out of character for very long. Sometimes a small group might meet to discuss how things were progressing, or to deliberate on a coded message sent by headquarters. Their instructions were most strict on one point, that they must do nothing to excite interest or suspicion. The project had taken two years to bring this far, and nothing was to be allowed to get in the way of its coming to fruition.

On only one occasion did they come close to being exposed. It was during a visit from PC Marsh, the policeman from Hexham Central who had responsibility for Middlewick. Marsh was a soft-spoken man of about fifty who had never aimed for the higher echelons of the force. He prided himself on his ability to relate to people, and endeavoured to use his skills to keep would-be villains away from crime. He wanted to be Dixon of Dock Green in a time so far out of joint it would never mend.

He headed straight for the post office, where Elizabeth Benyon once again spun her tale. On those rare occasions his steps graced the pavements of Middlewick, the post office was his first port of call. Margaret Ingram had always been happy to sit down and chat with him over a cup of tea and a couple of Hobnobs. He'd identified her early on as the village gossip, whose anecdotes about her neighbours formed the backbone of his knowledge about Middlewick and its inhabitants.

His friendly enquiries about several old acquaintances brought nothing but apologies: so-and-so was away for the day, another was in the Freeman Hospital, a third was on a course in Cumbria . . .

'That's a pity,' he said, wondering what the hell was going on. He spoke with a Hexham accent, not so very different from that of Middlewick itself. 'I hope Sammy Robson's not among your missing in action.'

'Sammy?' The woman who called herself Elizabeth Benyon did a double-take. Something had been overlooked. She had an uneasy feeling that the balding policeman sitting opposite her was about to stumble on the truth. No, she corrected herself, there was no way he could discover the truth. But he might be about to lay bare the lie.

'Sammy Robson,' he said. 'Has he done a runner?'

'I . . . I don't know. What do you mean exactly?'

PC Marsh was on his own territory again.

'Sammy sees his parole officer once a month. He's kept it up for over two years now. The officer thinks Sammy's a reformed character. Except that Sammy didn't turn up at his office last week. The parole officer let it go at first, expecting Sammy would be in touch, but there's been nothing. We've tried to get him on the phone a few times, but there's always an answering machine.'

It didn't matter what she told him now, he'd be back, and no doubt he'd be back with a partner. He wouldn't be talked out of asking questions all round the village, making enquiries of everyone, including the children.

They were in the cramped back room where boxes of postcards and aerogrammes jostled with a table, two chairs, and a hob devoted to the cooking of soup in winter and the brewing of fresh coffee all year round. She got up and walked to the drawer in which forks and knives were kept. There was no point in wasting time: give him a chance, and he'd be on his mobile back to base, asking for backup.

The gun was lying where she'd left it a few weeks earlier, still unused. To be honest, she hadn't expected to have to use it at all. But now her worst fears had been realized: a stranger, a man in a position of some authority, was snooping round, asking questions, and growing suspicious.

'Mr Marsh,' she said, turning and looking him right in the eyes. 'I'm sorry about this. We can't let you go, and we don't have the facilities to keep you safely, so it has to be this, I'm afraid.'

He didn't have time to feel an emotion, the whole thing was too unexpected and too gross. He'd never so much as set hands on a gun himself, let alone set eyes on a postmistress wielding one as though she'd always done so.

The two shots brought neighbours running. Within an hour, PC Marsh and his DNA had been removed from the room and given the same treatment Middlewick's previous victims had been accorded. The room was cleaned, the bullet holes covered up, and the policeman's bicycle taken apart down to the last screw.

The next weeks passed quickly. All day the inhabitants of Middlewick worked at their allotted tasks. At midnight, all of them, bar the children, would meet in the old barn that belonged to the man

14

called Roy Glattbach. They would all wear identical clothes, and show themselves to one another in their true mystical light. If anyone from outside had wondered just why anyone should want to steal a village, the simple sight of them so dressed and seated might have given more than a clue. But even then they could not have guessed. Could never have guessed.

Much went on under the cover of darkness. Different labours, different projects. A listener in the fields or a driver halting in the midst of the deserted village and switching off his engine might have heard them sawing wood or hammering nails or drilling holes. Their every action was tapered to a single end, and that end was approaching through the darkness like a hunter creeping through the night forest.

1

Simonsford Air Force Base
1 December

'You think he's as great in real life as he is in photographs?'

Laura Crawford could hardly believe she'd asked the question, as though she were some sort of groupie. But her cheeks felt warm, and she realized she was blushing.

'The President?' Brenda Rothstein looked at her in disbelief. 'Are you kidding? He has to be the best-looking incumbent ever. If you get too close, you'll faint. I guarantee it.'

'But I've got to be close . . .'

'Then you've got to get a grip on yourself.'

Laura was a special agent with the Air Force Office of Special Investigations, and she'd just been put in charge of arrangements for the coming presidential visit. Her boss, Special Investigator Paul Radisson, had been taken suddenly ill, and a senior officer at Third Air Force Headquarters at Mildenhall had given her the job. Over the telephone. Short and sweet. She was still reeling.

'Better than Kennedy?'

'Laura, this guy is Kennedy on ice. He's a stunner, he drips charisma the way I sweat, he's got so much money . . .'

'And Kennedy?'

'Kennedy what?'

'He was a charismatic stunner with stacks of the green stuff.'

16

'Come on, Laura, what's up with you this morning? Kennedy was a Catholic. Waterstone is Jewish.'

Joel Waterstone (his grandfather had been plain Wasserstein) wasn't just the youngest president ever (he had six months on Kennedy), or the best educated (PhD from Harvard Law School), or the fittest (he'd learned to row under Harry Parker, and in his thirties he'd sculled against Biglow and Wood and beaten them). He was also, as some of the commentators put it, 'the most Jewish'.

The first Jewish president: that was like saying 'the first black president' or 'the first female president', maybe even 'the first gay president'. To some voters, the only thing that could have been worse would have been a black lesbian rabbi. But in the end it hadn't mattered, they'd voted for him anyway, or at least enough of them to put him into office with a majority almost as handsome as the man himself.

He'd lasted over a year now, and that was in flat contradiction to everything the newspaper columnists had been saying ever since he'd announced his candidacy. It was astonishing how quickly the Jewish-Zionist conspiracy that controlled Washington and the media had evaporated into nothing. There'd been no coup, no sudden transfer of power to an imaginary Jewish fifth column, no rash of legislation. A year on, and Joel Waterstone was still the most popular president in American history.

The present tour was part of the popularization process. Kennedy had gone to Berlin at the height of the Cold War and proclaimed that he too was a Berliner. President Waterstone had gone on a tour of Europe, and declared that today we were all Europeans, whatever that was supposed to mean.

Meaningless or not, the phrase struck a chord back home. Italian Americans, Irish Americans, Polish Americans – above all, Jewish Americans – all took it as a cue to reassert their ethnic identity. If blacks and Hispanics could do it, why not the rest of us, they argued?

Some people claimed he was playing down their American identity. By way of retort, in every country he visited he headed straight for the nearest US air force base. The US military presence had been cut down since the end of the Cold War, but there were still

17

important bases across the continent, with over 14 installations, 30,000 personnel and 230 aircraft. Everyone with a television set had seen those planes in action at one time or another, whether over Serbia, or in the Gulf, or flying sorties over northern Iraq.

And now he was days away from Simonsford, the most northerly of the USAF bases in Britain, home to the 49th Fighter Wing and its stable of F-15E and F-15C fighters.

'Brenda, what if something happens while I'm in charge? I mean, this is the President of the United States we're talking about. What if . . . ?'

'What?' Brenda had never heard her friend talk like this before. Laura was usually so brimming over with confidence you wanted to puncture her with a large pin. And it wasn't just the confidence. At first glance, she seemed like little more than a woman in uniform. But then you might meet her on a day's leave, shopping for antiques in Hexham, or taking tea in Betty's down in York, and you'd know you'd never seen anyone quite like her before, and that you wouldn't for a long time to come. And the next time you saw her in uniform, you would wonder why you ever thought her ordinary.

'Oh, I don't know,' she said. 'I just had a batch of security assessments from the Air Intelligence Agency.'

'And . . . ?'

'I can't tell you what's in them, Brenda. But you already know there was that trans-European security alert from the 497th three months ago.'

The 497th Intelligence Group was based at Bolling Air Force Base in Washington. It supplied specialized intelligence services to Headquarters US Air Force and other US Air Force units throughout the world. Its job was to provide tailored intelligence assessments in support of Air Staff planning and policy-making, analyzing and reporting on hostile action against the US and its allies. September's assessment had included a warning against renewed threats to US interests by a consortium of Islamic terrorist organizations.

Nothing had happened so far, but with the president travelling abroad, and with London a haven for every fanatic who could recite the *shahada* and grow a beard, no-one was treating the warning lightly.

18

'Is there anything I need to know, all the same?'

Brenda was Simonsford's public relations officer. She'd been put in charge of coordinating the President's short visit to nearby Middlewick and his afternoon in Newcastle on the east coast, when there was to be a display by Thunderbirds, the air demonstration team, and a performance by the Protocol Combo at that evening's dinner with the great and good of England's North East.

'I guess everything was in order at Middlewick. My bosses give it a very low risk rating. Any chance of outsiders slipping in?'

Brenda shook her head. As she did so, there was a roar outside as an F-15E took off on a practice flight. She and Laura were drinking coffee in the officers' mess, next door to the base's commissary building. The mess was virtually deserted. Leave had been suspended until the President's visit was over, and now the entire base was busy making preparations for the big event. Everything that could be painted had been painted, everything that could stand an extra polish had been buffed till it squeaked. In one corner, a group of British pilots swapped jokes. They were here for a joint training exercise that was to be set in motion during the President's visit.

'Middlewick's fine,' Brenda answered. 'Have you ever been there?'

Laura shook her head.

'You should head over some day. You'd like it. I mean, it's nothing special, just a really sleepy English village. No thatched cottages or mossy church or a duck pond. This isn't exactly chocolate box territory. But Middlewick's the real thing. The people are friendly. They're looking forward to the President's visit. Hell, it'll be the biggest thing to hit the place since the Vikings landed.'

'Hope not.'

Just then, the door opened, letting in a blast of icy air from outside. They looked up to see a man approaching them, pulling down the hood of his windcheater and unzipping it.

'Hi, folks. Mind if I join you?'

Buzz Reynolds was the Wing Command's Chief Master Sergeant, the main link between the base commander and the enlisted force. He'd been in the air force for over thirty years, joining in 1971 as a basic trainee at Lackland and working his way up from there. Laura didn't like him.

Reynolds was old school air force, a tough guy type who should have joined the Marines. He was hot on discipline and rigorously enforced every rule in the book, including some he'd made up. The sergeant had never adjusted to the changes that had been taking place in the armed forces in the past decade, and he never lost a chance to make it clear that he tolerated women serving alongside him because the regulations demanded it.

He'd joined the force as a basic trainee at Lackland Air Force Base in Texas, taken their Law Enforcement Specialist Course, and developed a career in security and anti-terrorism. There'd been a spell with the 12th Security Police Squadron at Randolph, then he'd gone abroad, working with the Security Police Directorate at USAFE HQ, Ramstein.

Then something had gone amiss – nobody knew exactly what – and he'd wound up here in Simonsford, 'counting the sheep', as he put it. Since he knew more about it than anyone else, he still had responsibility for base security. But he wanted more, and he felt sure that none of the senior staff at Simonsford really trusted him.

Then news arrived that the President would be visiting. Since then, old Buzz had been filled with self-importance, as though the President was coming all this way to visit him in person. All he really did most days, however, was try to interfere with Laura's arrangements for security during the President's visit.

'We were just going,' said Brenda.

'You haven't finished your coffee. Or maybe you'd like it freshened.'

He sat, still uninvited, and set his own coffee cup down hard on the table. Hot liquid sloshed out of the cup into the saucer. Buzz poured the spillage back into the cup.

'Any news, girls?'

'Not for your ears, Master Sergeant,' said Laura. She too had a largely untouched cup of coffee in front of her.

'I heard the Ramstein visit went off well,' he said. 'I wish I'd been there.'

'C'mon, Buzz. You don't even like this president. He probably doesn't like you. Why are you so keen to be around when he visits?' Laura hated herself for always rising to Reynolds's bait.

'The President is my commander in chief. Or ain't y'all heard of that in your illustrious career in the man's air force?'

'I know perfectly well who the President is. The difference is, I don't just respect him because he's the commander in chief, I respect the man himself.'

'Hell, what's to respect? The guy's a scumbag. What's worse, he's some kind of Yid scumbag.'

Laura glanced at Brenda, but her friend didn't even flinch. Brenda had long ago made up her mind that Reynolds was a moron who really didn't get it, whatever it was. His racial and sexual jibes were, she reckoned, the product of a deficient brain, and, as such, they meant nothing to her.

'I know this is tough for you, Sergeant, but just what the hell makes you think Waterstone is a scumbag? Or was that just some kind of banter?' Laura could feel herself growing angry. Common sense told her to get up and walk away before this developed into something they'd all regret. But she couldn't just sit here and listen to a control freak put down the President.

'Lieutenant, I don't banter. If you want my opinion, Waterstone is worse than a scumbag, he's within this' – he held up a thumb and forefinger and brought them close to touching – 'of being a traitor. That's my democratic opinion.'

'Why don't you get real, stupid?' Brenda's cool was starting to desert her.

'Meaning?'

'Meaning, the man you're insulting has already shown himself to be one of our country's leading presidents. He's been in office just over a year, and in that time unemployment has fallen to record levels, violent crime has dropped by something like twenty per cent, and his popularity rating has gone up instead of down. He must be doing something right.'

'"Right"?' It was Reynolds's turn to get angry. 'You think anything the Yid Kid does is "right"? It's people like you who need to get real. He's bringing in a bill to take away our American right to carry weapons; he says he wants to abolish the death penalty

21

throughout the nation; he's giving full rights to gays, which means we're going to have shirt-lifters on this base within the next year. This guy doesn't do "right", he doesn't even know what right means, he has an entirely different agenda. Morality don't mean nothing to that guy. Did you hear what he had to say last week about abortion? Did you listen to that crap? Jesus, the little fucker must be some sort of Jew faggot that he wants to kill so many babies.'

Laura leaned forward. She was fighting hard for self-control.

'Leave it there, Reynolds,' she said. 'You're about to cross a line that doesn't need to be crossed.'

'This is a free country. Or has he stopped that as well?'

'He's stopped nothing. And this isn't America. We're guests on British soil, and if you look to your left you'll see some RAF types who are hanging onto our every word. If you go any further with this, I'll have you put on a charge.'

'No,' he said. 'You listen. This is a US base: those fuckers over there are only here because we let them come in. If we wanted, we could shut our gates, and what would the Brits do? The fuckers couldn't handle the IRA, do you think they're going to tell the United States what to do? I don't think so. And do you know why they're in the miserable state they're in?'

He left the question hanging. The silence in the mess was palpable. Laura thought to herself that he shouldn't really have been in here in the first place. It was just a courtesy that allowed him access to officers' quarters, because he was the liaison between them and the enlisted masses.

'Well?' he pressed.

Laura shook her head.

'I don't know,' she said.

'They've lost sight of God,' he said. 'Back home, whatever Waterstone and his crew try to do to us, we're still a God-fearing people. We go to church, and we mostly take heed of what our preachers tell us. Over here, it couldn't be more different. Did you know that only a few per cent of Brits even bother to go to church on Sunday? The Church of England is some kind of social club for the middle classes. It has women priests and half the clergy are openly homosexual.'

'Reynolds, this is Europe. Religion isn't that important. But I don't see many signs of moral decay. Who the hell are we to preach when we have one of the highest murder rates in the world, and the Brits have almost none?'

Just then, the door opened again and a man in flying gear stepped inside. Laura's husband, Major Jim Crawford, Leader of B Squadron, had just been up taking his F-15 through its paces. He took in the scene at a glance. Laura had told him more than once of her feelings about Reynolds, and personal experience had taught him to recognize when she was angry. From the look of her, she was very angry at that precise moment.

He strode across to their table, letting his flying helmet swing gently in his right hand.

'Everything OK?' he asked.

'Sergeant Reynolds here was just leaving. Isn't that right, Sergeant?'

Reynolds made as though he was going to stay after all. But he realized in time that his views might sting Crawford into attacking him. He wasn't so much afraid of getting hurt as of finding himself on a charge for fighting. All he wanted was to get through his time at Simonsford without a blemish on his record and be given a posting to a larger base, preferably one outside the British Isles.

'That's right,' he said, standing. 'Nice to see you, Major.'

Crawford said nothing, but just watched him go.

'He been annoying you?' he asked.

The two women shook their heads.

'Nothing we can't handle,' said Laura.

'What is that guy's problem anyhow?' Jim asked as he sat down.

'Wish I knew.' Brenda pushed her chair back.

'Can I get you something to drink, Jim?'

'A coffee will be fine.'

'Nothing stronger?'

He shook his head.

'I thought you were off duty now,' said Laura.

'Not any more,' he said. 'The Wing's been placed on stand by.'

'Stand by?'

'The base is being put on low-grade alert. Haven't you heard?'

'Heard what?'

'The Turks just declared war on Greece. Greek planes sank a Turkish warship just off Cyprus. The Turks retaliated by blasting six merchant vessels out of Athens harbour. They're both NATO countries. If the war can't be stopped by other means, we may have to go in.'

2

Air Force One
Somewhere midway between
Aviano Air Base, Italy
and USAF Simonsford, England
3 December, 08.55 hours

'Mr President, Richard Hope-Irwin is ready to tape his interview with you now.'

Mike Andrews, the President's press secretary, swayed slightly as the great aircraft dipped through a pocket of clear air turbulence. He was a plump man, with vivid red hair and a ruddy complexion. It was a generations-old belief with his family that there had been an anonymous Irish grandparent somewhere, for the Andrews genes were on the whole disposed towards red hair and ruddiness of face.

'Sit down, Mike,' said the President. 'I don't want you suing me for millions if you break your neck. The pilot just rang through to say this may go on for a few minutes.'

'Shall I tell him you've been delayed?'

'I'll handle that when I see him. Save your breath and tell me his agenda. I didn't like that piece he did last year about – what was it . . . ?'

'"Questions Hanging over the Presidency". I've heard he nearly won an award for it.'

Waterstone snorted. He was still finishing breakfast.

25

'He what? You must be kidding. It was a scurrilous piece of gutter journalism. He couldn't have gotten away with it back in the States. It was nothing but innuendo.'

'He says this won't be the least bit like it.'

'Then I expect it'll be worse. Do you really think it's worth the risk?'

'Actually, I do, sir. Don't forget, he's the London *Times*'s senior political columnist, and their United States expert. His column's syndicated to the *New York Times*, the *Boston Globe* . . . He's an opinion former. If you could get him on your side . . .'

The President grimaced and reached for a cup of coffee. It was almost cold.

'My side? He's a dyed-in-the-wool conservative who only wants to . . .'

Andrews shook his head vigorously. Strands of red hair fell over his forehead and into his eyes. The plane lurched more resolutely than before.

'Actually, sir, you'll find he's more complex than that. Word is that he's quite impressed by the way you've been handling some issues.'

'Such as?'

'Such as the political role of the religious right. He's constantly contrasting the way the Brits handle their churches and the way the churches get to run things in the States, and he thinks you're doing the American thing by excluding religious bodies from political activity. It's a kind of conservative position in England. They think it's a bit vulgar to let fundamentalists stir things up, and, of course, they're always worried about left-wing priests. And you won't be surprised to find that he backs you on gun control.'

'OK, you've convinced me. And, as you say, he is on the plane and I'm making a goodwill tour here.'

Waterstone stood. He towered about a foot above his companion, whom he'd known since they were at Harvard together. Andrews had watched his future president row on the Charles, first in the jayvee boat, then aboard the varsity, and finally alone in the most gruelling of challenges. In the year of his graduation, Waterstone had won the Head of the Charles in the single. Andrews had written pieces about his sculling successes for *The Oarsman* and the *Boston Globe*. It had marked his beginning in journalism.

They'd always seemed an improbable pair, the Abbott and Costello of US politics; but between them they'd proved a match for an army of Republican newspapers and magazines.

'You planning to sit in on this one, Mike?'

Andrews shook his head.

'I've still got to set up some photo opportunities for the British press. And we're fixing to have a news conference soon after we land. You need to make a statement about Turkey.'

The President opened the door that separated his quarters from the rest of the plane. Heads turned, bodies straightened, aides smiled. He smiled back. As he did so, he was seized by the elbow by Corrina Walters, his secretary.

'Sir, I have the Secretary of State on the phone.'

'Oh, Corrina, I have an interview lined up. Can't Jerry wait?'

'No, sir. He says he has to speak with you urgently about our position on Turkey and Greece.'

'Where is he?'

'He's just arrived in Brussels, sir. They hope to hold the first meeting of the emergency council at noon.'

Corrina held out a telephone handset. The President took it and turned to Mike Andrews.

'Mike, will you make my apologies to Richard Hope-Irwin? This won't take long.'

He pressed a button on the handset.

'Jerry, what the hell is going on? Corrina tells me you're in Brussels or something. This is way too early for you to be involved in this thing. Why didn't you send Jack Devalera?'

Devalera was the US ambassador to the North Atlantic Council, and permanently resident in Brussels.

'Joel, Jack himself asked me to come over. Things have been hotting up. The Greeks have retaliated by bombing Izmir harbour. Both sides have troops on either side of their mainland border around Edirne. Just after dawn, there was a clash between two Greek air force Corsairs and half a dozen Turkish RF-4s over Paphos. Two of the Turks were shot down. The Secretary-General

27

called a special meeting of the Council at noon today, along with representatives of the Military Committee.'

Jerry Kovaleski had been an academic teaching international politics at Princeton until the newly-elected President Waterstone had picked him out and appointed him Secretary of State. He was reckoned to be a genius of some sort and, many thought, better equipped to handle the rough and tumble world of day-to-day politics than many long-term politicians. He was thirty-eight years old, and suffered from amyotrophic lateral sclerosis, a rare disease that meant he could die before he reached forty. A cure was regularly predicted, but so far no-one had come up with a real answer.

'Why wasn't I informed of all this?'

'The Izmir thing only happened half an hour ago. I was informed of the aerial clash five minutes ago.'

'OK, listen up. I'm going ahead with my tour. I think we should play down the seriousness of this affair for the moment. But I intend to extend my stay in Europe, in case NATO wants to hold a head-of-states meeting in the next few days. Will that work?'

'It's perfect. I'll pass word on to the Secretary-General.'

'Tell Heinrich to keep it to himself for the moment. The same goes for you. Tell me, Jerry, has there been confirmation yet of the reason for the Turkish invasion?'

'Yes, sir, I had that checked by several independent agencies. Our original theory holds. You'll receive a full report later this morning.'

'Thanks, Jerry. Let's speak later. By the way, how's Judy?'

There was a long pause. When Jerry spoke again, he sounded tense.

'You want me to be honest, Joel? She's breaking up. This thing is killing her faster than it's killing me.'

'I didn't know this. I'm sorry. I should have asked earlier. Is there anything I can do?'

'You could divert ninety per cent of this year's health research budget to finding a cure. Or you could talk to that peculiar God of yours and try to pull rank.'

'God and I don't see eye to eye much. You should know that, Jerry. Look, this could turn into one of those discussions. Can I speak to you later, maybe this evening, take an hour to go over the whole thing?'

'Sure, whatever. But the only thing that will help Judy is for some scientist in a lab somewhere to unravel whatever genetic glitch that's responsible for this.'

'I have to go now, Jerry. Take care. And please don't be angry with me if I don't suggest you take a break. This situation is way too serious to have you take your eye off the ball, even for a minute. I'm sorry, but that's how it is.'

'Joel, you don't have to apologize. I knew how things stood when I took this job, and I promised you I'd do my best as long as circumstances allowed. I'm not dead yet, and I've no intention of being so for some time yet.'

The President hung up to find Corrina barely inches away, trying to attract his attention.

'Mr President, I . . .'

'I don't have time now, Corrina. Will you make a window this evening for the Secretary of State and myself to talk? We need an hour. And send some flowers to Judy Kovaleski. Whatever's in season. Spend money on them.'

Mike Andrews was waiting for him, and managed to snatch him away before another aide or secretary found his ear.

'Joel, we're going to have to fit a press conference in at Simonsford. It won't wait till we reach London. Every newsdesk and every bureau in creation is screaming for your opinion of the Turkish crisis.'

'It's not a "Turkish" crisis, Mike. Don't let anyone get into that, it's sloppy and it could do damage. I'd call it a Greco-Turkish standoff, but who the hell knows what "Greco-" means these days? "Turco-Greek" is no better.'

'Don't worry, I'll think of something.'

Andrews opened the door to the President's day room. Inside, Richard Hope-Irwin was already on his feet, hand outstretched, a satisfied smile on his face.

They greeted one another, and Waterstone showed his interviewer to a sofa, where he sat down beside him.

'Richard, some sort of apology is due to you. First, for keeping you waiting. I was on the phone with Jerry Kovaleski just now. I'm sure you can guess what about. And secondly, we're going to have to keep this brief. It's for the same reason. All my schedules are being changed even as we speak. So, what can I do for you?'

Richard Hope-Irwin looked like any self-constructed English gentleman from the Home Counties, though he'd come by his image somewhat irregularly. He and his wife had a small villa in Italy's Marche region. They bought their clothes in Milan, from Italian boutiques that pretended to be English, with fake English names and labels, windows stuffed with tweeds and tartans woven and stitched in a variety of sweatshops in Naples, and heavy brogues almost finer in quality than a decent pair of Church's.

'Mr President, I'm very grateful for this opportunity, especially at such a busy time.'

Waterstone smiled.

'It's no trouble. Maybe I can give you a scoop or two, who knows?'

'Mr President, before we embark on the interview proper, as it were, I have to tell you that my editor in London wants me to probe you on this Turkish crisis. I understand Jerry Kovaleski has just arrived in Brussels, and that a meeting of the North Atlantic Council is on the agenda. Any idea why you've all gone into such a flap over a fairly routine show of strength by the Turks? I mean, something like this has happened before, hasn't it? In '97 and again in '98. And I think . . .'

'Mr Hope-Irwin, we have a NATO press officer on board this aircraft. When this interview comes to an end, he will brief you on anything you want to know about previous tensions between the Greek and Turkish governments. Indeed, he'll supply you with more briefing papers than you can possibly need on the Cyprus issue. I'd prefer to concentrate on what's happening at the moment.

'The fact is, I believe we may be very close to open conflict along a border that stretches from the Balkans through the Eastern Mediterranean. If this does become war, it will be war between two NATO countries, and between a European Community member and a state actively applying for EU membership.

'Now, that is bad. When you look at it from a European per-spective, it could scarcely be worse. But, in fact, it could get a lot worse. If the Turks turn their military forces westwards in order to protect their borders with Greece, or, God forbid, to invade Greek territory, the Kurds in eastern Turkey will start the uprising to end all uprisings. And no doubt that uprising will sweep up the Kurds who live in northern Iraq and Syria. That, in turn, will provide all the justification Saddam Hussein may need to send forces back into Kurdish areas.

'In the meantime, if there is any trouble between the Greeks and Macedonia, it could heat up the Balkan conflict again. I could go on. But I will let you and your military advisers on *The Times* sort out the possible implications for yourselves. Does that help you understand why we appear to have gone into what you call a "flap"?'

Hope-Irwin winced.

'I'm sorry, Mr President. I honestly had no idea.'

'No, you're right. You were caught out like the rest of us. Maybe a stringer in Ankara lost the plot. Or maybe your Athens correspondent was on leave. Now, shall we continue with the interview?'

'Well, I . . . Actually, this does fit into what I was going to ask anyway. Let me think how to put this . . . Yes – are there any lessons for the rest of us in what's just happened?'

'Mr Hope-Irwin, you're old enough to know that this is a lesson-filled universe, even if most of us simply refuse to read the text. Of course there are lessons, although it may be far too soon for them to be clear. All the same, we can already be sure of one thing.'

'What's that?'

'This is yet another example of the dangers posed by religious fundamentalism. Modern Turkey was founded as a secular state. Islam was put firmly in the background. Women were taken out of the veil, modern laws were introduced instead of Islamic law, and Turkey slowly made some progress away from the middle ages. Then, a few years ago, things started going backwards. The fundamentalists were voted into power and started turning the clock backwards, so the military stepped in, kicked them out, and helped keep things straight.

31

'Two weeks ago, the religious right took power again. They used a series of coalitions to help get themselves elected, and the minute they were in power they dropped their allies and voted themselves sweeping powers. The day after they took control, they announced a state of emergency. Everybody thought the generals would step in again. But the fundamentalists weren't willing to be tricked out of power a second time round. They had it all very well planned.

'In the week after their comeback, they held a series of kangaroo trials, as a result of which they executed all the generals and other senior military personnel who'd been responsible for their original overthrow. By the time they'd finished, the only people with power in the armed forces were their own appointees.

'A week later, they declared holy war on Greece. It's a principle of Islamic law that any territory that has been under Muslim rule, even for a short time, must always remain under Muslim rule. That's why Israel is such a big issue. In this case, the new bosses in Turkey have decided to claim back all territory that was under the control of the Ottoman Empire. Starting with Cyprus.'

'Most of this hasn't been reported in the press yet.'

'I think it's time it was. It was kept under wraps till now, in the hope we could get somewhere just talking to these people. But I don't think that applies any longer. Be my guest, and treat this as an exclusive.'

'You still haven't told me what the moral of all this is.'

Waterstone lifted his eyebrows. He grew conscious that the plane was no longer being buffeted by powerful currents. They would be in England soon, and then the real pressures would begin. He did not want to be the president to get the US embroiled in a war from which there might be no easy way of extracting itself. And yet, if he failed to act soon, the consequences for mankind might prove disastrous.

'Mr Hope-Irwin, you have the reputation of being a perceptive commentator on the political scene. Stop thinking about Turkey, and ask yourself what I have been trying to achieve back in my own country.'

Joel Waterstone had ridden to power on the strangest ticket ever. All his advisers had told him he was heading for a huge political

32

disaster; all his advisers had been wrong, and he'd already ditched them long before he set foot in the White House.

The Democratic candidate had defied all expectations. He'd gone all out on a liberal programme, at a time when 'liberal' was still a dirty word in the States, and he'd won a landslide victory. Analysts were still trying to fathom what it was he'd done right and how he'd attracted such a high turnout of liberal voters.

One of the main planks in his platform – and one that everyone had thought would wipe him out at the primaries – was his opposition to the interference of the religious right in political and civil life. He'd had enough, he said, of state legislatures bringing in laws making it illegal to teach evolution in schools, and replacing it with religiously-biased 'Creationism'. The first amendment expressly prohibited the creation of an established church, rendering church and state forever separate in US law. When religious bodies tried to have books and films banned, when they used violence to force abortion clinics to close, when they interfered directly in the electoral process (by drawing up lists of candidates of whom they disapproved, for example), then they were, in Joel Waterstone's opinion, in breach of the Constitution.

No candidate for the presidency had ever dared go up against the religious lobby. And certainly no-one had taken on them and the National Rifle Association. Joel Waterstone had done that and more, and somehow he had tapped a second consciousness among the American people. They had voted for him in droves: blacks, gays, women, worried secularists, Quakers, Jews, and just about anybody who was concerned about free speech and liberty.

He'd broken all records, and he'd left the right divided and shaken. His popularity exceeded all bounds, and his opponents found themselves isolated and stigmatized. Abroad, some loved and some hated him. Muslim states like Saudi Arabia condemned him as a 'Jewish atheist', Thailand regretted his loss of personal faith, and the French awarded him the Légion d'Honneur.

'And do you intend to force your policies on the rest of the world, Mr President?' Hope-Irwin asked, thinking it best to be belligerent while the opportunity presented itself.

'By all means. You may tell your readers that whenever the forces of unreason threaten to draw innocent men and women into conflict, I will use all the powers at my disposal to bring those forces to heel. If we had acted against Hitler in the 1930s, or Khomeini in the 1970s, we might have prevented two of the greatest conflicts of the last century. If it is proved that Turkey was the aggressor last week, and if Turkey refuses to pull out of the war it has created, President Sina Yilmaz can rest assured that his days in office are numbered, and that the forces of reactionary religion in Turkey will suffer a setback from which they will never recover. Make that your scoop, Mr Hope-Irwin. I said it to you first.'

3

The sound of warplanes filled the soft December air, as though summer had returned, and swarms of giant bees were buzzing and droning over the grass. The branches of the trees in Wark Wood shook as jet followed jet, gently brushing their tops as they strained towards the sky. All across the broad back of Scannell Moor, a mess of shifting shadows was thrown slantwise by a host of black wings.

At ten o'clock all noise ceased, and Simonsford and the fields surrounding it were cast into a deep silence. The sky, so recently full of planes, was empty. On the ground, faces were turned upwards expectantly. Up in the control tower, of course, there was no need of eyes or ears: the base had already been in direct radio contact with Air Force One for over ten minutes.

A woman cried out suddenly, and stretched up on her toes, pointing skywards with a shaking finger.

'That's it!' she cried. 'He's coming.'

And when everyone else looked, there was a dark speck on the southern horizon. The presidential jet was on course.

All was silent too in Middlewick. Each of the three roads leading into the village had been closed, and traffic diverted. The main street

35

was alive with bunting, the stars and stripes repeated alongside the Union Jack, up one side and down the other. The street itself was almost empty of people. Most of the surrogate population of the village were up in the old Glattbach barn that they had come to call their Principal Place and their Glad Horizon. Some were praying, some were talking in low whispers, some were handing out arms.

'*O Lord, give us Light in Abundance, from the Morning of our lives until the Dark Night of our existence.*'

An elderly man stood at the head of the barn. Appropriately, long rays of light slanted their way through the gaps in the wooden planking that made up the walls. The greybeard's eyes were wide open, and his face seemed bathed in both physical and spiritual light. In front of him, half a dozen of his fellows knelt among heaps of straw.

'*Let your Spring Light and Summer Light and Autumn Light and Winter Light all shine upon us, let them show every Sin in its own measure, both large and small, let them reveal the true state of every Soul. And give us New Life in body and soul, that we may be hardened against the present World and softened towards the World of Thy New Creation. And that our hearts may be hardened against the people of the present World, and softened towards those who have come to dwell here within Thy New Creation.*'

Matt Pike had made his mind up. It just wasn't good enough, her not replying to his letters all these months, as though there'd never been anything between them, as though the year they'd spent together before that had meant nothing at all. If nothing else, he wanted to hear it from her own lips, that she didn't want him. For, to be honest, he had his own ideas about what had happened. Lorna had been barely sixteen when they'd met, and she was barely seventeen now. Her parents had never really approved of him, and if they'd found out he and Lorna had been going all the way since June, they'd have gone ballistic. He reckoned that must have been what happened, that she'd confessed or had the knowledge dragged out of her, and that they'd banned her from having any communication with him. Even so, what had there been to stop her sneaking at least a short letter to him?

Matt was eighteen. He'd just finished his first term at London university, where he was studying politics. When he'd gone down in September, he and Lorna had been an 'item', albeit in a rather huggermugger sort of way. Only his best friends had known, and they'd been sworn to secrecy. He'd written to her regularly over the first few weeks, and awaited her replies impatiently, but none had ever come. He knew her parents' opinion of him ('Too clever by far for the likes of our Lorna', 'A bit big for his boots, that Matt Pike'), and he imagined they had in some way intercepted his letters. Their hostility also made him shy of telephoning, and though he lifted the receiver more than once, he could never compose himself to dial her number.

They'd met at a disco in Hexham. It had been her sixteenth birthday, and she'd gone with a handful of friends to spend the evening partying. Her parents (as she told him later) had been 'out of their minds with worry' when she didn't return until well after one the next morning. They'd laughed about it when they next met, but he should have taken it as a warning, that her parents were overly protective.

Well, to hell with them anyway, he thought as he buttoned his Barbour against the chill. He lived in nearby Haydon Bridge. It was only a short bicycle ride from there to Middlewick.

'A and B squadrons are due to take off within five minutes of the President's leaving here.'

Major Jim Crawford looked as though life might have been easier. A presidential visit followed by a flight that would end close to a war zone wasn't his idea of a good day. His wife, Laura, couldn't have agreed more. Her husband had flown sorties in the Gulf, and later over Bosnia and Kosovo. He was highly decorated, and a knowledge-able eye could have made out ribbons for the NATO Service Medal alongside the Medal of Honour and the Air Force Cross on his chest. Laura was not unused to the thoughts or the sensations of danger.

But something about this business between the Turks and Greeks made her pensive. And their own lives had changed since the last conflict. Tina, their daughter, was eight years old now, and able to appreciate the nature of the risks her father ran.

It was hard to insulate a child on an air force base from the harsh realities that base had been built to protect against. Most of the other kids up in the DODEA school had fathers too: some flew planes, some sat at desks, some provided the engineering skills needed to keep the planes in good flying order. Already, the older children had started talking among themselves about the coming crisis, which had taken on sinister proportions.

'Do you know where you'll be based?'

'Cervia, like before. We'll be joining the F-15C Eagles from 48th Wing. Together, we'll form the 48th/49th Expeditionary Operations Group, alongside the Italian 5th Stormo.'

'Jim, do you think this is going to be a shooting war?'

'They're all shooting wars, honey. It just depends who's doing the shooting. The Turks won't be much of a match for us.'

'I still don't like it, Jim. I worry every time you go up. I worry a whole lot more when I think somebody may be shooting at you.'

Laura looked through the window, beyond which the grey weather had gathered, as though it had special business with her. She was on duty again in five minutes, but she'd taken a few minutes off in order to pick up Tina and get her ready to meet the President.

'Darling, there's nothing I can do about this, you know that.'

'I'm not asking you to. It's just that . . .'

'You'd rather I stopped flying, left the force, and went back home to Maine with you and Tina.'

The words came out gently. But Laura knew just how much force lay behind them. She said nothing. This was not the moment for another argument. But he was right, it was what she wanted, more and more intensely with each year that passed, each mission that he flew.

The phone rang. Laura answered.

'Captain? You'd better get your ass down here quick. Air Force One is on the ground and taxiing this way.'

'I'll be there.'

Laura hung up and smiled nervously at her husband.

'This is it,' she said. 'Oh my God, I've never been so nervous in my life. What if I say the wrong thing? Or do something awful?'

'You'll be fine, don't worry. And look who's here.'

Tina appeared at the foot of the stairs. She was small, beautiful, and quite unlike either of her parents. They'd adopted her at the age of two months, soon after learning that Laura could never have children of her own. There'd been no details available of Tina's background, except that she came from a Hispanic family, Mexican immigrants for whom life had somehow gone badly wrong in Texas, probably for financial reasons, or perhaps because of sickness.

'Hi, Mom,' she said. 'You look terrific. None of the other mothers will be half as well turned out.' She glanced at her father. 'Dad, what are you doing here? Shouldn't you be meeting the President?'

She was dressed in a long calico dress that had been bought for her a month earlier in York's exclusive dress shop, Droopy & Brown's. Catching sight of her in it for the first time, Jim felt the pang he always did when, all unsuspecting, he noticed how his little girl was a woman in miniature, and knew that, in time, he would lose her.

'The President can wait,' he said, reaching out to brush her cheek, a gesture she had recently begun to rebel against. 'I wanted to see how beautiful you looked.'

'And?'

'And you look stunning.'

'What about Mom?'

'Your mother is always stunning, and she knows it. Even in uniform. You, on the other hand, are frequently anything but.'

'Dad, I've got to go. We're meeting in the school hall in five minutes.'

She rushed off, overwhelmed by the prospect of meeting the President face to face: she'd overheard her parents and teachers talking about him with the sort of admiration people in her world reserved for pop stars or movie actors.

'Stunning?' said Laura. 'Can I have that in writing?'

'You can have it in triplicate. Or maybe you'd rather I took you to bed right this moment and demonstrated?'

'And miss the most important man in the world?'

He took her gently in his arms and pressed her against him.

'The most important?' he asked.

'Well, maybe the second most important.'

He kissed her then, a long, passionate kiss that reminded them both that today's real event would not be the presidential visit, but the flight that would take him back to the edge of war.

They drew apart reluctantly.

'God, Jim, I hate this. You've got enough medals already. You're an all-American hero, you could stand for president yourself. If this blows over, will you promise me you'll request a transfer?'

'I've told you, Laura, if I quit flying, I have to leave the force. I couldn't stand to be grounded.'

'And I've told you to ask for a job as an instructor. There's no shame in that.'

He reached out and brought her head forward until their foreheads touched.

'Maybe this isn't the best time to be discussing this. I've got to get over there now. So have you.'

She ventured a reluctant smile.

'OK,' she said. 'Let's talk when the war's over.'

Matt Pike stood outside his girlfriend's door, wondering what the hell was going on in Middlewick. He'd arrived in the village to find it deserted and the main street crowded with bunting. For several moments, he had felt as though he'd stumbled onto some weird film set, and almost expected to find that the buildings were nothing more than flats propped up against the grey sky. And then a faint memory had stirred, and he'd realized the US President was due to fly in to Simonsford USAF base some time around now. Had everyone gone over there to welcome him, drafted in perhaps by the Yanks, to represent the surrounding populace?

He rang the doorbell twice, setting off a jangling sound deep inside the house. In days past, he'd left Lorna here on many occasions, always hanging back so her parents would not know she'd been seeing anyone. Her father owned a small agricultural provisions store a few doors away from the house; Matt had seen him a few times from a distance, and had felt himself intimidated even then by Ron Howie's manifest bulk and furrowed brow. He was, according to Lorna, a drunkard and a wife-beater who only spared his daughter the back of his hand because he was frightened what they might say when she went into school the next day. Matt feared other forms of abuse, but had never been able to bring himself to ask Lorna, not even after they started sleeping together.

He was about to walk away and try in the shop instead, when he noticed the door was unlatched. Nervously, he put his hand to it and pushed. It swung back without restraint of any kind. He hesitated only a few more seconds, then steeled himself to step inside. In a sense, he thought he had a right. He was determined to find Lorna, and worried that something untoward might have happened to her.

The door closed behind him, leaving him standing in a dark and narrow entrance hall that led down to the kitchen. The house was silent, and a little cold, and Matt thought that, if he had been imaginative, he might have felt ghosts pass through the walls.

'Hallo, is anyone at home?' he called, his voice weakened by his own timidity. 'Lorna, are you here? It's Matt.'

But no-one answered. He thought to leave again, then felt prompted to dash upstairs and look for Lorna's bedroom. Something told him he might find some sort of clue there.

There was only one steep flight of stairs that led onto a landing, then three more steps and he was in the corridor off which the bedrooms and bathroom sat watching silently. The bathroom door was open. He opened the door next to it and found a medium-sized room stuffed with a large double bed, the parents' room.

The door next to that had a single bed, and for a moment Matt thought he'd found Lorna's room. Then he noticed the decorations and the photographs, and he realized that her parents must sleep in separate rooms.

There was only one more room to investigate. He pushed open the door to find what in part he had expected, a teenage girl's bedroom, decorated with boy band posters and soft toys and Newcastle United regalia. Lorna was a big Newcastle fan and mad about Alan Shearer; she tried to get up to town every time there was a home match, and many of their liaisons had taken place before or after a fixture.

It all seemed normal. Matt started looking round for a scrap of paper on which to write a note alerting Lorna to his presence. There was nothing on the dressing table. He crossed to the bedside table, and as he did so he looked up and realized something was wrong. Above the headboard, carved from naked wood and hanging by a two-inch nail was a crucifix, and above it a sheet of white card pinned to the wall by four drawing pins. The card bore a saying of some sort.

He shal not spare the Wyked.

Matt caught his breath. Never, in all the time he'd known her, had he heard Lorna express religious sentiments or entertain a belief in the supernatural. On the contrary, she'd expressed contempt for the Sunday school to which she'd been forcibly marched as a child, and had about as much an idea of Christ, the crucifixion, or the resurrection as the nearest Hindu.

He heard a noise behind him, a footstep or something similar. No-one said anything to him, but he knew for certain someone was there. Lorna, perhaps. Or her father. He turned slowly, bracing himself for the very worst.

The worst was more dreadful than he could have anticipated. It wasn't Lorna behind him, and it wasn't her father, and to be honest, he wasn't sure just what the hell it was. But one thing he did know, and that was that the gun pointing in his direction was real.

'Kneel down,' the figure said.

Matt felt a stream of urine pass down his leg. He tried to speak, but his mouth could not form words, and sounds would not issue from his throat.

'Kneel as if to pray,' the figure said.

Matt knelt. The figure lowered the gun and placed it against the crown of his head.

'Praise the Lord in all His Wonderments,' the figure shouted.

4

'Mr President, may I introduce you to Colonel Plato Perodeau, my vice commander.'

Harry Fujiyama had been commander of 49th Fighter Wing for three years now. He stood nervously beside his president, fervently praying that nothing would go wrong during the visit. There had been whispers that he was in line for promotion to Brigadier General and a transfer back to a major US base. But he knew that all it took was a cockup today for his entire future to be undermined.

'That's an unusual name, sir,' said the President. 'Looks to me as though you had philosophical parents.'

'Well, not exactly, sir.' Plato had gone red, although it was the sort of remark he had come to expect. He often wondered why he hadn't changed his name when he was younger, when it was still possible to get away with it.

'How's that?'

'Sir, my father thought Plato was a dog in a Walt Disney cartoon. If you understand me, sir.'

'I understand you one hundred per cent, Colonel. Where are you from? Sounds like Louisiana to me.'

'Yes, sir. Thibodaux, Louisiana, sir.'

'Hell, no. We're almost next-door neighbours.'

The colonel looked puzzled. Everyone knew that President Waterstone came from Boston.

'My family used to fly down there once or twice a year. We had an old cabin down on Six Mile Lake, just outside Morgan City. *Vous parlez Cajun, n'est-ce pas?*'

'*Mais, bien sûr.* Isn't that remarkable. You never can tell who's on the other side of the magnolia tree. I guess you don't get to go down there much these days.'

'Haven't been there since I was fifteen years old. I still send Christmas cards every year, though. You get back much, *cher*?'

Perodeau grinned. Being called *cher* by the President was the biggest compliment he'd ever had.

'When I can, sir. But the kids are growing away. More English now than Cajun. They speak English all the time and listen to rap music more often than Zydeco.'

'An old Louisiana friend of mine told me the *fais do-dos* are dying out.'

'They're pretty well dead. Some restaurants still feature that style of dancing, and the parish fairs.'

'Colonel, are you old enough to remember swamp pop?'

'Well, sir, not really, sir. But my daddy used to listen to it some. He had a big collection of records, old 45s. He'd play them some evenings during the week, then he'd take my mother dancing on a Friday or a Saturday night. They'd go down to the Purple Peacock in Eunice, sometimes the Green Lantern over in Lawtell, get back early hours of the morning. He always said he'd take me when I was older, but he upped and died when I was sixteen.'

'You ever hear Jivin' Gene sing "Breaking Up is Hard to Do"?'

'Yes, sir, my daddy had that record. Used to play it over and over. Believe it was the only hit old Gene ever had.'

'A great song all the same. Sometime, if you're back at home, I'd like to come down and relive some memories.'

'You're more'n welcome, sir. My mother still lives down there in the old house. You'd be mighty welcome.'

'We'll have to do something about that, Colonel. Well, I've got to move on. It's been good talking to you.'

'*Bon Ton Rouley*, Mr President.'

'Let the good times roll for you too, Colonel.'

Standing a few feet away, Laura watched her president take Plato Perodeau's hand and seal the bond he'd forged in those few seconds

44

standing on a strip of cold tarmac. It was now clearer to her than ever why people voted for the man. She could see that Perodeau, a crusty Southern-bred Republican, had been charmed out of his senses by Waterstone's easy manner and disarming smile.

As Waterstone moved along the line of the Wing's leadership, Laura saw it happen again and again. The President had something to say to everyone, and he made it seem that, instead of being driven by a punishing schedule, he had all the time in the world to chat with his fellow-Americans.

Laura was equally impressed by the President's wife, Rebecca. Up close, she was more beautiful than any of her photographs let on. At a distance, Laura watched her move among the junior ranks, shaking hands and smiling a radiant smile that did not for a moment seem forced. Laura noticed something else as well, something so discreet she almost felt embarrassed to have stumbled on it. From time to time either the President would look up, or his wife, and whichever way round it was, the other would look up a moment later, and their eyes would meet for half a second before it was time to move on to the next airman or airwoman in line.

'Colonel Sam Mercer is our Logistics Group Commander . . . May I introduce Colonel Hastings Byrne, the Wing's Support Group Commander . . . Colonel Samantha Bernstein, Medical Group Commander . . . Chief Master Sergeant Buzz Reynolds . . . My British liaison, Squadron Leader Dafydd Jones.'

'*Bora da*, Squadron Leader. *Sut yda chi?*'

The Welshman looked at the President in astonishment.

'*Bora da*,' he said. '*Roeddwn ddim yn gwybod eich bod yn siarad Cymraeg*. I didn't know you spoke Welsh.'

'I've about exhausted my vocabulary. But I wanted you to feel at home. You know how much we all depend on you Brits. And I hear you've been having something of a personal success recently.'

Jones looked puzzled for a moment, then it dawned on him what the President must be referring to.

'Oh, you mean the Eisteddfod? Our choir came first in the Male Voice finals.'

'I just love choral music. Welsh choirs are among my favourites, next to the Russians. Maybe you can send me a tape of your performance, see if you can beat them to number two position.'

Another promise made, another bond sealed. It didn't matter that he hadn't spent that much time in Louisiana, that aides had taught him Welsh, that he really disliked choral music, or that he had private misgivings about the role of the British within NATO: he put in the hard work necessary to show that he cared about the people he met, and treated them as individuals.

'Major Crawford is our most decorated pilot, sir. He fought in the Gulf, in Bosnia, and in Kosovo.'

'Well, Major, I don't often see a chestful of ribbons like yours. You must have done an awful lot of flying.'

'Yes, sir. A lot, sir.'

'That your wife back there?'

Jim nodded. His mouth felt drier than it had during the worst sortie he'd flown.

'Yes, sir.'

'Well, you're a lucky man. If I had a woman like that, I'd be tempted to ask for a desk job.'

'Yes, sir, thank you, sir. I'll do that, sir.'

'No you won't, Major. You love flying too much. What do you fly?'

'F-15C, sir.'

'It's one hell of a plane.'

'Yes, sir, it is, sir. Have you ever flown in one, sir?'

'I've not had that privilege.'

'Well, sir, if you'd ever like to go up in one, I'm at your disposal. There's a second sent on a 15D or E.'

'I'll take you up on that one day,' Waterstone laughed, as much to conceal his fear of flying as anything. 'In the meantime, I'm going to keep your wife close with me for the rest of the afternoon. That OK with you?'

'You're the boss, sir.'

'So they tell me. But ask *my* wife, and she'll tell you different.'

The President bent forward and scrutinized the rows of ribbons running like coloured bar code strips across Jim's chest. Jim saw the hesitation on Waterstone's face as he straightened. He could sense the other man's uncertainty, and he knew that whatever came next would not have been rehearsed.

'Major, I see not all your decorations are Air Force. What's this one? The Navy Cross?'

'If that's a blue and white stripe you're looking at, then, yes, sir.'

'And this looks like a naval version of the Distinguished Service Medal. Does this mean you were a sailor before you took up flying?'

'Not exactly, sir. I served with the Marine Corps a few years. I joined the Corps as soon as I could and stayed two years. By then I knew that, however good a Marine I might hope to become, I'd always be a better pilot. So I transferred to the Air Force, and here I am.'

'Tell me, Major – did you find the Marine Corps brutalized you?'

'Well, I . . .' Jim's answer petered out. Here he was, surrounded by an assortment of top brass and Secret Service work-out freaks, and he was being asked to shop the US Marine Corps. By the President.

'Don't worry, Major, you won't get into any trouble for an honest answer. You have my word. This is just between the two of us.'

Imperceptibly, the President's entourage dropped back.

'If I'm . . . well, sir, I . . . The answer is, yes, sir. I believe the Marine Corps is a brutalizing institution.'

'It produces good soldiers, doesn't it?'

'Yes, sir. But it also produces misfits and men with a hard-on for danger. If you'll forgive my choice of expression, sir.'

'No offence taken. Good soldiers, but brutes, is that about it?'

'Yes, sir, some of them, sir.'

'But in an emergency . . . ?'

'I'd want them around. I would definitely feel better knowing they were there. Or about to arrive.'

'Like the fifth cavalry?'

'Like that, sir.'

'Tell me something else, Major. A lot of servicemen your age,

47

when I meet them, a lot of them have Gulf War medals. As far as I can tell, you're not wearing one.'

'No, sir.'

'Is there a reason for that? Where did you win your Medal of Honour?'

'Fighting over Iraq, sir. I shot down some enemy planes, sir.'

'But you don't have a Liberation of Kuwait medal.'

'No, sir.'

It was obvious Jim was feeling uncomfortable, but the President would not let up.

'Mind telling me the reason for that, Major?'

'Between ourselves, Mr President?'

'It goes no further. Trust me.'

'Well, sir, I was offered a Liberation of Kuwait medal from Saudi and from Kuwait, but I had to turn them down politely.'

'Why was that? I'd like to know.'

'Sir, the Saudis treated our military personnel like dirt. They wouldn't let Jewish Americans on their soil, and they wouldn't let Christian Americans get together to sing hymns. My wife is Jewish, sir, and I was brought up a Christian, though I don't go to church much nowadays. I thought that was wrong, and I thought it was wrong to fight a war for a dictatorship like that. As for the Kuwaitis, they just jetted off to holiday hotels and waited beside swimming pools while we went in and did the killing and dying for them. I was willing to die fighting Saddam Hussein, but I'm not willing to wear medals from other dictators in the same row as American medals. That's what I think, sir. I'm sorry, sir.'

The President said nothing at first, then he took Jim's hand and shook it firmly.

'Thank you, Major. Thank you for being honest. That's between ourselves. I'll see it stays that way. I think the Air Force was lucky and the Marine Corps lost out. Keep up the good work. I'll talk with your wife later, see what she has to say about you.'

'Yes, sir, thank you, sir.'

Waterstone started to move on.

'Sir?' Jim had to know, even at the risk of causing offence.

'Yes, Major?'

'I have to know, sir. Were you . . . ? Did you . . . ?'

'Serve in the Corps? Yes, I did, Major. But it didn't brutalize me. I didn't let it. It's possible to be a man in spite of all that.'

Jim came to full attention and saluted. The President walked on. Laura looked at her husband with an expression of mock horror on her face. Near her, Chief Master Sergeant Buzz Reynolds stared at Jim with a look of pure disgust and ill-disguised hatred.

The seating arrangements for lunch had been made according to guidelines issued by White House protocol staff, and not on the basis of Air Force rules of precedence. Feathers had been ruffled as a result. Some individuals had gone into a sulk, others had protested to the base commander, and one had turned up uninvited and was being seated at the bottom table.

Laura found herself at the top table, next to the First Lady, with Tina on the other side.

'I really can't fathom how you do this, Laura. You both have demanding service careers, yet you have such a lovely daughter. Where do you find the time?'

'Well, um, the DODEA grade school here is really great. They understand the special needs of children on a base like this. It's a big compensation.'

'To hell with the school. Don't get me wrong, I'm sure they do a great job, but you created Tina, I can tell. You must spend most of your spare time with her.'

'Yes, we both do. It's not a chore or anything.'

'I'm sure it's not. I have two of my own. They're grown up now, of course. Russell just graduated from MIT, and his sister just started modelling. Seventeen, she acts like she's thirty. Can you believe it? They don't feel like my own children any longer. And now with all this president's wife nonsense, I honestly think I've lost them. There's never time to be around.'

'Oh, maybe later . . .'

Rebecca shook her head.

'I'm already down in history as the world's worst Jewish mother. Which is what my own mother said would become of me.'

'What did you do before you became First Lady?'

'Oh, I was the faithful spouse of a presidential candidate, and before that a Senator's wife, and before that a Congressman's wife. Try not to look so impressed. It's the only job on offer. But before that I taught high school for six years. That's what I was doing when I met Joel.'

'What did you teach?'

'Civics. It was the love of my life. Or so I thought. By the way, what is this?'

She spooned a portion of brown grains from her plate.

'Oh, that's something called haggis. It's more a Scottish thing. I understand this is the first kosher haggis in recorded history.'

'Good for it. It's quite nice. What's . . . ?'

'You don't want to know. Just eat and enjoy.'

'Now you sound like my mother.'

In the barn in Middlewick, no-one was eating. They had vowed to fast that day, to lend them strength of spirit over the days that were to come, days that might not have an end. The old man led the prayers as before.

Matt Pike sat on a stool in a dark corner, expertly tied with baling twine, and gagged with a strip torn from an empty feed sack. A man of about forty, his face stamped with authority, his dark suit a contrast to the white garments of the others in the barn, sauntered across and pulled up a stool next to Matt.

'Don't worry, son,' he said. Matt could not place his accent. Eastern European, perhaps? Or Scandinavian? 'There's not long to go. I'll make sure you die quickly, without pain. You will die in a cause, for a good reason. Rest assured. Your life will not have been entirely wasted. Even after you die, we have a use for you.'

Matt tried to speak, tried to plead for all that was left to him, the mere sensation of being alive, but all that issued from behind his gag were low grunts without meaning. Tears slipped from his eyes, but he could not wipe them away, and the stranger did not care.

'*O Lord Highest above High, Brightest above Bright, the Soft Murmur of Your Breath is in our hertes, and the Light of Your Herte is in our Breasts.*' The old man's voice droned on, punctuated from time to time by the ecstatic cries of his little flock. The time was upon them. Hallelujah.

5

Sorting out who went where at lunch had been nothing compared to knocking the President's visit to Middlewick into manageable shape. Back home, a presidential cavalcade involved something like four full-length limousines, a couple of staff cars, around six motorcycle outriders, a pair of surveillance vans, and a land cruiser carrying a counter-assault team. The President would be outnumbered by a host of Secret Service agents, some in vehicles, some on foot, their trained eyes scouring every inch of the street, while they spoke back to base or to one another through tiny lapel microphones. They dressed in dark grey suits, wore aviator shades, and made their one and only fashion statement through man-made fibres, narrow ties, and button-down collars. It was as though a special breed of Mormon missionary had been sent down from Joseph Smith heaven to baptize the entire north-east of England. The stuff of movies.

But out here in wildest Northumberland, it all seemed a bit heavy-handed. The President himself had wanted to do a simple walkabout in Middlewick that would allow him to shake every hand in the place.

'Who the hell is going to assassinate me in a place called Middlewick? Almost nobody knows I'm here. I don't need any of your rednecks boxing me in today.'

So he'd told the leader of the Secret Service team that was accompanying him on his European travels, a tall Lutheran called Agent Bergman, while they were still descending into their flight-path for Simonsford. It wasn't the first time he'd argued for something similar, and it wasn't the first time he found himself overruled. Presidents are precious commodities, and Secret Service officers don't stand in awe of them.

In the end, a compromise was reached. They'd use two Lincoln limousines, one for the President and the First Lady, the other as the Secret Service backup. There'd be four motorcycle riders, supplied by the Northumberland police, two several yards in front of the first Lincoln, two flanking it. A black Chevy Suburban with heavily tinted windows would follow up, carrying half a dozen SAS soldiers who'd been sent up from Herefordshire the night before. About a mile behind, there would be an ambulance. It followed the President everywhere, always at a discreet distance, ready to treat him in the event of an injury, stroke, or heart attack, and capable of rushing him to the nearest major hospital.

The Lincolns, the Chevy, and the ambulance had been flown in to Simonsford that morning, about four hours ahead of the President. They'd already been checked over, their bodywork polished to perfection, and their engines tuned to within an inch of their lives.

'I also want four walkers, two either side of your car,' insisted Bergman.

'No, no walkers. They're intimidating.'

'I still think . . .'

'Mr Bergman, this is a twenty-minute visit to Hicksville. These people are farmers who, frankly, could care less about me. I'm a passing curiosity, that's all. Believe me, they'll be back in their fields within five minutes of my departure.'

'Sir, you forget that there's nothing to stop outsiders getting in. What if the Iraqis wanted to have you shot? Where better than Hicksville?'

'The Iraqis in the UK are too closely watched.'

'Then the Turks. Sir, we're on the brink of a potentially major conflict. I've already had eleven reports of Turkish undercover activity here in Great Britain, all of which could be directed against US interests. Your visit here today isn't a secret.'

'Almost nobody knows about the Middlewick interlude except the villagers themselves. And Captain Crawford has done an excellent job checking security measures down there.'

In the end, it was agreed that there should be two Secret Service men to accompany the presidential vehicle. On account of the weather, the car would travel close-topped.

Dead on one o'clock, two policemen turned up from Hexham. They talked about Sammy Robson, the one who had absconded while on probation, but the official Middlewick response was that he had, indeed, done a runner. Which meant, of course, that police forces up and down the country were hunting for him, while Middlewick was ignored as being the last place anyone might hope to find him. In the back of their minds was PC Marsh, and the mystery that surrounded his disappearance.

They knew the area too well not to leave certain things alone, things that were outside the ken of the village's new inhabitants. A slow unease began to settle over the policemen and those near them. Suspicions gathered in the icy air, like flakes of unformed snow, drifting above the rooftops. All it would take would be for enough of them to fall, and Middlewick with all its dead would be buried beneath a thick crust of lies.

The little crowd that had gathered about the policemen thinned, then peeled away entirely. One of the policemen took out a mobile phone, and was about to punch in a number when two of the elders appeared and invited them to the Glattbach barn where, they said, they were holding a local lad, a burglar who'd been caught in one of the houses on the main street. Neither policeman was seen after that.

At 1.50 p.m., a small group of Secret Service agents descended on Middlewick. These were the advance team, six experienced members of an elite bodyguard division trained to sniff out would-be assassins in the windows of book depositories and grey hotels, or behind the low parapets of forgotten roofs. Today, all they did was check all the street-facing rooms in Middlewick. Outlying buildings, such as barns and stables, were given the most cursory of goings-over. These were serious men, with a serious mission in their lives, and they did not hang around for chitchat. They had to be back at the base, making last-minute arrangements for the President's security. The new people of Middlewick watched them go, then set to work preparing for the arrival of the President. They had a mission too. But no love in their hearts, unless it was for things they had never seen.

At 2.30 p.m. precisely, the President and his wife were on the parade ground, preparing to step into their limousine. The driver was outside, adjusting the little Stars and Stripes adorning the bonnet. The car had been highly polished, but a quiet Northumbrian drizzle had dulled it, as though concerned lest it appear conspicuous against the ploughed fields and wind-blown moors past which it was to be driven.

Just as Rebecca Waterstone made ready to get in, she looked round and caught sight of Laura Crawford among the crowd. With a quick gesture, she summoned her over.

'Captain Crawford, I thought you were accompanying us.'

'I am. My people are coming along behind you in a Jeep. But I'm sure everything will run smoothly without us.'

'In that case, why don't you come along with us? I'd like to have some company.'

'But don't you . . . ?'

'I've nothing to do on these visits but stand beside Joel looking wifely. Come on, you may as well get there in style.'

'All right. I'll just tell my team to go on without me. And I'd better warn Tina.'

'Oh, bring Tina with you, why not?'

'Is that all right?'

Rebecca nodded.

'But hurry up. Joel likes to keep on schedule.'

It took less than a minute to explain what was happening, and to snatch Tina from among her gaping classmates. They ducked inside the limousine, and found themselves on either side of the presidential couple, Tina next to the President, Laura on Rebecca's left. No sooner were they seated than the car glided off.

In Middlewick, prayers had come to an end. Everyone was in a state of preparedness. Brother Nathaniel, the old man who had led the prayers, had changed into the Sunday-best suit that had once belonged to the man whose place he had taken, old Albert Humble. It was a perfect fit, another sign of God's hand in their enterprise.

By now, any doubts had gone. It had not proved necessary to send anyone home. Any milder expressions of disquiet or an uneasy conscience had been addressed by a combination of beatings and night-long exhortations. All believed, all obeyed, all anticipated Judgement.

The road blocks, manned by a private security firm hired by the villagers of Middlewick, proved wholly effective in keeping casual visitors from neighbouring communities away. There were some angry scenes, and very nearly fisticuffs on one occasion down by Burnop crossroads, but on the whole things remained quiet.

At 2.32 p.m., the President's car left Simonsford base, accompanied by two outriders and a handful of back-up cars. Along the three-mile route, an occasional curiosity seeker stood by the hedgerow, bicycle to the rear or labrador to the front. Some waved, their hands held at about shoulder height, nervous fingers executing a slow-motion dance that signified 'welcome'. Others simply stared, determined to catch their glimpse of this strange trans-Atlantic creature, come all these miles to drive through the moorlands of northern England.

'You're so lucky to live in countryside like this,' said Rebecca Waterstone. On her right, the President was chatting volubly to Tina. 'I've only been to Europe once before. Mind you, I saw a lot more then than now.'

'It's what some of us women have to do, isn't it? I wouldn't be here if it weren't for Jim. I miss home.'

'You don't like it here?'

Laura shook her head.

'Oh, I didn't mean that. If you had a week or two, I'd take you round. We could visit the Lake District, then go up to Scotland, to see the lochs and mountains. There's some of the most beautiful scenery in the world all within a radius of a few hundred miles. And you're always less than a hundred miles from the sea. What I meant was ... Well, I sometimes think of a life where I can make my own choices. I had the feeling you have much the same problem.'

55

Rebecca nodded.

'Where I'm sitting gets more uncomfortable every day. You don't know what you have to give up at first. Then you discover you can never sleep in or sneak off for a burger or stay in to watch *Friends* as long as you're married to the president.'

'Do you resent him for that?'

'No, why should I? My life would be a lot less interesting if I weren't married to him. And, besides, I think he's the most wonderful man in the world.'

'Really?'

Rebecca leaned forward.

'Laura, if he had dark secrets, I couldn't tell you about them. He's the President, and I have to look after him. But the truth is, there's nothing dark about him. Did you vote for him?'

'Yes.'

'I thought you must have. Believe me, you'll never have cause to regret it. He's what he says he is. One hundred and ten per cent. He'll give everything he has to make this thing work.'

'This thing?'

'Oh, you know . . . In private he calls it his war against the fanatics. Given half a chance, he'll chase the loonies out of US politics. Wait and see.'

'What about – this is something that means a lot to me – what about capital punishment? I mean, is there any chance he'll try to ban it?'

Rebecca waited a few moments before replying. They were passing a country house hotel whose staff and guests had come out to watch the cavalcade pass.

'Do you know, dear, I don't think I can give you a simple answer to that. You don't say if you're in favour or not.'

'Oh, I'm opposed. So is Jim. It's just . . . We read about kids of seventeen or even younger getting gassed or electrocuted. What sort of society can do that to people?'

'Well, I can tell you that it's not on the agenda for this first term. Too many people support capital punishment to make banning it a safe objective, even for a president as popular as Joel. But he'll come to it in his second term.'

'You're sure he'll have a second term?'

Rebecca looked at her candidly.

'Short of treachery, he'll get a second term. Believe me.'

She took Laura's hand.

Tina pointed excitedly through the side window, showing the President where part of Hadrian's Wall ran away westwards. Middlewick was half a mile away.

6

Middlewick

At 2.41 p.m., the presidential car swung round an awkward bend and slowed to five miles per hour as it arrived in Middlewick. On either side, the street was lined with onlookers, but no-one cheered or hooted or showed any sign that they had noticed the new arrival.

Middlewick was too small a place to have a mayor or a town hall or even a village council. Decisions for everything were taken up the road in Hexham, and handed down as by a decree from above. Street lighting, rubbish collection, street sweeping – all were concerns of the district council, leaving the villagers of Middlewick with little to do but organize a dozen of their own number into a parish council. The real parish council having long ago been fed to some very hungry pigs, a surrogate council had been created under the supervision of the counterfeit Reverend Hunsley. It would be the duty of this council to receive from President Waterstone, and on behalf of the airmen and airwomen of Simonsford, a Letter of Commendation, thanking them for the part they played in providing a hospitable environment for the base.

The President could make out a low wooden structure at the far end of the street, on which the council members sat in a long row. Seeing that the platform blocked the street, the driver came to a halt within six feet of it and started worrying about how they would all back out of here when the time came.

58

Behind the President's car the other vehicles came into the street at an equal pace, and halted, their engines still running. Still no-one cheered, or showed in any way their awareness of their visitors.

But the English, whether urban or rural, are known for their reserve, and no-one in the cars noticed anything much out of the ordinary at first. It was Laura who, glancing out of her window, remarked on the oddity.

'There's something wrong,' she said.

No sooner had she spoken than a heavy tractor dragging behind it a heavy cattle wagon, groaned sideways onto the street at the rear, blocking any exit to the vehicles parked there.

None of this was visible up front. In the President's car, Laura, not yet knowing what was happening or about to happen, leaned across to where the President was encouraging Tina to push open the door.

'Stay where you are, sir. And I'd suggest you lock the doors.'

'Captain? I don't understand. Everything seems OK to me.'

'There may be nothing wrong, sir, but I think I should take a look outside first.' She looked through her window again. 'Nobody's smiling, sir. Absolutely nobody.'

At that moment, those who'd been standing along the pavement stepped back and turned to go back inside the houses and shops that lined the street. Within seconds, the street was deserted. When Laura looked forward again, the parish council had vanished from the platform.

Laura needed no more hints. With still no clue as to what was going on, she reached for Rebecca, trying to force her down between the rear seat and the partition.

'Get your head down, sir!' she shouted. 'Get Tina down beside you! For God's sake, hurry!'

Base Communications Center
Simonsford Air Force Base

'Come in, Papa Sierra. This is Sierra Alpha Bravo. Can you hear me? Come in, please.'

Charlie Profaci swivelled on his operator's chair to face his boss, Simonsford's Chief Communications Officer, Major Pete Albany.

'Sir, it's like there's some total blackout. I don't get it. There doesn't seem to be anything wrong with their equipment. I've tried all possible channels, but there's no answer from any of them. It's as if there's nobody out there.'

'I don't get this. This is the President's bodyguard we're talking about. They *have* to answer. For heaven's sake, it's not as if they're in the middle of some grand reception. What have they got to do out there? You're sure they're not answering?'

'Positive, sir. I've done a complete sweep: none of their receivers is out of order.'

'Then why the hell aren't they answering?'

'Maybe the President's got them Morris dancing, or whatever it is they do here, sir.'

'Not even the President can get those guys to take their eyes off the ball for an instant. Something's wrong. Did you try to get the President's car?'

Profaci nodded.

'I told you, sir, I've tried every possible channel.'

'OK, let's not waste any more time. Get me Reynolds. Tell him to drop whatever he's doing and get the hell over here.'

He leaned across Profaci to the next operator. 'Hooper, you get me Colonel Fujiyama. If he asks what it's about, say you know nothing, but you've been told it's urgent.'

'What about the Secret Service unit still on base, sir?'

Albany hesitated for a long moment, then shook his head.

'Let's not get them involved unless we have to. There's no need for this to get out of hand. We have no reason to suspect any kind of trouble out there.'

He crossed the room to where a recently-arrived RO corporal called Ann Kelly was talking the fighter wing through its takeoff for Italy.

'Corporal, will you instruct the Wing to stand down until further notice? Ask Major Crawford to bring B Squadron back to base and come to see me here as soon as possible.'

The Major was worried, but he tried not to communicate this to any of his staff. Even as he issued orders, his mind was frantically scrabbling through the options open to him. Foremost was the thought that radio contact with the President and his bodyguard had been severed. Until he knew the reason for the communications failure – if it was that – he had to act on the assumption that something had happened to the President and that the security of the United States was in danger.

But he was afraid to act without authorization from higher up. What if nothing was wrong at all (and that seemed most likely, given the very few risks the President was running here), yet he raised a false alarm and caused an uproar on both sides of the Atlantic? The US was practically at war, and it would only play into the hands of their potential enemy if any confusion was raised about the safety of the President.

Middlewick

It was still silent outside. But the illusion of stillness lasted only a few moments. Suddenly, there was a loud explosion right behind them, followed by a crashing of glass and what sounded like machine-gun fire. To Laura's astonishment, no shots hit their vehicle; but when she looked through the windscreen, she could see that the motor-cyclists in front had disappeared from view. Twisting round, she saw to her horror that the Secret Service limousine immediately behind had been turned to a charred wreck. There would not have been any survivors, and probably nothing much left of the men who'd been sitting there.

There was a twinkling in a first-floor window. Laura watched with her heart in her mouth as she saw men starting to spill out of the middle doors of the Suburban. One rolled out, followed tightly by a second on the other side, both dressed in full combat gear, with flak helmets, and holding M16 assault rifles equipped with M203 grenade launchers.

The rear door was lifted up and two more troopers leapt from the vehicle. Seeing there was no way to turn or manoeuvre, the driver switched off the engine and prepared to abandon the Suburban.

It normally takes about twenty seconds to reload a MILAN Anti-Tank Post. The two-man launch crew situated in the window above Salkeld & Sons Hardware Shop had worked hard to get this time down to sixteen seconds. It took another one and a half seconds for the missile to leave the window, and a fraction of that time to reach its target as it kicked into a travelling speed of two hundred metres a second.

The Suburban was torn apart by the force of the explosion. Pieces of hot metal and human body parts went spinning out of control in all directions, colliding with one another, smashing into doors and walls, sailing over the rooftops of what had been until now a sleepy northern village.

Simonsford Base

Albany crossed to another sector of the large room and sat down beside a black operator called Turner. Airman Turner was Simonsford's secret weapon in the base's ball games against other army and air force teams in the UK and Europe. It was said he'd been offered large amounts of money to play for a string of teams back home, but that he'd turned them all down in favour of a life in the Air Force.

'You playing this weekend, Turner?' There was a game against Lakenheath on Saturday. There'd been hopes of getting the President to attend, but with the current crisis the best they could hope for in grandees was the local mayor.

'Well, I should be, sir, but Sergeant Reynolds says . . .'

'If you have any trouble, son, come to me. I'd like to travel down, but my duty rota won't allow it. Now, Turner, I want you to treat this order in confidence. Will you get the White House on line? Just say who you are and that you're acting on my instructions, but don't say anything else about the situation here. Ask them to make contact with the Vice President, and ask him to stand by for a call from us, but don't speak to him until further orders. Is that clear?'

'Yes, sir. Has something happened to the President, sir?'

'You know I can't answer that question. And the truth is, I don't know. Whatever you do, son, don't give them that impression over there. If they ask, say the President wants to try out our facilities as part of his tour of the base, and that he'll be along as soon as he finishes his visit to Middlewick.'

The door opened, and Master Sergeant Reynolds stormed in. He was redder in the face than a plum tomato, and it looked as though red stood for danger. Catching sight of Major Albany, he came to attention and saluted.

'Sergeant Reynolds reporting, sir. I was told you wanted to speak to me.'

Albany dashed off a salute and asked Reynolds to come into his private office. As he was going inside, he popped his head back round the door and called to Profaci.

'Profaci, if the chief turns up while I'm in here with Sergeant Reynolds, just bring him right in.'

He closed the door and glanced at his visitor, standing straight as a meerkat in the middle of the little room.

'Sit down, Sergeant. And take that frown off your face.'

Reynolds sat. Albany looked at him and wondered if he had ever seen anything so polished before.

'This better be important, sir. I'm in charge of base security, and during the President's visit that means my team and I have some kind of responsibility for his security as well. I'm not a man who likes to take his eye off the ball, especially where women are involved.'

'Women?'

'I'm thinking about Captain Crawford, sir. In my opinion . . .'

'Yes, I think I know what your opinion is, Sergeant. But that isn't why I brought you here. We may have a more immediate problem on our hands.'

Middlewick

On the ground, one of the SAS survivors from the rear of the Suburban was torn to pieces by shrapnel. His companion had barely got himself behind a concrete box containing salt. The other two escaped serious injury by the narrowest of margins:

63

one had crashed through the nearest doorway, while his partner had managed to take shelter behind a metal lamppost.

The moment the explosion from the Suburban died away, the soldier behind the salt box tried to get a fix on the window from which the anti-tank round had come, hoping to lob a grenade through it with the help of the launcher attached to his attack rifle. As he did so, he tried desperately to raise someone on the internal communications network, using the microphone fixed in his helmet. But all he could hear was interference. Either the system was broken, or someone was jamming it, and jamming it hard.

The motorcycle policemen who had been flanking the presidential car had already stopped and shut off their engines when the firing had begun. Neither was armed, but they did have two-way radios aboard their BMWs.

'Joe,' called the one on the car's left side, 'try to establish radio contact. I'm going to make a run for it.'

He restarted his engine and pulled the heavy machine onto the pavement. It was a clear run to the far end of the street, provided his tyres didn't get shredded by shrapnel. Still trapped inside the presidential car, Laura watched as he revved up hard, then sprang forward along the pavement at high speed. He had almost reached the last house when a shot rang out from somewhere and the rider was thrown bodily from his bike to crash against the house wall. He did not move again.

The other motorcyclist looked blankly at his handset. Whoever was jamming his transmission knew exactly what they were doing. He was about to follow his companion back along the pavement when the door of the limousine opened and the surprisingly familiar face of the American President looked up at him.

'Hurry up,' said the President, 'get in here with us. You'll be safe.'

The policeman hesitated only briefly, then stepped down from his bike and made for the car door. A second shot rang out, eerie against the all-engrossing silence that held the village in its grip. The policeman staggered, tried to take a second step, and fell face forwards, striking his dead face against the edge of the door. Laura threw herself over Rebecca and pulled the door closed again.

'Please, sir,' she pleaded, 'don't do that again. So far they've left us alone. Let's just see what they want.'

'They want me. I just wish I knew what for.'

Simonsford Base

There was a knock on the door, and Colonel Fujiyama was shown in. Albany and Reynolds scrambled to their feet, saluting. He nodded them back down to their chairs and leaned his back against the door. The commander had always been comfortable with seniority. He treated the officers and men under him with genuine respect, and expected the same in return. One look at Pete Albany told him something was up. He felt a sensation as though a steel band had fastened round his chest, and his breathing grew tighter. If he'd had any sense, he'd have gone with the President across to Middlewick, but the wing was flying out to Italy today, and he had to be with his men to ensure everything went smoothly.

'What's up?' he asked.

Reynolds, who had nothing but contempt for the Japanese, and who privately considered his commanding officer an unAmerican threat to the security of the free world, opened his mouth to venture an opinion, but he was halted by Pete Albany.

'Sir, we seem to have lost contact with the President.'

Fujiyama looked back at his communications chief as though he'd just been e-mailed to another planet.

'Will you please say that again, Major?'

'Sir, we can't get him or his bodyguard on any of their radio channels. We've tried the President's satellite phone, but there's no response there either.'

'What about their mobile phones? Any luck there?'

'No, sir. But I'm told this isn't a good reception area.'

'Don't rely on that. Is there some sort of interference, is that what you mean?'

'No, sir. All the bands are clear. There's no problem at this end, and we don't think all their equipment could have been damaged simultaneously.'

'Could they be refusing to answer during the walkabout at Middlewick?' Fujiyama looked at his wristwatch. 'Which should be under way right now. For the past ten minutes, in fact.'

Reynolds half raised his hand and butted in.

'Sir, that would be in contravention of the communications protocols that were set up for this visit. The President is never to be allowed out of contact for a second. Or his bodyguard.'

'Then why won't they answer?'

'What if something's happened to the President, sir?'

'Such as?'

Reynolds shrugged his broad shoulders.

'Maybe he was taken ill.'

'If that had happened, every radio set between here and Middlewick would be bleeping and blaring the news. The ambulance would be in Middlewick by now, and feeding back a second-by-second account of what was happening.'

'Shouldn't we be getting someone over there, sir?' Pete Albany knew that time was of the essence. It would probably take a fast motorcyclist five minutes or so to ride out to Middlewick and see what was going on.

'Yes, I think you're right, Major. Reynolds, would you mind getting a despatch rider over there? Make sure he has a functioning radio and a satellite phone.'

Reynolds, who could not have cared less what happened to the President, his wife, or their dog – if there'd been a dog – nevertheless resolved to snatch whatever shreds of glory there might be in this for himself. If something bad happened, he'd be the first on the scene, the first official person to lend assistance. He reckoned he could steer a motorcycle across muddy fields as well as any despatch rider, and if there was any trouble from anti-American protesters, he knew he could give a good account of himself.

'I'll get onto that right away,' he said. 'And you might try making contact with the local police. They have a couple of their men down there too. Maybe they can get through to them.'

With an audible click of his heels and a crisp salute, he headed out on his one-man mission to find a place in early twenty-first-century history.

7

Middlewick

There was a light explosion to their rear as the SAS man behind the salt box fired a grenade into the window containing the Milan post.

He had already made visual contact with his companion behind the lamppost. Using a modified form of sign language, he indicated that they should make their way down opposite sides of the street and try to get to the presidential car. If only they could hold off their attackers until someone back at Simonsford realized something was wrong and sent in a backup team.

The fourth SAS man had hurled himself hard against a front door, which had collapsed under his weight, leaving him sprawling in a dimly-lit hallway with a kitchen at the far end. Still winded, he sat without moving for several moments, trying to get his breath back. As he started to get to his feet, he realized that he must have dropped his M16 as he crashed through the door. Quickly, he reached for the Browning Hi-Power that he carried in a holster. He was about to go back outside for the rifle, and to see what was happening in the street, when he heard a light sound behind him.

He spun round, lifting the handgun, ready to aim and fire. Long training in Stirling Lanes' Killing House, where live hostages are mixed with cardboard terrorists, and the rounds are live, had taught him the skills and virtues of restraint. He found himself face to face, not with a gun-wielding man in a balaclava, but with a little girl in a long white dress. He guessed her age at ten or so, and he was astonished that she showed no sign of fear though faced with the terrifying figure he knew he presented. She had a serious, pretty face and long black hair that fell almost to her waist.

He put his finger to his lips, took it away, and smiled, but her expression did not change. As he looked, wondering what to do with her, a second girl appeared, dressed much like the first, but with blonde hair. A third followed, and others, until he counted eight of them. Only then did he notice what they were holding in their hands: long knives with blades of steel.

Simonsford Base

The door had no sooner closed behind him than it swung open again to let in two Secret Service agents, Reilly and Shapiro. Introductions were quickly made.

'Gentlemen,' Fujiyama said quickly, before the Secret Service men could take the initiative, 'I think we should all head back into the main communications room. Major Albany here will fill you in on what's been happening.'

'You can see for yourselves,' said Albany, leading them to where Profaci was still trying to summon a reply from the presidential party. Reilly and Shapiro watched in silence until the full gravity of what was happening sank in on them.

'Gentlemen,' the Colonel broke in, 'I think it's my duty in this matter to hand total responsibility to you and your team until such time as we know exactly what's happening.'

Shapiro, who sensed that he and his colleagues were being set up to take the blame for something that could turn out to be their worst nightmare, hesitated to say 'yes'.

'With respect, Colonel,' he began, 'before I took on that responsibility, I'd need to be sure this really is a Secret Service matter, and not simply a problem relating to this base, its personnel, and its communications systems.'

Fujiyama, on the other hand, was not disposed to let the other man slip out of the noose he'd prepared for him so easily. In any case, he genuinely believed this was going to be the Secret Service's responsibility long before the day was through.

'Agent Shapiro, we have tried every which way to communicate with the President or his staff, including the vehicles driven by your own people, and we have had not so much as a squeak. You're welcome to try for yourself.'

Profaci turned, removing his headphones, and speaking to Albany.

'Sir, I think I've come across some sort of jamming device. It could be what's interfering with our communications.'

'Where is it? Somewhere on the base?'

Profaci shook his head.

'More likely down around Middlewick. It seems quite a powerful device, sir – we should check it isn't interfering with our base-to-aircraft transmissions.'

'I'll get someone on to that right away. For the minute, stick with the President.'

'Yessir.'

Albany hurried off to find someone to track down the jamming device and its range. Fujiyama used an emergency phone to order the immediate return to base of any aircraft still within possible jamming range.

Reilly, whose job was to concentrate on the safety of the President and the First Lady whatever else was happening, whipped a mobile phone from his inside pocket. It was a secure phone capable of sending and receiving encrypted signals via satellite. He speed-dialled the number that would connect him to the main Secret Service team at Middlewick. The sound of ringing filled his handset, and he got ready to fire off some well-chosen swearwords when someone answered. But the phone just went on ringing. In the end, he pressed a flashing red button to cancel the call. It should not have happened. The system was supposed to be invulnerable to jamming.

Middlewick

On the street outside, the SAS man's two companions made their way cautiously down the street. One was called Evans, the other

69

Lorimer. They'd done this sort of thing before, but never in an English village. Smoke issued from the upper window where the Milan post had been put out of action. The street itself was covered in a pall of smoke from the two main explosions. Evans wondered if the smoke would rise high enough to alert a watcher back at the airbase.

Lorimer carried a night sight in his webbing, a Schmidt & Bender 6 capable of seeing some way through smoke. He took it out and examined the scene ahead of him. The Secret Service limo burning like a tank in the desert, and the presidential limo, scarred and dirty, but miraculously (as it seemed to him) intact. He couldn't understand why their attackers had not finished the job by lobbing some sort of heavy explosive at it. This had to be a hostage-taking rather than an assassination attempt.

He thought quickly. There was a slim chance that he and Evans could make a dash for the limousine, take the wheel, and ram their way through the wooden platform ahead of it. He signalled his plan, Evans gave it a thumbs up, and they came out, zigzagging down the narrow pavements towards the limo.

Laura watched them come, watched them twist and turn as they ran towards her. On the floor beside her, Rebecca Waterstone lay huddled, her hands across her head, as though to protect it from harm. Next to her crouched the President, murmuring words of comfort and reassurance to Tina, whom he held tightly in his arms. Next to him was the briefcase containing all the codes for US nuclear missiles, and the button that would fire them.

Laura's heart felt tight inside her chest. Silently, she urged the soldiers on, not knowing what earthly use they might be against bombs and missiles. As they neared her, they grew bigger and more powerful in her eyes, and she half believed they could save her and her daughter. It was disloyal of her, but she knew she'd let the President and his wife die, if she could carry Tina alive out of this carnage.

Her hope died in a single burst of machine-gun fire that raked the street from side to side, peppering the two SAS men with round upon round of Glaser bullets, throwing them on their backs, and tearing them to shreds.

The machine gun stopped. Silence came. Two minutes had passed since the arrival of the President.

Simonsford Base

Albany came back to where Reilly and Shapiro were waiting.

'Any luck?'

Reilly, whose Irish features had gone as red as a ripe lychee, looked like a child who has just discovered for the first time that life doesn't always work out quite as you plan it.

'I don't understand it. I got a ringing tone. They should answer on the first ring; this just went on ringing. What the hell do you make of that? I mean, what the hell? Could jamming do that?'

Albany shook his head thoughtfully.

'Don't think so. It sounds more like nobody answered.'

'I can't believe that. How could they do that, not answer? Those guys aren't just among the best-trained bodyguards in the world, they've got total commitment.'

'I'm not questioning that. But maybe they've become separated from their handset.'

'Anybody who tried to separate a Secret Service man from his gun or his communications equipment should have seen a priest beforehand. No way is that possible.'

'Suppose it was possible. It would explain a ringing tone instead of interference.'

Shapiro was about to make his own contribution, when the door opened and Jim Crawford came storming in. Catching sight of Fujiyama, he slowed his pace and saluted. Then he made straight for Albany. The Secret Service made a hurried exit without saying where they were headed.

Middlewick

He pointed his rifle at them, but he couldn't bring himself to do it. They were just little girls, surely more frightened of him than he

71

could ever be of them. Their ages varied between about eight and fourteen, as far as he could judge.

'I'm not your enemy,' he said, removing his helmet so they could see his face properly. 'I've come to help you.'

He lowered the rifle. That was when they came for him.

Simonsford Base

'Just what the hell is going on, Major?' Crawford demanded. Heads turned, then returned to their computer screens. 'My squadron was ten minutes from first take-off. We were all ready to go when I received orders to stand down and was asked to report to you. Couldn't you just have spoken to me while I was in my cockpit? It's been known to happen, you know.'

If he hadn't known Jim Crawford well, Albany would have put him on a charge. But he understood how tense many of the pilots became when on the brink of flying into a potential war zone.

'Jim, we're under some pressure here as well. The fact is, somebody is jamming our communications with the President and his staff over in Middlewick.'

'Jamming? You're sure of that?'

'Not entirely. But we've lost contact, whatever the reason.'

'Jesus. Is there no way of getting someone down there?'

'Reynolds is sending a despatch rider over now.'

'A despatch rider? What fucking good is that going to be if the President's under attack? Can't you get some military police down there right away?'

Fujiyama, who'd been taking a back seat while thinking things through, came to life again.

'Major, get Reynolds at once and order him to take a detachment of Security Police to Middlewick at once. Tell him to make sure they're armed.'

'Sir, they're not supposed to carry arms on British soil.'

'Major Albany, the President's life may be at risk.'

There was a polite cough next to them. Fujiyama turned to see

72

Arnold Turner saluting him. He returned the salute and told Turner to stand at ease.

'Turner, isn't it?'

'Yes, sir. I was looking for Major Albany, sir.'

'He's busy right now. Can I help?'

'Maybe you can, sir. I have the White House on hold, and they tell me they have the Vice President waiting. I'm told he can't stay waiting much longer, he has an appointment in five minutes.'

'Tell him to cancel his appointment. Say I'll speak to him personally in a few minutes.'

Turner, worried about what reception he'd get, hurried off.

'The Vice President, sir?'

Fujiyama nodded.

'It was Albany's idea. It may be premature, but if anything *has* happened to President Waterstone, the VP will need to know immediately.'

'Sir, I think you should speak to him now, without waiting to hear what's going on.'

'I'd rather be certain something has gone wrong. There are dozens of innocent explanations for why this may have happened.'

Jim shook his head.

'I don't think there are, sir. You have to speak to Vice President Heller at once. He has to place the US military on nuclear alert.'

'Isn't that jumping the gun, Major? We can't be sure that anything is seriously wrong. But if we raise an alarm, tell the Vice President, maybe even get the National Security Council involved, we might do more harm than good.'

'Sir, only the Vice President can call the shots on this. If anyone is trying to take advantage of the President being uncontactable, then the only way to convince them to call their plan off will be a phonecall from Heller. We have to get our move in first. I for one would rather be safe than sorry.'

'Major, you're panicking. The Turks don't even have a nuclear capacity.'

'I wasn't thinking about the Turks, sir. This is way out of their league.'

'Who, then?'

'The Russians. Their ICBMs could already be on the way, and we have no response so long as the President is out of touch and unable to make use of his nuclear briefcase. Speak to the VP now, sir. We may have only moments to spare.'

Middlewick

A door opened opposite the presidential car, and a tall man stepped out. He was followed by five more men. All carried powerful-looking assault rifles which Laura recognized as Heckler & Koch MP5s. The six men surrounded the car. As they did so, the street seemed to come to life. Villagers appeared from every doorway and moved off in small groups, some this way, some the other. A group of men started dismantling the wooden platform that had been blocking the way out of the village.

A seventh man followed his companions and approached the limousine. He was tall like the others, but his manner conveyed an air of indefinable authority. From his pocket he took a small package about the size of a paperback book. He peeled a sheet of oiled paper away from the top of the package and slapped the whole thing onto the side window facing the front passenger seat. Casually, he walked back to the rear of the car and waited. One second later, a small, controlled explosion took the window out, sending shards of glass whistling through the driver's section.

The glass all but severed the driver's head from his shoulders, and turned one side of him to mince. The entire driving area filled with blood, as a juicer, turned on suddenly, fills with the juice of red tomatoes.

The seventh man returned and got in on the passenger side, after throwing a heavy tarpaulin sheet over the seat. He bent over and pressed the button that operated the glass window separating front and rear sections.

Laura's hand shook as she tried to bring her handgun to bear on the intruder. She pushed herself in front of the First Lady, pressing her back into the plush, upholstered seat.

'This place is going to be surrounded any minute now. You'll be outnumbered. If they know you harmed either the President or his wife, they won't forgive you. They'll hunt you down wherever you go. Just leave things as they are. You can still get away. In six months, all this will have been forgotten.'

Laura knew that, if he fired into her head or chest, the bullet would travel on into the body of the First Lady, and she suspected this was something their attackers did not want.

The gunman drew back and pressed the partition button again. As it closed, he pressed a second button, sending the side window next to Laura downwards. As Laura spun round, one of the other gunmen stepped up to the window and fired a single shot with the H&K.

Laura died in a shower of blood that drenched Rebecca Waterstone and sprinkled with fine droplets both the President and the little girl he was trying to shield.

The partition slid open again.

'Now, Mr President, please get out of the car at once and climb aboard the vehicle you see in front.'

Someone had parked a Ford Transit van directly in front of the presidential car.

'I'm not moving without this little girl. She's under my protection, and I will sooner let you shoot me than break my promise to her.'

Tina, her eyes covered by the President's shaking hands, had seen nothing of what had been done to her mother, but she had heard it all, and put together in her mind as bloody a scenario as any that might have been enacted in the flesh. She was sobbing softly now, her little girl's grief held in check by a wholly adult terror.

The seventh man hesitated for only a fraction of a second. His whole purpose at this moment was to get the President and his wife as far away from Middlewick as possible, in as short a time as he could manage. Delays could be fatal.

He nodded, and President Waterstone rose slowly, with what little dignity he could muster, and took Tina's hand, and led her to the waiting van. His wife, visibly shaking, her face and hands and clothes covered with Laura Crawford's blood, followed her husband. Her grandparents on her mother's side had survived the camp at Majdanek; the rest of her family, like Joel's family, had died in the same years by bullet and cudgel and boot and gas and knife and stone. Some their killers had buried alive, some they had operated on without anaesthetic, others they had harried to their deaths on the electric wire.

She looked at the van, and her mind was filled with thoughts of heavy locomotives carrying endless trains of the dead and dying and condemned. She joined Joel as he placed his foot on the first step. He looked round and saw her, bloody, frightened out of her wits.

'Not this time,' he said, as if he had been thinking the same thoughts. 'This time they picked on the wrong man.'

And he stepped up, then turned again and took her hand, and lifted her into the van beside him. Two men slammed the doors behind them. The van moved off, picking up speed by the second.

8

Buzz Reynolds encountered no-one but thin grazing sheep on his way to Middlewick. He'd requisitioned a powerful BMW K1200 RS from the Security Police garage, and set off in high spirits, wishing only that he'd driven the route more often, and worrying that he might get lost among the labyrinthine circuits of back roads and farm tracks that hemmed the village in. For what might have been the first time in his life, he configured something quite imaginary in his head, a black spider squatting at the heart of its web, a fearful image of Middlewick and its complex pattern of public roads and private dirt-tracks.

He'd gone about two miles when he saw a plume of black smoke far ahead of him. When that first plume was followed by a second and a third, he knew something was badly wrong. Taking his mobile from its pouch, he rang the Security Police office. Nothing happened. Not having been told about the possibility of a jamming device, he attributed the non-communication to a weak signal, without noticing that a hill half a mile away sported a telephone boosting mast.

Frightened now, he threw caution to the winds and pushed the bike faster and faster, oblivious of the sharp bends and narrow tracks along which he was speeding. Helmeted and hunched over the body of the huge machine, he could hear none of the sounds of shooting and explosions that would have alerted him to the true situation at Middlewick. But if he looked up, he could see smoke mingling with smoke, rising from the same spot out of sight beyond a blurring of moors and hills and forests.

In Middlewick itself, no-one was wasting time. The bodies of the dead had been left lying where they were. Those few outsiders who had slipped in to see the President were made to kneel and then shot in the back of the neck in a series of summary executions. Matt Pike's body was dragged outside to the street and dumped there, another innocent bystander caught up in a rage he could never have understood.

As if from nowhere, cars and trucks appeared and were rapidly boarded by the surrogate residents of Middlewick. The whole procedure had been rehearsed so many times it went off as smoothly as a stage production. In no instance did a vehicle belong to an earlier resident – all those had been sold under false ownership certificates at auctions the length and breadth of the country. The vehicles into which people were now climbing had been registered under a whole batch of new names. These belonged to living people as far apart as Cornwall and Inverness, none of whom had any idea that they'd become the proud possessors of these Range Rovers and Volvos and Mercedes lorries.

One of the first to leave was a red bus carrying the village children. Dressed in pretty frocks and freshly-pressed trousers, they could have fooled anyone. The destination board declared this to be the 115th St John the Baptist Sunday School Outing. On board sat the Reverend Hunsley, benign and ecclesiastical-looking, and the Sunday-school mistress, the substitute Mrs Boustead, her permed hair and lace blouse several generations behind the present.

It set off first. Next to where it had been standing was a large blue Ford Transit van, on whose sides white letters proclaimed it to belong to the Hadrian's Wall Museum at Corbridge and the Department of Archaeology at Newcastle University. Inside, it was filled with archaeological tools, and what seemed like Roman artefacts, recently disinterred from one of the wall's many forts.

A quick examination – such as one might expect in a roadblock – would turn up nothing of interest. The fact that the rear of the van was a mess of objects, some looking rather sharp, others fragile, meant that only the most determined investigator would take the trouble to dig his way through the heap as far as the bulkhead separating the interior from the cab. Even then, he would have seen nothing out of the ordinary unless he'd been equipped with a table of dimensions for Ford Transits.

In reality, the bulkhead was about two feet back from where it should have been. The interior of the van, excluding the cab, was about nine feet long by six feet wide. By moving the bulkhead back just that small amount, the van's owners had been able to create a space two feet wide by six long by four feet high.

Two men appeared from further back, where the presidential car had been stopped. They carried the inert body of Joel Waterstone between them. The President had been rendered unconscious by a strong dose of Thiopentone Sodium, intravenously injected. The men dragged Waterstone into the rear of the van and fitted him carefully into the tiny compartment that would be formed when the bulkhead was replaced. Two more men arrived with the First Lady, similarly drugged. And finally the body of the little girl whose life the President had saved was brought and placed between them. All three were dreaming. And their dreams were nightmares that never ended.

The bulkhead was fitted carefully into place. The only air that would enter the cramped space behind it would come from a compressor fitted in the cab. The compartment in which the President would be riding was completely soundproofed. A small bomb could have gone off in there without anyone noticing a thing.

The van driver made a last check of his vehicle. His co-driver joined him in the cab, while two men and two women, dressed to look like archaeologists fresh from working on an outdoor site, climbed into the rear of the van, slamming the doors behind them with a crash that echoed round the village as though signalling the end of the horror. Or perhaps its beginning.

Buzz Reynolds glanced skywards in time to catch a flight of Warthogs swooping down a path that would bring them back to Simonsford. Just what the fuck was going on? he wondered. At that moment, he came to a rise from which he could look down across the little valley in which Middlewick was situated. He braked quickly, skidding half across the road, then straightening. As the bike steadied beneath him, he turned his eyes on the village.

He saw nothing at first but the world he had always seen there, houses and trees, and a fishing stream set back from everything, as though some part of his mind was working hard to blot out a world he could not have foreseen or for any reason wished to behold.

And then he blinked or woke or fell into dream. What he saw he simply could not believe. Who could have done? He was in the middle of the English countryside, in one of the world's few places not given over to violence. But the scene below him seemed like something familiar to him from Kosovo, or from film footage of Chechnya. Vehicles burned like funeral pyres, the fronts of some buildings had been smashed inwards, cars, buses, and vans scurried hither and thither. The smoke drifted in his direction. He could smell gunpowder.

'Jesus,' he whispered beneath his breath. 'Jesus.' It was his first thought that the President was dead, that he had been stopped here and killed, like Kennedy. Except . . . and he realized that there was no shooting, only the sound of motor vehicles, which must mean that the Secret Service and the SAS and the British police must be dead or taken prisoner. And he thought that there would be no widow to walk after her dead husband this time, since she would have died beside him.

It was the first time in his life when he did not know what to do, or whom to turn to for advice. With a trembling hand, he pulled out his mobile again and carefully tapped in a secure number at the base. And, as before, there was not even the faintest signal. If he had known it, he wasn't alone. For a wide radius around the nearby Cellnet mast, mobile phone users were champing the bit with frustration, and their host companies were inundated with landline calls.

He looked down towards Middlewick again, and saw a car move out of the village and into the road that led in his direction. He switched off his bike engine and moved the machine into the centre of the road, laying it flat and sideways on to the traffic. The sound of the approaching car grew rapidly in volume.

He took his gun from its holster. As chief of security, he had authority to carry virtually any handgun or rifle he chose, and today he was carrying a snub-nosed 38mm revolver known as a Dan Wesson .38 Special. Quite against USAF rules, he had loaded it with KTW armour-piercing rounds. Thinking about them and what they could do to most materials made him feel more confident.

The car came into sight, and he knew that the occupants would have seen him already. Their speed did not change, and for a moment he wondered if they would simply try to ram him out of the way. But he stood up, adopting the classic law enforcement officer's stance, holding the heavy weapon tightly in two hands. The car continued on its unswerving course.

Just as he was about to shoot, the driver either chickened out or simply made up his mind that discretion was the better part of valour. He slammed on the brakes and screeched to a halt inches in front of Reynolds's improvised barricade. The car was a large Volvo, an 850, and the driver could have side-swiped the bike without sustaining too much damage. But his orders were to avoid anything that would get him or his car noticed.

Reynolds had stood his ground. The moment the car came to a stop, he shouted loudly, keeping his pistol firmly pointed at the driver.

'Out of the car! Now! Put your hands on your head, and don't try anything. Move slowly!'

Several seconds passed. Reynolds did not take his eyes off the driver, but he was ready for any sudden move on the part of the passengers, one in front, two in back.

The driver stepped out. He wore a green loden coat and a scarf that might have been silk. His expensive-looking shoes were freshly polished, and he wore tan leather driving gloves. He looked rich and worried, and nothing in his appearance or behaviour suggested a threat to Reynolds.

'Can I help you, Officer?' he asked. Reynolds had heard RAF officers speak with much the same accent.

'Keep your hands on your head.'

'Of course.'

'Make sure nobody in your car does anything stupid.'

The man turned his head a fraction.

'Did you all hear what the gentleman said?' He turned back to Reynolds. 'Believe me, neither my wife nor my children will do anything to disturb you.'

'Can you tell me what's been going on down there?'

The driver looked down towards Middlewick, then back at Reynolds. A curious smile played across his tanned features.

'Good Lord, you don't think . . . ? Officer, I think you've got entirely the wrong idea. No-one's been hurt. The smoke's coming from canisters. But your President and his party are perfectly safe, I assure you.'

'I asked what's going on.'

'I see what you mean. Thing is, the good folk of Middlewick got hold of the idea that they'd like to entertain your chief. They got some Territorial Army people over to stage a mock ambush. I thought your people knew all about it.'

If Buzz Reynolds had not been brought up in the city, he might have lived longer. As it was, he knew nothing but city streets and alleyways, and the windswept grids of a dozen air force bases. He hadn't calculated on the watchers who would be the last to leave the stricken village, and he never so much as thought to look anywhere but the road. Meanwhile, a man in hunting jacket and boots, and carrying a rifle, had made his way across a muddy field, through a rain-swollen brook, through a copse of evergreen trees, and up to a position about 500 yards from Reynolds.

The rifle the shooter was carrying was a long-barrelled Barrett .50, the best sniper's rifle on the market. It had a tremendous range, and was chambered to take .50-calibre rounds that could punch their way through the toughest Kevlar vest. Quickly setting the rifle on a bipod, he trained it on Reynolds's back. His only concern was to prevent the bullet exiting from Reynolds and hitting the driver of the Volvo.

The driver, meanwhile, could see all this. Reynolds continued to question him.

'I'd like you to ask your family to step out of the car as well, sir. Same procedure, hands on heads, no sudden movements.'

'Do they really have to, Officer? It's freezing out here, and young Polly has had flu recently.'

The sniper signalled to his colleague, who threw himself sideways suddenly, leaving Reynolds a standing target. As he started to swivel after the driver, a tap tap of two bullets hit him in the middle of the back, entering fast and exiting through a wound many times their own size. Reynolds's body was flung forward by the force of the blow, striking the bonnet, then flopping back to the ground like a dead fish. A trail of bright red blood traced his path.

Getting to his feet, the driver swore. The blood would have to be washed off before they went another yard. His family – a woman and two teenagers, a boy and a girl – hurried into the road. The woman checked Reynolds's body, giving a thumbs-up once she was satisfied he was dead. The driver passed the message on to the sniper, who broke from concealment and hurried back in the direction of the village.

The blood was fresh enough to be wiped away with tissues, which could be tossed into the ditch. The 'family' – and, who knows, perhaps they really were a family – dragged Reynolds's body off the road, and pulled the heavy motorbike right out of the way of any traffic that might still come.

Down in the village, the van containing the President, his wife, and Tina, started its journey in a different direction, heading eastwards, towards the coast. In the air above, a jet plane made a low pass, then headed on to Simonsford.

9

'Two seven one to base. Two seven one to base. Can you receive me? Over?'

'Base to two seven one. Receiving you clearly. What can you see?'

'I've made several low passes over the target. It's very hard to see anything very well. The village is covered in smoke. On the ground, I've been able to make out several vehicles. Most of them are badly damaged, as though they've been hit by anti-armour ordnance of some kind. Over.'

'Is the President's car one of those hit? Over.'

'I don't think so. It's further along, and as far as I can tell it's untouched. Over.'

'Can you see if the President's inside? Over.'

'Negative, sir. Visibility is way too poor. Over.'

'OK, thank you two seven one. Come back to base now.'

Albany removed his headphones and turned to Fujiyama, who was standing on his left. Behind the Colonel stood the Secret Service agents with faces like those of men on death row.

'Worked like a dream, sir.'

'Thank heavens for that. Check that the anti-jamming system is up and running on the helicopter. If it is, tell it to fly there now and use its rotors to disperse the smoke.'

Airman Turner came hurrying across to the Colonel.

'Sir, I have Vice President Heller on video. He wants to speak to you again.'

'Tell him I'm on my way.'

'And he wants agents Reilly and Shapiro with you.'

'We're coming.'

Fujiyama turned to Jim Crawford.

'Jesus, Jim – is your wife there?'

'Yes, sir. So I believe. And my little girl Tina, sir. The President wanted her along for the ride, so I've been told.'

Fujiyama put his hand to his forehead and pressed hard.

'Christ Almighty! I didn't know that. But you shouldn't go ahead of things. Don't give up hope. That last report said the President's car was untouched. This looks like a kidnapping.'

'Sir, I need to do something. I just can't sit around here waiting for news.'

Fujiyama hesitated for a moment. There seemed to be too many things to think about at once, all of them urgent.

'Jim, go to the administration block, tell Plato what's going on, and set up an incident room. Get Albany to make a link with the White House Situation Room. From here on in, we're on a twenty-four-hour alert. Whatever has happened down there, this will be the European centre for the search, whether it's for the President or for his killers.'

'Sir, I think the local police have to be alerted immediately. There should be roadblocks up and down the region as of now.'

Fujiyama nodded.

'That's Reynolds's job. Jim, why don't you find him, then get on over to Colonel Perodeau? Good luck.'

They shook hands, and Jim found an internal phone from which to ring Reynolds. Two minutes later, he'd been told that the Master Sergeant, instead of putting together a security team, had requisitioned a bike and headed on over to Middlewick alone, and was now uncontactable. Jim spoke quickly to Corporal Jose Gallardo, Reynolds's second-in-command.

'Get your entire team together and drive out to Middlewick now! Take as many weapons as you need, and expect opposition. If you're fired on, fire back.'

There was a brief silence as Gallardo took this on board. The Corporal wondered if he was being tested in some way, while his immediate superior was off base.

85

'Sir, you know I can't do that, sir. We're forbidden to carry arms on British soil. And we sure as hell don't have any authority to open fire on anyone. You'd better get hold of the local police, bring in their SWAT team, if they have one.'

'Corporal, the United States is very likely in a state of war even as I speak. We have reason to believe that the President has been killed or taken prisoner on his visit to Middlewick. Do you understand what I'm saying?'

The silence that followed seemed fraught with tension.

'I . . . Is this some sort of joke, sir? May I speak with Colonel Fujiyama? I want to know just who my orders are coming from.'

Gallardo was right, but he was wasting precious time.

'Gallardo, none of this is happening by the rule book. We're all breaking rules. But if the President's life is in danger, none of us has a choice.'

'Sir, how can I be sure you are who you say you are?'

'Fuck you, Gallardo. If you refuse to obey my orders, I will have you on a charge so fast you will enter orbit. Now, get this thing moving.'

Jim slammed down the handset. He hadn't waited for Gallardo's reply. It was a mistake he would come to regret. But an understandable mistake, given that his wife and daughter were down there with the President and might be dead.

'Where's Fujiyama?' he asked, of no-one in particular.

'He's in the blue room. I think the VP got back to him.'

Jim hesitated for about half a minute. Fujiyama had asked him to stay on the base, and without his permission he couldn't leave. But Laura and Tina might be dead or wounded, and at the least badly frightened. To hell, he thought. He was a pilot, not a security policeman.

'Colonel, I'm sorry you've been placed in this position. But if the airplane reconnaissance showed what you say . . .'

Vice President Heller looked like a man who'd been kicked in the stomach hard. If the President was dead or out of contact for the long term, responsibility for everything now fell on his own shoulders. And that wasn't something he wanted. He'd known since his teens he would never amount to more than vice-presidential material, and he'd gone on to fight hard to manoeuvre himself into that position. The thought of instant presidency made him want to get in a car and drive all the way to nowhere.

'Sir, I have a helicopter on the way there now. We should be able to get better details from it.'

Colonel Fujiyama didn't look much better. It was one of those moments when one of his samurai ancestors might have contemplated *hara-kiri* with a short-bladed sword. Being an American had its disadvantages.

'Good. Pass that to me the minute it comes through. Colonel, you're in a hard spot. You have no US military on the base, and even if we could fly some in from Germany or the Balkans, you still could not deploy them on British territory. I'm going to get permission to do that, but first you have to get other things moving.

'I want you to contact the local police and military, saying that you're speaking with my authority. Bring them up to speed and get them out there. We need roadblocks across the entire country. I'll ring Downing Street and bring them into the loop. But don't wait for me to do that. There's no time for diplomatic formalities.'

The video screen went blank, leaving Harry Fujiyama staring at nothing. He picked up a telephone and asked to be put through to Northumbria Police Headquarters at Ponteland.

Jim got to the officers' mess just in time to find half a dozen members of his squadron rolling in for coffees. Booze was still off limits: no-one had yet given orders to stand down from duty. Jim didn't know what to tell them.

'Major!' called out Jed Wawro, who was sitting at a wall table with six espressos lined up. 'What the fuck's going on?'

The others joined them. Everybody wanted to know what was going on.

Jim did not sit down.

'I'm looking for Bud Kramer, guys. Anyone see where he was headed?'

'He said he was coming here. There was something in the cockpit he needed to see to first.'

'I'll go over there.'

'Hey, Major, just what the hell is going on? Are we at war or aren't we?'

Jim shrugged.

'Nobody's declared a war, have they?'

He knew they hadn't heard about the President.

'Then how come we're told to fly back to base like twenty minutes after the goddam Turks launch an attack on Greece?'

The question took Jim entirely by surprise. Nobody had said anything about an attack the whole time he'd been in the communications room.

'I don't know what you're talking about.'

'Turkish planes hit a port in the north of Greece. Place called . . .' Jed looked round for assistance.

'Alexandroúpolis,' Dave Hallit, a new addition to the squadron, put in. 'About an hour ago. We've been listening to the BBC news. How come nobody is telling us?'

Taken completely by surprise, Jim just shook his head.

'There's more going on than that,' he said. 'Somebody just attacked the President's cars over at Middlewick. He may be dead or taken hostage, we just don't know. One of you should get over to the communications room, set up a link with the Wing. I've got to get hold of Bud.'

Before anyone else could ask a question, Jim was off, haring towards the airfield as fast as he could go. He found Bud just climbing down from his plane.

'Jim? What's up?'

Jim told him.

'Laura was in the car with the President. Seems he took Tina along for the ride. I'm going over there, Bud. But I need your bike.'

Bud just stared at him. He was Jim's oldest air force friend, he'd been best man at his and Laura's wedding, and he and his wife Lolly were the Crawfords' weekend companions. Their girl Heidi was in Tina's class at school. And Jim and Bud were combat veterans who spent time together knowing just how precious it was.

'Say what?' Bud hadn't even let the possibility of a prank cross his mind: Jim would never joke about something like that. So it must be true. But if it was, it wasn't something he thought he could take on board very easily.

'You heard me. Look, I need to talk about this later. But now I need to get there and see what's going on.'

'We'll go together. You got your gun?'

They both carried handguns, Browning Hi-Powers, in case they ever got shot down in combat and had to defend themselves against enemy forces.

Jim patted his holster, and they were off. Bud commandeered an airfield buggy and headed straight for the shed in which officers kept their motorbikes.

Since coming to the UK, Bud had acquired a couple of vintage Harley-Davisons. Jim wasn't a biker, but he knew how to ride. He took the less powerful machine, a red and black Road King Classic with a Twin Cam 88 engine, and followed Bud.

'Have you alerted security?' Bud asked as they headed for the main gates.

'Reynolds is over there already. I told Gallardo to get his ass down there as well, along with his entire unit. They should be there by now.'

They took much the same route that Reynolds had followed. If a police patrol car had been anywhere around, they'd have been pulled over for doing speeds far in excess of the fifty-mile-an-hour limit. But the roads were mysteriously empty, as though the countryside had been swept clean of humanity.

Their road in to Middlewick was the same that Reynolds had taken, and as they passed, Bud, who was in the lead, noticed Reynolds's machine where it lay in the ditch. He raised his hand and braked, then they both turned and rode back to the spot where the BMW was lying. It was only a matter of seconds before they found Reynolds's body.

Jim looked around. There was no sign of other casualties.

'He must have come out here on his own,' Jim said, as though speaking to himself. 'I told the stupid bastard to take a team.'

'Well, it's too late now. Whoever shot him knew what he was doing.'

'How can you tell?'

'Saw some like this back in Kosovo. Remember the Brits had some SAS types over the border, taking pot shots at key Serbs? They coptered one or two dead guys back to our side. I saw them laid out on the tarmac. The Brits were using snipers' rifles, heavy-duty bastards. They'd punch a small hole in the chest, and the round would come out through a barn door. Don't it look to you like Reynolds got in the way of something similar? Conclusion: some wacko sniper killed Reynolds. But a pro. Whoever did this was a pro.'

'Let's get moving.'

The White House Situation Room
Washington, D.C.

'Any idea what we're here for?'

Elaine Somerville looked across the long table at which an aide had seated her. Her companion, Charles de Rossi, shrugged. They knew one another well enough, both having been appointed deputies to Marvin Dickens, Assistant to the President for National Security Affairs. Neither had been in the White House Situation Room before. In their short time as Dickens's aides, there had never been a crisis sufficient to require it.

As newcomers, they were ill-equipped to notice that something out of the ordinary was going on. In the body of the room, men and women scuttled backwards and forwards, lights flashed on computer consoles, telephones rang, and lines and arrows marched across the giant map of the world that took up most of the right-hand side wall.

Next to arrive was Karen Sutherland, newly-appointed Coordinator of the ECHELON intelligence gathering network. Beautiful, unmarried, and forty-five, the tabloid press had greeted her appointment with barely suppressed glee that turned rapidly to frustration as they found her beyond any reproach their twisted minds could configure. She looked at Elaine and Charles, asked the inevitable question, and received two well-coordinated shrugs in reply. Shrugging in return, she sat down and set her briefcase on the table.

'By the way,' she said, 'I'm Karen Sutherland, Coordinator of ECHELON. What's going on? This place is pretty busy.'

They introduced themselves, united in their newness. Their eyes strayed from time to time to the large clock on the far wall. Each wondered just how long they were going to have to wait until somebody else arrived.

Elaine tried to fill the uncomfortable gap that followed the introductions.

'My guess is that something has happened in Greece or Turkey. Perhaps the Greeks have retaliated for the raid on Alexandroúpolis.'

'I don't think we should talk about that until everybody else is here and we know the whole story.' Karen tried not to sound censorious, but she could see that Elaine had been made uncomfortable by her mild rebuke. 'There's bound to be a satellite link with the President. He'll explain everything.'

She noticed that Elaine was wearing a Peruvian Connection pima cotton dress identical to one she had in her own wardrobe. What were deputies getting paid these days, she wondered. She changed the subject, leaving Charles to scribble notes on his pad and glance at the clock.

About three minutes later, General Sainsbury Patch, Chairman of the Joint Chiefs of Staff, made a grand entrance, accompanied by his own aides and by William van Buren, the US Representative to the United Nations. They were followed by an assortment of National Security Council assistants and John Habibi, Chief of Staff to the President. As these new arrivals took their places, the doors opened again, and the Vice President came in with a gaggle of aides, all carrying files and looking grave.

Heller took the seat at the top of the table which would normally have been reserved for the President. Nobody thought this strange, since the President was abroad, but Heller himself knew that his sitting there constituted an almost historic gesture.

'Gentlemen, ladies,' he began without preamble. 'Thank you for coming. I know this is unorthodox, having you meet here in the Situation Room, but I want us to have direct access to whatever information comes here. I'm constituting this meeting as a special sitting of the National Security Council. I know we're several

91

members short, but I wanted to get as many of us together so we can get moving with the crisis now facing us.'

'Which is?'

Stanley S. Rawes, the Secretary of State for Defense, was the least deferential member of the Council. He had arrived a few moments after Heller, and slipped into his own seat almost unobserved. With him he had brought a freshly-prepared statement for the President, which included a declaration of war against Turkey. Caught unawares by Heller's initiative in calling this extraordinary meeting of the NSC, he wanted to know what the hell the Vice President thought he was doing.

'Be patient, Stanley. You'll know everything in a moment. I just want to get Jerry Kovaleski on board first.'

As he spoke, a large screen on the rear wall flickered into life, and a huge image of the Secretary of State appeared above their heads. All eyes turned in his direction.

'Jerry, thank you for joining us. I think as many of us as can be here have arrived.'

Heller looked round the table. Most of those seated were strangers to him. He had to trust in his belief that the President had made the right choices. These men and women, he thought, and a handful of others, were about to walk straight into the biggest political storm their country had ever known.

'Thank you once again for coming,' he went on. 'By no choice of my own, I am coming to you as the bearer of bad news. Before I tell you what I've come here to say, I'd like us all to bow our heads in prayer. We are all of us about to set foot in a time of grave peril, and each of us will be tested to the limits of our strength. Let us pray.'

They bowed their heads. All round them voices called softly, telephones sang out like birds, and paper spewed from a score of electronic mouths.

10

Middlewick

Had it not been for the smoke, and the red flames that still spurted up from time to time from the shattered wrecks of motor vehicles, and the bite of real cold on their cheeks, and the wind moving with ice-cold fingers in and out of everything, they would never have believed the scene before them to be anything but a painting of hell's inner chambers.

From an open window above the greengrocer's, there came music, 'Sympathy for the Devil', sung by the Rolling Stones. The song, its words blurred by distance, floated through the smoke like a blind thing. It seemed as though the cars and burning buildings were all part of a massive stage set, among which unseen performers walked and were silently consumed.

Jim and Bud stopped their machines side by side and flipped the rests down.

'Let's leave the bikes here,' Jim suggested. He took his gun from its holster and led the way into the main street. They walked past twisted metal and the unmoving bodies of the dead. Flames had taken hold in several buildings. Jim paused and made an emergency call on his mobile, using the local 999 service. When he told the operator that half of Middlewick was alight – or would be by the time any fire engines arrived – he thought the man might hang up on him, so unlikely did this sound.

They passed the cars occupied by the SAS and Secret Service.

Charred bodies everywhere. Bodies on the pavements. Mothers and fathers, little children. Jim didn't hurry: he didn't want to see what was coming.

The President's car was covered in ash and bits of metal that had sheared off other vehicles. Its windows were covered in thin lines, but remained unbroken. It alone had been spared the worst excesses of the attack. For a moment, Jim's heart leapt, thinking that this indicated abduction and not assassination, in which case it was possible that Laura and Tina might still be alive, taken hostage along with the President.

And then he looked down and saw Laura's body, half in and half out of the car, part covered in blood, part untouched. He could not see her face, but he knew her right away.

'Keep me covered, Bud, while I go over there.'

Bud, who had not yet recognized his friend's wife, nodded and took up a defensive stance.

Jim walked to her slowly, as though she was sleeping after all, and he might wake her. He bent down and lifted her body away from the car, smearing himself with blood, drawing her in to himself, while his own body remained rigid, and his breath stopped moving, and he was in a certain way dead. He expected tears to come, or an animal cry, or some great expression of his unbearable rage, but nothing like that came, nothing but rigidity and silence, while the music floated from the broken window above his head.

He felt a hand on his shoulder, and his breath moved, giving him life again. Bud had knelt down beside him.

'Is it Laura?'

Jim simply nodded.

'What . . . what about Tina? Have you looked?'

Jim shook his head.

'OK, you stay there, I'll take a look round.'

As Bud got to his feet, he heard a faint sound crisscrossing the music. Within moments it had become recognizable as sirens. Someone was coming at last.

He looked everywhere, in and out of the car, but could see no sign of Tina, nor of the President and First Lady.

94

'Jim,' he said, 'I think they've taken Tina with the President. She's nowhere to be seen.'

The sirens grew penetrating. Bud looked round and saw motorcycles coming into the village, four or five of them. The riders, who were wearing USAF Military Police uniforms, started to weave their way through the debris. Bud stood and watched, thinking how much more easily they could have come through if they'd ditched their bikes and walked.

The first rider was Jose Gallardo. Seeing the President's car, he braked to a halt. As he switched off his engine, his right foot kicked down the rest. He dismounted and removed his helmet. In spite of the weather, he was wearing shades.

He straightened and looked directly at Bud.

'You!' he barked. 'Have you got permission to be here?'

Considering the circumstances, Bud thought this was the stupidest thing he'd ever heard a cop say.

'I'm sorry?' he asked. 'Are you talking about a pass or something of that kind?'

'That's exactly what I am talking about. Do you have one?'

'Reckon not.'

'You realize this place is out of bounds?'

The other riders started to arrive. Observing the evident confrontation between their leader and a man in flyer's clothing, they hung back.

Bud laughed out loud.

'Has it occurred to you to look at this place?' he asked. 'Corporal, I am an Air Force major, you are a corporal. I outrank you by several degrees; you do not order me off someone else's property. When I last looked, Middlewick was a public town on a public highway.'

'That's enough, Major. I have overriding authority here. Now, if you and your companion don't get your act together and leave pretty damn quick, I will have you on a charge so fast you won't see your feet moving.'

Suddenly, Jim Crawford got up, leaving Laura's body where he'd found it. Bright with her blood, he took several paces until he was face to face with Gallardo. It was immediately obvious to him that neither the Corporal nor his men had thought to arm themselves for their outing. He lifted his own Hi-Power and put the barrel against Gallardo's forehead.

'OK, fuckwit, enough's enough. Any idea who the woman is back there, the one with the bullet wounds? Recognize her?'

'I . . . ?'

'That is my wife, Laura. Captain Crawford to scum like you. Now, if you value your life, you'll leave her be, and you'll leave me and my friend be. Otherwise you will become another casualty of whatever fucking war this is. Understand me, Corporal?'

Jose Gallardo's working life had, until now, been devoted to speeding offences and Saturday-night brawls. With a gun pointed at his head while he stood in a wilderness of burned-out cars and murdered bystanders, he hadn't a clue what to do. He just nodded once and backed off.

More sirens sounded, coming from the opposite direction. Bud looked round, but it was too early to see anyone. He joined Jim, and together they took Laura's body and laid it gently inside the presidential limousine. Jim got in beside her, and Bud walked away self-consciously, knowing his friend wanted no-one with him at such a moment.

The first police cars came into the high street from the far end. Two came in together, then a third, then a fourth. Policemen and policewomen got out, English bobbies who had seen heads bust open on a Friday night at Newcastle's Bigg Market, and knife wounds in a set-to at one of Whitley Bay's infamous night spots, but who'd come unprepared for this.

Inside the limousine, Jim brushed Laura's hair, making it as tidy as he could. He'd found her handgun, and now placed it in her hand. She'd died trying to protect her President. Her eyes had been wide open, but he closed them now, gently, and they did not open again. That was when he vowed revenge, that whoever had killed her would die by his hand and no-one else's. And vowed he would find his daughter, even if it took him to the ends of the earth. He bent and kissed Laura's bloody cheeks, and as he did so felt the gentle hand of a policewoman on his forearm.

'Don't worry, sir. She'll be all right. Best to let her be till forensics get here. We'll look after her.'

'She tried to fight them off, tried to protect the President. That was her job. They had to kill her to get through to him.'

'I can see that, sir. I can see the gun in her hand. But don't worry, we'll look after her now.'

She took him gently by the shoulders, and he let himself be taken away, like a child in its mother's arms, tottering.

They buried her three days later at Arlington, at the edge of a storm, among raindrops. No birds sang, and when the bugle finally sounded, it rang out clear and august among the gardens of stone.

Vice President Heller had given permission for her to be given Armed Forces Honors, something normally reserved for presidents and secretaries of defense or others of that ilk. But Heller had been given no choice. Several of his aides had advised him otherwise, but he'd known instinctively that this was a time to listen to the public, not political insiders. In three days, Laura Crawford had become a symbol of what was great and good about America, and Heller wasn't going to be the VP who played down her death.

Her father and mother were there, her brothers, and an elderly aunt. The only indication that she was Jewish was the presence of her rabbi, summoned all the way from Boston. Jim stood between the Vice President and his mother-in-law, fighting back hot tears and memories that came with every breath. They buried her in her dress uniform, and they gave her the posthumous rank of colonel, and they drove her to her grave on a caisson drawn by six horses.

Only once did Jim show signs of breaking, when the gun salute rolled out nineteen times over their heads, and he was pulled back in seconds to Middlewick and the storm that had broken there.

All passed as it was meant to pass. The Old Guard took care of every gesture, every small part of grief, as they had done so many times in the past. CNN covered the event for an already stricken nation. Its footage went round the world, transforming America's grief into a curiosity for others. Israel broadcast the entire funeral, the rabbi's address, calling on the kidnappers to return, at the very least, Laura's daughter, her father stepping forward to say *kaddish* and to place a handful of rocks on the headstone, then stepping away again, leaving a lone soldier to stand vigil over the grave.

As Jim walked away, hand in hand with his mother, his father a few steps behind, a uniformed man stepped out of the crowd.

'Jim, I can't tell you how bad I feel about this.'

Until now, Jim had handled himself quite well. But the shock of seeing one of his oldest friends among the mourners unmanned him at last. They fell into one another's arms, old soldiers weeping for the death of a comrade-in-arms.

When they drew apart at last, Jim looked straight into Greg Hopper's eyes. Greg and he had been close buddies during the years Jim spent in the Marine Corps. Each had saved the other's life more than once, and their parting – when Jim left the Corps in order to enter the Air Force – had been difficult.

The Old Guard – men of the Third Infantry Regiment – walked away discreetly. The sun was going down in the west, like it does in the movies sometimes, restless to be away. Its light turned whitened marble to rose and nectarine, and raddled the Greek columns of Arlington House, where it stood overlooking the graves on its green hill to the west.

The two men pulled apart. Jim saw his parents and in-laws watching him from a little distance.

'Greg, I . . .'

Greg followed Jim's gaze.

'Yeah, I can see you've got folk to attend to. I shouldn't be sticking my nose in at a time like this. But I need to talk. Can we meet later?'

'Sure. I'm staying in Georgetown. The Air Force has some apartments over there, for single officers visiting the capital. Here, I'll write down the address.'

Jim took a small notepad from his pocket and scribbled a couple of lines.

'Telephone number's on there as well.'

'Fine. I'll meet up with you there.'

Greg made to go, then turned back to Jim.

'Jim, I'm so sorry about Laura. She was a great person. We're all going to miss her.'

'Thanks. I miss her already. I can't think how I'll cope without her.'

'You've got friends, Jim. Friends can help more than family at times. Here, you'd better take this.'

He reached into a small pocket situated below the long rows of medal ribbons that covered his chest. From it he brought out a small card, inscribed with his name and a telephone number. There was no address, nothing to indicate Greg's identity in either personal or geographical terms.

As Jim slipped the card into his jacket pocket, he became aware of Greg's fixed stare.

'You get my letter, Jim?'

Jim looked puzzled.

'Letter? I don't remember. When was this?'

'Back last October. I wondered how come you didn't write back.'

'I got no letter from you. Honest to God. Was there anything . . . ?'

'Nothing much. Just that I left the Marine Corps.'

Greg's news, told so abruptly, and coming so hard upon present grief, rocked his friend.

'Jesus, Greg, I had no idea you were thinking this way.'

'Hell, I'd no idea myself till it came on me, sort of sudden. I'll tell you about it when we meet. All I want now is to tell you I'm here. Jim, if you find nothing's going much forward with this investigation, if you discover the CIA and FBI and all those other know-it-all agencies are no closer to finding Tina than when all this started, then I want you to get in touch. I mean it. I know some good people, some heavy duty people who don't work for Uncle Sam. If you think you need us, ring me any time.'

The first of two cars drew up to take the families back to their hotels. Jim took his friend's hand.

'OK, Greg. I know you won't fuck me around. I'll be in touch.'

11

It was the first time the two families had gathered together for Christmas. With Jim's folks in Wickenburg and Laura's in Boston, there'd been a distance problem, one made worse by Jim's successive postings to air bases further and further afield. Now, it was grief that brought them together and grief that kept them apart.

Laura's parents had sat *shiva* for a full seven days after the burial, staying at home, as was recommended by the Talmud; but although they had now returned to public life, their clothes were still torn and their hair dishevelled. A host of reporters had turned up at their house in Brookline, clamouring for interviews, photographs, blatant grief. But by nightfall of that first day, their neighbours had spoken quietly with the reporters, and the following morning showed an empty street and an empty drive.

Nevertheless, the first days had been hard. Every newspaper that carried a story on the President's abduction (and which newspaper did not?) also ran syndicated pieces about the heroic Laura Crawford and her missing daughter Tina. The *Arizona Republic* and the *Phoenix Gazette* both treated the Crawford family as their own, and ran 'exclusive' feaures which they then tried to syndicate worldwide, usually with success.

Every time a TV studio broadcast something about the President and his wife, there would inevitably follow some words about brave,

100

beautiful Laura and little Tina, presumed to be with the President, wherever he might be.

Every school in the country, with the exception of the more evangelical Christian institutions, had its 'Help Us Find Tina' campaign. In every school foyer you could find a stand plastered with Tina's portrait. Money was collected and sent on to the White House, where a sizeable fund was accumulating; but nobody knew what to do with this largesse, because nobody knew where Tina was, or whether she was still alive, or how to find her if she was.

When they couldn't get footage of Laura's parents or other relatives, the press would run and rerun film of her Jewish funeral, and above all her Gentile husband wearing a yarmulka, reciting the kaddish for his dead wife. Meanwhile, back in Arizona, every church held daily services for the safe recovery of the President, his wife, and Tiny Tina. The Vice President declared it a sign of how the nation was united, that Christian churches prayed so fervently for the safe return of three Jews. Jim just wanted to get his little girl back.

Synagogues everywhere were packed. Some non-Jews pressed themselves inside, trying to expiate wrongs they could barely iden- tify. People talked about the Holocaust on television chat shows. Vice President Heller called it a defining moment in America's self-understanding. His opponents on the far right, and committed Christians of an anti-Semitic persuasion (often the same people) went onto the streets to burn the stars and stripes in rage and to chant of a coming apocalypse.

Jim, his parents, and, after some persuasion, Laura's parents, had attended the First Presbyterian Church that morning. Aware of their presence, the minister had preached of healing, trust, and tolerance. A television crew, discreetly placed, had filmed the service and its worshippers overflowing into the street, and the recording had been broadcast to the nation later that day. After it, the Vice President made an address to the nation.

Back at the house, Jim's mother set about preparing the late lunch. She took pleasure in showing Miriam Moskovitz how to set about making a Christmas feast. Jean Crawford's own family, the MacIntoshes, had come from Scotland originally, about five

101

generations ago, and Jean had retained vague notions of a Scottish Christmas, some genuine, some more the result of watching tartan-coloured Hogmanay shows on television down the years.

Relatives from both sides had wanted to be there, but after much heart-searching they had all agreed to restrict their numbers to the four grandparents, Jim, his brother Bob and sister Mary-Beth, and Laura's two older brothers, Danny and Moshe.

It was a strange and potentially volatile mixture, and the first time the principal members of both families had got together since Jim and Laura's wedding. They would never have got round to doing it if it hadn't been for the events of the past few weeks. Jim had just wanted to stay at home with his parents, but once his mother got it into her head that a family reunion was essential in times of adversity, everything from world affairs to the internal politics of her local church had conspired to make this happen. Jim just hoped it wouldn't turn out to be a dreadful mistake.

The Crawford home was too small to accommodate so many at one time, so his father asked the Moskovitzes to stay along with Jim, who had his own room, where 'he needed to get things out of his system'. Everybody else was put up at a nearby motel. Jim had gone out there in his rented Land Cruiser when he went to pick up his siblings and his brothers-in-law the previous evening. The foyer had been filled with plastic holly and artificial snow, there had been a cracked plastic reindeer whose red nose flickered violently, and a jolly crib of wood and straw, from which successive Christmases of children had filched everyone but the baby Jesus. The air had been laden with ersatz carols sung by custom-built choirs, Bing Crosby, and a host of electronically-manufactured elves and chipmunks.

His parents' home was not much better. The tree, hung with lights and trimmed with ancient baubles and tinsel, stood in the living-room window like a beacon of fidelity and despair. But, numbed as Jim was by grief and constant fear, it just washed over him, much as it must have done when he was five or six, and never thought to complain about the way his parents saw the world. Later, he'd found everyday life on the fringes of Phoenix City a mite restrictive, and in the end he'd fashioned a new one for himself.

His brother Bob had dropped out of high school first chance he had, and had never really got to grips with life since then. He was twenty-five now, and had done time for petty theft. He'd find a job for a while, then do something stupid and lose it, then spend six months or more complaining about life's injustices. People in town looked out for him on account of Jim, their local war hero, but a lot of the time there was nothing any of them could do. Bob had lived with a teenage girl on Phoenix Row for a few years, on and off. There was a rumour that he'd gotten her pregnant, but insisted on her having an abortion, much against her wishes and those of her family. Jim hoped that wasn't true.

Mary-Beth, Jim's sister, was in her first year of college, at Arizona University in Tucson. She was planning to major in photography and science fiction, the only two subjects in which she had any real interest, and for which there happened to be good collections in the university library. Maybe she'd build something out of it, maybe not. The photography had come about by mere chance. She loved the early Patti Smith recordings, and had read some of her poetry. A slim book on Smith's life had followed, one that contained photographs of Smith by Robert Mapplethorpe, and details of their time together. Mary-Beth had grown fascinated by Mapplethorpe, and now harboured ambitions of becoming a controversial photographic legend herself.

Jim didn't know if she had the dedication to make the course. Mary-Beth was pretty, extremely pretty, with a body that had sex sprinkled all over it, and she would always have a thing with men. Of course, she liked men, and she liked sex, which meant life would never be too hard; but her lithe body and the high she got from sex put a career and long-term stability at risk. That, at least, was how Jim viewed it. He didn't even ask what sort of career might be available to someone who liked science fiction.

He'd tried to talk about it with her a couple of times, but she'd always wound up shouting at him to stay out of her life, and stormed off, saying she'd rather have sex with a psycho than drop bombs on innocent people from one mile up. It was never any use telling her he was a fighter pilot.

The other half of the Crawford–Moskovitz junior divide, Danny and Moshe, had none of these problems. Danny had moved to downtown Boston, where he worked for the important law firm of Kopf Tremain, specializing in European trade law. He shared an expensive apartment in Quincy with his brother Moshe. Quincy was the now place for young Jewish professionals tired of Sharon and Canton.

Moshe was a paediatrician practising at Beth Israel Hospital in Brookline Avenue. Whenever possible, the two brothers lunched together, dined together, and attended performances together at Boston Concert Hall.

Beneath the surface, though, it wasn't all happy families. The older Moskovitzes still attended *shul* at the Kehillath Israel, a Conservative synagogue on Harvard Street. Danny and Moshe had stopped going there a few years earlier, and were now affiliated to an Orthodox Lubavitcher congregation, the Beis Menachem Mendel in Brighton. Everywhere, young Jews were becoming hardliners, observing the Talmud in its fullness, and coming down on non-observant Jews. Danny and Moshe were still half-baked, but year by year their parents noticed signs of growing fervour. They were both planning to get married to Lubavitcher girls recommended by their *rebbe*. Their parents thought it a strange world in which a mother and father were more progressive than their sons.

It quickly transpired that Christmas lunch had been a bad idea. They'd all wanted to share their grief, to find a focus for the unnameable thing that had killed a daughter and snatched away a grandchild. But it didn't work like that. They all had different griefs, and were trying to work them out in different ways. Jim and the Moskovitzes were the most truly bereaved. Jim's parents had never really got to know Laura that well, so all their anguish was focused on a granddaughter whom they loved only from the brief visits she'd paid to them over the years. Neither Bob nor Mary-Beth could have cared less. The Moskovitz boys had been shattered by Laura's death. It and Tina's disappearance had triggered off the beginnings of a neurosis, that it was their Jewishness that had singled them out somehow.

At first, it fell to Laura's parents to take the conversation in its inevitable direction, talking of how hard it was to adjust to the fact of a child's death, even when that child was grown up and had a child of her own. They talked about her childhood, bringing up anecdotes that the Crawfords had never heard, many of which were even new to Jim.

'What sort of food did she like when she was a kid?' Jim's mother asked. 'I remember when she stayed here, she enjoyed her food a lot. She was a good eater, know what I mean? She'd eat chilli and beans, and I'd make sweetcorn to go with that, big cobs with lashings of butter. She eat anything like that when she was younger?'

The Moskovitzes looked at one another, cautious of straying into difficult territory.

'She was what you just said, a good eater,' Mrs Moskovitz replied. 'Sometimes I thought I could never fill her. You expect boys to eat a lot, and sometimes these two nearly drove me crazy; but Laura could make a dinner plate look like it was a coaster. Of course, it isn't so easy for Jews. You know, we eat kosher. Back then, Harry and I were more observant than we are now, we kept a kosher kitchen. I still do now, for the boys, but Harry and I cut corners a bit. Laura used to like all sorts of foods, and we always used to have to tell her not to eat stuff that wasn't kosher. I'll never forget the day she found the Shalom Hunan. It's a Chinese restaurant on Harvard Street, but it's strictly kosher, a meat place, it serves terrific food that even Jews can eat. You can imagine the queues in that neighbourhood. Other times, we'd take her to Rami's Felafel, they do mostly Israeli-type food – felafels, pita bread, hummus, and hot sauce that hits the roof of your mouth.'

'Didn't she find it hard in the Air Force, keeping kosher?' Vince Crawford asked. There was a ball-game later on TV, he hoped the talk wouldn't go on long. In any case, he didn't feel too hungry, like he hadn't felt hungry in weeks. He noticed that nobody else except Mary-Beth seemed to be doing justice to their turkey.

'She'd moved a long way by then,' Harry answered. He'd barely picked up his fork. 'We worried about her. Naturally, we were proud of her, how she was serving the country and everything, but she was losing her Jewishness. She'd become so liberal . . .'

'Jews shouldn't work in situations like that,' Moshe broke in. He looked flushed, as though the subject disturbed him. 'Places they can't get regular kosher food.'

'The Air Force provides kosher meals,' said Jim, wondering where this was all leading. He wished his mother hadn't opened the subject.

'It's light kosher, it doesn't really count,' Danny said. 'In the Air Force, you get moved around from base to base, country to country. You can never be one hundred per cent sure where the food comes from.'

'Hey, you guys, cut it out,' their father snapped. 'Thirty already, and they think they know it all. Next thing is lectures on the Talmud and what the *rebbe* said last week. Boys, we're here on account of your sister is dead and your niece Tina went missing. This is Laura's husband sitting beside me. These are his family. Show respect. Behave like *menschen*.'

'They're nice boys, they don't mean no harm.' Jean Crawford tried to pour oil on troubled waters that she did not really understand. 'I bet they're missing their girlfriends back home? Is that right, boys?'

'Please, Mrs Crawford, you shouldn't call us "boys".' Danny seemed troubled by this piece of awkwardness, as though the word 'boy' had true legal significance and might one day soon be trotted out in court in front of him. 'We've been grown men for some time now. Only our mother calls us "boys" nowadays.'

'I'm sorry. But I expect that makes no difference to the girls up in Boston.'

Danny smiled.

'I'm sorry to disappoint you, Mrs Crawford, but there are no girls in our lives. Moshe and I don't date. We think that would be a sin against the Torah. But we both have plans to marry once our *rebbe* gives the green light. He's already got a couple of Lubavitcher girls lined up for us.'

'Jeez!' exclaimed Vince. He was feeling so far out of his depth, he could sense an empty sea opening up before him. Here, at Christmas, at his dinner table. He turned to the older Moskovitzes. 'You all right about that? Them having, what's it called . . . ?'

'An arranged marriage?' Harry shook his head. 'You want my

honest opinion, I think they're both crazy. Miriam does too. That sort of thing was fine for my grandfather's time. You brought in the *mohel* to circumcise your son, you'd ask the rabbi to instruct him before his *bar mitzvah*, and you'd pay a *shadchen* to find him a good wife. But nowadays only my sons want an arrangement.'

'They had girls in college you wouldn't believe,' Miriam added. 'Beautiful girls, like models some of them, and Jewish. Jewish princesses, they could have had any of them, but these perverts go making a thing about keeping themselves holy. For what, I should ask?'

'Mom, what's a *mohel*?' Mary-Beth, who'd been eating with one hand and scratching herself with the other, pretending to ignore the conversation.

'Don't ask me, dear. I think Mrs . . .'

Mrs Moskovitz tried to pass the question off, but Moshe broke in.

'A *mohel* is Yiddish for the circumcizer. He . . .'

But Mary-Beth just ignored him. Now she had Ma Moskovitz's attention, she sensed her way into deeper waters.

'Mrs Moskovitz . . .'

'Call me Mom. This is family. No "Mrs", please.'

There was a slight pull round the table. Nobody but Mrs Moskovitz seemed to feel it was time for such intimacies. Still, Mary-Beth shrugged and made the best of it.

'OK, Mom. Did it give you grief when Laura got married to Jim. Him not being Jewish. *Capisce?*'

Bob leaned back in his chair and sniggered. His father shot a look at him that might have worked five years earlier, but meant nothing to the tough guy who'd taken his son's place.

A little disturbed at first by the bluntness of Mary-Beth's question, Miriam was brought face to face with something she'd spent years trying to blot out.

'Yes,' she said. 'It hurt me immensely. I thought she'd betrayed me and her father, betrayed our community and our faith. And even though she's dead, and even though I still love her so much, the truth is, I still think so. But I said nothing to her. She'd made her choice, and she'd found a good man. So what if he was Gentile? That's what I tried to persuade myself. Her children would be Jewish, maybe she'd teach them enough, show them enough of what it's about to be Jewish. I won't pretend it doesn't still hurt me today, but I'm reconciled. She was such a lovely daughter, and now such a loss. Maybe one day you'll understand that, what it is to lose a daughter. If I could have her back, I wouldn't care if she was a Buddhist or a Hindu, just as long as it was Laura herself. My . . .'

'Don't get yourself worked up, Momma.' Danny left his chair and went to put his arm around his mother, whose tears were dripping onto the untouched turkey and potatoes on her plate.

'Jim,' broke in Vince, who was despairing of getting the conversation back on track. 'Have you had any news today? I haven't spoken to you since you were on the phone.'

Jim had been on the phone to a secure number in Washington, which he'd been ringing every day since Tina's disappearance. He shook his head.

'Still nothing, Dad.'

'Nothing? What's wrong with them? They spend billions of dollars on all these spy satellites and God knows what, and they can't track down the President of the United States. What kind of goddammed operation is that? It sounds to me like they couldn't find their own pricks if they had to.'

'Dad, I happen to know that they are working very hard on this case. It's the biggest criminal investigation ever. Not just in the States, but over in Britain, and a whole lot of other places. The reason they can't find the President is that whoever took him has gone to ground and is waiting for the fuss to subside before popping their head back above the parapet.'

'C'mon, what sort of excuse is that? If you'd just kidnapped the President and his wife, you wouldn't want to hang around, would you? You'd make your ransom demand, get your money, and push on.'

'It isn't that simple, Dad.'

'Oh, c'mon!'

'I'm telling you, they get maybe three thousand ransom demands a day. On top of that, a few thousand letters from people who think they've seen the President, or seen his body, or have heard something from someone who heard it from a friend, who had it from her mother . . . You get the idea.'

Vince nodded, but Jim could see he wasn't really convinced. An ordinary man like his father, caught up in a drama that touched on the fate of millions, could not understand why his government, in alliance with other governments round the world, employing the best minds across two hemispheres, and spending money like it hadn't been invented yet, could not track down his granddaughter's abductors and lead her home to safety.

'Don't they even know who was behind this thing? They must have left clues behind.'

Again, Jim shook his head. He understood his father's bitterness, he felt it himself every day when he lowered the telephone to its rest.

'Dad, they've got a thousand theories, and so far nothing sticks.'

'You think they're telling you the truth? Huh?' Bob opened his mouth for the first time. He'd been drinking while the others were at church, and until now had kept the fact fairly well concealed. But as the strained conversation across the table had gone on, his mask had slipped, and now he was careless and dangerous.

'Bob, it don't seem you're eating much. Why don't you . . .' His father managed to get a few words in, but he was too late. Bob was getting his dander up, and moving in for the kill.

'Why don' you jus' keep out of my hair, old man. You don't have a clue what goes on in this fuckin' country. Old Jim here thinks he knows jus' 'cause he's some power-crazed war hero that they speak to up there in Washington. But the truth is, you don't know your ass from shit, do you Jimbo?'

'That's enough, Bob.' Jim was getting angry, but he didn't want to lose his rag in front of the Moskovitzes. They'd always treated him kindly, even when they must have hated him for taking their daughter away.

'Ain't enough. Ain't half enough. You ever been told what this hell-to-tarnation government is up to? You heard of ZOG, hmmm? Zionist Occupied Government? Heard of that? Bunch of Jews and Freemasons and assorted motherfuckers got their hands on our blessed US Government, got their claws fixed right in the flesh of these United States. Straight people like you don't have a clue.'

'Bob, why don't you just cool it? Nobody here wants to hear your junk theories. Nobody in their right mind believes that sort of thing. Just a few lonely freaks spend all their time browsing the web and ain't never seen a shred of real life.'

'Go boil your ass. You think this stuff ain't been well researched? You think there aren't books and papers exposing the whole fuckin' thing? Like how there never was no Holocaust, just some fat-ass Jewboys telling the rest of us we should be sorry for something that never happened. You know that, don't you, you Jew cocksuckers . . .'

Danny was first on his feet. Jim watched him head for his brother, and didn't do a thing to stop him. Despite appearances, Jim had noticed earlier that the Moskovitz boys carried muscle. He wouldn't have chosen to go up against them.

By the time Danny had his hand raised and was about to strike laughing Bob full in the face, Moshe was on his feet, backing his brother up.

'Danny!' Miriam Moskovitz's voice was shrill with horror. 'You don't touch him, do you hear me? Put your hand down and come back to your seat.'

Danny held his attack position.

'Momma,' he said, 'I'm not a Christian. I don't have to turn the other cheek.' He faced Bob directly. 'Listen to me, punk. The Holocaust happened. It happened because Jews were weak and Jews were easily led. After we came out of the camps, we swore it would never happen again. There are no more weak Jews, Bob. If I had to kill you in order to protect the truth, I would do so. But since we are in your parents' home, and since they have extended hospitality to us, and since my beautiful sister Laura is dead, and since my lovely niece Tina could be in the hands of loonies just like yourself, I will not hurt you. Please do not say or do anything else that might provoke me. I hope you understand.'

'You should leave the table, Bob, and bring no more shame on our family.' His mother didn't know what to do to retrieve the situation.

Bob nearly risked it. But Danny's demeanour, and the looks of everyone round the table told him it wasn't worth doing. He got to his feet, casting a look of what he considered cool contempt round the table. As he stormed out of the room, Mary-Beth stood as well, and followed him through the door.

Jim watched him leave. He'd let Bob go for now, he thought. But he swore to himself that later, when it was dark, he'd take his little brother for a walk, and talk to him some about his behaviour, and when that was done, he'd give the kid the beating of his life.

'I think we'll have to leave,' said Harry Moskovitz. He looked genuinely sorry. 'Miriam and I can spend tonight in the motel with our sons. It isn't your fault. But I think we would find it hard to stay another night under your roof.'

12

Washington
White House Situation Room
4 January

It was January. The American people had just passed their first Christmas and New Year without a president, like a nation fast asleep. Today, a flame burned on the lawn in front of the White House, put there by order of the Vice President. On every tree and lamppost, on doorknockers and fences, on flagpoles and car aerials, someone had tied a yellow ribbon. Tourists came to gawp at the ribbons on George Washington Memorial Parkway, and most of them added one or two of their own. All round the White House, you could see people praying or just focusing their thoughts on the man who should have been living there.

It was the same in every town; not even the most far-flung gas station in the country was without its ribbon or its photograph of the President and the First Lady. And almost always, next to them, there would be a photograph of a smiling schoolgirl, Tina Crawford, daughter of a war hero, whose mother had given her life to save the President.

For as many leafless trees as sported a ribbon or a photograph, there were theories as to what had happened to the trio. Almost every passer-by had his own explanation, or at least one he'd picked up off the web or from some mass-circulation magazine. Most popular by far were theories of alien abduction, but these enjoyed no support among the better-educated sections of society. The *X-Files* were not flavour of the month. The weapons used on what had come to be known as 'the grassy knoll of Middlewick' had been anti-tank and other armour-piercing guns that had torn the heart out of a peaceful parade and the life out of dozens of families. There had been no gamma-ray projections, no Martian-built projectiles, no thought-transmitted particles of doom. It should have been a matter of simple detective work, but everyone involved could see that this was rapidly turning into the crime of this century. In the self-perpetuating world of conspiracy theory, no-one talked about Kennedy any more, or Diana, or the Tsar of all the Russias.

The room was packed. So many agencies, so many heads of state were involved in this thing, that Vice President Heller had decided to bring as many as possible together for a summit meeting. The sole purpose of today's conference was to bring together the results of all the investigations made so far. Faces around the room were grim. Everyone knew, one way or another, that weeks of work had so far led to very little result. A lot of hands were being shaken, and a lot of papers rustled, but nobody looked as though he or she had an answer to the questions that pressed on them all: had the President been killed or abducted (ditto for his wife and Tina Crawford)? If abducted, where were they now, and why had the kidnappers not been in touch? If, by some chance, one of the thousands of ransom demands being submitted every day turned out to be genuine, how could they hope to single it out?

'Gentlemen, ladies, please be seated.' Vice President Heller called the meeting to begin.

A lot of people were pressuring him to take on the mantle of the full presidency, but he insisted that to do so could put the real president's life in jeopardy. He reckoned that the President and his companions were of use to their abductors only so long as he remained nominal President of the United States. Heller believed his superior was still alive, and considered it immoral to usurp his position simply because he wasn't here in person.

'I understand that Prime Minister Manwell has a preliminary report on the British side of the operation.'

Joyce Manwell looked tired. She had not been in the prime

minister's shoes very long, and fought a daily battle against a tabloid press at home that considered her dowdy, intellectual, and liberal. Dean Heller liked her. He'd met her once before, at a joint summit on the continuing Northern Ireland crisis, when she was still Home Secretary, and had found her views refreshingly candid. Her directness over the kidnapping, and her willingness to place all British resources at the disposal of the United States, had been the only real relief there'd been for him in those first, horrid days.

She got to her feet slowly.

'Mr Vice President, I wish I could say that I'd come here bearing more than a report. Sadly, that is not the case, and I cannot honestly say how long we expect it may be before we can give you some positive results. I understand that you are having similar problems. By pooling our resources, I hope we can finally make some progress.

'Our primary problem is this: we do not know whether the President is still in the UK or not. For all we know, he and his wife may be holed up somewhere within a narrow radius of Middlewick. But it is just as likely that he may turn up in the Himalayas or Siberia or here in Washington. Every police force in Britain has been given orders to make the hunt for the President a priority, and I believe they have responded very well to the challenge that represents. House-to-house searches are being made, beginning with any property lived in by relatives of the erstwhile inhabitants of Middlewick. I'll return to them in a moment.

'On the day of the abduction, all our sea, air, and land forces, along with our customs services, coastguards, and others kept a close record of all planes, boats, and motor vehicles leaving Great Britain. That process still continues. All data are automatically dispatched to security services around the world, and every departure that we have not been able to intercept has been followed up at the next airport or seaport of entry. So far, nothing has come up.

'A second course of enquiry is our hunt for the villagers of Middlewick. They seem to have vanished into thin air. There have been sightings up and down the country, but none has held water once investigated. They may, of course, be abroad, with or without the President. However, we have been turning up some anomalies that may provide a key to what happened. The ambush

114

and abduction present us with a most implausible conundrum. Why would the inhabitants of a small English village turn into hardened killers, buy and ultimately use lethal weapons against the head of a foreign state, and then contrive to vanish into thin air? It's so unlikely, so obviously hard to contrive, that we are starting to wonder if that's really what happened at all. We would be grateful for suggestions that may get us closer to the solution to this particular mystery.'

A hand shot up almost opposite her. Dean Heller sighed. He hadn't wanted to proceed this way, hands being lifted, comments aired, and the meeting prolonged way beyond anything reasonable. He wanted to find the President, but he and the rest of the attendees had other priorities. Nevertheless, recognizing the would-be speaker, he nodded.

Gottlob Fischer was Secretary-General of Interpol. His father had been a high-ranking Gestapo officer who had worked for Interpol in the years it was based in Berlin. After the war, Fischer senior had found a ratline out of Germany to South America, leaving his son and mother behind to scrape an existence out of the ruins of the Reich. Whether from a desire to get even with his father, or from deeper motives best known to his generation of young Germans, Gottlob joined the West Berlin police on leaving school, and proceeded to make a career by clearing neo-fascists out of the city, and later in West Germany. This bias had already encouraged him to build theories about the group behind the President's disappearance, but, unlike so many others, he'd said nothing about his ideas to anyone.

'I'm sorry to interrupt,' he said, 'but I'd like to put something forward while it's fresh. Mrs Manwell, I do have a suggestion. I think – and I say this with all due respect for the extraordinary efforts you are taking – that it may be a mistake to think that the villagers of Middlewick are the culprits in this matter. As you say, how likely does this seem, that a small group of farmers and small shopkeepers in the north of England suddenly become so desperate to kidnap the President of the United States that they take the most elaborate measures conceivable and carry out a massacre in order to further their ends?

'Villagers are like other small geographically determined groups: they agree on the price of grain or whether or not they like the new vicar. But it's hard to think that they will all vote the same way, they may have a range of religious opinions, and so on. How come they agree on such a dangerous matter, a matter that will involve every single one of them, including the smallest child, a matter that could end in death or imprisonment for some or all of them?

'I'd like you all to think again. The people responsible for this outrage were not the villagers of Middlewick, but a group of indeterminate size who had an overriding need to carry this out. A political group possibly, perhaps anti-Semites who wished to take prisoner a Jewish president, or a religious sect who wanted to use him as a pawn in some wider chess game they are playing.'

Manwell broke in.

'Gottlob, I'm grateful for the suggestion, but our information shows that the villagers were going about their daily routines on the day the President arrived. They were there when the milkman did his rounds, when the postman delivered mail, and when various routine deliveries were made in the course of the morning.'

'Check more carefully,' Fischer said. 'There's an anomaly here that has to be solved. We will waste months if we don't solve this part of the mystery. Do you want to know what I think? I think the villagers of Middlewick are dead and that another group took their place. When this happened, I really don't know. But it may have been some time ago.'

Martin Vance, Director of the FBI, got to his feet.

'Gottlob, your head's too high in the clouds for the rest of us. Just how on earth do you wipe out an entire village and allow things to go on as usual? Don't you think somebody outside the village would notice that something out of the ordinary had happened?'

Before Fischer could reply, someone else was on his feet, Dick Cohen, head of the CIA.

'Mr Vice President, since this is a secure gathering, and we all possess the highest security rating, I would like to share with you an item of information dating back to the sixties, but still classified Above Top Secret. Do I have your permission to continue?'

116

Heller, already sensing that he'd lost his grip on the meeting, nodded.

'These are very unusual circumstances, Mr Cohen. Our priority is the President's life, so go right ahead.'

'Thank you, sir.'

Dick Cohen had been America's keenest legal brain in his day. By the age of thirty, he'd started picking and choosing clients the way a spoilt cat picks his food. If you'd had the money, you could have committed murder and mayhem up and down the United States, and Dick would still have got you off. Then, one day in spring, it had gone wrong. He'd successfully defended a client from Seattle, a man accused of killing a little girl in woodland along Puget Sound. In the course of the trial, the defendant had got to know Dick's daughter, ten-year-old Karen, and a week afterwards he'd picked her up from school and driven out of the city with her.

Dick's marriage had broken up soon after that, and he'd allowed his practice to go to pot. When he started practising law again, it was with the National Council for Civil Liberties, drawing down a salary that would have paid one of his secretaries in the old days. But he was good. The energies he'd previously put into defending the guilty now served the innocent. Judgments were overruled, appeals were heard, and woe betide the state governor who tried to send an innocent fifteen-year-old to the chair.

It wasn't much of a surprise, then, when newly-elected President Waterstone asked him to take charge of the CIA. He'd been given to believe he might expect a post in the FBI, but when the call came it was for the biggest job there was in foreign intelligence. His was not a popular appointment within the agency, but it restored public confidence, which was what Waterstone strove for above all else. Being top honcho at Langley wouldn't kill his demons – nothing would ever do that – but it helped keep them at a more comfortable distance.

'I don't know if this will be any help, but we've uncovered something in CIA archives which might just shed light on what happened. There's a bunch of files dating back to the mid-sixties, a few years after the Cuban Missile Crisis. The files relate to three

117

neighbouring Russian villages in the Saratovskaya Oblast', near the Kazakh border: Oparino, Storozhevsk, and Kraznozatonskiy.

'In June of '65, one of our spy planes reported unusual activity around this region. We managed to fly over the area again twice within a few days. When the photographs the planes brought back were studied, we saw something very odd. The second set of aerial shots showed a total absence of agricultural activity in the region. More than that, there was no sign of human beings anywhere, although farm animals were still visible in the fields.

'At that time, we had a mole in the Soviet Ministry of Agriculture, a woman codenamed Flamingo. She'd been giving us high-grade product over a course of seven years, and we knew we could rely on her as a perfect antidote to whatever official pronouncements might be made about agricultural policy or productivity statistics. It took her six months on this occasion, and we later learned she'd come within a whisker of being exposed and executed.

'She told us that the original inhabitants of the villages in question had been taken away in a series of convoys organized by the KGB. All this took place at midnight. By morning, nothing of the villagers could be seen.'

'Excuse me,' put in Joyce Manwell, 'but do you have any idea what happened to these originals?'

'They were taken somewhere in Western Siberia and put into labour camps. There was no particular reason. Meanwhile, new inhabitants were shipped into their villages. In the course of time, they became the genuine occupants.'

'But what on earth was the purpose of all this?' asked Peter Broderick, director of the National Security Agency.

'We don't have all the details, but it goes something like this: the plan was to create the illusion that nothing in that region had altered, when in fact the Soviet Ministry of Defence was building some huge project for which the villagers and their daily routine were part of the camouflage. It all came to nothing in the end. The ministry buildings are still there, but as far as anyone knows, they've never been used.'

'This is very interesting, Dick, but I don't really see what help it is to us.' Broderick, an old hand, had not yet cottoned on to the

118

need for full cooperation between government agencies involved in the search for the President. Vice President Heller, noting his tactic, decided to have a word with him afterwards.

'It means that something of this order has been done. If somebody did this back in the sixties, then somebody else could do it forty years later. I don't see why not.'

'It's an interesting theory,' Joyce Manwell broke in, 'but I don't think it's plausible. England isn't the Soviet Union. You couldn't just turn up with trucks and take an entire village away.'

Cohen shook his head.

'With all due respect, Mrs Manwell, but I've thought hard around this thing, and in my opinion it could be done, provided you planned it well enough ahead and left absolutely nothing to chance.'

The Prime Minister, intrigued, just nodded and asked Cohen to talk with her afterwards about his theory.

From the far end of the table, a hand was lifted. Jerry Kovaleski, the Secretary of State, had been listening carefully to the exchange.

'Excuse me, but I think we may have overlooked another significance in Mr Cohen's report. It may not be so much that this has been done before, but that there may well be people out there who remember doing it.'

Silence worked its way round the room.

'They could be in their seventies, maybe their eighties, but they'll be there in their retirement homes and lakeside dachas. Who knows what other crimes against humanity they may have committed? But all it would need would be for one of them to be in contact with one other person, perhaps a person outside Russia. I agree with Dick, it could be done.'

13

More hands went up. But before Heller could select one of them to speak, an aide entered the room and approached him, bearing a large white envelope in one hand.

'Sir, this has just been delivered to the White House. It was left at FBI Headquarters. The man who handed it in was some junkie, the security team nearly refused him entry. He told them a stranger had paid him twenty dollars just to walk across the road and hand a parcel in at the desk. The guards opened it and reckoned it was safe to hand over.'

Heller looked at the front of the envelope. It was a standard Fedex pack, stiff card designed to take small consignments of papers and slim objects. It had Heller's name written in bold black letters on front.

'Anyone get a description of the stranger?'

The aide shook his head.

'No, sir. Seems the junkie was too far gone to recognize his own mother. They're holding him in custody for now, but the man has his legal rights and they may have to discharge him soon.'

'We'll get back to him later. What was in the packet, and what makes you think it's worth your career interrupting a top-secret meeting just to hand it to me?'

'I . . . I'm not . . . sure, sir,' the young man stammered.

'Why don't you tell me what's in here? I take it you aren't wasting my time with something that hasn't been checked out . . .'

Everywhere, heads were craning to catch sight of the envelope.

'No, sir. The FBI agent who brought it round is a senior officer. He says that he and some of his colleagues checked this out at headquarters, and that you'd better look at it urgently.'

The envelope had already been opened. Heller put his hand inside and drew out a small, silvery disc.

'What the hell is this?' Heller asked.

'It's a DVD disc, sir.'

'Audio?'

'No, sir, it's a video disc. It contains about five minutes of video, sir.'

'How do I watch it?'

'You can access it through any one of the computer consoles in this room, sir. Or you can place it in the DVD drive in your own console and play it on all computers simultaneously.'

The Vice President weighed the disc on the palm of one hand for a few moments. It astonished him that something so light could be the centre of so much attention.

'Show me how to do that, son.'

The aide took the disc and fiddled about for a few moments on the Vice President's console. Finally, he inserted the little disc and pressed a button.

'Gentlemen, ladies, I think we're about to see some important film.'

Someone dimmed the overhead lights. Around the room, all eyes were focused on the tiny screens that ran along the table top.

The screens flickered for a moment, then a picture formed, clear and confident from the beginning. It showed three people sitting on armchairs, a man, a woman, and a little girl: the President, the First Lady, and Tina Crawford. The simultaneous intake of breath was immediately followed by a cheer that rapidly subsided. Then silence.

A date and time ran along the bottom left-hand corner of the film: *3 January 14.15 p.m.* The President was holding a copy of the *Washington Post* which was clearly dated the same day. Just to make sure, the cameraman zoomed into the newspaper masthead; he kept the lens focused there for about ten seconds, then pulled out again.

All three hostages looked exhausted. Tina's eyes were bright red, and she clung to Rebecca Waterstone as though she was her real mother. The President and his wife were trying to smile, trying to send messages of reassurance to loved ones and supporters round the world. But it was clear that, underneath, they were worried.

The President was wearing a charcoal-grey suit, quite different to the one he'd put on first thing on the morning of the day of the abduction. His new suit looked as though it had been tailored for him. The shirt and tie could have been taken from his wardrobe. His face was more pinched than usual, but immediately recognizable. Rebecca's clothes were likewise unfamiliar but well tailored, and in keeping with her style; she was obviously doing what she could to keep up appearances: her hair was washed and combed, and held in place by pins, her face was carefully made up, and her fingernails had been recently clipped. Little Tina elicited the greatest sympathy. Her abductors had obviously not been expecting her, so she was still wearing the school dress she'd had on that day; it was covered in caked blood, blood that everyone watching interpreted as her mother's.

From what the camera showed, the room in which they sat was extremely luxurious. The chairs were upholstered in what seemed to be the finest of fabrics, there were curtains in the same fabric that must have cost thousands of dollars, vases that seemed to be Chinese antiques held intricate arrangements of flowers. A Tiffany lamp glowed softly on a table next to Rebecca's elbow.

When a minute or more had passed, the President raised a sheet of paper from his lap and began to read from it.

'My wife, Tina, and I are well, though somewhat tired by our ordeal. We have been treated properly by our captors, and adequately fed. Our quarters here are cramped, but sufficient to our needs, which are not many. Neither my wife nor young Tina has been . . .' – here he hesitated for the first time – 'interfered with at any time. In fact, the people holding us are uniformly polite and courteous. Needless to say, they have certain demands about which they will seek to negotiate. Please be helpful, do not obstruct these negotiations, and please call off your hunt for me. Once your talks have finished and their demands are met, they promise to release us. I believe them, as does Rebecca.'

He paused and reached for what appeared to be a small mineral water bottle, and drank. His voice when he spoke continued clear, yet dead, as though he was some sort of living computer terminal, incapable of reading anything except in a low, deadpan fashion.

'However, if their demands are not met promptly and in full, they promise terrible consequences. My wife and I shall be put to death by the worst means. Tina will remain with them, to be raised in the ways of the Lord. There will be no peace anywhere until the thing is done. The suffering shall continue, day and night, until the land of unbelief becomes the land of His covenant again. They have the means and they have the will. As you have seen, their hand will not tremble when it is time to strike. I, who speak these words, did not write them. Listen and wait, then perform the Lord's work with your heart and soul and mind, according to the scripture. Wait, then, and when you speak remember to place honesty on your tongue and the ear of God on your hearts. Rejoice, we shall make of you a new nation.'

The President put the paper down. His expression had not altered the whole way through, nor did it alter now. Then, clearly by some prior agreement, the camera zoomed in on Tina. Hesitantly, her voice always on the verge of tears, she began to speak.

'Daddy, I hope you're listening to this tape. And Mummy too, if you're . . . still alive. I love you both, and I just want to be home with you again. The people here treat us real well, but it's not so comfortable, and there's no TV or playstations or anything, and all we do all day is sit about and listen to the engines. Please, Daddy, I want out of here. Do everything they tell you to do. Will you make sure all the other people in the government do the same? You mustn't upset them in any way, they are real serious about what they will do.'

Suddenly, she turned her head. A man's voice could be heard faintly, just out of shot. She nodded and turned back to the camera.

'Daddy, they say this is enough, and I have to go now. Give my love to everybody, Mummy and everybody in Wickenburg, and Auntie Miriam and Uncle Harry . . .'

The sound ceased, the camera pulled back, showing the trio for the last time, sitting together on their green and gold chairs, watching an unseen audience of millions.

Then the screen went blank.

14

They might have been anywhere. Their dead voices and their dead hearts were carried along in nothing. There was no sense of movement, but they all sensed that they were being taken somewhere. Whenever the lights went out, there came upon them a darkness no human eye or brain could fathom, as though they lay deep beneath the earth, or far beneath the waves, in a place natural light could not reach.

Every morning, on waking, it was like *Groundhog Day* again. The same bedroom, the same king-sized bed, the same soft music piped through their suite. They might have been in any luxury hotel in the world, except that the books in the little cabinet at the back of the sitting room were all in English.

A muted alarm would ring and they would wake out of a troubled sleep. Each would look for a while at the other, as if to make sure he or she was still there, then they would get up and dress from the range of clothing hung up in the large built-in wardrobe facing the bed. There would be hot tea and hot coffee awaiting them on a low table, with dark chocolate biscuits and chocolate-covered orange slices.

There must have been a hidden camera somewhere (though they had been unable to find it so far), because each morning as they were finishing their tea and coffee (Earl Grey for her, French Roast for him), there would be a discreet knock on the door and a young woman would enter to tell them breakfast was ready. The waitress spoke very little English, and their many attempts to engage her in conversation had ended in either giggles or silence.

Immediately outside the bedroom was a well-proportioned and comfortable living room, through which lay a small dining chamber. This last room had a peculiarity, which was that it had two tables specifically, they were told, to accommodate the need for kosher eating, one table being devoted to meat and the other to dairy produce. Throughout their married life, Joel and Rebecca had observed *kashrut*, except when away from home. They were not particularly observant Jews, but kosher eating meant something to them that they would not readily give up.

For this reason, they had always eaten apart at breakfast, Joel preferring meat dishes, Rebecca sticking to dairy. Naturally, they kept a kosher kitchen, and one day Joel left a note asking about this. A typed answer had awaited him the following morning, on his breakfast table, indicating that that had indeed been taken into account. Someone was going to a lot of trouble to ensure that the presidential couple was treated well.

When they entered the dining room, Tina would always be there, waiting for them. She acually slept in the living room, where a temporary bed was made up for her every night. At first she had caused their kidnappers considerable difficulty, since she had not figured in their original plans. They had no clothes for a girl of her age, which meant that she had at first been compelled to wear her own blood-spattered uniform. Rebecca had made a lot of fuss about that until, out of the blue, new clothes had arrived for her, along with a small wardrobe to put them in.

Tina's greeting each morning was enthusiastic. They were, after all, the only human beings between her and insanity. That day, they'd been total strangers, by now they were closer to her than anyone except perhaps her Mom. It was an unwritten rule that they spoke of Laura as alive. No-one knew for sure she was dead, and no-one wanted to add her name to the list that troubled Joel's brain so much.

The tables had been set in such a way that they could all chat between themselves while Joel ate his beef sausages and Rebecca and Tina tucked into yoghurts, Actimel, and potato bread topped with butter and salmon eggs, and washed them down with glasses of creamy milk while he downed a large glass of chilled Nesher Malt, a non-alcoholic beer that had been imported from Israel. Unless they were in Israel, of course.

But he'd discounted that, along with many other possibilities, some time ago. They'd been driven for miles after the massacre, shut off in their little compartment, quite unable to guess which way they were travelling. The van turned and twisted so many times, there was no way they could second-guess their abductors. Perhaps they were driven far north into Scotland, perhaps west to the Lake District, or more likely south into the heart of England. The reality was more bizarre, but they had no way at all of guessing what it was.

In a perverse way, Joel derived some pleasure from these breakfasts. He could not remember when he had last sat through a long breakfast like the ones he was offered, relaxed, peaceful, knowing he would not have to leap up at any moment to go back on the never-ending campaign trail, or to give himself over to the role of being president.

As each day wore on, however, these sentiments of indulgence changed. He fretted at being confined like this, unable to communicate in the simplest way with the world outside. And by 'the world', he meant exactly that. What if the war between Turkey and Greece had escalated, and US pilots and – he feared even to think it, but could not rule it out – even ground troops had become entangled in it? By now, Russia might have thrown its weight behind the Turks, might – and this was what frightened him most – have provided its allies with nuclear weapons. Heller would not be up to such a situation, Joel was sure of that. He needed to be there in Washington, not stuck here in some anonymous hotel, however luxurious.

Rebecca did her best to reconcile her husband to his enforced idleness. She never faltered in her resolve to get them all through this time of peril.

'Joel, you have to stop fretting,' she said to him on the night after the filming. 'It's bad for you, and it doesn't help the child. Think of her more than you think of yourself and being president. She

127

needs reassurance, but when she sees you with your head in your hands, when she senses your despair, it makes her confused.'

'I'll do my best.'

'You'll do better than that. As long as things continue like this, we're down to basics. That makes all our decisions easier. Tina Crawford has become, to all intents and purposes, our child. Certainly, she has no other parents, no other human being to turn to.'

He took her in his arms, gently, each of their limbs knowing its way around the other, until they nestled perfectly.

'I said I'd do my best. I'm very fond of her, she's a delightful child. But I have my worries, you must understand that better than anyone.'

'I understand it well enough. I just want you to take on board things you can actually do something about. Leave the rest to one side, there's nothing you can do about them. Dean Heller's a good man. He'll have every agency in the States looking for us, practically every security agency in the world. It'll be the biggest manhunt in history. Just be patient. Let them do their jobs.'

'And if they don't find us? After all, we must be very well hidden, and it's not impossible that we are unfindable. We've just made a video that will be used to make some sort of ransom demand. I don't think our keepers will be asking for money. They're obviously religious extremists of some kind, and their demands are bound to be impossible. But the only way for us to get out of here will be for those demands to be met.'

It was hard for Rebecca to keep her spirits up in face of Joel's growing negativity. She spent most of her days in the living room with Tina, while Joel stayed in the kitchen reading. Their captors had provided them generously with means of entertainment. There was a large Bang & Olufsen TV set with its own video. The TV was incapable of receiving transmissions, but they could play video tapes from a small library in one of the living room's cupboards. There was a complete set of *Friends*, everything Audrey Hepburn ever appeared in, romantic comedies with Meg Ryan, all the episodes of *Frasier* to date and a collection of BBC costume dramas. But nothing horrific or violent.

Besides the videos, they were supplied with an even larger collection of CD-ROMs catering for a vast range of music. Tina, whose musical tastes were poorly formed, played some records through and through in the first days, as though to distract herself from what was happening. Later, Rebecca talked to her, and out of that conversation was born Tina's musical education. Rebecca knew more about opera than anything, so they started with opera, supplementing the CDs with video tapes of the more popular operas. Either way, Rebecca would go through the story in detail, showing her passages from the librettos, showing how the music and the story developed together. Within days, the Spice Girls had been consigned to a corner of Tina's heart reserved for false loves and wasted affections.

And so a semblance of normal life continued for them, even if no-one was for a moment deceived. There were no windows to the outside world, not so much as a crack. Any doors giving external access were permanently locked. When the lights were switched off – ten minutes after a courteous announcement that this was about to happen – it was awesomely dark. Nightlights eased the sense of total gloom, but nothing could ease the feeling all three had to conquer each night, a hopeless ache of claustrophobia that sometimes woke one or another of them in the middle of sleep, an oppressive sense of something bearing down and in on them, something that threatened to obliterate them at any moment.

They possessed no sense of time. Their wristwatches had been removed early on, leaving them with nothing to tell the hours by, except for the arbitrary click that indicated the going on and off of the lights.

Possibly connected to this determination that they should not open their eyes to natural light or experience any sense of natural time progressing, there had been a number of occasions on which they had been knocked unconscious by injection and then allowed to come round slowly. It had first happened after a drive of what must have been hours on that first day. Whether they were in the Scottish Highlands, up a mountain in North Wales, down a Cornish tin mine, or had just gone round and round in circles and wound up more or less back where they came from, they had at least come to a halt, uncomfortable and desperate to use a toilet.

They'd been let out into the main interior portion of the van, where a chemical toilet had been put in place. They took it in turns, and were returned, one at a time, to the narrow space, then, after several minutes, out to the larger section once more, where car seats had been fitted. While they were seated in these, hungry and aching in every limb, a man entered with a tray of hypodermics, swabs, and plasters. He made quick work of the injections, and refused to answer any of their questions. Minutes later, they had all succumbed. When they awoke from their stupor, hours seemed to have passed, and they found themselves in the rooms they were now in.

After that, the man returned a number of times. They demanded to know what was in the injections, but he refused to say anything, and it was clear that any kind of resistance would be sorted out quickly and efficiently. Joel thought he understood whatever rationale lay behind the first use of drugs, since they were clearly in the process of moving them from the van to wherever they were now. But after that? Hard as he tried, he could not fathom it. If they were ever moved out of their apartment, for however short a time, it was, presumably, only in order to hoover their rooms or change their bedlinen. But all that could be done easily enough with them all in one room.

Something had to happen that required their absence, and however hard they thought their way around it, the answer never came.

Without windows, without time, without a sense of change or movement, the days began to blend maddeningly into one another, until life became one never-ending parade of the same thing. It was much worse than being in any prison, or locked inside a single room. Prisoners had days to mark off, real rooms had windows and views of something, if only a chimney stack. It was a strain not to go mad.

And then, one morning, as they sat down to breakfast, Tina looked up from her Cinnamon Grahams.

'We're on board a submarine,' she said. 'I've been thinking it over, and it's the only thing that makes any sense. They knock us out to prevent us from finding out we're on board a submarine. We're going somewhere after all.'

And she was right. They were going somewhere.

15

The Presidential Task Force Room
CIA Headquarters
Langley, Virginia
7 January

CIA Director Dick Cohen looked like a schoolteacher whose pupils have run amok, some of them carrying guns, the others dope. He was in that impossible position of someone who knows he has nobody else to turn to for help. The Vice President had already made it clear that he was getting on with the task of running the country, that he was not to be disturbed unless absolutely necessary, and that, in any case, he didn't have much of a clue what to do about the crisis.

The authorities had just made public the video of the President, Rebecca Waterstone, and Tina, leaving off the demands made by their captors. Within minutes of its first showing, the American people had gone into overdrive. If they'd been praying before, they now prayed overtime, ten or twelve times a day, invoking the names of more gods than a sane universe could have had room for. They prayed in twos and threes, in dozens and scores, in small congregations and nationwide assemblies conducted by television show hosts. The nation's televangelists stayed prudently clear; having duly considered their position, they had tacitly agreed that their prayers were best reserved for their regular cash appeals, rather than the earthly salvation of a Jewish president.

With greater generosity, every football match, every ball-game, every basketball tournament and every stock car race was opened and closed with prayers. Elsewhere, Pope Urban IX recalled his predecessor's millennial apology to mankind, and again preached reconciliation with the Jewish people. In Israel, the Chief Rabbi led daily prayers at the Wailing Wall for the safe return of 'Israel's most blessed son'. In the Hawziyya Ilmiyya in Iran's holy city of Qom, Ayatollah Mesbah Yazdi denied Islamic involvement in the kidnap, but called on the American people to repent and to take the crisis as an opportunity to see off the Jewish parasite that had so slyly battened on their minds and hearts.

Across the globe, mouths buzzed with speculation. Every would-be sleuth and secret service agent bent to one preoccupation, the hunt that would lead to the ultimate prize, the reward that would turn mere lotteries to sand.

More practically, men across the States formed vigilante groups and offered their services to the National Guard or the FBI. Others chartered planes to fly to England, where no arrangements had been made to receive them, and where no-one was very pleased to see them. Britain had gone into a guilt-induced funk since the kidnapping, and had set its face hard against anything that might be interpreted as an admission of involvement in the crime.

In Washington, a task force had been set up to coordinate international efforts to find the President. Its members sat together for the first time in room B#19, set aside in the basement at Langley. B#19 had been built along the lines of embassy Kremlins around the world, impervious to bugs or long-distance spying techniques. It was swept for all the usual bugs every hour, and for the less common once every twenty-four hours.

The international nature of the manhunt had made it inevitable that overall control pass to the CIA, though all other important agencies were involved. Interpol, Britain's MI5, the United Nations, and many others from outside the US had observer status.

Dick Cohen was the only directorship-level member of the task force. The rest had been carefully chosen, some because of their professionalism and skill in conducting operations of this kind, some because they could be relied on to report everything back to their bosses, and others for their political acumen.

'OK,' said Cohen, after getting through the introductions, 'let me spell this out. The twenty-five of us in this room have been designated the Presidential Task Force. Since there has never before been any organization of this kind, I have no more idea than you do how to go ahead with it. But I will tell you what Vice President Heller wants from us. He wants us to find the President.'

Something very like a moan went round the room. Cohen put up his hand.

'Wait a minute, wait a minute. Try not to get too far ahead of me. You're perfectly correct if you think finding the President is the most thankless task of the new millennium. President Waterstone could be anywhere in the world right now, and until we get better information, I think we just have to forget him for the moment.'

'Are you crazy?' Matt Liu, a computer systems analyst from the National Security Agency, looked shocked.

'Matt, please don't jump off the wall at me. I'm trying to do a job here. That job is to find Joel Waterstone, his wife, and a little girl who was kidnapped with them. To achieve that end, I propose that we forget about them for the minute, since we have nothing – and I mean nothing – to go on that looks likely to lead their way. Instead, I think we look for the people who kidnapped them, since that is, at present, a more realistic project.'

'You know something we don't, Mr Cohen?' The speaker was Brian Quinn, an Irishman who had served Interpol for several years as Head of their Fugitive Tracking Programme. Dick had been warned that the Irishman was blunt but honest.

'In a way, in a way. But I'd like to get some other things out of our path before I come to that, if you don't mind. I was instructed to tell you that Congress has voted you the largest ever peacetime budget for a single operation. No real limit has been placed on what we spend.'

Eyebrows went up across the table. Then a loud voice interjected from the far end.

'Mister, I've heard the words "spend as much as you like" more times than my sainted mother had sex with the postman, but when it came to it, I never got close. Before you get to order so much as a box of blue paperclips, there come the memos warning that

134

all Federal budgets will be subject to revision and that you should exercise caution in everything you spend. Check it out! "Spend all you want, but don't come to me at the end of the day with a deficit the size of Texas." So what can we expect to spend?'

'That really has to be determined. For the moment, behave as if it's true. We've also been promised direct access to all police and security agency files. You can act on that as far as this country and most of the Europeans are concerned. Apparently' – and he shot a look at the MI5 representative, Dennis Wadham – 'the British Official Secrets Act prevents their disclosing items covered by the Act. You won't be surprised to learn that the Chinese regret that they cannot engage in anything likely to expose their state secrets.

'It's not impossible that someone out there apart from the criminals already knows where President Waterstone is. And we'd do well not to rule out the possibility of a rogue regime being directly involved in what happened.'

He took a deep breath and let it work its way round his lungs and out again. The truth was he felt tense. Chairmanship of the task force was beginning to take its toll, yet he knew it was likely to prove the greatest responsibility of his career.

'Fact is, we can't afford to waste much time checking out the Chinese or anybody else. To offset that, the Vice President has given this group full access to ECHELON.'

Across the room, looks were exchanged. It was as if a loving father had just told his child he could spend all day in the toyshop and buy anything he wanted. Anything. There was only one drawback – which was yet to be mentioned – and it was that you couldn't tell anyone about your day shopping, or about what you did afterwards. Not ever, not even when you were a little old man and writing your memoirs. Everyone knew what would happen if you did. They'd kill you. And if you had a wife and children, they'd kill them as well. And if your children had wives and husbands and children, they'd kill them too. ECHELON was the biggest secret in the world. Once in, you were in for ever, with no way out. In silent offices across the world, they called it the Echelon Taint: once you came in contact with it, it would leave its mark on you for good.

135

16

Washington
8 January

It had been a season of funerals. In England, they had buried their dead by Christmas. It had been a long task, first identifying the bodies, then carrying out the post mortems, each attended by a medical examiner flown in from the States, and finally consigning the dead to earth or flame. Forty-four bodies in all, seventeen men (including SAS and police), fourteen women, thirteen children. Their tombstones – if they had any – said nothing of their way of death. But the afternoon of Northumberland's holocaust was already graven in local memory and would remain that way until the stones had lost their inscriptions and the graves had become invisible among tall grass, and the great wall of the Emperor Hadrian no longer stood there.

Twelve members of the Secret Service had been killed in the blasts that destroyed their cars, or in machine-gun fire. After a few weeks in the possession of the coroner for south Northumberland, the red tape that kept them in England was torn to shreds after some stinging words to the Foreign Office from the US embassy. Two weeks after Laura's burial, Arlington Cemetery shivered once more to the sound of rifle fire and the snap of leather soles on its pathways. Jim was there. He did not have to be, and several of his friends advised him not to go. But it would have been a betrayal of some sort for him to have stayed away, or so he reckoned, or felt it in his heart. They were buried together, shoulder to shoulder, near the Tomb of the Unknowns, and ground was cleared nearby, where a memorial could be erected in their honour.

Jim stood and saluted as each body was lowered into darkness. He looked round from time to time at the huge crowd of relatives come to bury their dead. They'd come to Washington from every corner of the Republic, ageing mothers, grief-crippled wives and girlfriends, and, behind them, pale within their unhappy rows, the endless cemetery dead, whole generations murdered for their country's sake. He thought at first he was simply another mourner, with a shade at his side, like all the rest. But as he walked away at the end of the ceremony he knew he did not belong to them after all: his wife was dead, but his daughter was alive and waiting to be released from her nightmare.

He turned and looked back. The crowd was breaking up. In minutes, they would all be heading back to some sort of normality, to grieve and, in time, recover from grieving. He would have gone with them, and spent his days remembering his dead wife, and showing her photograph to old men on the street and drunken men in bars. But he had a daughter to find and free from her captors. Something came down in his mind when he thought of her, like steel bars. He took her photograph from his wallet and stood staring at it as though it was an icon and he its worshipper. When he looked up again, the crowds had largely dispersed, escorted from the cemetery by members of the Old Guard. A uniformed Guard officer was walking towards him.

'You all right, Major?'

He slipped the photo back into its place, and put the wallet in his pocket. His fingers fumbled as he did so, and he realized he was growing cold. A sharp wind was running in off the Potomac, turning the air in the graveyard to ice.

'I'm fine,' he said. 'Just thinking my thoughts.'

The soldier was closer now, and Jim saw him catch sight of his name badge.

'I'm sorry, Major Crawford. Didn't know it was you.'

'That's all right. You did no harm.'

'We try not to.'

137

The soldier was a kid, maybe twenty-four, twenty-five; same age he'd been when he'd met Laura.

'You must see a lot of this sort of thing, son.'

'Sir, yes sir. I attended your wife's funeral. I hope we did well for you.'

'You did a good job. Maybe you'll be there one day to put me with her.'

'I hope it's long after I leave the service, sir. Sir, it's getting dark. Can I help you in any way? Whereabouts are you headed?'

He did not answer at once. All around him, the graves reddened in the dying light. And the light gave way to the coming darkness. And high above the Washington Monument, a small star shook, as though it lay sunken beneath rippling waters in a vast sea.

'I'm going to find my daughter,' he said. And he walked aside to find a way out of that place.

Public Liaison Office
Presidential Task Force
E Street
Washington, D.C.
9 January

He edged his way through sullen winter crowds, earthbound, wishing he had wings to fly above it all. When he'd first started his daily routine of asking whether there was any news at all about Tina, he'd been made welcome at the White House. The Vice President had seen him on the first occasion, and spent half an hour talking about the situation. Then it had been a succession of aides, until he'd been told to see a senior agent at FBI headquarters. Now they were sending him to some newly-opened office that doubled as the press bureau for the Presidential Task Force, where he was to see a minor official called Saul. They had lost interest in him, war hero and father to the nation's lost child, and he prayed that did not mean they had lost interest in her.

He stopped at a steel door set in the grey concrete of a brutalist

138

building. Only a small label next to the door revealed the building's identity. They certainly weren't encouraging visitors. He lifted his finger reluctantly and pressed the bell. If it rang, it rang too far away to be heard.

Several seconds passed, then a woman's voice crackled emptily through the intercom grille.

'Please state your business.'

'My name's Major Crawford. I've been authorized to come here in order to check on progress in the search for my daughter. I was told to speak to an agent Saul. I'm sorry, but I don't know if that's his first or last name.'

'I don't know anything about that, sir.'

'I have the authorization of the Vice President.'

'Sir, I believe I'd have to see that in writing.'

'Well, I believe I don't have it in writing, since I had it from Mr Heller face to face. Perhaps you'd like to put that to the test. Why don't you just pick up the phone on your desk and call the White House?'

It seemed absurd to him to be standing on this strange street, arguing with a voice in the wall while passers-by gave him the once-over and walked on. There was silence from inside, and for a moment he thought the woman had just abandoned him. Then her voice slid through the grille again.

'What did you say your name was, sir?'

'Major Crawford, USAF. Jim Crawford. My . . .'

'You may as well come in while I check this, sir.'

There was a buzz, and he pushed the door open. At least I'm inside, he thought. The door closed with a snap behind him.

He found himself in a small lobby, much smaller and shabbier than any he'd seen before in Washington. It seemed to indicate very low priority for the operation. He wondered who had decided to relegate the search for the President to this level.

A young woman in a regulation FBI jacket was seated behind a low reception desk. Behind her, the wall was decorated with portraits of President Waterstone and his smiling wife. Yellow ribbons were tied across the frames. There was no sign of Tina anywhere. Back in the White House, Vice President Heller had hung

139

pictures of both Laura and Tina next to those of the Waterstones, a black ribbon on Laura's frame.

'Yes, sir,' she said. 'Can I help you?'

'We already spoke. I'm Jim Crawford. I'm here for my regular report on my daughter.'

'Forgive me, sir, but I don't think I know anything about this.'

She was young and blonde, and she had a voluptuous chest, and Jim felt embarrassed leaning forward to read her name badge. Her name was Agent Hopkins, no first name.

'Agent Hopkins, did no-one tell you I would be coming?'

'No, sir, no mention of you. Perhaps you can tell me your business, then I can see whether we can help you in any way.'

He felt himself being held at a distance by a bland bureaucracy. Agent Hopkins was just the first uncomprehending face in a limitless line of blank faces. If he didn't bring her round, he'd be in here for days until they threw him out.

'Hopkins, you most assuredly can help me, but only if you engage the gears in your brain. Shall we see if they taught you anything at Quantico? For example, are you aware that the President and his wife were kidnapped several weeks ago?'

'Major Crawford, that's the whole purpose of this office. We were set up to . . .'

'Yes, of course you were. Now, do you remember anything about a little girl being kidnapped with the presidential couple?'

'You mean . . . I'm sorry, but I forget her name. Yes, Major, there was a little girl.'

'Exactly. She is my daughter. Her name – and please tell me you won't forget it again – is Tina. Tina Crawford.'

'I'm sorry, sir, I . . .'

'No, I haven't finished yet, Miss Hopkins. Tina's mother was Laura Crawford. I attended her funeral in Arlington a few days ago. The Vice President was there in person, and a hell of a lot of other top brass. You may have seen it on television.'

'No, sir, I . . . My boyfriend wanted to watch the Skins game. Turk was playing again at number one, with Conway in five. I'm a fan too. What can I tell you? But I know who you mean. Laura Crawford. It must make you feel kinda special.'

'No, miss, it makes me feel lost. But that isn't your concern. The White House gave me this address as a place to come to for information about the search. Am I to get it from you, or is there someone higher up . . . ?'

Her golden hair swung like a bell as she contradicted him.

'No, sir, I'm sure I can deal with this . . .'

'Because, if you can't, maybe I can speak to one of your superiors about it. They would remember who I am, who Tina is. I was introduced to your boss, the Director of the FBI, at the funeral. He seems a nice man, though that might not be your experience. I gather he can be unpleasant.'

'Sir, just tell me what it is you want.'

'I don't want much. Just to know what progress has been made in the search. Are there any fresh clues, any breakthroughs? Has an informant come forward? You must have information.'

'It's possible we do, sir. But you need proper authorization before we can disclose it to you.'

'I just told you who I am and who sent me here.'

'Sir, I understand that, sir; but you must have that authorization in writing.'

'If you think I have the time to run back and forwards between here and the White House . . . If you're so desperate, why don't you just pick up your phone and ring Walter Glenpatrick at the White House press desk?'

'Sorry, but I'll have to pass on that one, sir. It would be a breach of security if a third party learned you'd been making enquiries here.'

'So, you're freezing me out?'

She smiled at him furtively. Beside her, the inner lobby door opened and a man came out. While the door slowly swung back on its hinges, Jim could make out a long grey corridor in which low-voltage lights flickered and faltered. The man deposited a buff file on the reception desk, turned on his heels, and was gone back through the door before Jim had a chance to say a word.

'Did someone instruct you to fob me off like this? I'd like to know: my daughter's life is at stake.'

'Sir, I already told you, we require written authority. It's Bureau policy.'

'Very well, I'll come back with a piece of paper this time tomorrow. But it's only fair to warn you that your job is on the line as of this minute.'

She flashed a big smile at him; he wondered what sort of dentist could have produced such wonderful teeth. Or maybe she'd never visited a dentist in her life.

'You'd be wasting your time to come back here, sir. This office will be closing shortly, and will not be opening again.'

He looked at her as though she'd just laughed in his face.

'Don't bet on it,' he said.

That night, he hit the bottle for the first time since Laura's death. He wasn't a drinker by nature, and he never touched booze when he was on duty, so it took only a few whiskeys to send him into a spin.

He'd ridden a cab straight back to the apartment in Georgetown that the Air Force had laid on for him as long as he was in the capital. The rest of the day had been spent making phone calls, at first with the assurance that a word with this or that person would change things, towards the end with the certainty he was out of the loop. That was when he'd started drinking. Because he was a fighter pilot, and because fighter pilots don't drink when they're planning to fly, he thought he had the control to handle it. He started with a few light beers, but soon found his hand reaching for the bourbon that had come with the apartment.

He was still the worse for wear when the telephone rang. It rang ten times before he managed to find it, and another three before he managed to pick it up.

'Daddy?'

The room wobbled. He felt hairs move on the back of his neck, as though a ghost had spoken. When he looked down, he saw that the bourbon bottle was empty. Had he drunk that much? Had he brought tormenting ghosts into his world, and with them God knows what other graveyard horrors? The phone crackled again, and the same voice wriggled into his ear.

'Daddy? Can you hear me? It's me, Tina.'

He should have put the phone down then, but he couldn't. Not in a million years could he have hung up. He summoned up every ounce of energy and sense in his being, and spoke. Already he could feel himself sobering. Very carefully, then, he spoke to her.

17

He let the receiver fall back on its rest. It fell into place with a click that filled the room. His hand was shaking, and he thought he was about to be sick. It had been Tina, his daughter, live at the other end of the phone; not a recording, not the auditory component of a drink-induced hallucination. Unnoticed at first, tears were coursing down his cheeks, and without conscious control his hand went to his face and wiped them away. Moments later, the vomiting started, with a violence that took him by surprise. He didn't make it even halfway to the bathroom, but threw up all over the carpet. While it lasted, he felt more ill than he'd ever felt in his life, and part of him thought he was about to die, while another part feared he was not.

In the end, he did not die, but emerged from the bout of vomiting feeling he'd just emptied his body of gallons of black bile and intestinal poisons. His head was pounding, and he felt simultaneously hot and cold. His stomach, on the other hand, felt emptier, and he was clearer in his mind than he had been all day, perhaps for weeks.

Ignoring the pools of vomit, he went back to the telephone and lifted the receiver. It seemed some sort of betrayal when he heard merely a dialling tone, and not Tina's voice. He'd been given a Presidential Task Force emergency number, one that was manned twenty-four hours, in case he should stumble across anything that might lead to the President. Earlier, he'd decided against using it, but Tina's call now made it vital he did.

'Task Force Helpline. How can I help you?'

144

For a moment he thought the voice on the line was that of Agent Hopkins, then realized he was in danger of becoming paranoid.

He plunged straight in.

'This is Major Jim Crawford. My daughter Tina was the little girl who was abducted along with the President and his wife.'

'Yes, sir. What can I do for you?'

'I've just received a phone call from my daughter. We spoke for about three minutes, then she was told to hang up.'

'I see. And you're absolutely sure this was your daughter? That it wasn't some sort of hoax?'

'I know my own daughter's voice when I hear it. Take my word for it, this was the real thing.'

'Very well, Major, I'll assume you're telling the truth. Will you hold the line, please?'

For a sickening moment, he thought she was about to hang up on him. Then a burst of music heralded a long wait. The machine played Paula Cole singing 'I Don't Want to Wait'. Jim winced. The song was the theme tune for *Dawson's Creek*, Tina's favourite TV show. Jim and Laura had teased her that she was turning into a teenager years ahead of her time.

'Major Crawford? This is Dick Cohen, Director of the CIA. You may remember we met briefly at your wife's funeral.'

'Yes, I remember.'

Jim had shaken hands with Cohen and exchanged a few words. There had been assurances of unflinching resolve to catch Laura's killers and to bring Tina home safe and sound; but Jim had immediately sensed that Cohen could not really be trusted. He guessed that Waterstone must have had faith in the man, but perhaps that was just misplaced trust. On his part, it had been pure instinct, but instinct honed by Jim's years as a Marine and then as a flyer. You didn't stay alive in combat, whether on land or in the air, just by keeping your boots polished or by looking at the control panels in front of you.

'Did I say that Vice President Heller has put me in charge of the task force he set up to look for the President?'

'Not just the President, surely . . .'

'No, no, of course not. When I speak of the President, it's a sort

145

of abbreviation. Your daughter is as much in my prayers as the Waterstones, believe me.'

Jim said nothing.

'You say your daughter rang you tonight.'

'Yes, that's correct.'

'And you're certain it was your daughter?'

'Yes.'

'Because there are some people who would not stoop even at impersonating your child's voice. Perhaps even the kidnappers themselves, in order to throw us off their trail.'

'Mr Cohen, I . . .'

'I have to be sure. Did she ask or say anything that might indicate her authenticity?'

'I don't think so. She . . . she was crying, telling me she missed me, that she wanted to be home.'

'Did she give any clue as to her whereabouts?'

'No, I don't think so, no. She said they wouldn't let her say anything about that, that she actually didn't know where she was. But she said the President was unhurt, and the First Lady. They were both well, she said.'

'Good. If that's authentic, it's good news. Did the kidnappers make any demands through her? Or pass on any information?'

'Information, no. She asked about her mother, asked if she was still alive.'

This was where he had to hold on tight. The alcohol had not entirely left him, and when he recollected Tina's voice, forlorn and lost among the world's empty telephone lines, it threatened to over-power him again. It had been the hardest thing in his life, answering her with a half-truth, that her mother was hurt and in hospital, fighting for her life. He wondered if Tina had been fooled. She had, after all, been present at the ambush. She must have known.

'And this lasted how long? From beginning to end.'

'The phone call?'

'Yes, of course, the phone call. How long?'

'I don't know. I wasn't timing it. Would you have done, in my position? I didn't so much as glance at my watch. I was scarcely thinking. I'd have to guess . . .'

'There's no need . . .'

'I'd say about three minutes.'

'Who hung up first, can you remember?'

'She did, of course. Why would I hang up on her? They gave her no choice. Whoever was with her took the phone out of her hands and cut off the connections.'

'Didn't they want to speak to you?'

'If they did, they didn't say so. No-one said a word. I spoke with no-one but Tina.'

'What about the President?'

'She said nothing further about the President or his wife.'

'You didn't ask her?' Cohen's voice was growing snappier the more he realized he wasn't getting the answers he wanted.

'She's my daughter. She asked the hardest question I've ever been asked in my life, she asked if her mother was dead. By the time we'd come to that, our time was up.'

'Any idea why she was allowed to ring in the first place? I mean, come on, what was it? Was it just to reassure her daddy she's still alive?'

'Sure. That was what she wanted to do. But it wasn't the main reason for her being allowed to ring. She also passed on a message from the kidnappers.'

'There was time for a message?'

'Sure there was. It was a short message. Tina said that if you don't call off your search for the President, they will begin to mutilate her, and in the end they will consider themselves forced to kill her.'

He woke late the next morning to a raging headache and a stomach like old lead. Breakfast consisted of a prairie oyster and a couple of paracetemol washed down with instant black coffee. He swore never to touch alcohol again. When he went into the living room, the first thing to greet him was the all-pervading stench of the vomit he'd left on the carpet overnight. Feeling like a diseased Thanksgiving turkey left around till January, tough, mouldy, and utterly inedible, he set about cleaning up the mess. When he'd finished, the carpet – which had been a uniform shade of serviceable beige – looked as though Jackson Pollock had just created another timeless masterpiece on its pristine surface.

The doorbell rang. When he opened the door, he found a man and two women standing on his doorstep. They were dressed for the cold weather that had followed them to his apartment, and in their young arms they carried what looked like a shopful of electrical equipment.

'Major Crawford? My name's Otis Clark.' A tall black man with the air of a hungry basketball player stepped forward and saluted. 'I'm accompanied by agents Holly Miles and Anita Gonzales.'

Jim cast his eye over them in turn, then returned his gaze to Agent Clark.

'Yes, Otis, what can I do for you?'

'Sir, we've been sent here in order to set up a trace on your phone line. In case your daughter rings again, sir. From now on, there'll be a twenty-four-hour vigil on your line.'

He looked at them, young FBI agents keen to get to work, warriors in a worldwide crusade against evil, none of them old enough to remember the wrongdoings of their own organization.

'A twenty-four-hour vigil? Are you serious? Can't you run a trace from the exchange?'

'I've been ordered to set it up here, sir. If you want to make some sort of complaint, I can only suggest you take it up with Mr Cohen. We were briefed by him in person this morning.'

Jim hadn't spent years in the Army and Air Force not to recognize when it was useless to argue.

'You'd better come in,' he said.

They were so eager to play their part in the Great President Hunt that Jim could not find it in his heart not to like them. He told them about Tina, and they listened politely and vowed, not only to find her, but to bring her persecutors to justice. Jim listened to them talk, and nodded, but privately he expected little justice to come out of this, and perhaps much evil. He said nothing about Laura, and they did not ask; he never knew whether they'd been told of her, and he didn't care. Her public death had given way to his private grief, and that was how he wanted it to stay.

They took a little over an hour in which to set up their equipment. Jim watched them work, efficient and proud of their skills. Anita Gonzales was petite and dark-haired, and went about her work in silence and with an attention to detail that left nothing unchecked. Holly Miles was . . . Every time he looked at her, Jim found himself confused and bothered. She operated the computer system that made sense out of all the other bits and pieces. Jim delighted in watching her type and click her way through layer upon layer of databases. It reminded him of the quick responses he required in the air, reading the onboard computers and overriding them where necessary.

But it was not her computer skills that confused him the most, it was herself. She threw him, that was all there was to it. He found her attractive, immensely attractive, and he knew he shouldn't be finding another woman so engaging this soon after Laura's death. She was auburn-haired and honey-skinned and long in limb, and he thought she was the most beautiful creature he'd ever seen. He tried hard to ignore her; sometimes he thought he'd succeeded in putting her out of his mind entirely, then she'd say something, or move her head in a certain way, and there he'd be again, torn with guilt while watching her slim fingers move across the keyboard as though skating on ice.

When everything had been set up, Otis took a mobile phone from his pocket, asked Jim for his phone number, and punched it in. The phone rang, the equipment came to life, and within moments the call had been traced back to Otis's mobile.

Watching, Jim was suddenly struck by a disturbing thought. How had Tina known what number to reach him on? This apartment had never been used by him before, and the number was strictly ex-directory. The only way either Tina or her captors could have obtained the number would have been for someone with access to it to have handed it over. That could only mean someone within the USAF, or perhaps one of the security agencies, maybe even the Presidential Task Force.

Holly apart, he felt a dogged indifference to the presence of these newcomers, and the flashing and spinning of their magical machines. Whoever had organized that bloodbath at Middlewick and spirited a president away with the wave of a wand would not be caught

149

by a child's grief and the momentary joy of a brief telephone call home.

They broke for coffee. Anita found the percolator, Jim handed her a bag of Costa Rican coffee, while Holly rummaged through a cupboard to put together some cups and plates. She came up with a collection of Starbucks coffee mugs and placed them proudly on the table. Otis produced a box of chocolate biscuits from one of his bags. When the coffee was ready, they all sat round the kitchen table, sipping at it and thinking of things to say. About a minute's silence had passed when Otis piped up.

'Major, I hope you don't mind my saying this, but that living room of yours stinks.'

'It does, I know. I had something of an accident last . . .'

'That's not my business. But if we're all going to spend some time out there, we need to do something. If you like, I can make a phone call and ask for some cleaners to be sent in. They will roll up that carpet and dump it somewhere, and an hour later they'll lay a new one identical or near-identical to it. How's that sound?'

Jim shrugged his shoulders. He wasn't too enamoured of the smell in his living room either.

'Be my guest,' he said.

Otis made a quick phone call on his mobile, then sat down to enjoy his coffee.

Jim took another sip from his, and followed it with a chocolate biscuit.

'These are good,' he said. 'Better than Orios.'

'Got them in Hecht's,' said Otis.

'He's a chocolate magician,' Holly ventured. 'Take your eye off those for ten seconds, and they'll reappear in Otis's stomach.'

Jim laughed. Her remark hadn't been so funny, but she had a way of saying it that overcame his reluctance to relax.

'Otis,' he said, 'can you tell me something?'

'Maybe. Depends what it is.'

'I just wanted to know if your people had any luck tracing last night's call.'

'The one your kid made here? There's no way we could trace that, not once the call was finished.'

150

'You don't have any idea where it came from?'

'Nothing. We just have to hope she rings again and that we can catch the call in time.'

'Does that mean the task force is pushing on with the search for the President?'

'What do you think?'

'I told Dick Cohen they'd threatened to mutilate and kill Tina if the search continued.'

Holly frowned.

'Nobody mentioned that to us. Are you serious? That's what they said they'd do?'

Jim nodded.

'Christ,' she exclaimed. 'Isn't there anything those guys won't do?'

'What have they done?'

'Cohen just told us they're stepping up the hunt. Congress has just voted to double the task force budget. And I think they have a lead.'

18

The call came at five minutes past ten. It was not what any of them had expected. Everyone jumped the instant the phone rang. As arranged, Jim picked up the receiver. His hand was shaking suddenly, and he had to grip the handset tightly almost for fear of losing it.

There was a hush, then hissing on the line. Outside in the street a dog barked. Jim ignored it.

'Am I speaking to Jim Crawford?'

The voice that spoke was a man's, and the accent American.

Jim spoke hesitantly. He was thrown by the possibility that this was just an ordinary phone call, from someone who'd been given his name and number by a mutual friend. Then he remembered that it was after midnight.

'I'm Jim Crawford,' he said. 'Where's Tina?'

'Tina's fine. Try not to worry about her. She sends her love.'

'Can't I speak to her? I need to be sure she's OK.'

'I'll see if they'll let her speak.'

It was slowly dawning on Jim just whom the voice belonged to. Beside him, Otis and his team were bent over their instruments. The computer screen was filled with colours and moving shapes. A sound of rapid clicks filled the air.

'Will you do that, please?' Jim responded. 'And could you please tell me whom I'm speaking to?'

There was a slow pause, then the voice came back again.

'This is Joel Waterstone. Am I right in thinking this conversation is being recorded?'

'I . . .' Jim looked up and caught Holly looking at him in astonishment. 'Yes, I . . . Yes, sir, Mr President. I have some people here at this moment. They're making a recording.'

'That's what I wanted to hear. Tell them to run a check, just to be sure it's my voice. Though I expect they've already thought of it themselves.'

Jim saw Holly flash a huge grin at him.

'Mr President, I think you're right.'

'Good. And please stop calling me "Mr President". I can assure you I don't feel anything like a president at this moment. Jim – do you mind if I call you Jim? I . . . They want me to pass on a message, maybe you could call it an order. But that can wait until I tell you how deeply indebted I feel to you and your family. Your wife died a heroine. She put herself between my attackers and me, without thinking of herself for an instant. You're with me in my thoughts all the time, Major, you and your lovely daughter.'

'She is all right? You said she was fine.'

'They haven't touched her, you can be sure of that. As long as I'm alive, nobody will so much as set a hand on her. That's why I'm making this call. I want Vice President Heller to call off any search he has set on foot for me. Our kidnappers have made it clear that, if the search is not called off, they will hurt Tina, and eventually kill her. I believe them. They seem capable of anything. What happened in Middlewick demonstrates that only too clearly. And when they have finished with Tina, they will start work on my wife. They will hurt her and they will kill her if the hunt is not cancelled. Please see that this tape reaches . . .'

Suddenly, the line went dead. All that remained was a humming. Holly gestured to put the receiver down, and Jim did so with fingers grown numb from pressing hard on it.

Otis removed the headphones he'd put on as the phone rang.

'Shit, man, this is going to make a lot of people angry.'

'Any way we can keep it quiet?' Jim too knew only too well the reaction they might expect.

'No way. They've been monitoring that conversation down at the exchange. Every syllable that passed your lips or the lips of the chief will have been heard and duplicated many times by now.'

'So we can expect another phone call?'

'In about five minutes, I'd guess. Give them time.'

'What about the trace? Can you say where they are?'

Holly shook her head.

'I've never seen anything like it,' she said. 'We should have had a firm handle on the call within seconds, but instead it went bouncing all over the place. One minute it was coming from Peking, then from Oslo, then Buenos Aires, then Dublin. Need I go on?'

'At least that suggests somewhere outside the States.'

She shook her head again. He had not noticed before how her auburn hair caught the light.

'I'm afraid not,' she said. 'They're playing tricks, and those tricks could be played from the next apartment and still make the same imprints on my computer. If there's a next time, I'll have some fresh software in place that may outmanoeuvre them. But only if we're very, very lucky.'

'We'll never be that lucky,' said Anita. 'Whoever put in that call is too clever for us. Your software won't make the slightest difference.'

'Even the cleverest people make mistakes,' said Holly. 'There's a lot at stake, which means they're under heavy pressure. If they make enough calls, we'll get them.'

Jim admired her optimism, but he did not share it. A mood of despondency had taken hold of him. The effects of last night's alcohol binge were wearing off, but leaving blackness in their wake. Jim reflected that organizing the Middlewick slaughter and the mass getaway that had followed could not have been easy. They'd have been under enormous strain then, but they'd not only coped, they'd whisked the President of the United States out from under the noses of a watching world. Even if a phone did happen to be traced, they'd probably have ample time in which to slip away before anyone came to find them.

The telephone rang again. Holly tapped out a command on her keyboard, and her computer answered with a series of clicks and beeps.

'It's OK,' she said, turning back to Jim, 'it's a local call.'

'How's that OK? You already said they could be in the next apartment.'

She laughed.

'Actually, it's coming from somewhere inside the CIA complex at Langley.'

'That's a possibility,' said Anita. 'Those guys are always up to something. I wouldn't put it past them to steal their own president.'

'Go ahead, Jim,' Otis said. 'Pick it up.'

He picked it up and placed the receiver against his ear.

'Jim Crawford.'

'Major Crawford? This is Dick Cohen. I understand you've received another communication.'

'You probably know that better than I.'

'Major, I know you have your special problems, and I sympathize. But I have my own difficulties, difficulties which have just escalated with this phone call.'

'What difficulties? You heard the President. Just call your dogs off.'

'It isn't that simple.'

'It couldn't *be* more simple. The President issued instructions, and I believe it's your duty to obey them.'

'Don't be so naïve. For one thing, we haven't yet established that the voice on the phone was actually that of the President. A tape's being sent to Quantico for the FBI's experts to analyse. Everything hinges on the voice's authenticity.

'But that is not my only problem. I have a serious difficulty with accountability. The Presidential Task Force was set up as a means of bringing together the capabilities of all the main US intelligence and law enforcement agencies. I was appointed director because we had to carry out intelligence gathering outside the United States, which is mainly a CIA responsibility. But anything that involves working on US territory has to be handled by either the FBI or state police. That's why you have a team of FBI agents in your apartment right now. It keeps things legal and above board. But it also fucks up my chain of command and makes it very hard for me to keep control of any information that is actually gathered.

155

'As for you, Major, you are yet another thorn in my flesh. Your chain of command runs through the ranks of the USAF, which is not involved at this stage in the president hunt. Strictly speaking, I have no authority over you; only your own superiors have that. You're here as a guest of the task force, or, to be more precise, of the Vice President. That leaves me with a dilemma, as I'm sure you understand.

'What dilemma? Let me tell you. I want to keep knowledge of the President's orders to as narrow a circle as possible. I'm still not sure exactly what Joel Waterstone's status is. I have constitutional lawyers who say that, as long as his whereabouts are unknown, and he himself remains uncontactable, he cannot be considered president. I'm still taking advice on that. But what if you four or one of you decide to go public, or get a separate investigation moving through the FBI? Hmmm? Don't you see why that could be a problem for me?'

There was a pause. Jim said nothing. His veins and nerves were turning to ice. It was sinking in on him just how complex the search for a president might become. Despite all the yellow ribbon hanging on old oak trees, there were those who might not want to see him back again. Who would not care if Tina died a dozen times.

Cohen's voice came on again.

'Major, will you please hand the phone to Agent Clark?'

Jim held out the receiver.

'Mr Cohen,' he said. 'He wants to speak to you.'

Otis grimaced and took the phone. Over the past few weeks, rivalry between the CIA and FBI had been strained.

The conversation, if it could be called that, lasted less than half a minute. Otis's side of things amounted to no more than a couple of 'Yes, sir's', two 'No's', and a string of 'Yes'es'. When he put the receiver down, his face looked slightly ashen.

'He's not too happy,' he said. 'He considers us to blame for not tracing the call. I've got to go out to Langley. Can I leave you guys in charge?'

'We'd rather be here than out there,' said Anita. 'Best of luck.'

'If we never see you again,' Holly piped up cheerfully, 'it's been good working with you.'

Otis paused only to pick up his briefcase, then hurried through the door like someone pursued by hounds.

They could hear his feet pounding down the stairs outside, then silence.

'That guy will go far,' she said.

'Provided he transfers to the CIA,' Anita chuckled to herself. Jim guessed they'd all worked together before.

'God, I'm famished,' Holly exclaimed. 'Let's order in.'

Anita looked up from a tangle of wires she'd been extracting from a metal box.

'I'm not hungry,' she said. 'I had too much earlier. Anything more right now would screw up my diet. You guys go on out for a real meal. Charge it up to Mr Cohen.'

'Sounds like a good idea. I know some terrific restaurants in this neighbourhood. Is that OK with you, Jim?'

Jim shrugged.

'I've got nothing in but beer,' he said. 'Some salted cashews. A bag of potato chips.'

'Anita can have those. She needs to put on a few pounds. Haven't you noticed the resemblance to Callista Flockhart? Check it out – the Hispanic Ally McBeal.'

'I think you just sealed our fate,' said Jim. 'No way will she let you stay after this.'

'OK, Major, lead the way.'

157

19

The Cosmos Club
Massachusetts Avenue
Washington, D.C.

'Gentlemen, I've called you here for one purpose only: to decide on our next course of action given the developments of the past few days, and this evening's somewhat startling message from President Waterstone. I take it you have all had a transcript of the latter?'

Eleven heads nodded.

'In that case,' said the speaker, a grey-haired man who occupied a senior position at the State Department, 'you will be aware that we may be facing a serious problem. The President's order that we call off the search puts us in a difficult position. If we climb down now, we more or less give up any possibility of locating and rescuing the President. At present, the task force is inundated by letters from concerned citizens and foreign nationals, all claiming to have seen Joel Waterstone or to be privy to knowledge of his whereabouts. These will have to be sieved and filtered over a period of weeks or more. Fresh staff have been drafted in from police forces, the universities and colleges, and libraries, just to sift through the mountain of papers this has created.'

'Thomas, is it really necessary to trawl through this stuff?'

The man – they were all men – asking the question was a Supreme Court judge of long standing.

The gathering had been called here in an inner room of the

158

Cosmos Club, to which all those present belonged, and had belonged for many years. The Cosmos was one of Washington's oldest societies, founded in 1878 to provide a haven and meeting ground for the capital's intellectual elite. It had been and remained a very private place where statesmen, lawyers, judges, senior civil servants, ex-presidents (and, not infrequently, presidents), and others could meet to talk and exchange ideas or formulate policy. It was, in many ways, more central to the running of America than the White House or the Capitol.

'I think it's essential for the moment, Henry,' the first speaker responded. He was calling the shots tonight, but only because he had access to all the information. 'Ninety per cent and more will be garbage, written out of greed, or self-aggrandizement, or mischief. But there could be a single letter in there which might turn this whole thing upside down.'

'I accept the force of your argument, Thomas, but have you given enough consideration to another possibility, that it was not the President on the telephone tonight, but an impostor?' This was a small man in his fifties, a former Senator who now spent his days on his horse-breeding ranch in Wyoming, while working behind the scenes to ensure the political future of his party in Washington.

Thomas shook his head.

'We have considered that. It isn't a possibility. The man on the phone tonight definitely was the President. I can give you two reasons for my confidence. First of all, we've had the tape of the call run through computerized voice analysis, and it matches the President's voice perfectly. Secondly – and I have to urge the extreme sensitivity of this information – I received this by hand about ten minutes after the phone call. It was delivered to my office by someone on a motorcycle. They were long gone by the time I thought to go after them.'

He reached into his pocket and drew out a small bottle filled with clear liquid. In the liquid, something short and thin was floating. It took a few moments to see that it was a human finger, the small finger of the left hand. A child's finger. Thomas set it down on the table in front of him.

The bottle was passed round the table. Each man took it in turn

159

and held it up against the light, in order to see its contents better. No-one flinched: they'd all fought in one war or another, had seen infinitely worse than this. The finger had evidently been severed by a sharp implement, probably a knife.

'What makes you think this belonged to the Crawford girl?' The questioner was the oldest of those present, a ninety-two-year-old who was still the sharpest mind at the table.

The combined age of the men assembled in that room was eight hundred and eighty-six years. Their overall wealth, so far as it could be computed, amounted to at least $40 billion. What nobody could have calculated was their collective influence on the US government and the American people, or even the immense power they exerted abroad, in NATO, in the Organization of American States, or in the world at large. Some of them had children and grandchildren, the rest scarcely knew what children were.

'The fingerprint checks out. The Air Force keeps a record of the fingerprints of all base personnel for security purposes. There's no doubt the finger is genuine, and no doubt that others will follow in due course, unless we settle this business.'

'Thomas?'

'Yes, Warren.'

'Am I right in thinking that the finger did not come unaccompanied? I'm not referring to the motorcyclist.'

Thomas nodded, almost as if caught out in a deception.

'Of course not. And, yes, you are perfectly correct.'

Warren had been brought up here in Georgetown, a wealthy socialite who, as a young man, had enjoyed unlimited money, good looks, a brain sharper than Kissinger's, and – which counted for more than all the rest – contacts with an international coterie of men and women of real influence. He had joined the Cosmos Club the moment he was old enough to do so, and had over the years formed a sort of court there, to which presidents and secretaries of state resorted in time of trouble, or to which they were secretly invited should their behaviour or policies give cause for concern in those quarters where power was handed down and taken away.

'And I take it you wish to tell us about what it was came with the bottle.'

Thomas nodded again. If he feared anyone across that table, it was most certainly Warren.

'Yes,' he said. 'I brought it with me. In fact, I made copies for all of you.'

Saying which, he reached inside his briefcase and brought out a thin folder. From it he took several sheets of paper. One he laid on the table in front of him, the others he distributed to the other members of the cabal.

'This is the original,' he said. 'So far, only I have seen it. It is typewritten and written in reasonably good English. You will see that the writer refers directly to Respice Finem. Whoever is behind this thing knows of our existence, and makes proposals to us, rather than to the government.'

Respice Finem ('consider the end') was the name their predecessors had thought fitting for their tiny group. To achieve their ends, they frequently had to commit actions that were morally reprehensible. They knew that, if their activities ever became public knowledge, outrage would sweep like a storm over all they had ever accomplished, and devastate each and every good thing they had brought into being. And they understood that, should that ever happen – though they had taken careful measures to ensure that it did not – and they no longer able to use their boundless power, then the United States (and, very likely, other countries too) would descend into anarchy and chaos. 'Consider the end' was the only justification they had ever been able to offer one another for the acts they committed or caused to be done. As they read slowly through the demands made by the President's kidnappers, it sank in on them that, were they to respond in full, no-one would forgive them.

'Gentlemen,' said Thomas, 'you've had time to read this document now. You will need some time to take it all in, but I have to have your answers to some questions before that. May I, in principle, have your agreement to deal with these people?'

'My dear Thomas, the financial settlement alone beggars belief.' For Warren, the finances were always the crucial thing.

'We can bring that down. But for now, I believe these people can deliver.'

'Is it entirely essential that they do?'

161

'I don't understand, Warren.'

'Oh, of course you do. Is it essential that we secure the release of Waterstone? Should the kidnappers kill him, Heller will be able to take over the helm. That way, we could save a vast amount of money and . . . avoid liaisons that could bring this country into jeopardy.'

'I agree, the demands are outrageous.' Thomas spread his hands. 'But I don't accept your argument about putting Heller in Waterstone's place. Heller's an incompetent, and I'd as soon not have him in a position of influence. National morale would suffer greatly should Waterstone not be returned to the White House alive. The impact could be greater than the Kennedy assassination.'

'So, you'd be willing to go along with these people and their egregious demands? You'd abandon more than half of our nuclear arsenal, make cuts in the military, and whatever else they may choose to ask for?' Henry, the Supreme Court judge, had started his career in the Judge Advocate General's department during the Nuremberg trials, and continued to show a pious concern for the welfare of the US military.

Thomas put up his hand.

'Henry, please. There's plenty of time to work out the fine details. Once we've discovered who these people are, we can find ways of exerting pressure of our own. But I remain convinced that they represent – what's the expression? – the only game in town. If we can't find and rescue the President ourselves – and I don't believe we're any closer – then I can't see that we have a choice.'

'Thomas,' Warren broke in. 'Can you assure us that you haven't already done some sort of deal with these people yourself?'

There was a stillness throughout the room. It wasn't the done thing for a lone member of the Cosmos Club, let alone Respice Finem, to call into question the probity of another member. Had the questioner been other than Warren, Thomas's reply might have been less temperate.

'Warren, I hope you already regret the tenor of that remark. No, I have not benefited in the slightest from my contact with the kidnappers. So far, that contact has been one-way. But once we have a two-way street, we can start talking sense. And I do believe there is no reason why Respice Finem and its members should not be beneficiaries of whatever goodwill these people possess. We shall have the thanks of a grateful nation on the one hand, and the money and help of the thankful kidnappers and whoever is behind them on the other. Do I have your agreement?'

One by one, heads nodded round the room. The last to dip was Warren's. When he raised it again, he was smiling softly.

20

Café Milano
Prospect Street
Georgetown
Washington

'Made your mind up yet?'

Jim just looked at her and shook his head. He'd never set eyes on a menu like this before. When they'd left his apartment, he'd suggested somewhere within reasonable walking distance, and had asked her if she knew any of the neighbourhood eateries. She'd nodded and he'd followed her, thinking they might end up in some small Ethiopian place, or maybe somewhere Vietnamese. He liked Vietnamese food, just as he adored Chinese and Thai food. Then she'd turned and suggested they eat Italian.

'You like Italian?'

'Sure, why not?'

By that he'd meant that he ordered in pizza back at the base, or when he was home.

'I know a great place not far from here. They open till one or two o'clock most nights.'

'What's it called?'

'The Café Milano. You haven't heard of it?'

'No, why? Should I?'

'It's OK, you're not a native, you can't help it.'

She'd said that with such a pleasing smile he'd gone along with it.

164

'A café,' he said. 'Sounds OK. Think it's big enough to serve a real dinner? I'm feeling famished. I guess I threw up most of my stomach last night.'

She smiled again.

'Don't worry,' she said. 'The Milano's plenty big enough for both of us. Even if it's crowded, I know the owner can always get us a seat. He's a great guy, Franco.'

They went on walking. The streets were still full of people, late-night diners, tourists soaking up the atmosphere, strollers come from the Key or the Biograph after watching an intense foreign movie, jazz fans on their way to Blues Alley.

Holly took a mobile phone from her pocket and pecked in a number.

'I've got to tell Anita where we're headed. Just in case something comes up.'

She spoke briefly and hung up.

'Let's go down here, it's faster.'

'How come you know Georgetown so well?' he asked, after she took yet another short cut. 'You don't live round here, do you?'

'I was brought up here,' she said. 'Over on 31st Street, not too far from Dumbarton Oaks.'

One glance at the entrance, and all hope of a small local trattoria faded in him. A stiff white awning overshadowed flowers in pots and planters, flanked by a white trellised fence. In the centre, a long carpet led to the door. As he helped Holly through, he was in time to catch sight of Demi Moore and a small party on their way out. Once inside, he noticed half the Redskins standing at the bar, and a well-known talk show host chatting with an equally famous model.

'Where have you brought me?' he whispered to Holly in horror. 'I can't afford to eat in a place like this.'

'This is my treat, Major,' she said. 'I spent most of today helping ruin your domestic peace and quiet. And besides, it makes a change to come here with a real celebrity in tow.'

'You've been here before?'

'I already told you.'

At that moment, the maître d' advanced, quite formal at first, then smiling with recognition.

'Miss Miles. *Buongiorno. È molto bienvenuta.* It's so long we haven't seen you.'

'I've been very busy, Ricardo. Do Mother and Father still come?'

'Yes, yes, we see them almost every week. Your mother she is still so lovely. But won't you introduce me?'

'Ricardo, this is Major Jim Crawford. He's an Air Force pilot.'

She leaned forward and whispered quickly into Ricardo's left ear. His eyebrows went up, and recognition dawned in his eyes. Celebrity did not usually unsettle him, but this was special.

'Wait, please,' he said. 'Wait. Signor Nuschese has no seen you for very long.'

Suddenly, he was gone, then just as suddenly back again, sheltering this time behind the graceful figure of the restaurant's owner.

Franco Nuschese was all over Holly in seconds, kissing her on both cheeks, gripping her hands in his, and exclaiming loudly his devotion for her.

He then treated Jim to a lower-key version of the same.

'You are very welcome. I will see you have one of the private rooms. Please, come with me.'

They followed him to a small room off the bar. Waiters were already making the table ready for them. Ricardo was snapping out instructions in Milanese Italian, while turning every so often to smile in their direction. Nuschese chatted with the couple amiably for several minutes, then made his farewells. His pager had summoned him back to other duties.

'Sharon Stone is arriving any minute,' he said. 'She always expects me to be there to welcome her. Let me know when you are leaving.'

Moments later, they were being seated at their table, while large menus were thrust into their hands.

Holly put her hand over her eyes and bent her head.

'I'm sorry,' she said, 'I didn't think we'd get the full treatment. I thought we could just blend in.'

'In that case, why the hell did you make such a thing about who I am?' Jim was feeling angry about how Holly had transformed a simple meal outing into a major event. He dreaded reading the morning papers lest they run stories about 'bereaved war hero dates Washington socialite'.

'I'm sorry, I didn't think. I just wanted to get a good table and see you were treated properly. That's all. I didn't think it would make you uncomfortable.'

'You just didn't think. Jesus, Holly, my wife is freshly buried and my daughter is being held to ransom, and you take me out dining in what is presumably this city's top restaurant. And the most expensive.'

'I'm sorry. To be honest, I brought you here because I wanted you to have fun. You've been through something terrible, and I thought you needed to get away for a while. Just try to relax. This is a private room, and I guarantee we won't be disturbed by anyone. The food is good, and, believe it or not, this is not the most expensive restaurant in town.'

'OK, but how come a Federal agent can afford to eat in the same dive as Sharon Stone and Demi Moore?'

'Yes, right, I'm sorry about that as well. Shall we just say I have resources above and beyond those the state provides me with?'

'Come on, Holly. I need to know. If your parents are eating here on a weekly basis, I presume they are what is known in my neck of the woods as loaded.'

She put down her menu and looked at him across the table.

'All right, yes. My father is one of Washington's top lawyers, and my mother is a Daughter of the American Revolution. Wise up, Jim: this is Washington. A lot of people in this city are rich or powerful, and usually both. As it happens, I don't particularly like wealthy people or politicians or, for that matter, lawyers. My parents and I are not closely connected. I see them as seldom as I can manage, and they make that easy for me to do. We don't respect each other very much. They wanted me to marry well, so they trotted me around all the balls and presentations, where I would be introduced to a series of seriously rich young guys. I ended up dating just about every eligible bachelor in town, and found them to be, without exception, the most godawful bunch of pompous, stuck-up nonentities it has ever been a girl's misfortune to know. When I was twenty-three I had an affair with a married man twenty years older than me. He

167

was a writer. Not a very successful one, but I thought his books were beautiful and maybe even profound. My parents have never forgiven me for that.'

Jim couldn't think what to say. He didn't know what age she was, whether she was still in the affair or long past it.

'You're still with this writer?'

There was just the slightest of pauses before she spoke.

'He died,' she said. 'Three years ago. We were together for two years, but they were the best years of my life. He used to say they were his best years as well. Just two years out of more than forty.'

'How did he die?'

She shrugged.

'A heart attack. Nothing out of the ordinary. Funny how something so banal could take somebody so remarkable.'

'What was his name?'

'David. David Bernstein. You haven't heard of him?'

'What did he write?'

She opened her mouth to reply, then closed it again.

'We've talked enough about me. Let's choose something from this menu and get down to eating. You told me you were famished.'

They stopped talking and started to read the extensive dinner menu. After two minutes of silence, Holly put down her copy – which she had scarcely bothered to read – and asked if he'd made his mind up yet. He shook his head, then put down his own menu.

'Holly, I don't know about you, but this menu has me beaten. I mean, what the hell is this?' He turned the menu round and pointed to an entry among the *antipasti*.

Holly smiled.

'It's not as bad as it looks. Just because it's long doesn't make it unreadable. "*Alici con salsa di capperi e prezzemolo su indivia e crostone di pane.*"'

She read the Italian without affectation, like someone who has spoken the language since childhood.

'It means "Anchovies in a caper and parsley sauce on endive, with crostini bread." But personally, I'd recommend the San Daniele ham with pears.'

She chose his main course too, a roasted veal chop with truffle and radicchio, and he let her do it because his fascination with her was growing in spite of the anger he had felt.

As they ate, he tried to loosen the awkwardness that had come between them. Without knowing why, he found himself talking about what had happened on Christmas Day.

Just then, the waiter arrived to take their orders, and was followed by the wine waiter. Holly had already advised Jim on what to order. In the end, they settled on a Piedmontese Barolo by Sori Ginestra, at ninety dollars a fine balance between cheap and pricey. The waiter bowed and went away a little let down. He knew that Holly's favourite wines were a bit more up-market.

'I think your brother owes everyone an apology,' she said once the waiters had left them alone again. 'Have you been in touch again since the incident?'

'I rang the Moskovitzes a week or so after New Year. They tried to make light of it, to brush the whole thing off as a misunderstanding; but they were badly hurt, I could tell. I'll visit them once this is all over. When I get Tina back, I'll take her to Boston. Wickenburg just doesn't come into it at the moment. In fact, I really don't want to go back down there till Bob clears out.'

Their starters arrived.

'What about you?' he asked, picking up his fork and twisting a slice of thin ham round it. 'Any brothers and sisters?'

She was eating a small pumpkin risotto. At first he thought she had not quite heard his question. She moved her fork gently in the rice, lifting and dropping it as if she had suddenly lost her appetite. Then she let her fork drop and looked him full in the face. Somewhere in the main dining room, a troupe of roving guitarists were serenading the customers. The strains of their music came gently to their ears.

'I have a brother,' she said. 'His name is Leonard. Always Leonard, never Leo. He's twelve years older than me. I was never close to him when I was a child. Then, when I was about fifteen, I suddenly became interesting to him. Every night for over a year, he came to my bedroom and got into bed beside me. I won't go into details. When he left, he'd threaten to tell our parents, to say I'd led him on. For a long time I thought precisely that, that it was all my fault, that I had led him on.'

She stopped talking, as though old memories were threatening her.

'Why are you telling me this?' asked Jim. 'We scarcely know one another.'

'Yes, I know. But I trust you. It's a rare thing for me to trust any man so quickly, but I think I can depend on you.'

'Isn't this rushing things a bit?'

She went on looking at him, quite without reserve.

'Yes,' she said. 'And yet . . . maybe not. I feel as if I've known you for months.'

'Why did your brother stop?'

'Our parents found out. I'm not sure how. I think maybe one of the maids . . . Anyway, they found out and my brother was sent away. Oddly enough, no-one tried to blame me. I was even sent for psychotherapy to help me over the trauma. It was my parents' way of evading responsibility for what had happened, but I had a good therapist, and I think I was helped. What really mattered to me was that my brother no longer lived in the same house.'

'What happened to him?'

'Nothing, really. Moving out had been on the agenda for far too long anyway. Leonard had followed in my father's footsteps. He graduated *summa cum laude* from Yale, and by the time he was pushed out he'd built a successful career in an upcoming law firm here in the city. He was appointed an Appeals Court judge three years ago. It's predicted that he'll make the Supreme Court in about ten years' time. I can believe it.'

'But you could ruin him.'

She shook her head.

'No way. You don't know what this city is like. My brother is connected. If I made an accusation, they would ruin me, not him. They know how to close ranks faster than a regiment of Marines, believe me.'

'Did he marry when he left home?'

She laughed.

'Leonard? My brother has affairs. He's often quite indiscreet about them.'

170

'With the wives of other judges?'

'Oh, no, nothing so mundane. Leonard has discovered that he is gay. His partners are drawn from the best social class: politicians, lawyers, judges, doctors. He once told me to my face that I was responsible, that my prepubescent breasts and narrow hips gave him a taste for the male form. It upset me for a long time, now it just sickens me. Everything about him sickens me. Do you know, soon after I joined the Bureau, I hacked into the computer files that are held on him. I found out things that shocked me. The Bureau uses its information to lean on him. Sometimes an appeal will come before him, somebody the Bureau wants to see sent down for a long time. Before the hearing, somebody has a discreet word in Leonard's ear. It's the only thing that lets him survive.

'But I've talked enough about myself.'

'I'm very content to go on listening to you. Tell me how you came to be a Federal agent.'

A waiter came and took away their plates. Another brushed away their breadcrumbs. A third laid a fresh tablecloth. And a fourth brought their main dishes.

'It happened because I was such a spoiled brat. When I was sixteen, my parents bought me my first computer, a little Macintosh Classic. It changed my life. Before that, I'd never been much good at anything in school. But I took to computing like salt to water, and I never looked back. When I was seventeen, I chose to go to MIT to study computer science. My parents were not happy, believe me. But I just said '*vafanculo*' and headed on up to Cambridge. After graduation, I enrolled for a Master's and planned to go on to a PhD, but one of my teachers ratted on me to the FBI. The Bureau made me an offer I could have refused but didn't. The money was neither here nor there, except that earning my own income meant I could stay free of the family. What brought me in was the promise of some very special coaching at the computer laboratory in Quantico. I did basic training, learned to shoot straight, and was taught more about computers than most programmers learn in a lifetime. I haven't regretted it once.'

Dessert was Sorbetto alla Pesca for Jim and a Frutti di Bosco sorbet for Holly. They talked throughout. There was no small talk: their situation did not permit it. He talked about his days in the Marines, and his decision to join the Air Force. She listened carefully as he spoke of his career as a pilot. And at last he spoke to her hesitantly, first about Laura, then about Tina. He told her about their life together on different bases. But he said nothing about the growing tensions and increasing distances that had been developing between them, for they were things he scarcely dared admit to himself.

It was well after midnight when they left. Their host was still on the premises, waiting to see his last guests go. Holly whispered something in his ear, and within moments the paparazzi on the pavement outside waiting for whatever photo opportunities might present themselves were discreetly shunted off.

They walked slowly back towards Jim's apartment. It was very cold, and the streets were practically deserted. They walked in silence with their collars turned up against the cold. From time to time they would pass another couple bound in the opposite direction. Shops and restaurants were closed, not many residences were still lit. Their feet sounded cold and echoing against the pavement.

'We'll go back this way, remember?' she said, leading up through a side street.

They never saw their attackers coming. There was barely a rush of hard feet, then they were on them. Holly was thrown heavily to the ground by a large man who proceeded to lie on her, stopping her from getting up. The other attackers, three men, concentrated on Jim. One held him from behind while the other two set about him, kicking and punching him mercilessly. He tried to fight back, but his assailants were professionals. The man behind had pulled a length of tape across his mouth, preventing him from calling out.

They hit him so many times he was sure his limbs were broken. One man would beat him on the face, then his companion would turn to his torso or his arms and legs. He wanted to collapse, and felt himself near passing out, but the man behind went on holding him upright.

Then, as suddenly as it had begun, the assault stopped. The man at Jim's back released his hold, and, as Jim sank to his knees, he bent down and whispered in his ear.

'Keep your nose out of things from now on. Go back to your base and fly your fucking planes. Just leave this other thing. There's nothing you can do about it, understand? Leave it, or next time we won't go half so easy. You understand what I'm saying?'

Jim summoned up his strength to nod. The man stepped away, nodded at his fellows, and ran off down the street. The other three followed. Holly pulled herself to her feet and drew a gun from her pocket. She started to run after their attackers, but she'd barely reached the end of the street when she heard a car cough into life and go screeching off into the darkness.

Painfully, she made her way back to Jim. He was on his back now, moaning, but moving very little. By the time she reached him, she had her mobile in her hand and had already dialled 911.

'I'm a Federal agent. I need an ambulance at once.'

21

'Major Crawford, can you hear me?'

The voice was male, young, dispassionate.

'Can you hear me, Major Crawford?'

This time he burst into giggles. He felt lightheaded and abandoned. The words of an old Bowie song started running through his head.

'I can hear you.'

'Good. Can you open your eyes?'

He tried, but a bright light made him close them again at once.

'The light's too bright.'

'That's OK. I can have that turned down.' The voice paused, then Jim heard it speak a little further off. 'Nurse, could you get these lights down?'

This time when he opened his eyes, there was little pain. But the moment he thought of pain, he came back to the agony that was his body.

'Everything . . . hurts.'

'We know. We can see your bruises.'

'What the hell happened? Was I in an accident?'

'Not really. Agent Miles has given us a full account. You were attacked while walking home. The men who attacked you probably just wanted to frighten you, not injure you badly. As far as we can tell, you're in fine shape despite the way you look. I've asked for X-rays. They should be back here in about ten minutes, then we can see if you need surgery or work on fractures.'

His eyes came into focus. Standing over him was a young doctor, his stethoscope slung round his neck like a cross on the neck of a priest, his white coat marking him out from more lowly forms of life.

'Where am I?'

'Suppose you tell me. I want to know how much you remember.'

'I can't remember anything after the restaurant. Obviously, I'm in a hospital.'

'You got that right.'

'Listen, I'm an out-of-towner, I've absolutely no idea what hospitals you have in Washington.'

'You're in the emergency room of the George Washington University Hospital. Believe me, this is the best place you could be. This is one of the top ERs in the country. It's what we call a Level 1 Trauma Center. You're in very safe hands.'

'Where's Holly?'

'She's all right. They didn't hurt her, just crushed the breath out of her. It's possible she may have cracked a couple of ribs, but otherwise she's fine.'

'Can I see her?'

'She's here. She's been waiting for you to wake up. There's a couple of police officers in the corridor. They want to interview you.'

Jim groaned.

'Tell them I'm not up to it. Tell them I can't remember a thing.'

The doctor grimaced.

'You'll have to tell them yourself. Maybe you can pull rank on them. What are you? Army?'

'Air Force.'

'Better still. You guys are number one ever since that dumb blonde put herself between a machine gun and the President. She could just have stepped aside and saved herself and the rest of the country. Maybe I'm just prejudiced, but I don't think women should be put in that sort of position. Bodyguarding a president is a man's work.'

'Which is probably why you'll never be asked to do it.'

Holly's voice came without warning. It was like steel, and as cold as the back of the universe.

'If you don't know, your patient was married to the dumb blonde who lost her life back in England just because she was too stupid to recognize the virtues of self-preservation. Get out of here; you don't deserve to be around human beings, much less tend to their wounds.'

The doctor scuttled out of the room as though a shark was swimming fast in his direction.

'He won't be back.' Holly smiled and sat on the edge of the bed. 'How are you feeling?'

'I'll live.'

'I don't doubt it. Did you know this was the room they put Ronald Reagan in after his assassination attempt?'

'You're kidding me.'

'Actually, I'm not. There's a plaque outside recording the event. If they could save him, I reckon you're a pushover. Jim, those guys weren't out to kill you or even hurt you badly. If you really want to cause injury, you weigh in with some iron bars or baseball bats. You come down hard, you break a lot of bones. The guys who attacked you were quite gentle, as these things go. Which leaves me asking, what the hell was going on?'

'Some of it's starting to come back.'

'That's good. You care to tell me what you remember?'

Jim told her what the man had told him when the beating came to an end. Holly did not reply at first. She just sat on the side of the bed, thinking hard. Finally, she reached up and stroked his cheek. His face felt rough with stubble, and the little pressure of her hand made him wince.

'You're in a lot of trouble,' she said. 'And I think you could be in a heap of danger. Maybe the man was right, maybe it's time for you to step aside and leave the rest to us professionals.'

'Don't ever say that.' He raised himself in the bed. There was no part of him that did not ache. 'As long as Tina's alive, I'm staying with this. I want to be there when they rescue her. That's not negotiable.'

'I understand that. But I still have to do my job. Part of it is bringing these people to book, them or whoever sent them. Another part is making sure you're safe.'

176

'You can start by helping me off this trolley.'

'The hell I will. You're not going anywhere.'

'That's for me to decide. Either you help me or you make yourself scarce. You can do what you like, but I don't want you getting in my way.'

He made a tremendous effort and managed to get his legs over the edge. Holly grabbed his feet to stop him and the trolley from crashing over.

'What the hell do you think you're doing?'

'I told you, don't get in my way.'

'OK, stay cool. What do you want me to do?'

'You got a car?'

'No, but I can get one. Where are you planning on going at four in the morning?'

He grinned.

'Just a little visit,' he said.

'You got anyone particular in mind?'

'You bet I have. We're going to have a few words with the Vice President. You got a problem with that?'

The Vice President's house is a private residence set away from the hustle and bustle of downtown Washington. Unlike the White House, it remains a proper home. It isn't open to the public, and it doesn't appear on maps. To get there, you have to drive to the north of Georgetown on Wisconsin, passing Dumbarton Oaks Park to your right, up onto Observatory Circle, the perfectly circular road that lassos the US Naval Observatory and, at its heart, the house of the Vice President. This is a white-painted structure of three storeys that brings to mind a French chateau stripped of all but one of its peaked towers. It is a fine house, but not ostentatious, planted among gardens that are almost suburban in tone.

They arrived at the entrance to the Observatory to find a manned barrier in place. Holly stopped and turned off the engine. She drove a small European car, a Fiat or a Peugeot, Jim hadn't noticed. The naval guard on duty came across, and Holly wound her window down.

'Can I ask your business, ma'am? The Observatory opens again at eight o'clock. I'd suggest you come back then.'

'Sergeant, this can't wait till you reopen. Major Crawford here has urgent business with the Vice President. I'm sure you're aware that he's the father of the little girl who was kidnapped with the President.'

'Well, ma'am, I know about that, and it's an honour to meet the Major, but I don't have no authorization to let anybody up to the house. I'd have to ring through, and, to tell you the truth, I don't intend to do that at this time in the morning and find myself on a charge by noon. This is nothing personal, it's just the way things work round here.'

Holly reached in her pocket and took out her ID, which she held under the Sergeant's nose.

'Sergeant, my heart bleeds for you and your trouble, but the truth is, I just don't have the time or the patience to worry about what sort of charge they may put you on. This is Federal business; the Vice President knows the Major personally, and any delay may lead to the death of the President. Now, I leave it to you to work out what sort of charge they'll put you on if that should happen and it be found to be your fault.'

Sergeant Treponti didn't know what to do. He'd been brought up in an Italian family that regarded the Feds with a mixture of fear and loathing. You didn't mess with them if you wanted a quiet life. On the other hand, he'd been in the Navy long enough to know that you didn't mess with the rules either. If he let them in, he was finished; and if he kept them out he'd probably be doubly, trebly, and even terminally finished.

'OK, you can go through, but I'd appreciate it if you said you'd sneaked in some other way. I've got kids, I've got a wife, I get seasick if I have to go to sea.'

They drove on. Holly knew how to find the Vice President's house – she'd been there more than once to attend receptions, and on one occasion to a private tea party for Al Gore's family and her own.

'There it is,' she said, pointing past some trees to a wide lawn at the back of which sat a white house with a long veranda and a high roof, barely visible through the darkness. A few security lights

178

marked it out, and the steady radiance of the street lighting on the paths that led from one Observatory building to another lifted the darkness a little.

Holly drove up to the front door and switched off the engine.

Jim turned to her.

'Go on home, Holly. I'll deal with this.'

'The hell you will in your condition. I've brought you this far, I'm going to see it through.'

They argued briefly, but in the end he was too weak to contradict her. In any case, he reckoned that the good Sergeant, once he got over the shock of tackling a Federal agent, would be hot on the telephone to his base, wherever that was situated. Any moment now, there would be flashing lights in the distance, and Jeeps with armed guards ready to fire at the slightest sign of a threat to Heller and his family.

There was a sound of racing engines from not far away.

'I think we should get going,' Jim said. He opened the car door and ran for the front door of the house. Holly followed him. Glancing back, she could just see the blue lights flashing far over the trees. This, she thought, had been a big mistake. She'd been warned more than once about acting on impulse, and now she'd done it once too often.

He rang the bell five times in a row. That should get somebody moving, he thought. But for the present, all within remained silent. He pressed the bell again, a single long ring. All the time, he thought it was madness, but he concentrated on the aches and stings that covered his body and decided maybe it was not.

A light went on above the fanlight. There was a quick sound of slippered feet coming towards the door, then the rustling of a chain and a series of hard clicks as locks were undone. Behind them, a Navy Jeep came rushing up the drive with a squeal of brakes and a blue lamp spinning like a latter-day dervish on its roof.

The door opened to reveal a startled housekeeper, a grey-haired woman in her mid-fifties dressed in a padded robe. She stared at Jim as though he was the devil incarnate come to fetch her to an eternity of pain. His cuts and bruises, not to mention the appalling state of his clothes, all served to enhance this impression.

179

'My name is Major Jim Crawford, USAF. I'm accompanied by Federal agent Holly Miles. We've come to see Vice President Heller on an urgent matter.'

Behind them, another vehicle slammed on its brakes, barely in time to avoid crashing into the Jeep in front. There was a slamming of car doors.

'It's out of the question. You can't come in.' She could see quite clearly a group of four armed guards coming towards the door.

Jim didn't wait to be arrested. He pushed the housekeeper out of the way. Holly, frightened now that he'd gone beyond all that was reasonable, hared inside after him. She had to stop him attacking the guards when they came in.

'Heller, where the fuck are you? I want to see you now. If you won't come out, I'll come and find you.'

Suddenly, he felt himself restrained from behind. One of the guards had grabbed him round the waist, and was trying to pin his arms to his side. Meanwhile, a second man appeared in front of him, holding a heavy pistol to Jim's face.

'Just stay calm, motherfucker. If I see you so much as wrinkle your shit-ugly nose, your head will become empty space. Now, put your hands on your head.'

Jim could have floored both guards, maybe the others too, but the beating had left him weak and inflexible. And he reflected that fighting back was probably not a clever thing to do under present circumstances. Reluctantly, he raised his hands and placed them squarely on his head. The guard behind him reached for his wrists, clipping one half of a set of handcuffs onto his left wrist.

At that moment someone appeared at the top of the main staircase. Everyone looked up. Vice President Heller was there, dressed in pyjamas and looking dishevelled.

'Will someone tell me what the fuck is going on here?'

It was as if the Admiral of all Admirals had appeared on deck. Mouths fell open, and then the naval guards, realizing what was happening, snapped to attention and saluted. The one who had been holding the pistol to Jim's head was the first to speak.

'Mr Vice President, sir! We've just apprehended this intruder. You don't have to worry, he's no further threat to you or your family. We'll see he's made secure, and hand him over to the police. Or the FBI, whichever.'

'Sir, I'm an FBI agent. I came here . . .'

Holly's attempt to restore the balance was immediately squashed by the guard.

'This woman is also under arrest, Mr Heller. She brought the other intruder here. We think she . . .'

This time it was Heller who interrupted.

'Are they armed?'

'We don't know, sir.'

'I think you should hurry up and find out.'

Two guards secured Holly while a third quickly frisked her. He found her pistol and, at her suggestion, fished her ID out from an inner pocket.

Meanwhile, the fourth guard searched Jim. When he finished, he stepped back, opening his hands in front of him to indicate that he'd found nothing.

The man who had frisked Holly held up her ID.

'It's an FBI badge. Looks genuine. Gives her name as Agent Miles.'

'I'm more interested in the man,' said the Vice President. 'How'd he get in this state? Have you been beating him?'

The guard in charge shook his head.

'No, sir. This is how we found him, sir.'

'He doesn't look too dangerous to me. What is he anyway, some kind of vagrant?'

Jim snatched the chance to take a step forward.

'Sir, I can speak for myself. I haven't come here to hurt you or anybody else. I just want to speak to you. You owe me that. You owe me ten minutes to talk about this thing.'

'I'll be the judge of that.'

'You don't have a choice, things have gone too far. Maybe you don't recognize me, but we have met before, and you know who I am. I got beaten up about four hours ago, that's how I come to look like this. My name's Crawford, Jim Crawford. I'm a USAF major. Does that help?'

'I know who you are.' Heller spoke in a neutral voice, a voice that said he wasn't too pleased to see Jim at this time in the morning, maybe wasn't pleased to see him at all, but was leaving his options open.

'Then you'll talk with me. I have some rights. Maybe I have more rights than anyone.'

'What exactly is this about? Is it about the President?'

'About him. About my daughter. Take your choice.'

'OK, we'll talk.'

He came down a few steps lower on the stairs, and spoke to the guards.

'It's all right. I know who he is: he doesn't represent a threat. Will you please take those cuffs off him?'

The guard who had cuffed Jim's wrist now went into reverse, fumbled for his key, and nervously released him.

'Gentlemen, I'd like you to leave me alone with Major Crawford and Agent – what was it?'

'Miles.'

'Sir, we're obliged to protect you at all times. This man could still be a danger to you.'

'I asked to be left alone with him. He's no threat to anyone. He's just upset about something. Now, I want you to leave him alone. I won't be preferring charges, and I advise you not to plan on arresting him when he leaves this house. Have I made myself clear?'

'Yes, sir, perfectly.'

The guards came to attention and saluted again, then turned and made their exit, inwardly seething.

'You choose your moments, Major. I had a very late night. But I can see you can't have slept much yourself. Let's go to the parlour. Maria, could you bring us hot coffee and cookies?'

The housekeeper, still frightened, scurried off towards the kitchen.

Heller led the way along a short corridor and into the parlour. This was a small, comfortable room where the Vice President took tea with his family when he could. A small white-painted fireplace was flanked by tall bookcases, also painted white. In them Heller had placed part of his collection of rare editions. He had been

182

an academic before moving into politics, and his choice of books reflected a careful and probing mind.

Jim and Holly sat on a sofa from which they faced Heller across a low table.

'OK, Major. What can I do for you?'

Jim proceeded to give him a run-down on what had happened, culminating in the beating he'd received earlier. He spoke about how he'd been snubbed at the task force office, about the risks to Tina if the search for Joel Waterstone continued, and about how he'd been warned by one of the men beating him to keep his nose out of things.

Heller listened carefully. Even when coffee was served, he remained intent on what Jim was telling him. When Jim came to a halt, he asked Holly what she knew about the matter. Finally, he sat back, eyes closed as though asleep or thinking hard.

He opened his eyes and looked at Jim for a few moments.

'You should get home,' he said. 'Miss Miles can drive you. She doesn't know it, but I'm aware of exactly who she is. I see her parents from time to time. But she knows that.'

'But what about . . .'

The Vice President raised a hand.

'I'll look into those things. They worry me greatly. But for the moment, there are more pressing matters.'

'What could be . . . ?'

'More pressing than your embarrassments? The search for the President. Major, I want you – and Agent Miles – to treat what I am about to tell you as Top Secret information. The fact is, we've had a strong lead. I believe we now know who the kidnappers are, and where they may be found.'

22

The fog had come down on them fast, about an hour earlier. It had been thick at first, and they'd taken shelter in the lee of Stuart Island for a spell, south of Reid Harbor. Then holes had started to appear in the fog canopy, and the team leader had urged them back onto the water. They had fallen behind schedule, and now he wanted them to reach their target while the fog lasted. It had been unasked for, but a blessing just the same.

On the water, it was bitterly cold, despite their padded clothing and the spray skirts on the kayaks. Jim struggled to keep warm, setting his paddle down on the bow section from time to time in order to clap his gloved hands together in short thunderous bursts. The little boat felt heavy in the water. Alongside his own equipment, he'd stowed guns and other hardware to lighten the loads on some of the other kayaks. They hadn't allowed him to carry any weapons, even though he was qualified to fire them.

Every so often, Jim noticed he was in danger of straggling behind the others. He'd put on a spurt for a while, but he could never catch up with the lead group. There were twenty of them altogether: sixteen were men selected from Navy SEALs. As an ex-Marine, Jim acknowledged that SEALs were the toughest fighting force in

184

the world. Their training in hostage rescue left other HRUs looking like rank amateurs.

The rest of the force was made up of Jim (eligible on account of his Marine training and experience), somebody high-ranking from the FBI called Figueras, a hardnut named Markham from Joint Special Operations Command (hurried up from Pope Air Force Base, North Carolina), and the now unavoidable Dick Cohen. Cohen had never been a field agent, but he knew this was one operation he could not afford to run from his office in Langley.

The special forces team had been flown from their HQ at Dam Neck, Virginia, leaving early that morning on board two C-20B Gulfstream IIIs out of Andrews AFB in Maryland. The Gulfstreams were normally reserved for state officials and dignitaries, but a phone call from the Vice President had removed all objections to leaving the machine in such uncouth hands. Instead of the regular five-man crews, the planes were flown by men from the 8th Special Operations Squadron, who'd flown up several hours earlier from Hurlburt Field in Florida. They'd chosen the Gulfstreams because they could make the journey to Washington State at about twice the speed of their regular insertion aircraft, the MC-130E Combat Talon I.

Jim, Cohen, Markham, and Figueras had joined the sixteen-man team at Andrews shortly before takeoff, and had spent the flight being instructed on kayak skills and the ground plan for that night's raid.

The Gulfstreams had landed just over four hours later on the other side of the United States, touching down in a snowstorm at McChord AFB, near Tacoma. This left them with plenty of time to check their equipment – including the black Klepper folding kayaks they'd brought from home – and to run through their plan for the raid, using satellite photographs that had been taken over the past twenty-four hours and updated all the time they were in the air. While they were busy fine-tuning the rescue mission, their four civilian colleagues were out on Puget Sound being schooled in the use of sea kayaks by an instructor from the base. Snow was still falling, more gently now, and every island and every stretch of coastline and every forest had grown white with it.

The SEALs would be doing the shooting, if there was any, while the other four had come along as observers. Jim was really there should the raid prove entirely successful: the last thing anybody wanted was for Tina to panic and run into trouble. The Vice President had suggested that a familiar face and a fatherly voice would help prevent a tragedy.

Cohen had fallen yards behind. Too many years in a desk job had left him unfit, like Figueras. Markham was paddling furiously up ahead somewhere, trying to keep close to the expedition leader, Major Carl Jurgensen, a grizzled old warrior of thirty-seven who could still outrun, outgun, and outpunch any of the men in his crew. He was semi-retired, but his CO had brought him back to lead this mission. Jurgensen had been brought up on Puget Sound, on Fidalgo Island, the grandson of a Danish fisherman who'd settled in Anacortes in 1930.

After dark, their aircrew had flown them in a couple of Pave Lows up to deserted Johns Island, just west of Stuart Island. They hadn't wanted to make use of any of the island landing strips around the San Juans: all it needed was for word to get out that a Special Ops team had arrived in the north Sound, and folks would soon begin to wonder, and ponder, and make up their minds that something was going on. And maybe some of them would put two and two together, and add in one and three, and get eight. This had started as the most secret mission imaginable. If it got blown, there would be far more than careers at stake.

The fog pressed in on them harder and harder, freezing, bitter-edged, dark with an unforgiving northern cold. There had been no snow since nightfall, but they knew it lay all around them, and that it would be their first enemy once they landed on Forrest Island. All the time, the waves were growing higher and louder, while a deep current ran across their path, pushing them south-west, towards a string of islands due south of Prevost Passage. They were already in Canadian waters, and entitled to be there following a conversation between Dean Heller and the Canadian Prime Minister, Hugh Calvert.

Everyone was equipped with a helmet and radio headset, supplied by the SEALs. This allowed them to keep in close radio contact.

186

Before leaving McChord, they'd spent time poring over local tide books and current tables, calculating their best route and a timing that would spare them the worst the sea had to offer.

They were on the open sea now, struggling across Haro Strait, tossed and harried by the conflicting tides created by the juncture just north of them of Boundary Pass, Swanson Channel, and the Strait itself. These were shipping lanes normally reserved for large vessels, log and grain carriers, oil tankers, enormous factory trawlers the size of ballparks. In the dark this was dangerous enough, with only a few lights to give warning of a great ship's passing; but in the fog it was near-suicidal to venture into these waters. Direct collision was one hazard, but a small boat could just as easily be overturned and sunk by the vast wake surging out from a freighter or a tanker. The great ships prowled the seas, capsizing and drowning canoes and kayaks and one-man fishing smacks as though they were no more than minnows in their path.

'Listen up!' It was Jurgensen's voice running through their headsets. 'We're in danger of breaking up. My current GPS position is 123° 16' 10" by 48° 40' 30". That puts us close to Rum Island. Let's get over there now, and make sure the team's intact. There's a small beach on the south side, big enough for us to haul our asses on to.'

He'd hardly spoken when they heard it coming, somewhere far off in the fog, but moving fast. Heavy engines were running at something like full speed, in defiance of the weather conditions.

Jurgensen thought quickly. He was under orders to observe strict radio silence. But the ship was coming closer every second, and represented an immediate threat to his team and his guests. In the fog, they couldn't even tell which direction it was coming from, much less take action to avoid being swamped or ground into matchsticks.

'The hell with this,' he muttered, and selected channel 16, the emergency and distress call band.

'This is a message to the motor vessel somewhere between Sidney and Stuart islands. A team of twenty kayak boatmen are scattered across your bow. Please slow down at once and place lights on your vessel ahead. Please return my call on this channel and let me have your coordinates and speed of approach.'

187

The engines went on turning, louder now, and still unfocused. Every member of the team was concentrating intently, ready to be the first to pin the sound down and warn the others.

'Come in, whoever you are. This is a US military operation, and I am issuing an official warning to stop your engines until our kayaks are safely out of your path.'

Still no answer. The drumbeat of engines came songlike across the pelagic darkness. And with it, the waves suddenly boiling, then rising, then surging beneath their keels like some giant sea creature woken from a long sleep on the ocean bed. Jim flailed with his paddle, not sure what was the best thing to do, terrified that the ship itself might at any moment bear down on them and sweep them beneath its hull and down, breathless, beneath the waves. These were deep waters, and he dreaded all that salt darkness lying ready to suck him pitilessly down.

He slapped the water hard repeatedly in a desperate attempt to brace it against the surging wake. Whether the ship was driving past or through them, there was no way of knowing. Everything was vibrating now, the waves as they slapped against Jim's hull, the sea around him, the kayak, and his own body. He peered through the fog, now in this direction, now in another, scared that any moment he would see the ship's prow coming out of the mist and only yards away from him. Thoughts of Laura and Tina rushed through his brain, like a drowning man's whole life compressed into moments. And another thought followed them, frightening him more than his being this close to death, and that was the thought of Holly somewhere in Washington, fast asleep and naked, and dreaming of him.

The sound of the passing ship began to fade. The disturbance of the waters continued long after it had passed.

'Report back to me, please.' Jurgensen's voice filled their headsets again. 'A Team in order. Andrews?'

'Sir!'

'Carlucci?'

'Sir!'

The litany of names went out into the fog, and each response brought its release of tension. Jurgensen quickly finished the A

Team, then rehearsed the B Team, name by name again. No-one had drowned.

Then he began on his four guests.

'Cohen?'

'Yes.'

'Crawford?'

'Here.'

'Figueras?'

There was no reply.

'Figueras? Can you hear me?'

No answer. The only sound was that of waves cresting and falling on the open sea. Then the boom of an orca near the surface, echolocating now that the ship had gone. But no answer from Figueras.

'Figueras, we can't hang around. We're in a shipping lane, and the next boat could drown us. We're making for Rum Island. Like I said, there's a small beach on the south shore; we're going to lie up there till the fog lifts. The coordinates are 48° 39′ 50″ by 123° 16′ 20″. Catch up with us there, if you can. If you can't make it, go a bit further to Gooch Island, where there's more shelter. Stay there till the operation's over.'

They moved on after that, steering their independent courses for Rum Island. It was just a lump of rock in the middle of ice-cold seas, but to Jim it sounded like paradise.

There was the unmistakeable sound of waves crashing on rock. Jim used it to help locate himself. Minutes later, he saw the white, snow-covered beach appear through a rent in the curtain of fog, then a flashlight switching on and off. Jurgensen was there ahead of everyone, waving them in and counting them as they dragged their kayaks up onto the pebble beach.

Jim landed and pulled his kayak back out of the reach of the tide. He'd stowed a small bottle of whiskey in his rear storage compartment. It took only moments to find it, and less time to taste the first mouthful.

'Mind if I have some?'

Jim looked round to see someone standing over him. The voice had belonged to Jurgensen.

'Be my guest.'

Jim handed the bottle up to him. Jurgensen took a swig and handed it back.

'Needed that,' he said. 'Mind if I sit down?'

'It's your beach as much as it is mine.'

'Still, not much of a beach, is it? Wouldn't want to come here on holiday.'

The commander lowered himself onto the pebbles.

'Guess not,' said Jim. 'Good thing we aren't on vacation.'

Jurgensen laughed.

'You kayaked before?'

'Some. With the Marines mostly. Once or twice on my own.'

'How long ago is that?'

'Long enough. Oh, I don't know, eleven, twelve years.'

'You get out of practice, huh?'

'Some. These aren't the best conditions for relearning. But I've made it this far.'

'Think you can make it the whole way? I mean, being an ex-Marine is something, and being an ace jet pilot is something too, but out here you're on a different edge.'

'I've got to be there, Major. I want to see my daughter safe, whatever you have to do.'

Jurgensen picked up a small rock and tossed it into the waves.

'What will you do if something goes wrong out there, and they hold her at gunpoint and threaten to kill her, and you have to call the shots, you have to say, let's back off, or go ahead and kill her? I mean, can you handle that? Because the President's life could depend on that, on your strength of will.'

'I don't think I can sacrifice my daughter, not even to save the President. Don't ask me to do that.'

'I hope to hell I don't have to. I don't want you involved in the fighting, not unless someone is threatening your own life. What you carrying?'

Jim patted the shoulder holster in which he kept his handgun.

'P9,' he said. 'First weapon I trained on.'

'You rusty?'

'No. I shoot three times a week. An hour on the range each time.'

'OK. I'm going to give you an MP5. Know how to use one?'

'I've used one.'

Jurgensen vanished, to return moments later carrying a compact sub-machine gun, which he handed to Jim. He also handed over several magazines.

'You may need it. This could turn vicious if we lose the element of surprise.'

Jim stowed the MP5 and the magazines in his front compartment.

'These folding kayaks are something,' he said.

'They're babes. You can fold the big ones into three bags, but they handle rough conditions like they were gliding on some duck pond.'

Jim took another swig of the whiskey, wiped the neck, and handed the bottle back to Jurgensen.

'Gets into your bones, this fog, don't it?'

He poured a dram down his throat and passed the bottle back to Jim.

'I hear these are your home waters,' said Jim.

'The Sound? I've known it since I was a boy. One of my first memories is going to Seattle with my father. He'd saved up for years, and he took me with him to the Dock Street Brokers in Ballard Avenue. Hell, I'd scarcely been in a shop before, let alone one like that. We left Seattle on board his purchase, a thirty-foot gillnetter that had seen better days. She was built by Crawford Bros. back in 1929, so she'd been to sea more times than a rabbit has sex. But she was the best my father could afford back then, and he loved her to distraction. He called her *Dorothy*, after my mother, and went out fishing in her that same night. Of course, she soon became *Dot*, which is what he called my mother, except on Sundays.

'He'd come home around dawn every day, and I'd try to be up to see him. Then I went to school, and that got harder to do. On weekends, he'd take me over to the North Beach on Guemes Island, and we'd dig for clams. I always hoped to find a geoduck or two, and if they'd dug themselves down deep, there'd always be butter clams, native littlenecks, macomas, and manilas. Dad showed me how to tell one type from another. Eastern softshells

191

were my favourites. My mother made all kinds of chowders with them. Now, half the beaches are poisoned. You can die just from eating a geoduck. What's the world coming to?

'Once I was old enough to be safe on deck, he started taking me with him, said he'd make a fisherman out of me. He'd started going out to the Strait of Georgia, or west into the Strait of Juan de Fuca. We fished for salmon mostly – Pink round the San Juans, Chinook and Coho further out. The stocks hadn't been exhausted back then, the way they are now. We'd know which stock kept to each river, and we'd fish clear of stocks that had been worked over too much. Nowadays, nobody gives a damn. The purse-seiners come in and lay down walls of net, so nothing gets out, not even sharks and seals.'

'What made you join the Navy?'

'Seemed the way to go. My family had been in the fishing business since way back, home in Denmark. None of us had gotten rich, though. I didn't reckon I'd get rich either, but I thought I could do something with my life, see the world. That's the way it looks when you're sixteen, and you've been brought up in a place like Anacortes.'

He took a cigarette from his vest and lit up.

'You smoke?'

'No, thanks,' Jim replied. Jurgensen put the pack away.

'I understand what you mean about Anacortes, though,' said Jim. 'I was brought up in Wickenburg, Arizona. We didn't even have water to go sailing on. Wherever you went, it was still Arizona.'

'So you joined the Marines?'

'Only way out. So I thought then. And maybe it was true. I just never liked the Marine Corps.'

'You never thought of becoming a SEAL?'

'I thought of it. I even applied for the BUD/S-SEAL training course. Had it all set up. But I backed out a week before I was due to report to Coronado.'

'You don't seem like a quitter to me. Man who flies a jet fighter has to be made of guts.'

'It was the drownproofing test. I can cope with water, but not like that. So I backed out.'

'Drownproofing' was part of the basic SEAL course. They'd tie a

192

candidate's hands behind his back, and his legs at the ankles, then throw him into a full-size swimming pool and leave him for half an hour. The only way to survive was to kick up from the bottom, snatch a breath, then go down again until they pulled you out.

'Damn shame. You handled yourself well in the water tonight.'

'Thanks. And thanks for getting us through that.'

'I didn't get Figueras through. This damn fog . . .'

'Don't blame yourself. He may still be out there somewhere. These FBI types . . .'

Jurgensen laughed, but Jim could tell he was still worried.

'I'm sorry about your wife,' he said. 'Dreadful thing that happened. All those people killed, and for what?'

'I think they were killed in a game with very high stakes. Laura was just in the wrong place at the wrong time.'

'She tried to save the President's life. I don't much agree with Waterstone and his fancy liberal ideas, but he is our president, and in my book nobody gets away with that. I take it personally. So do the men in my team. Don't worry, we'll get your little girl out. That's a promise.'

He stood and tossed his cigarette butt on the beach. It glowed for several moments, then went out.

'Fucking environmentalists don't like you doing that. But I don't see no ashtrays round here, do you?'

'You're the fisherman,' said Jim, thinking of what his jets did to the stratosphere.

Jurgensen walked off a little way, then turned back.

'Listen, Major. Things could get hot where we're going. Leave the shooting to us, unless you're attacked. But I think it's best to warn you to watch your back. That's all I can tell you. Watch your back.'

Jim made to question him, but when he looked closely, Jurgensen had already gone. On the shore, the waves expired in troops, and in the sea at Haro Strait a lone whale cried out in the darkness.

23

The President's Quarters
Location Unknown

With each day that passed, he reflected ever more deeply on the Holocaust. It was not that he thought of himself as a victim like those victims. He did not seek to compare himself with other Jews. But he was a president, and a man of the people, and he knew that his abduction had inflicted a blow on his people, those who had voted for him and those who had not, Jew or Catholic or Protestant or nothing at all. If he compared himself, it was with other men. No-one could have foreseen the attack at Middlewick, and he knew he had no personal culpability for it. There was simply nothing he could have done. But he remembered how so many in Europe had pleaded that Hitler had taken them by surprise, and then the Nuremberg Laws, and then Kristellnacht, and so on to the gas chambers. It was not that they shared any guilt for that. But it was a context he understood, and a basis for his comparisons.

And perhaps he should have seen it coming, not only him, but his advisers too. Now that he understood it and knew what his abductors' ultimate aim was, and who they were, he knew they had been negligent.

He looked through the window into darkness. Snow had fallen earlier, white and crisp and very cold. He shivered. They were a lot less comfortable here than they had been on board the submarine. He'd been astonished when they finally disembarked. It had been a private luxury submarine, designed for a magnate and his chosen friends to roam the oceans in, and adapted for the purpose of keeping prisoner a man, a woman, and a little girl.

They'd been handed warm clothes the moment they stepped out of the sub. They'd worn them ever since, sometimes even indoors, when the stove wasn't working, or when the weather outside grew particularly inclement. Little Tina found it hard, and stayed indoors most days watching videos. He and Rebecca did their best to get her outside, encouraging her with snowball fights or walks on snowshoes.

A few times they'd seen other children around Tina's age, but their captors would not let them get close, much less speak. Tina's grief had gone inward, in spite of their best efforts, and they feared for her if she had to endure this confinement much longer. In all honesty, they feared for themselves too, but being together did a great deal to dispel the worst feelings.

There was a knock on the door, and Tina came in.

'My finger's hurting again,' she said, holding out the stump for him to examine. It had been bleeding again. He removed the dressing, cleaned and re-dressed the wound. She tried her best not to flinch, though he knew it must hurt a lot.

'You can have more codeine,' he said, making some up for her. At least their captors had not expected her to suffer without some form of relief.

'Perhaps they'll let you speak to your father again,' said Rebecca.

'I won't let them. They'll only cut another finger off.'

'No, dear. They've made their gesture. There's no point in their amputating any more.'

'Isn't there? They could start on you, or Mr Waterstone.'

'Yes, they could. But they've presented their demands now, and I'm sure Mr Heller will do all he can to respond as they want.'

Privately, she knew that wasn't true. The demands were just too lavish. Money would have been simple, however much they'd wanted. But their captors wanted power more than riches, and she suspected that they were just a front, and that their real kidnappers were waiting to tighten the screws further.

'I wish the sun would come out again,' Tina complained.

'Would you go outside then?'

'I might.'

'Good. I'll hold you to that. Now, Joel and I want to get some sleep. Off you go.'

Tina kissed them both goodnight and left.

'Rebecca ...' He stood away from the window. Something was worrying him. 'There's something I need to tell you. It's about Tina.'

'I know.'

'How ... ?'

'I've guessed. They'll kill her if Heller turns down their demands. Is that right?'

He crossed the room to her. Had his grandparents, Grandma and Grandpa Wasserstein, held conversations like this in the early hours, before their escape? He guessed they must have done.

He sat down beside his wife and stroked her hair.

'Yes,' he said. 'It's not an idle threat. They'll do it. I think they'll do it tomorrow.'

24

Miners Channel
Gulf Islands
Canada

It was within an hour of dawn when the fog began to lift, shredding at first, then drifting off in fat clumps that left the sea bereft and prowling. The high winds that had accompanied the fog – a natural phenomenon more frequent in the Strait of Juan de Fuca – now began to whisk the heavy mists away. Watching the waves, Jim wished the fog would re-form and cover them again. With the fog's passing, the snow returned, bitter and ruinous, as though it had come down direct from the Arctic. Jim imagined that, if he looked hard enough behind the great white curtain, he would see polar bears and ice floes.

Jurgensen gave them no time to think about just how cold it was going to be out on the ocean again. They were travelling due west towards Forrest Island now, and as he carved a path for himself through the waves, Jim found his heart beating, not from exertion, but from the sick anticipation of violence to come. He knew they would not achieve their objective without some degree of fighting. The kidnappers would be armed, as they had been in England, and they would not give up such a great prize without a fierce struggle. Jim remembered the times he had travelled one way or another towards a similar destination, as a Marine, and as a pilot. More than once he'd gone head first into gunfire or an anti-aircraft barrage. It mattered very little at the time, when there was adrenalin to take him through; but afterwards, when reflection took the place of the fighting urge, he would be left with feelings of emptiness and irritability that he could not easily understand.

The water ahead of him was changing. Small patches of silver appeared on its surface; the wave caps were suddenly bright. He looked up and saw that patches of night sky were shining through the cloud cover, which was breaking up slowly, but at a steady pace. Stars grew in the blackness, as though evolving in a matter of moments. There were great clusters of them, and among them, if he looked very carefully, he could make out the moving pinpricks of man-made satellites.

Suddenly, the moon was whisked out from behind a veil of cloud, and the sea became bright with its light, as though the entire world had been transformed. A full moon was every Special Ops soldier's nightmare. They'd been forced to set out tonight, knowing the moon might betray them, but praying the fog would stay down, as the forecast had promised. Jim looked out across the sea, and there, spread out around him, lay a scattering of kayaks, like a miniature invasion force. They were within reach of Forrest Island now, and if anyone was watching, they would see nineteen kayaks bearing down on them out of a silver sea.

Looking up again, he saw a string of shadows passing across the surface of the moon. Snow geese heading out to sea. Their honking was the loneliest sound in the world. It tripped him up and threw him on his face. He thought of Laura, and he thought of Holly, whom he'd never see again.

There was a crackling in his headset, then Jurgensen's voice came through, clear as glass.

'That's Forrest Island ahead. We've been pushed a bit to the north. Before we get any closer, I want us to get round that little island off the south point, then make our landfall on the west side as planned. Keep a low profile, and remember not to cut too hard or splash when you paddle. Our intelligence report says these people don't keep any sort of watch, but I don't want to take any risks that aren't necessary. And for God's sake, tighten up: I don't want anybody else to get lost.'

198

They called him Emmanuel. It was the name the All-Father had chosen for him on his entrance to the community, a few years ago, back in England. They called themselves the New Pilgrim Fathers, or New Pilgrims for short, and they'd travelled all the way here to set up God's new community on earth. That had been their first name, and Emmanuel had been one of the first to set foot on Forrest Island, God's given home. He'd been here all through the first hard winters, fighting wind and cold and high seas while they went about building and planting crops. His wife and children had joined him later, when things were easier. Even so, it was a hard life, and the children had complained a lot at first, until he'd subdued them.

'There is so much to subdue,' he thought. In himself, ambition, pride, and lust. In his wife, vanity, a love for trivialities, and ill-becoming lust, as in himself. He slept with her now every forty days. And in his children, who were ten and fifteen, there was all of nature to subdue: loud laughter, high spirits, a great lack of sobriety, inattention to God's word, inattention to his own counsels, and to the counsels of the All-Father, frivolity, an attachment to the vanities of the world, and, in the older, the first stirrings of lust. The boy would have to be watched before he discovered pleasures that went counter to the sacred text and to the admonitions of the All-Father.

Emmanuel had left the compound directly after prayers, in order to start the job of milking the goats. One of the All-Father's first decrees following their arrival on the island had been that they should drink goats' milk, and make cheese and butter from the milk of goats, as had been the rule in Bible times. The original herd, brought over from Vancouver Island, had been sold off for a loss when they went to England towards the end of the previous year. These new goats were still unfamiliar to him, and would not always be milked. But no woman was allowed to touch them, for did it not say in scripture that no woman should set her hand to the flock of the Lord?

He made his way to the little paddock they kept the goats in. Thick snow, replenished every day now for the past three days, lay on the ground, catching his steps, forcing him to lift his knees high each time he moved forward. He did not begrudge the others their breakfast in a gradually warming hall indoors. This was one of several tasks given to him by the All-Father in person, and it was a blessing to him to be allowed to perform it.

The All-Father assigned tasks to each one of his followers, choosing their occupations, not on the basis of qualifications, but of spiritual signs. He also gave them their names, new names taken from scripture and bestowed on them in the course of their baptisms. When asked, he explained how Christians of all folds had strayed from the true Biblical names, and would call a child Elvis or Buzz as soon as Isaiah or Ezekiel.

The name problem was just another of the innumerable signs that marked the modern world as ungodly. A man might be called David, yet know nothing of King David or the psalms he wrote. On Sundays, the congregation sang metrical psalms, as taught them by the All-Father. Their leader had been a Scottish Presbyterian minister on the Isle of Lewis, in the town of Stornoway. His given name had been Iain McLeod, and he'd been a stuttering, whey-faced nonentity of a preacher until the Lord appeared before him late one Sunday afternoon and summoned him to bring His chosen ones to the sure promise of eternal life.

He'd been expelled from the island after being declared a heretic by the church's ruling council. That had been seventeen years ago, when he was forty. One month later, in Birmingham, he'd found his first convert, whom he'd named Joshua. After that, the new church had grown rapidly. The Reverend McLeod had become Nehemiah for a time, then All-Father, to distinguish him, and to indicate that he was the spiritual father of his people.

Emmanuel found the goats huddled in a corner of the paddock, their backs weighted down with thick carpets of snow. He cleared the snow from their flanks as best he could, then started to drive them back towards the milking shed. All the time he shivered in the freezing cold. Somewhere in the darkness, a black brant called out twice.

Coming near the shed, he paused to look out across the sea. A bright moon and stars had replaced the fog of an hour earlier, and the channel seemed alive with divine purpose.

They'd come to this inhospitable place following a revelation granted the All-Father, in which God appeared before him in a burning bush, ordering him to take his people out of Sodom and Gomorrah. Such was the evil of the times that there was no hope of saving more than a small remnant, and this the All-Father did. They gave him all their worldly wealth, and with the proceeds he bought Forrest Island and bricks and mortar to build a settlement on it. But it had proved hard going, for not everyone was of the mettle needed for life in such a remote and unforgiving place.

Then, two years earlier, the All-Father was offered a very large sum of money to spend on the Mission. With it, he would be able to build churches throughout North America, and send preachers to each one, ready to bring new flocks to join his first congregation. They'd gone to England, where they'd worked their elaborate plan to trap and destroy that embodiment of Satan's falsehoods, the Jew and Christ-killer whom Lucifer had made President of the United States.

Since their return, the All-Father had bidden them be watchful. They knew there would be men looking for them, that a treacherous world sought them everywhere. So, while he looked out across Miners Channel, he scoured the face of the sea for signs of strangers.

That was when he saw the kayaks, beating a slow path across a deep swell, and coming in his direction. He left the goats standing where they were, and started running towards the main house.

The first light of dawn appeared on the eastern horizon, erasing whole galaxies before working its way down Boundary Pass, then tiptoeing on the wide stepping stones of Brethour, Domville and Forrest Islands. A world of pure white shimmered before the rescue party. Not far away from where they'd landed, a compound made up of a central building and several outhouses dominated the first rise. There was no sign of commune members going about their labours, though one intelligence report had led them to expect one or two. Old man Jurgensen put it down to the weather: they'd be crazy to come out in this snow if they didn't have to.

'They must be crazy enough just to live in this place,' ventured Dick Cohen. He was still shivering from his journey on the open sea. This was the bleakest spot he'd ever set foot on in his life.

'Crazy or not, they carried out that stunt back in England,' Jurgensen retorted. 'We can't assume they don't know what they're doing.'

Jim was inclined to agree. He'd just been given a full briefing about the Watch, the name used by church members among themselves. The official name for the community was the Church of Christ Imminent. The shorter name indicated much the same thing, that group members were watching for their Lord's return to earth.

The central part of their message, according to an FBI report prepared a few years earlier, was that of dozens of survivalist and fundamentalist groups round the country. McLeod preached that the United States had been conquered by Satan, that the government was run by Jews and demons, and that its great cities were uniformly sinks of iniquity, in which the evils of homosexuality, abortion, child abuse, prostitution, pornography, and drug abuse ran riot. Its politicians were mired in every sort of corruption, from the President down, every arena of public life was overrun by Jews and Zionists, and the media, when not in the grip of Jews, was in thrall to a conspiracy of homosexuals and radical feminists.

Apparently, the Reverend McLeod had gone ballistic when Joel Waterstone was elected president. Not only was he a Jew, but he was hurrying to implement a programme of political and legal reform which would make the most heinous practices permissible. He wanted to let people smoke cannabis for medical purposes, which was another way of saying: 'Here's the thin end of another wedge, boys: come back for more in four.' And if he had his way, guns would be strictly controlled, capital punishment would be suspended, and gays would start serving in the armed forces.

All of which, a more recent report argued, was sufficient to send cult members on their deadly mission to England, and to explain some of the demands now being made to secure the release of the President.

Jurgensen came over with a heap of pebbles he'd scrabbled up from the beach, digging beneath the snow as though searching for clams. He used them to weigh down his map of the island, a composite based on satellite and low-level aircraft photography. Everything was marked on it: the main building, the cookhouse, the bakehouse, the little church in which they offered up their devotions, the granary, and a cluster of other buildings whose use was harder to guess.

Jim could not stop thinking about the Watch and its goals. It was significant that they did not number among the evils of modern life such constant threats to the American way of life as race hatred, anti-Semitism, crimes against women, or plain old-fashioned murder.

He continued watching as the commander went over the main features of the compound, trying to relate each landmark to what they could see from their vantage point just above the beach. As he spoke, two lookouts kept a steady watch ahead, scanning the buildings with binoculars. Jim knew that his own role would be restricted to this, keeping lookout while the others (with the exception of Cohen) formed the attack. But if they breached the main house quickly, and succeeded in locating and securing Tina, then Jim would hare across the intervening space and be with her in seconds.

The entire force now covered their sea clothing with white camouflage suits, complete with hoods and trigger-finger mittens. Once this was done, the soldiers used camouflage paint to turn their faces white. Weapons were taken out of the pouches in which they'd been keeping warm. Extreme cold like this was potentially fatal to guns of any kind. Metal could become brittle, but once a gun was fired, the barrel and the rifle itself would rise to somewhere between 200° and 750° Fahrenheit.

Feeling his eyes grow tired, Jim let his glasses drop to his chest. He stood and went down to the beach. Near the water's edge, the snow had been unable to lie, and the wet sand lay covered in a glistening sheet of near-freezing water. A little higher up, patches of frost had started to form, blanching the tops of sand dollars and starfish. Jim reached down and came up with a sand dollar in his hand. He slipped it into his pocket – maybe it would serve as a souvenir of the morning, should all go well.

As he straightened, he noticed something out at sea. A small boat riding at anchor, about half a mile from the shore. He raised his binoculars and trained them on the boat. It was a motor cruiser, between twenty and thirty foot in length, with a displacement of around five tons. A small cabin protruded above the deck, concealing whoever was on board. Jim didn't think they were fishermen. The boat carried no name, and a small flagpole at the stern bore no flag.

He went back up the beach.

'We're ready to go in,' said Jurgensen. 'Keep an eye on things back here, will you? I'll contact you as soon as I have a situation. Don't worry, she'll be fine.'

The SEAL squads had moved off in different directions, so they could approach the compound from several angles at once. They'd rehearsed this back at base so often they could do it in their sleep. But after Middlewick, no-one was complacent.

Jim watched Jurgensen walk up the ridge to the vantage point he'd established to give him the best possible view of the compound's rear. Snow still fell. It fell on trees and grass and roofs, on water and fences, and on the three crosses Jim could make out in what he reckoned was the commune's cemetery.

As Jurgensen reached his post, Jim saw another figure head towards him. A second look told him it was Cohen. The CIA Director went right up to Jurgensen and started talking to him in a huggermugger sort of fashion, his mouth close to the other man's, as though engaged in some kind of conspiracy. Cohen pulled back a little and started to make stabbing signs with his right hand, pointing in different directions one after another. Jurgensen rounded on him and started shouting, but not loud enough to be heard above the waves crashing on the shore. The two men seemed to argue for several minutes, then Jim saw Jurgensen nodding and seeming to comply with whatever it was Cohen was instructing him (and perhaps his men) to do. For the first time, Jim began to wonder who was really in charge of this expedition.

Cohen went off to the right and vanished behind a clump of weather-beaten trees. Jurgensen watched him go, and seemed to hesitate, as though uncertain how to proceed. Then Jim heard his voice come over the helmet receivers.

'Start moving in. Take your time and don't make any breaches till the whole unit's in place. Horovitz, start counting down now.'

Jim came up to the ridge from which Jurgensen was directing the attack, and placed himself about one hundred yards to the commander's left. He saw the men moving across the snow in pairs. They seemed conspicuous and exposed, yet their movements were confident. Jim's heart was beating hard now, in hope of a quick rescue and a bloodless release for everyone.

Suddenly, his attention was distracted by a sound to his left. It was the sound of a motor, and when Jim turned he could see the little motorboat coming into the shallows off the island, a little distance down the beach. He raised his glasses, and as he watched, four men jumped from the boat into the waves and started ferrying boxes from the boat to the shore. The boxes seemed heavy, and the men stumbled more than once as they walked on rocks and sand.

Jim turned back, meaning to draw Jurgensen's attention to what was going on, when he heard a loud crack. He turned his gaze back to the compound in time to hear more cracks. Someone was firing on the SEALs. Jim turned his binoculars on the commune buildings and made out flashes of gunfire coming from the main building and the church steeple.

'Go in!' shouted Jurgensen. 'Go in now!'

The SEALs stopped pacing themselves and, throwing caution to the winds, ran for the main building. One went down, shot in the neck, another stumbled and picked himself up again.

Next thing he knew, Jim was up and running, his MP5 in his hands, his breath pluming in front of him like a war banner.

25

Almost the first thing Jim noticed as he advanced towards the compound was that the shots coming in his direction were small arms fire, and sporadic at that. So far, none of the attack squad had been hit, and from the disarray evident in the sect's defence, it didn't look as though any would be, or, even if one of the riflemen on the roof got lucky, that it would hurt too much. The light rounds being fired would just bounce off a Kevlar vest.

Jim had seen the devastation wrought at Middlewick, vehicles blown into fragments, human bodies peppered with heavy-duty ammunition, whole buildings with their fronts ripped off. He found it hard to reconcile those images with what was happening on Forrest Island today. He didn't stop zig-zagging, but he began to think he was not in any real danger. As far as he could see, the Watch didn't pose much of a threat to anyone, unless this was just a feint to bring their attackers closer so they could unleash hell on them at the last moment. They'd done it at Middlewick, why not here?

It was hard to form an overall picture of what was happening. Jim had not been made privy to the plans of the breaching force or its support teams. He was a little out of range of the guns up ahead, and for the moment, nobody seemed to be aiming at him. He crouched down and put his binoculars to his eyes. The falling snow was still an irritation, but it was already slackening, and he could see well enough.

The sixteen SEALs had divided into two squads, each of eight men, with each squad working in a series of four pairs. Squad A was making for the main building. It was their job to secure it and to locate the President, if possible. Squad B had been detailed to provide backup and, more importantly, to ensure that the compound buildings could not be used by the Watch for a counter-offensive.

As Jim watched, one of the men at the rear knelt in the snow. Jim knew that each squad carried a sniper, and he'd noticed earlier that they were using Barrett .50s, chambered to .50 calibre rounds that would snuff out a target even at a great distance. He saw the sniper raise his weapon and take aim at the church steeple. There was a loud report, and a gunman fell from his vantage point and plunged to the ground.

Jim was growing more and more terrified. Knowing they were being raided, the cult leaders would be using some sort of fall-back plan to get the President and his wife out. Whether Tina went with them or not might depend on mere chance. It was just as likely that over-confidence meant there was no fall-back, and that their captors might simply kill the presidential couple and the little girl with them, before taking their own lives.

An instant later, his fears were intensified. All eight members of Squad A halted as though at a single order, yet Jim had heard nothing through his helmet. Had they switched to a different channel? Suddenly, they had their M16s in their hands, each one underslung with an M203 grenade launcher. It was these that were now brought into play, as each trooper fired one explosive shell after another at and into the building. In a couple of places, intense flames sprang into life immediately, and Jim recognized the unmistakeable features of white phosphorous. It would keep burning until copious quantities of water were thrown on it to douse the flames.

Squad B had started to breach the outbuildings, and from each one there came a loud explosion.

'What the fuck is going on?' Jim shouted into his laryngophone. 'There are people in there.'

Even as he spoke, two figures emerged from one of the outbuildings, each wreathed from head to foot in flames. They stumbled blindly for a few seconds, then two quick shots put them out of their misery. Jim watched the whole thing in horror. The victims had not been holding their hands up in surrender, but equally they had not been carrying visible weapons, nor had they posed a threat to anyone.

'Fuck you, Jurgensen!' he shouted. 'Your men are out of control. Pull them back, for God's sake.'

No reply. An awful silence while weapons fired and explosives thudded. Jim ran forward, pulling his MP5 from round his shoulder, not knowing what to do. No fire came in his direction. The nearer he got to the main building, the stranger the sounds became. He heard loud cries of pain and fear, someone was weeping uncontrollably, a child was screaming, then another. His feet stumbled on the uneven ground; he was half blinded by tears. They were slaughtering everyone inside. He heard the repeated ripple of machine guns, the rapid stuttering bursts that reminded him of the lawn mower back home, cutting through flesh like spinning blades through grass. He went on forward in utter desperation for his daughter's life.

Suddenly, two crisp shots rang out. He felt one pass within millimetres of his ear, and the next strike him in the left arm. With an instinct born of long training, he threw himself to the ground, breaking the fall as well as he could with his right arm and dropping his rifle to the ground. As he fell, he struck his right hip hard on the frozen earth that lay so treacherously beneath the snow. A third shot followed, throwing up the powdered snow like smoke as it thudded at high velocity into the ground an inch or two from his left leg.

He brought himself round quickly. Prone, he knew he could hardly be seen against the snow. He looked up at the building, but could see no-one but the advancing soldiers. His wound was leaking into the snow, creating a patch of red that would soon draw more fire down on him. A fourth bullet ploughed through the snow ahead of him. That was when he first realized that something was very wrong. He found his field dressing and, despite the pain in his left arm, discovered that he could use his left hand to help pull it apart.

He made to place the sterile side of the dressing to his wound, and, as he did so, noticed that there was an exit wound to the

208

front of the arm. This could only mean that the bullet had come, not from the commune in front, but from someone behind him. His first thought was that some of the sect members had managed to work their way round to the beach, in order to come on their attackers from behind.

Then he remembered two things. First, the map of the island showed that there was no easy communication between the beach landing area and the commune buildings. Second, Jurgensen's words as they rested on Rum Island earlier that morning: 'But I think it's best to warn you to watch your back. That's all I can tell you. Watch your back.'

He turned, facing back the way he had come, but there was no-one there, no-one whom he could see. For all he knew, his would-be assassin was still lying there camouflaged, taking careful aim for his next shot. Jim turned and bent down hurriedly, picked up his rifle, and began to run, zigging and zagging, towards the main building. Some instinct told him that, if Tina was being held here with the Waterstones, it would be somewhere in there.

The firing continued, punctuated by cries and occasional explosions. He saw dead and wounded animals on both sides, a woman, dead eyes staring, her hair on one side black as seaweed against the whiteness of snow, the other side of her face blown off, and the blood spread out in a frozen crimson pool, and in her hand a Bible, its pages fluttering back and forwards in the wind. Near her was a child, a boy of ten or eleven, Jim guessed, flat on his back, his face and limbs twisted and blackened by flames.

He ran on. Two SEALs were bringing a man out from the rear entrance. They stood him against a wall and started questioning him. Jim came close, but nobody paid him the least attention.

'Where's the President? Where've you been keeping him?'

The man just shook his head, whether out of fear, defiance, or just plain ignorance it was impossible to tell. The soldier who had asked the questions struck him hard across the face.

'Fuck you!' he said. 'We don't have time here for sitting around. We need to find the President. Just tell us where he is.'

Again no response. This time, the second soldier fired three or four rounds into the man's upper legs, causing him to collapse against the wall. Jim stepped across, pushing the soldier's gun to one side. He bent down and tried to get the man's fading attention.

'I'm the father of the little girl, Tina. I've come to take her back. Please tell me where she is.'

The man just stared at him. Before Jim could ask again, the first soldier took his handgun and shot the man through the head.

Jim, his clothes spattered with blood, got angrily to his feet.

'What the hell do you think you're doing? You're an American soldier. You can't shoot an enemy who doesn't pose a threat to you.'

The soldier smiled back at him.

'You got a lot to learn, buddy. This ain't the fucking Air Force, today ain't Christmas, and the fuckface I just shot helped kidnap my President. Don't get involved, or you may get hurt.'

The two soldiers ran off round the side of the building. The bulk of the rescue force was now inside the building, Jim reckoned.

He hared off in the direction the two SEALs had taken. Flames were coming out of windows on all floors now, and Jim feared they would burn the whole place down before he could ensure Tina was safe. As for the President and his wife, he wondered if their safety was on the minds of their would-be rescuers at all. It was as if the special operations force was working to a very different agenda to the one that had originally been set out by Heller when Jim spoke to him back in Washington.

He turned the corner and ran to the front door, which had been smashed open and torn from its hinges. Several bodies lay in front of or just inside the gaping hole that had been left. Some were clutching small-bore rifles and what looked suspiciously like air guns. A child who seemed to be around Tina's age and build was lying face down among the adults. She was wearing a grey dress, and her dark hair was netted at the back of her head in a snood. She looked very like Tina. For a moment, Jim's heart slumped. He reached down and rolled the body onto its back, and at once felt ashamed at the surge of relief that passed through his mind on seeing it was not Tina after all. He laid her down carefully, wondering if the man and woman nearest her had been her parents. One side of her face had been torn away, as though a giant claw had ripped her.

Beyond the entrance, chaos reigned. Short bursts of machine-gun fire alternated with screams and whimpers. None of the soldiers cried out, and if orders were being given, they were silent to Jim. The squads were going about their business with quiet and determined efficiency. Men, women, children and babies were being killed systematically. Jim swore to himself that he would stand up one day as a witness to these events should he succeed in returning safely home. If there was ever a home again for him to return to.

There was a wide lobby in which the bodies of sect members lay in bloody heaps. Jim was reminded of the main street of Middlewick, and the thought flashed through his mind that what he was seeing today was a direct reprisal. There were soldiers everywhere, moving in and out of the doors that led from the lobby into the rest of the ground floor. More frightened than ever, Jim ran up the stairs, taking them two at a time.

'Tina!' he shouted at the top of his voice, trying to make himself heard over the firing and banging all around him. 'Tina, can you hear me? Stay where you are, and I'll come find you. Just shout back so I can know where to go.'

He stood still, listening intently, but there was no reply. From the landing on which he stood he ran up to the main upstairs landing, calling Tina's name. Still no-one answered or ran out to him. The landing split, a left-hand corridor going down into a section labelled 'Women', its right-hand counterpart leading to 'Men'. Evidently, the sleeping quarters here were divided between the sexes.

He ran into the female corridor. The further end was in flames. All the doors had been kicked open, and Jim went to each one, calling for Tina. In one room, four women lay dead, bright red spots on their foreheads, the backs of their heads blown away. Two still held crosses in their right hands, one held a Bible. It was much the same in other rooms.

Coming back into the corridor, he realized that the flames were spreading with great rapidity. Several times he attempted to break through the fire into the remaining rooms beyond, but each time he was beaten back. At last he made his way back to the landing. He was sure now that Tina was dead, or that she had never been here. In which case, perhaps the President and his wife had never been here either.

Deciding this, he fell silent, knowing it was useless to call Tina's name any more. Men in white snow suits passed him as he made for the stairs, some still going up, the rest down. The sound of firing ceased, and there were no more explosions. For a few moments, all Jim could hear was the roar of the fire as it took firmer hold of the wooden building. Then footsteps sounded, and seconds later Jurgensen appeared, followed by half a dozen soldiers. Two of them were dragging between them an old man with long white hair and a beard. There was an open gash across the old man's forehead, and he staggered as they hurried him past Jurgensen and down the stairs.

Jurgensen pulled up hard when he saw Jim.

'What the hell are you doing here, Major?' he asked.

Jim found himself lost for words. All the things he wanted to say, all the biting phrases that were on his lips, he knew he could not say and stay alive. Getting back to Washington in one piece was now his only concern, if only so he could bring these men to book. More than ever, he had to keep a cool head.

'I'm doing what I was sent here to do, just as I expect you've been doing what they sent you here for.'

'I asked you a question, Major. You know you had strict orders not to enter the compound.'

'My orders were to help my daughter. I came here to find her.'

'Your daughter isn't here, Major. She was never here. Not her, not the President, not the President's wife. Come on, Major, let's get you out of here before we both wind up hamburgers.'

26

They walked down the stairs together, accompanied by the four remaining SEALs. Above them, the roof timbers were giving way, and burning debris was collapsing onto floors that were already on fire.

Leaving the house behind them, they started to head back towards the shore. Until now, Jim had been uncertain as to how they were to get off the island, but looking off to his right, he could see a V-22 Osprey hovering as it came in to land. He'd seen Ospreys before, and had spent some time learning to fly one during an exchange visit with the Marines about a year ago. The Osprey was a state-of-the-art tiltrotor plane, capable of taking off and landing like a helicopter, yet flying as a turboprop the rest of the way. It carried twenty-four troops, and this one would have been perfect had they found the President and his two companions. Jim reflected on the fact that there was only one Osprey, enough to get them all home: had it been decided from the start that they were taking no prisoners?

He could see the SEAL force already making its way towards the aeroplane. Their movements were unhurried as they gathered together arms and other equipment. The kayaks were being folded up and put into their carrying bags.

'We're going home in that,' said Jurgensen. 'We've got to get a move on: meteorology say the weather's going to get worse. There's a storm building out at sea, and it's headed this way.'

Jim looked up. The sky above was the colour of lead, dark and threatening. If a real howler came on, they might not be able to get off the island. He'd be alone with whoever had tried to kill him. He'd sooner paddle back across the open sea than take that risk.

The Osprey touched down. Jim recognized it as the CV-22 version, a long-range model built for US Special Operations Command, brought into service to replace the ageing Pave Low helicopters. He watched as the rotors spun to a standstill.

It was only as he took his eyes away from the plane that he noticed the old man, still flanked by two soldiers, standing a few yards away. Jurgensen turned to him.

'That's their leader,' he said. 'Man called McLeod. Considers himself some sort of prophet. Crazy by any standards. His people set up the whole thing over in England. We don't know how they did it, but they were responsible.'

Abruptly, Jurgensen took several strides, winding up facing McLeod. Jim noticed that the prophet had a remarkable face. He was perhaps seventy, or a little above, and for all his features showed his age in wrinkles and little blotches, the eyes that glared out at them were those of a man of twenty. Jim went closer in order to hear what McLeod might have to say.

Jurgensen went behind the old man and took a hunk of hair in his hand, yanking upwards and pulling back. McLeod cried out, an inarticulate cry that he quickly suppressed.

'They tell me you head up this group,' Jurgensen began. 'Is that right?'

'The head of our Church,' McLeod replied in a strong Scots accent, 'is Jesus Christ. Above Him is God. There is no-one else.'

'But you are God's prophet, isn't that the case?'

'He speaks through me, that is all. Why have you come to us like the Romans, wounding, killing, destroying the innocent? Who gave you this authority?'

'I'm not here to answer your questions, mister. But I have a few to put to you. Such as, where's the President? Where's his wife? Remember them? You were keeping them here till recently. That's right, isn't it?'

The old man laughed softly and shook his head.

'You're misinformed,' he said. 'The President was never here.'

'Then where did you take him?'

'What makes you think I took him anywhere? Or any of my people, for that matter? Your President means nothing to us. He's the ruler of a corrupt nation, that's all. He is not on my conscience.'

There was a momentary pause. Jurgensen's face went bright red, then deadly pale. One might have thought anything could happen.

'You telling me President Waterstone is dead?'

The old man stared ahead stoically. His God was talking to him. Inside, he was at peace. Everything he had laboured to build had been cast down, but the fine and rhythmical utterances of his long-affectionate divinity brought calm to his heart.

'The truth is, I don't know. He was never here. None of them were brought here. Our duty ended the day God took him prisoner.'

'I don't understand.' Jurgensen was steaming up now. He'd missed his chance to return a national hero, he had the killings on his mind, he had no God to shore him up. 'There was no God in that fucking hell you created in Middlewick, just like there's none here today. I don't want to hear about God, mister. I want to know who took the President and his wife, and if I don't hear what I need to hear in the next few seconds, you're a dead man.'

Before Jim could stop him, he took his pistol from his holster and held it to the prophet's temple. McLeod just smiled at him.

'God is about to turn this nation from ungodliness to godliness. Millions will die, but those who remain will have been chastened. They will know that God is real, and that He speaks through the tongues of men such as myself. If you shoot me, you will die very soon. I do not know where your President is. You should ask the ones who took him.'

Jim saw Jurgensen's finger tighten on the trigger.

'Leave it, Major,' he said. He didn't even think of moving on the gun. 'He's no good to you. Take him back to Washington. Let experts question him.'

'To fuck with that!' Jurgensen spat. And he pulled back on the trigger. Almost before the explosion could be heard, McLeod's skull shattered and emptied its contents, along with chunks of bone, on the untouched snow. Jim watched in horror as the old man's body

215

shook violently from head to foot and toppled sideways into a drift of snow. Though dead, the body refused to relinquish movement. Spasms passed through it, and once Jim saw the mouth open and close, as though the inner God had not yet departed, and sought to communicate further through the tongue of His dead prophet.

Jim swung round and watched as Jurgensen checked his handgun, a Heckler & Koch MK23, and put it away trimly in its leather shoulder holster. The commander took several breaths, then turned to Jim.

'What the fuck are you looking at? Want me to waste you as well?'

'I was wondering what turns a brave man into a killer. What makes a fisherman into a monster. Do you really think all this will go unnoticed back home?'

Jurgensen sneered.

'You're out of your depth, Jimbo. I could shoot you right here, and nobody would ask any questions back in Washington. You'd be a casualty of war, and so what? So fucking what?'

'This was a massacre,' retorted Jim, 'that's fucking what. Your men went on a killing spree. You know damn well no US soldiers get away with that, not even their commanders.'

Jurgensen burst into loud laughter.

'You're living in your sweet fucking dreams. Just think some. These people kidnapped the President of the United States, along with his wife and your kid. We don't know but that they already killed all three of them. We don't know but that we'll find their bodies when we do some digging round this shithole place. They also killed a heap of Secret Service agents. All I know is, nobody back in Washington is going to shed any tears to know nobody came out of this thing alive.'

'You killed women and little children. The children did nothing. Why did you have to kill them?'

'Because they were there. You think Mr and Mrs Middle America who just came in from tying a yellow ribbon round their fucking oak tree, who spend Sunday mornings in church praying for the safe return of the President and the First Lady, you think these good people are going to grieve for one second just because some kids got in the way of crossfire out here?'

216

In the distance, just behind the Osprey, Jim could see men coming from the beach, dragging boxes on sleds, and heading for the burning building. Jurgensen followed his gaze.

'Don't worry about those guys. They're just making some late deliveries to the grocery store back there. So later on people will know the defenders were fully equipped. Some of it's stuff we took out from Middlewick, we're just putting it back where it belongs.'

'Like putting a gun in the hand of an innocent man you just killed?'

'Listen, you fuck, I just might blow your fucking head off if I hear any more about innocence. The bodies back there belonged to some serious felons. President-killers come about as low as you get. You got some arguments with that, mister? 'Cause I can settle them right here. Believe me, one more corpse don't matter shit. Now, I'd appreciate it if you were just to hand me that MP5 and your handgun. Don't want you getting no funny ideas during our flight back home.'

Reluctantly, Jim handed his weapons to one of the white-faced troopers who had been guarding McLeod. He knew when he was outnumbered and out of his depth.

'And don't go getting any fancy plans about how you're going to blow the whistle once you get back to Washington. I warned you before this to watch your back. I haven't told you to stop watching, and I don't intend to. You're on my list, asshole, and believe me there's only the one way off that list. Do I make myself clear?'

'I guess you do.'

'You ain't seen nothing, you ain't heard nothing. Let's keep it that way. Maybe your daughter's still alive. Maybe she still misses her Daddy. Guess it's up to you to make sure she sees him again.'

The Osprey's rotors had started to turn. One of the crew stood on the step and called blindly to Jurgensen and Jim. Above their heads, the storm was coming in.

'Let's go,' said Jurgensen. 'We're done here.'

27

Washington, D.C.

She felt angry, more angry than she'd felt in her life before. They could have given her a month's notice, which was required in her contract, or a one-off payment in lieu of that, or just asked her politely if she wouldn't mind leaving. Of course she would have minded, but it could have been made to seem like her own decision, instead of being carpeted, dressed down, and kicked out on her butt. Which was why she was angry. She could feel the anger seething inside her, in her toes, in her heels, in her thighs and groin and belly, a whole heap of unresolved anger boiling up like hot lava. And all because she'd been a little impetuous.

She ran the whole scenario through her mind for the fortieth or fiftieth time since leaving FBI Headquarters that morning. The note that had landed on her desk first thing, summoning her to the Director's office, the long, embarrassing wait outside Martin Vance's office, her admission into an atmosphere so charged she could hardly breathe.

'Shut the door behind you, Miss Miles. I won't ask you to take a seat, I'd rather you stood.'

'Sir, I . . .'

'Don't even think of answering back. I won't have that, do you understand? If you haven't already guessed why I hauled you up here, I'm sorry for you.'

'If it's about . . .'

218

'One more outburst like that, and you'll wish you'd joined the Marines. Maybe you think the FBI isn't tough enough for you, maybe you like to spend your time dreaming up ways of making your life a whole lot tougher. Well, sweetheart, you just did. What the fuck did you think you were doing, turning up like that on the Vice President's doorstep in the middle of the night? He was trying to sleep, or maybe that's something you tough types don't understand. But let me tell you, he was not pleased, not pleased at all.

'He has specifically asked me to take you off the case you are on. Period. Consider yourself so off it, if you even say the word "president" again, you are likely to see the inside of a State Penitentiary for a very long time. But to make things easier for you, I have personally decided that you are no longer a serving agent with this Bureau. I want you to leave your badge, your ID, and your weapon on my desk.'

'Sir, my father . . .'

Holly wasn't sure what she had meant to say; but Vance had got in ahead of her.

'Don't try to play that card with me, Miss. I don't give a sweet fuck who your father is, or your mother, or your sick brother. I'm doing this because the Vice President asked me to. Don't think you can take this any further.'

She took the badge and ID from her pocket and dropped them on his desk, then unbuckled her shoulder holster and laid it, with her gun inside, next to them. Vance did not even reach out a hand to touch them.

'What got into you anyway? Did you think because you'd been up at the house a couple of times you could go in there any time of the day or night you pleased? Like you didn't have to make an appointment like other people? Like being an FBI agent gave you rights nobody else, myself included, has got? Well, wake up and welcome to the world the rest of us live in. You're dismissed from your job with this bureau as of this moment, and you needn't waste your time looking for employment elsewhere, because you won't find it, not in the public sector at least.

'Now, you've got a life to lead, I've got a job to do, so get out of my sight.'

219

There'd been no point in answering back. She'd left the building without looking back. Back in her apartment, seething now that the initial shock had worn off, she'd rung her father. He'd hung up on her the moment he heard her voice. After much heart searching, she'd rung her brother at his office. His secretary had asked for her name, then come back to her thirty seconds later saying that Mr Miles was too busy to come to the phone, and, no, she couldn't suggest a good time to ring back.

The next call she made was one that no FBI agent, current or former, should ever have made. But Holly Miles was angry, and somebody would have to pay.

28

10 January

The Osprey had flown them back to McChord, where a C-21A jet
– the military equivalent of a Learjet – was waiting to take Jim
and Dick Cohen back to Andrews AFB. They'd given up hope
of finding Figueras alive, and Markham had flown back in one
of the Gulfstreams. Whether they'd gone to Dam Neck or further
on to Coronado, or some other place the ordinary military had no
knowledge of, Jim neither knew nor cared.

Like Cohen, Jim was wrung out after the night and morning he'd
just passed, but whereas the CIA boss fell asleep within minutes of
takeoff and snored loudly throughout the flight, Jim did not close
his eyes once. If he did, all he could see were images of the dead
and wounded lying among the drifting snow of Forrest Island.

At the airport, Cohen had been whisked away in an official car.
Jim, whose brain was hardly functioning by this stage, pulled what
rank he could and was told he could have a car and a driver to take
him back to his apartment.

A chief master sergeant named Rooney came to tell him when the
car was ready.

'Sir, before you go, I . . . The thing is, I can't help asking you
this question, even though I'm probably not even allowed to speak
to you.'

Rooney was maybe thirty-five, intelligent-looking, and diffident.

'It's all right, Master Sergeant, you can ask whatever you want.'

221

'Well, sir, I just have to know. Did you find the President? Is he all right? And his wife, sir. And the little girl. I don't remember her name.'

'Tina. Her name is Tina. And the answer is, "No", we didn't find the President. Or anyone else.'

'I see, sir. But there's still hope, is there?'

'Hope? I really don't know. And I'm too tired even to entertain it. But why not? Why not?'

Just then an officer wearing a captain's uniform approached them.

'Major Crawford?'

Jim turned and they saluted.

'Would you mind accompanying me, sir? This won't take a moment.'

'I'm very tired. I haven't slept in a very long time. Can't this wait till tomorrow?'

'I'm afraid not, sir. I'm acting under orders.'

'I'm sure you are, Captain. Provided this thing doesn't take long.'

The Captain, whose chest badge gave his name as Bronovski, led Jim to a Jeep that was waiting to take them to Base HQ. It was a short drive from the main gate to the west gate, then down Command Drive to the semi-circular Headquarters building. The Captain did not attempt to start up a conversation once during the trip, and Jim was in no mood to engage in chitchat.

He was shown – marched might have been a better word – directly to a small interview room in the personnel section. Waiting for him was a man in a civilian suit, a dark suit with hand-stitched lapels, and a shirt that must have been pressed ten times a day. The man himself was of middle age, yet with none of the defects of the state. Wealth, a serene mind, and a body well honed by expensive sports and European spas, all gave him the appearance of a much younger man, and had it not been for the frontal balding coupled with a certain gravity of manner, Jim might very well have mistaken him for a junior functionary in a government department.

'Please take a seat, Major.' The other man did not rise, or make any gesture of welcome.

Jim sat facing him. Air Force bases did not, as a rule, let civilians interview USAF officers without agreement.

'Excuse me, but what is going on? I've just come back from a mission, I'm dog-tired, and I want to go home. You'd better have a good reason for this delay.'

'There's no need to be aggressive, Major. I'm only trying to help you.'

'Have you any idea where I've come from, what happened there?'

The balding head nodded twice.

'Of course. That's what this is about, or are you too tired to guess?'

'Then why the mystery? You haven't introduced yourself . . .'

'You don't need to know my name. As for my face – you'll never see me again.'

'I assume you work for the government.'

Over towards the east side of the base, a jet took off, screeching as it lifted to the sky. Jim realized how much he'd been missing the sound of high-performance planes.

'In a sense, yes. Think of it like that, if it helps. All I want you to do for me is sign a piece of paper.'

'My death warrant?'

For a moment, the nameless man was shocked. But he rallied and came back at Jim, as cool as ever.

'Not exactly. Although a refusal to sign could well have undesirable consequences. That would be stupid and unnecessary.'

He reached into his inside jacket pocket and brought out a folded sheet. This he unfolded before placing it on the little table that separated him from Jim. A vase sat on the table. It was filled with water, but the huge red peonies in it were artificial.

Jim took the sheet and read what had been typed on it. It was an agreement without heading or reference, at the foot of which a dotted line had been typed above his name. The text ran to only a few lines. If he signed it, he committed himself never to speak or write or hint or allude in any form, or by any symbol, token, or recondite method to the events he had witnessed earlier that day. On pain of imprisonment for an indeterminate period.

He stopped reading and looked up.

'Sir, I don't know your name, but I don't think you or the person who drew up this document can be properly familiar with the Bill of Rights. I'm not just speaking of the First Amendment, but the Fifth and Sixth. This infringes my rights as a US citizen.'

'Major, you are a serving Air Force officer. You knew when you joined the service that you would have to give up many of the rights your fellow-citizens enjoy. The First Amendment has no bearing on what the government considers secret, Top Secret, or above Top Secret. Today's events, as you can well imagine, have been classified so tightly that they will never be made public, not in your lifetime, not in your child's lifetime, and not in her children's lifetimes. As for the Fifth Amendment, you should remember that the right to trial by Grand Jury is not extended to the Navy or militia in time of war or public danger. We are living in a time of public danger more critical than you will ever know.'

'If what happened today is an example . . .'

'Major,' the suited man broke in. He had small eyes that perplexed Jim by their frankness. 'We do not want a second Waco, with every conspiracy theorist in the world seeing a deliberate plot to take innocent lives. As you're well aware, the occupants of the commune on Forrest Island opened fire when they saw our rescue party approaching. We still have to determine whether anything was done to conceal or move or – and I'm sorry to have to say this to you – kill the President, his wife, and your daughter under cover of the rifle fire that was laid down in the early part of the engagement.'

'You have evidence they were there?'

The man shook his head sympathetically.

'I'm afraid not. But we do have evidence that this sect was the one that took them prisoner in England. You can be shown that evidence if you like. There's no harm in it now, provided you've signed that paper and are willing to abide by it.'

Jim felt the room swimming round his head.

'If I sign, what guarantee do I have that you'll leave me alone after that?'

'None whatsoever. The people I work for will not accept to have their hands tied. Believe me, Major, you are not safe with them. Your

224

life, your freedom, your well-being are all at risk. If it were not for the fact that your daughter may still be held with the presidential couple, and that the nation would be troubled if she came out of imprisonment to find not only her mother dead, but you vanished, and your fate wholly unknown, you would already be dead.'

'Meaning that I am your prisoner, your kidnapee, as much as the President and the others are theirs.'

'You may put it that way if you like. Now, will you sign?'

The fight had gone out of Jim. He could barely keep his eyes open now he was back on terra firma. And he guessed what he was up against. If he was right, not even the President, should he ever return from his enforced absence, would be able to get him out of his present trouble.

'Yes. Have you a pen?'

The stranger passed him a gold-cased fountain pen. Jim scrawled something that might pass for his signature along the dotted line. The ink dried slowly. Jim replaced the cap on the pen and returned it. Then he folded the paper and handed it over.

'May I go now?'

'If you wait here, I'll have them bring a car. The driver will take you back to your apartment.'

'Will you at least tell me which agency you work for?'

The man shook his head.

'I thought you knew better than to ask that question. The agency I belong to does not exist. No amount of probing will bring it into the open. I advise you not to waste your time. Not if you wish to see your daughter again, and live a long and healthy life.'

29

The President's Quarters
Location Unknown

There was no knock on the door, just the sound of heavy feet approaching, then the outer gate being unlocked, opened, and locked again, and finally the inner door snapping open and slamming with force.

It was the auburn-haired woman, the one they called Barbie behind her back, on account of her real name, Varvara. They had been given no second name. Varvara was the biggest loss Hollywood had sustained since the death of Marilyn Monroe, and it was probably better that way. She stomped over to where they were sitting, talking between themselves. The little girl was nowhere to be seen.

'Get to your feet!' Varvara shouted. She seemed to know only this one register; if – improbable as it seemed – she ever came to whisper sweet nothings in a lover's ear, what came out would still have been a bellow.

'What's wrong?' Joel Waterstone asked.

She ignored his question.

'Hurry up. Get your wife and the child, and put on your outdoor clothes. You're being moved. You have five minutes.'

The President got to his feet.

'Where are you taking us?'

'That's not for me to tell you. Now, look sharp, *pizda*. There's no time to waste.'

226

She turned and headed back to the door. As her hand touched the handle, Waterstone spoke again.

'We can't go anywhere. Tina is ill. Rebecca is looking after her in her room.'

A slow double-take, then Varvara turned.

'We know she has been ill. But her wound will heal.'

'No, it's not that. Come and see her, if you like. She has a fever, possibly from an infection that may have started in the wound.'

'When did this begin?'

'About an hour ago. We've been telephoning since then, trying to get someone to come, a doctor, perhaps.'

'We have plenty of doctors, you know that.'

'All the same, no-one answered. No matter how often we tried, there was never an answer. And now you arrive, telling us to clear out.'

'Everyone has been busy. You are not always our first thought, you know. We have greater preoccupations. However, it is not good if the child comes to harm. I would like to see her, please.'

They led her to Tina's bedroom, a cramped space occupied almost entirely by her bed. Rebecca had squeezed herself into the space between the top end of the bed and the wall, and was holding Tina's hand and talking soothingly to her.

'Joel,' she began, catching sight of her husband. 'She's starting to grow delirious. Have you had no luck getting a doctor to come?'

Before he could answer, the President was pushed aside by Varvara, who told Rebecca to make room for her.

'What's she doing here?' Rebecca asked.

'She says we have to leave. Looks like something's come up. Maybe they've tracked us down at last. But our hosts are taking us somewhere else.'

Varvara bent to examine Tina. She finally straightened and looked at the Waterstones in turn.

'I agree, she is very ill. Nevertheless, our departure cannot be delayed. You will have to make her ready. Your transportation is already here.'

'We can't take her in this condition.'

'*Ëb tvoju mat'!* You have no choice.'

227

'What about a doctor? She needs treatment urgently.'

'There will be a doctor where you are going. But not now. The doctors here have already gone. If you don't leave immediately, I cannot answer for the consequences. Now, help me get Tina out of bed. We have about three minutes.'

Washington, D.C.
11 January

Jim woke about six o'clock, quite unrefreshed. A fellow-pilot had once told him it's a fallacy that, when tired, the human body makes up for loss of sleep by sleeping more, and now Jim had proved the truth of that assertion, for he had hardly slept at all. His recovery would take days, not hours, and that would only deal with the sleep factor. All night long, he had tossed and turned, sometimes in a deep sleep, sometimes surfing along the tops of dreams, aping reality. His dreams had seemed too real and too long, and were packed with incidents from Forrest Island, each more vivid than the one before.

It was as if all the dead had gathered in his head, wailing, swearing, sobbing, lamenting, unquiet every one of them, all calling for redress, calling his name, calling him alone out of all their killers.

Once he thought he was paddling through ice-cold waters, and that the sea was filled with the bodies of the dead, so that he was paddling through bodies instead of waves. Every time he looked beyond the prow of his ocean kayak, their eyes would stare up at him, and their open mouths, and their gaping wounds. And their long white hands would reach up for him, as though to pull him down into the freezing sea.

Another time, he saw himself land on the island, and everywhere, standing as still as statues, he saw the old Indian dead, the Chinook, the Makah, the Salish, the Coast Salish, among them the Skwaks-namish, the S'Hotleemamish, the Sahehwamish people, the Sawamish of Totten Inlet, the Skwai-sitl, the Stehtsasamish, and the Nuhsesatl people. They were wearing long bearskin robes

228

against the cold, and they showed signs of hunger, and signs of whips and axes on their backs, and some had wounds in their foreheads made by musket balls.

Waking out of all this, Jim could not even think of Tina. His motives had undergone a great change, and he knew that, whatever the people on Forrest Island had done, Jurgensen and his men had had no right to visit vengeance on babies and children.

Struggling to clear his head, he made himself a strong coffee and dug inside the fridge until he came up with a packet of waffles and a jar of maple syrup. The waffles were a bit over their sell-by date, but he popped them in the toaster anyway. He was suddenly starving, and ate voraciously; but even as he chewed his breakfast he had to shut out all images of ice and snow and slaughter.

After breakfast, he tried everything to clear his mind: television was too ridiculous to hold his attention for more than a few moments, reading required more concentration than he could give it, the news channels had much to say about efforts to find the President, and absolutely nothing to report on yesterday's expedition to Forrest Island. In the end, he put on a singlet and shorts and went out to Montrose Park, working his way along to Rock Creek Park, where he joined the other early-morning joggers. It was only as he left the park, sweating, but much more himself, that he noticed the man watching him from a distance. It didn't take brains to know that any surveillance agent who let himself be seen must want to be seen. Just how long was this going to continue? he thought.

He went back to his apartment, showered, and got dressed again. It would be intolerable if he started to fear going out just because he knew there would be a watcher somewhere.

The phone rang just after eight. He picked up to hear a familiar voice greet him, the suited man from Andrews Base.

'Major Crawford, I think you will be relieved to hear that we have had a confession. You were probably unaware of it, but Major Jurgensen's team succeeded in arresting the assistant head of the commune, a man called Emmanuel Beckett. We don't think that's his real name, so we've instigated enquiries in Britain in the hope of identifying him properly.

'Mr Beckett did not want to say anything to us at first, but he was spoken to very persuasively, and about an hour ago admitted on tape that his church, which they called the Watch, was responsible for what happened in Middlewick. It seems they murdered the original inhabitants, took their identities, and made everything ready for the President's arrival.'

'You mean, he knows where the President is?'

There was a long silence. The stranger's voice, when it came, was no longer quite as self-confident as it had been.

'So far, we've been unable to get that information from him.'

'Did he even say how they got the President and the others out of Middlewick?'

'No, I'm afraid he keeps quiet on that as well.'

'He's not much use, then, is he?'

'Oh, I wouldn't say that. We've scarcely started on him. He'll cough it all up before very long. I'm ringing to let you know this as a favour, and as a reminder not to run off to some whistle-blowing rag with what you know. It will all come to light in due course. Once we have the President back safely, nobody – and I include yourself in this number – will want to know anything about some abortive attempt that went wrong. I'll let you know the minute I have information. And, by the way, I'd get new running shoes if I were you. What you were wearing this morning won't do for Rock Creek. Look around while you're here: the stores have all the latest styles.'

Coming off the phone, Jim felt his sense of unreality increase. If this man Emmanuel knew where the Waterstones and Tina were . . . But that could only be another dream.

On his way back from Rock Creek Park, he'd slipped into a corner grocery and bought some supplies. The long run had made him feel hungrier than ever, and now he set about cooking some real food: eggs, ham, hash brownies, mushrooms, and some garlic-stuffed Italian sausages that the store owner had recommended ('*son' queste molto, molto piccante, signore. Credime, signore, non trovate altrove salsiccie come queste* . . . and so on and so forth for about five minutes, while the sausages were picked and weighed and wrapped in brown paper, Jim all the while not understanding a word). The mushrooms had been grown in the city somewhere, in dark, dank cellars far beneath the everyday streets.

230

He threw everything into hot olive oil and fried the life out of it, all the while censoring thoughts about saturated fats, cholesterol, and heart attacks. Laura would have taken the pan from his hands and dumped the contents into the trash can.

That was when he broke down for the first time since Laura's death, huddling on the floor in a corner of the kitchen, like a baby or a madman. He would have thrown up several times, but there was so little in his stomach, he only retched after the first time. The crying jag lasted a long time, and when he finally recovered and got to his feet, his meal had long ago incinerated itself, and the pan was showing signs of bursting into flames. He took it from the hob, turned off the gas, doused everything in a sinkful of water, and sat down at last, thoroughly exhausted.

After a spell, he went into the living room. His skin was crawling, and his thoughts gave him no peace. Sitting, he wanted to stand, standing he wanted nothing more than to sit. Hunger nagged at him, but he could not bear the thought of food. Above all, he wanted to get on board his beloved F-15, take off at desperate speed, his body crushed by the forces of gravity, with nothing but the blue and empty sky wherever he looked.

He made up his mind in an instant. He'd report for duty at Andrews AFB, and ask to be flown back to rejoin his squadron at Simonsford. It was time he got off his backside, he thought, stopped moping, and did something useful. If Tina was still found, surely he could be flown to the spot from England. And what if she had been there all along, he wondered, all the time he'd been here in America?

He only had a dress uniform with him, but he guessed that would be fine at this stage. The uniform had been hung up in his wardrobe after the funeral. He found it and put it on. As he slipped on the jacket, he slipped his hand into the pockets to check for rubbish, and came out with the telephone number Greg Hopper had given him.

He sat down on the edge of the bed. Rain, brought in from the Atlantic by an east wind, was drumming against the window panes. He listened to the downpour for a while, then got up and went to the window. On the opposite side of the street, half-hidden by a doorway, a man stood waiting for the rain to stop. He looked up once, then, catching sight of Jim, looked away again.

Jim sat down on the bed once more, and picked up the telephone. Greg's card had been in his hand all the time. He dialled the number, expecting a voice mail recorder, or to find that Greg had left town, heading for inner Africa or some part of Asia that doesn't exist on the maps.

The phone rang just twice before being picked up.

Jim managed to fire off a coded phrase that warned Greg they were speaking on a bugged line.

'Seventeen five. Repeat seventeen five.'

While serving together in the Marines, they and five friends had formed a loose grouping that communicated by means of a letter and number code. Jim started the conversation, dredging up half-forgotten memories of the code as he spoke.

'Greg, this is Jim Crawford. I'm on an insecure line. Can you use the old code?'

'Of course I can. I was wondering when you'd ring. I'd thought, a day or two more, but here you are, large as life. What can I do for you?'

'When can we meet up?'

'Any time you like, old buddy. Your place or mine?'

'I think mine's being watched.' Jim remembered the man in the street.

'Then mine probably is too.'

'I reckon.'

'Then here's where we'll meet . . .'

30

Washington, D.C.

There was a phone booth about one hundred yards down the street. Jim rang Barwood Taxi for a cab to come pick him up from outside his apartment and take him downtown.

'I want an empty cab,' he said, knowing as he spoke that his telephone line was being bugged, less now in the hope of hearing the President, more to know what Jim Crawford was up to, and whom he was speaking with. 'No other passengers on the way either. I'll pay extra for the privilege. You got that? I won't stand to be messed about.'

'OK,' came a woman's voice over the line, 'keep your cool. Is there anything else we can do for you? A nodding dog in the rear window, maybe? We got poodles, we got borzois, we got Afghans . . . .'

'Do I sound like a dog lover to you? Just be sure the driver gets here in exactly ten minutes, and make sure he knows how to drive.'

He did know how to drive, but only in the sense that he could start the engine, find the gas pedal, and drive off. An automatic shift took care of the rest. His driving style was all his own. The car was a 1985 Plymouth Reliant, the four-door sedan. Jim's Uncle Larry had driven one back in '81.

As they pulled away from the kerb, Jim looked back through the rear window to see a black Volvo peeling off from the opposite side near his apartment, and then a grey Ford from further back. He leaned back, smiling, willing them to come after him, while, in

233

front, his driver embarked on a monologue couched in a strange form of English that he seemed to be making up as he went along.

'Not espeak English so good. Sorry. Been refugee one year. Ees hard for work on tawksi. All time, estart, estop, estart again.'

'Where are you from?'

'Iran. You hear of my country?'

'Yes, I've heard of it. Been close to it more than once.'

Another backward look: his pursuers were struggling to stay behind the erratically driven taxi. They were hanging back as if they had not been sighted, but Jim's driver would shoot forward, pull in, weave in and out through slower cars, and generally break every rule of safe and polite driving. He used his horn a lot, and swore in Farsi repeatedly.

'In Iran not so poor. Live Tehran, in Qolhak, very nice espot, live house it has garden, plenty of carpet, esweem place . . . What you say?'

'Pool. Swimming pool. You must have been rich. What did you do?'

'Do?'

'What was your job?'

'I was lawyer, very good lawyer.' He braked suddenly. '*Pedar-sukhta! Ahmaq! Mana na-didi?*' He ranted quite happily for half a minute or more.

Jim looked back. They'd be working a three-man formation, with an eyeball one or two cars behind, a backup further down, and a third man holding the rear. That would give them enough flexibility at junctions and circles. In all likelihood, they'd have further backup available, but it wouldn't be much use until they knew where he was finally headed.

With the help of a good map, he set out to improve his driver's knowledge of Washington.

'What's your name, by the way?'

'Reza. Like Emam Reza.'

'Emam Reza?'

'Very holy man for Persians.'

He tapped a luridly coloured picture that had been taped to the right-hand side of the windscreen.

'OK, Reza, we're coming up to Washington Circle here. I want you to take the second exit onto New Hampshire. You got that?'

'Sure, ees not hard. You being followed?'

Jim hesitated.

'What . . . makes you think that?'

'Same two cars been keeping close to me since we leave. Move in and out, but always same. And you not estop looking through back window. You some sort criminal, maybe?'

'Something like that. When you get to Dupont Circle up ahead, make second left again, and head for Kalorama.'

'You go there?'

'No. You just keep driving.'

Half an hour later, Reza screeched to a halt outside Union Station. The arched entrance seemed to invite Jim to any number of destinations. More usefully, eight streets led away from Columbus Circle.

He paid Reza what was on the meter, then added twice that again.

'They'll come after you,' he said. 'They'll want to ask you if I said anything about where I'm going. Tell them what you like. And remember, they can't hurt you. You haven't done anything wrong.'

'Ees this paradise you talking about, or my old friend the Great Satan?'

'This is a democracy, Reza. There's something called rule of law.'

Reza laughed.

'Iran too is democracy. And I know what is rule of law. Maybe you will get away. You ees jet pilot, maybe you ees big hero. But I am refugee. Maybe they will send me back to Iran.'

'What did you do that makes it dangerous for you to go back?'

'I prosecute molla for rape. He has powerful friends. Ees old estory.'

'Stay alive, Reza. Become an American. Forget you ever met me.'

He dashed in through the main entrance, and was at once drawn into a swirling mass of travellers, some leaving, some going, others just waiting for their train to arrive. He plunged into the maelstrom, looking up from time to time like any tourist at the remarkable ceiling, as though he was in a cathedral.

So distracted, he might almost have missed the public toilets just off the main concourse. He hurried into the men's room. Looking not a little awkward, a man of his height and hair colouring stood just inside the entrance. A quick glance told Jim that the stranger was dressed in almost identical clothes to his own, as Greg had said he would be.

Jim dropped the holdall he'd been carrying, and picked up an identical one that was sitting on the floor next to the stranger.

'Guess this must be the Elvis lookalike contest,' he said.

The other man smiled briefly, then bent and picked up Jim's bag. He waited until Jim had dived into a cubicle before leaving. Outside the men's room, he paused long enough to be sighted, then hurried off to catch the 11.05 to Baltimore and Wilmington.

The bag contained a change of clothes, a wig, and a Colt automatic. Jim wondered why Greg had thought he should carry a weapon, then he thought about Forrest Island. The advice he had given Reza had been stupid and arrogant.

He got rid of the small holdall and its contents by flushing the toilet, then ramming the bag into the cistern and forcing the ballcock to a high position. The lid went back easily, and Jim stepped out of the cubicle. Heading for the washbasins, he caught sight of the tail out of the corner of one eye. He felt himself given the once over, and turned his head in time to catch the appraising look. Turning the hot tap, he returned the look, somehow managing to suggest a homophobic attitude that could turn to violence. The man turned aside.

He dried his hands and made his way back to the concourse. People were milling everywhere, a high school party had taken over the centre of the space, shoppers were threading their way through the crowds on their way to the station mall, and queues were forming at most of the gates. Holly had told him they held inaugural balls here, and he tried to picture it to himself now. All he could see was Holly turning and spinning while everyone else stood still to watch her. He felt terrible, knowing he would never see her again, and could not bring himself to admit why.

He took the third cab in line, and fished in his right-hand pocket for the sheet of paper that held his directions.

'Can you drive me to Theodore Roosevelt Island?'

The driver shrugged and headed out. Jim kept a careful eye behind, but could see no-one in obvious pursuit. Maybe Greg's ruse had worked.

The island proved another clever touch. His driver explained that vehicles aren't allowed on any part of its eighty-eight acres. It is connected to the mainland only on the Virginia side, by a footbridge.

They drove down Constitution Avenue west. Jim could see signs for Interstate 66. He looked behind again, but could not make out whether they were being followed or not. The cab moved onto the Roosevelt Bridge and moved into the right-hand lane. None of the vehicles travelling immediately behind imitated the manoeuvre. Once across the river, the driver took the first exit right and followed a ramp down to a car park. There were no other vehicles. In February, hiking through miles of wilderness is a pastime that attracts few car drivers.

Jim paid the driver and watched as he drove off. The footbridge was nearby. Walking across, he was able to get a good view of his surroundings. Nobody else had arrived at the car park, and, short of taking a rowboat or flying in by chopper or descending by parachute, there just wasn't any other way to get there.

Greg was waiting for him at the Roosevelt Memorial, just a short walk from the bridge. Dressed in a black parka, he almost blended with the statue of Roosevelt that dominated the little plaza.

'Let's go for a walk, Jim. I've got men in all the right spots. Good men: you won't see them. They'll see to it we don't have any visitors.'

The island was crisscrossed by paths that led among trees, the view opening to the river from time to time, then closing up again. Winter birds sang. There was wildlife everywhere. Jim talked, and talked some more, travelling deeper and deeper into the nightmare he had brought here inside his head. Greg said nothing, but listened intently. Nothing Jim said seemed to shock him, but once or twice he detected on his friend's face a dark expression that went far beyond shock or rage.

They must have walked for over an hour. His story had left Jim's mouth like a poison that had been threatening his life. It would never be entirely gone, but he'd spat a lot of it out, and felt a little cleaner as a result.

They came back to the plaza at last, and sat down side by side on the statue's plinth. A chill wind was coming across the Potomac.

'I knew Jurgensen,' Greg said. 'Used to be a regular guy. A tough bastard, but his heart was in the right place. He's changed a lot. That SEAL unit he runs ain't regular SEAL. It's hush hush; not even ordinary Navy SEALs know about it. They spend most of their time on stand-by, or training. Only certain very top people can call them out, and then only for very special operations. Like the one you were on.

'They'll kill you in the end. At the moment they daren't touch you, not, at least, till they get the President back, along with his wife and your little girl. But if you were to have an accident . . . My guess is they'll just assassinate you with a gun or a bomb, and put it down to the people who are holding the President.'

'Would they try?'

'It wouldn't be Jurgensen's people. You're small fry to them. There are other people who can do a job like yours. They were following you today.'

'What the hell can I do?'

'You don't go back to your apartment. You stay away from any USAF base. If it can be arranged, you die.'

'I what . . . ?'

'We fake your death, and you go underground. Then we start our own search for the President.'

'We?'

'I'll introduce you. We're a bunch of special ops guys who got together to clean some things up. There's a lot of shit out there. You've seen some of the worst of it. But Forrest Island ain't the only one, and maybe not even the worst.'

'You aren't some kind of survivalist cranks, are you? Conspiracy theorists of some sort? You think the US government's working to hurt the American people? Is that what I'm getting into here?'

'We're all sorts of things, Jim, but one thing we share is being

238

American. We believe in this country and its government, don't be in any doubt about that. But behind the government there are shadows who think they run the country. Almost nobody knows about them, but believe me, they're there. Even we know only a little about them. But I think it's time we started to find out just what they know about the President's kidnapping, and what they're doing about it.'

'What about me?'

'You're one of us now. You don't have no place else to go. We have a couple of safe houses here in D.C. It won't be comfortable, but we can try to keep you safe there. And there's another possibility I'd like time to consider. I need to speak to someone, see if he's happy. In the meantime, I think we should get you to one of the Washington houses. I'll drive you there.'

Jim nodded.

'What if they find Tina?' he asked.

Greg smiled and squeezed his arm.

'Hang in there, Jimbo. We're going to find her long before they do.'

31

They had been driving for ten hours now, without respite. Darkness had given way to a brief lightening of the sky, only to reveal endless snow wastes. Nowhere was the snow very deep, but they might have been in the Arctic. The road was the merest of tracks marked by occasional posts, barely picked out by the sidelights of the heavy truck in which they were travelling. Varvara said they could travel like this for days on end, never seeing another human being, let alone any sign of habitation.

She rode in the rear of the Kamaz alongside a man who turned out to be her superior in the FSB, the Federal'naya Sluzhba Bezopasnosti, the second successor kingdom to the late KGB. Gennady Tolbuzin was a KGB veteran. He'd served with the Arkhangel'skaya Oblast' counter-intelligence unit until the organization was disbanded under the Security and Internal Affairs Ministry. In 1993, he'd been appointed an FSK major, and now he was a highly decorated FSB colonel, no longer at *oblast'* level, but federal, and poised for greatness, if all ended well. He'd been in charge of the Waterstone operation from the start, and was riding it out now, in circumstances he had feared for several years.

Varvara, his subordinate, had been with the FSB since its foundation in 1995, when she'd joined Directorate T, the anti-terrorism unit. Up front, the three drivers were all former members of Alpha, Russia's premier anti-terrorist detachment, now part of Directorate T. They took turns driving, and the rest of the time either dozed or stared out at the flat, unchanging landscape running beneath their wheels like sleep.

Tina was getting worse. At the last minute, a doctor had turned up, a young woman fresh out of medical school, who had never treated this condition before. She was, at least, able to diagnose it.

They were in the back of a small truck that seemed to have shed its springs some years earlier. As they bumped and skidded along the ruts and frozen tyre tracks that meant 'road' in this country, Rebecca cradled Tina's head on her lap.

'How dangerous is it?' she asked.

'Very dangerous. If she does not get proper treatment, she will die.' The young doctor seemed shocked to find Tina's condition so far advanced.

'What sort of treatment?'

'At the moment, her symptoms suggest septicaemia: the fever, the occasional chills, the rapid breathing, the half-consciousness, the headache she complains of.'

'Septicaemia?'

'It means she has bacterial toxins in her blood.'

'Blood poisoning?'

The doctor nodded.

Rebecca drew Tina's hair back from her eyes.

'I presume she got this from the wound when they cut off her finger,' she said.

'Partly. But I've asked, and I'm told there was a swelling at the site of the wound. The doctor who treated her used a corticosteroid drug to help bring the swelling down, which it did. He prescribed prednisolone, and because he only had 25mg tablets, he gave her 50mg per day, which is too high. Corticosteroids are immunosuppressive, which means . . .'

'I know.' Rebecca smiled. 'They suppress the immune system, and leave the patient open to infections.'

'In this case, bacteria which managed to escape from the site of the wound and started multiplying elsewhere.'

Rebecca examined the young woman's ragged features. She'd be attractive if she put on some pounds and lost her tired and wasted look. Instead, she was out here, in one of the world's last wildernesses, aiding and abetting a gang of criminals.

'You said she should have "proper treatment". What did you mean?'

'She needs an intravenous infusion of glucose and saline, along with the right antibiotic drugs. She may need to have surgery to remove the infected material that has gathered on the wound.'

Outside, the landscape renewed itself endlessly. A black sky sucked all the available light into its own body. No trees stood against the horizon, no bushes broke the line of the track, no birds flew past, no wildlife stirred out of their dens.

'And if she can't get this treatment?'

'The septicaemia may turn to septic shock. Tissue becomes damaged, blood pressure drops. You'll find her hands and feet getting cold, maybe some cyanosis, perhaps some vomiting and diarrhoea. If it goes further, her urine production will drop, and there may be kidney failure. There could be heart failure as well.'

'But you said this was because the corticosteroid was suppressing her immunity. Won't it turn round if you just stop the drug?'

The doctor shook her head.

'It's not that simple,' she said. 'Withdrawing a corticosteroid abruptly can be very dangerous in itself. Fortunately, she hasn't been on the drug very long, but it will take me a few days to bring her dose down. In the meantime, if she does develop septic shock, she'll need intravenous infusions and oxygen therapy, along with the things I already mentioned.'

The truck lurched as it hit an obstruction, then found the road again.

'How long before we reach wherever it is we're going?'

The doctor shrugged.

'I don't know.'

'But you know where it is?'

She shook her head.

'I've been told nothing. All I know is, they wanted someone to look after your child, and to speak to you in English.'

'She's not our child,' Rebecca started to explain, but her husband placed a hand on her shoulder.

242

'She belongs to us for now, dear. Let's keep it simple.'

Suddenly, Tina began to cry out. The doctor bent down and examined her. When she lifted her head, her expression was serious.

'We have to make a detour,' she said. 'Otherwise she will die. I doubt it will be long before septic shock sets in, and even if we could treat it, she would still have only a fifty-fifty chance of survival.'

They looked at one another.

'Ask the driver to stop,' the President said. 'We need to talk to someone.'

32

The Dirksen Building
Capitol Hill
Washington, D.C.

'What do you mean, he got away?'

Thomas Ellison was furious. So angry, in fact, that he was totally composed. Neither his face nor his voice betrayed the dark emotions coursing through his veins. Only someone who knew him very well – his wife, perhaps, or one of his mistresses – could have recognized the mood and the danger. Ellison had been president of Respice Finem ever since the death of Harris Quinn in 1993. In public life, he was known as a former director of the National Security Agency turned Senator, now in his second six-year term. Behind the scenes, he was known as a man who could (and did) make and break the careers of even the most successful politicians. But here in the presence of his fellow-Respice Finem members, he was acknowledged to be one of the most powerful men in the secret life of the American nation.

'Thomas, they did their best. They tailed him to Union Station. He must have switched clothes with someone there, because when the tails caught up with him, it was the wrong man.'

'Is he in custody, this wrong man?'

Henry Bremahide, the Supreme Court judge who was regarded as Ellison's likely successor, cut in.

'The stand-in took out the tail who tried to arrest him.'

'Took out?'

'He hit him very hard. It's likely he had some form of Special Forces training. He vanished after that. They were in Wilmington by then, without backup.'

'I see. And what about Crawford?'

'We don't know. Most likely he took a train too.'

'More likely he did nothing of the sort. I take it there's a stakeout at his Georgetown apartment.'

'Of course. He hasn't been home.'

'He won't be. He's gone to earth somewhere, and he has someone helping him. I want the search party increased. And this time, make it clear there are no second chances. Shoot on sight.'

'Thomas, you can't . . .'

'We can do what we like. The way things are going, it won't be long before Heller is forced to declare a state of national emergency.'

'What would be his reason?'

'He doesn't have to have one. We are the only reason he will ever need.'

'Thomas,' said Warren Patrick, newly-elected head of the National Rifle Association, millionaire arms dealer, and go-between for the State Department and over a dozen foreign governments with whom diplomatic relations were generally strained. 'Could we please pass on? We have just received another communication from the kidnappers. They're moving house, and they're under pressure. They need our collaboration now. I think it's time to start giving them some answers.'

'What's their position regarding Waterstone?'

'Their position? I don't quite follow you.'

'Of course you do. We've talked about it at length before this. Are they willing to kill Waterstone so long as we can reach a mutually satisfactory agreement with them?'

'I don't think there's any question of that. But we still have to weigh the pros and cons. If it goes wrong, the consequences could be horrendous.'

'Then we shall just have to ensure that nothing goes wrong, gentlemen, won't we?'

245

33

Cranberry Wilderness
Monongahela National Forest
West Virginia
12 January

Greg took him out of the city in a dull-looking 4X4 that turned out
to be a Grand Cherokee V8 with every conceivable extra on board.
Outside, it was shabby and mud-spattered, inside everything was
sparkling.

'This car looks a mess,' said Jim, thinking of his own shiny BMW
back home in England. 'How old is it?'

''Bout a month. Got her for a good price from a dealership in
Baltimore. Which is not where I live, by the way.'

'But it's a mess.'

'Jim, you're gonna have to move quicker on this learning curve
you're now on. When this baby came out of the showroom, it was
shining like a new dime, wheels and all, like it had never spent
an hour on the road, let alone off-road. People notice a car like
that, remember it, maybe even talk about it to their friends. "Hi,
Norman, saw this brand-new Jeep drive past me this morning. Like
to get me one of them babies, if'n I had the dough. Guy drivin'
reminded me of my old Uncle Clem." So I got it in my garage the
moment I got it home, and I worked it over for a couple of days
till I got it like this. Shame to spoil a good car, but this way nobody
so much as gives it a second glance. On the other hand, I've got

246

a brand-new machine that will take me over some mighty tough terrain.'

Jim sat back as they drove west out of the city on Highway 66. He hadn't felt this cocooned in years. Anybody else but Greg, he'd have mistrusted the situation. But he'd come to know his old Army friend well, twice in combat. They'd been sent down south together on a couple of occasions, taking part in counter-insurgency campaigns designed to prop up a couple of corrupt Central American regimes.

Greg and Jim had been assigned as each other's buddies, vital for survival in jungle warfare, where no one man could see everything that was happening. Twice, Greg had saved Jim's life by being in the right place at the right time. He seemed to have a knack for that, and now he seemed to have done it again.

Greg had stayed on in the Marines after Greg defected to the Air Force. Two years after that, his wife Diane had died of breast cancer. There had been no children, and Greg had lived bereft from then on, forming no attachments, unburdening himself to no-one but Jim. For a few years, they'd met up on leave and gone hunting or climbing together, but as time had passed, Greg had found more frequent excuses for not turning up, until their close liaison had felt a thing of the past. Now that was changing again.

As Greg drove, Jim took his turn to unburden his heart, speaking about his grief for Laura and his anxiety about Tina. There was nothing he hadn't said before, but it felt good telling it to Greg, the way it had felt right opening up to Holly.

They joined Interstate 81 at Strasburg, and headed south. It was midday, and a lot of cars were involved in some kind of lunch-time dash that was leading to frayed tempers and some snarl-ups. Greg was practising a discreet form of evasive driving, and was at times more interested in what he could see through his rear-view mirror than in the road ahead.

'Don't worry,' he said, noticing Jim's interest in his driving technique. 'We're being covered by a second car about six back, and I've got cars in the other carriageway. If we had a tail, they'd have telephoned by now.'

The road headed on down into mountain country. They were in

Virginia, coasting the eastern flank of the Allegheny Mountains. Nobody gave them more than a cursory glance. Rigs like theirs were a dime a dozen out in these parts. They could see tall mountain ranges on their right, and a sky above them that looked as though it had all kinds of weather stored up in it, and none of them good.

'Jim, I can still remember the day my Diane came back from that clinic the first time. The doctors had done something called a needle biopsy, and they'd told her she had the big C. Jesus, I can see her looking at me with those big eyes and saying that word, and it felt like one of them TV shows where folks come out and tell half the world that they're gay or they gave their girlfriend the pox, whatever. It was like I was watching it all on a screen. Hell, we were both in something my doc calls denial, like we couldn't take it in, neither one of us. Later, after they removed the breast, she started to come to terms with it. Hell, Jim, she was the bravest person I ever met, in or out of the Army.

'It came back, of course, out of nowhere, and she died soon after. I watched her die, I was with her every minute, I peed in my pants sooner than get up and go to the toilet. It was hard for her, I know it was, but she got through it, and she died like a lamb, never a bad word to say about nothing. And I was still in that denial thing, I couldn't cry, I couldn't get nowhere with my emotions, didn't know I even had any. You probably remember.'

'Yes. Yes, I remember that time very well. Laura and I sat up at nights, talking about what to do with you. We knew you must be in some sort of hell, but we didn't know how to reach you.'

'You did what you could, you both did.'

'We always thought there was more, that we should have done more.'

'It wouldn't have done me much good. Not as long as I was a serving Marine. Shit, Jim, you know what it's like. They turn you into a killing machine, and they expect you to keep your emotions buried deep down in some sort of coal mine. Remember that?'

'I remember. It's the main reason I left. Air Force training's different. You're mostly on your own up there. The guys I worry about are the bomber crews, they never get to see the people they kill.'

248

'Do you?'

'No, but it's personal up there, just you and another guy, and you know at least one of you is going to get burned or fall all the way back to earth.'

They turned west just before a little place called Buena Vista, taking Interstate 64. The traffic was thinning out now. They were well into the Alleghenies now, and all ahead of them mountains rose like watchtowers, white and eerie.

'Where the hell *are* you taking me?' Jim asked.

'Up there a ways. Mountain country. You'll see.'

Greg turned on the radio and started searching for a suitable station. He'd scarcely touched the knob when a preacherly voice came on air, asking for a donation to help spread God's word.

'This is WJLS AM, broadcasting out of Beckley, West Virginia, with a message for all clean-living folks. Jesus is . . .'

'Shit! Don't these guys ever take a holiday?'

He twisted the knob violently to the right, where he found a weather forecast.

' . . . and most of West Virginia was covered in cloud today, with little sign of it lifting. The storms which have been moving across this way from the mid-Mississippi valley all week are now in the Ohio valley and expected to reach us by tomorrow evening. The latest weather map shows a cold front extending southwest from a low centred over Maine. Meanwhile, more snow is expected across the Allegheny Mountains tonight. Keep wrapped up well, and remember to take special care if you're out hiking or climbing. Now, back to you, Lori.'

Another voice came on. Greg nodded approvingly.

'We got WTNJ, the big country station in Beckley. I seem to remember you like country music.'

'That was more Laura than me.'

'This is Lori Vecellio. You're listening to WTNJ FM, the home of country music. And this is our own Fiddling Van Kidwell with the Hotmud Family, with some West Virginia hornpipe music. Stay with me, we've got an afternoon of local greats to come.'

At Lewisburg, they switched to WKCJ, another country station, and turned north onto US 219. Rain had started to fall, turning

249

quickly to hail. A cold wind from the north blew the rain hard against them.

'Where are we headed, Greg? Don't keep playing this secret thing.'

Greg switched off the radio.

'OK, Jim. Up ahead is the Monoghela National Forest. It's a huge damn thing that covers most of the Alleghenies. We're going in there, to a wilderness tract called Cranberry. That's where the house is.'

'Greg, you know you can't build in a wilderness area.'

'This is an old house. It was built there long before the US government ever thought to name places wildernesses.'

At Mill Point, they turned left and drove down a side road for another six miles. Signs said they were in Pocahontas County now, and advertised the Pocahontas Trail ahead, but there was no sign of any happy hikers anywhere.

'There's a forest road just off here,' said Greg. 'FR102 runs up the Cranberry River valley, takes us some ways into the forest if the track's good. There's snow higher up, but for some reason there hasn't been much on the lower slopes or the valleys this year. Global warming, I guess.'

The road was barely more than a track, and if there'd been anyone coming in the opposite direction, pulling in would have been a problem. They drove for almost eight miles, following the course of the little river as it increased in size, swollen by numerous brooks and urgent runs that trickled into it from the surrounding mountains.

Greg turned off into an old clearing that he'd obviously used before.

'There's things in back,' he said. With civilization far behind, he was changing back into a backwoodsman. 'Hurry and get dressed, I don't want to hang around here.'

For the first time, Jim realized he hadn't been followed. Greg had been as good as his word. He found mountaineering kit and passed half over to Greg before slipping on his own. He dressed in bright yellow nylon trousers and a nylon parka, with heavy boots and large gloves.

'I guess we don't need these snowshoes,' he said.

'Don't guess anything out here, Jim. You could wake tomorrow morning and find yourself snowed in. Don't pay no heed to those weather forecasts. Those guys are all in training to write for Hollywood.'

They set off, leaving the car covered by fallen branches. No casual passer-by would stumble on it.

'How far to this cabin?' Jim asked.

'Five miles. But that's uphill miles I'm talking about. Just remember your basic training, and we'll be there in next to no time.'

By uphill, he meant some of the steepest walking Jim had ever faced. There was no visible trail, and the terrain was uncompromising. He felt squeezed between rocks and a grey sky, with nothing between but the driving rain. By the time they'd passed an hour like this, both men were feeling the strain.

Then, as though it had never been, the rain stopped. The cloud was still there, and it was colder than ever, but it was as though they had passed some invisible barrier, beyond which no rain could fall. Standing upright, Jim became properly aware of his surroundings for the first time. On every side, broad, massive mountains roared up into the heavens, towering over everything like white ghosts grown tall and fat through centuries. Clouds swirled around their peaks, and one distant example wore an electric storm like a black hat, peculiar to itself. Their flanks were covered by stands of red spruce high up, with hardwoods of all sorts lower down, mixed with thickets of dark laurel. Jim could make out cherry and maple trees, with oak on nearby ridges, and yellow poplar.

'Good hunting round there,' said Greg, pointing to a valley running east away from them. 'If we ever find time, I'll take you. In the early summer, this area's full of rhododendron. It's a good time to be here.'

'Didn't know you were a nature lover.'

'This is where I learned to feel, how to get over my grieving. The mountains give you space to think. Even on a day like this.'

They rested briefly, then set off again. Greg set a hard pace, and Jim found it hard to keep up in places. He regretted not working out quite as hard as he should have done in the years since leaving the Marines. But every time he looked like giving up, Greg would

251

be there, never shouting, like a Marine sergeant, but easing him on, talking him into using a little extra strength, a little more effort.

'Look,' said Greg suddenly. Panting, Jim stopped and screwed his eyes to see what his companion was pointing at. A house came into focus, almost camouflaged against a stand of oak trees. It took another ten minutes' hard walking to reach it.

The lodge was two storeys high, eight-sided, and built entirely of wood. The first storey was completed by a matching part-roof, and the smaller second floor topped by an eight-sided roof atop which sat a wood and glass lantern big enough to let light drop down to the interior. Moss covered the structure in parts, and here and there Jim could see where it had been repaired over the years. He guessed it was old, but made no attempt to put a date on it. Looking up, he wondered how the upper windows and the lantern were cleaned.

Dark woods embraced the cabin from behind, without actually encroaching on its space. The sombre trees and silent snow reminded him of some endless northern European forest in whose depths lurked the flint gods of man's darkest past. Not even the presence of the lodge could dispel the overpowering sense of wilderness, and behind that a feeling of wildness always standing at a man's shoulder, its cool breath on his open face.

'Who lives here?' he asked.

Greg shrugged and smiled.

'I'll let him introduce himself. I guess he ain't around at the moment, but if you go on in he'll turn up soon enough. He's expecting you, you don't have to worry he'll shoot you for an intruder.'

'But I am an intruder, in a way.'

'He'll make you welcome. Don't worry about that. And you'll be safe here. I can guarantee that. Officially, this place don't even exist. Given time, you won't exist either.'

'Greg, what the hell am I going to do here? When you said "safe house", I thought you meant somewhere in town, somewhere surrounded by other houses and people.'

Greg raised his eyebrows.

'Hell, what'd they learn you back in the Air Force? I guess they trained you how to tolerate more gravity than a spaceman, but they sure as crikey taught you nothing about personal security. If you were in a safe house back in D.C. or some other urban location, believe me, it'd be like being under house arrest. You wouldn't be allowed to go out, you'd have to be moved every few days, you'd just be stuck indoors watching daytime television. Here, weather permitting, you've got a whole national forest at your disposal.'

'Greg, I don't give shit about the forest or hunting or skiing, or whatever else you've got up your sleeve for useful occupations. I just want to get out there and find my daughter. What if she telephones again, or Waterstone? I'm afraid they may do something to her, that they may have done something already.'

'Listen, Jim, this safe house thing is just something we set up for your benefit. You may not have too much time for hunting once your host shows you round. Listen to me, OK? My friends and I don't mean to sit around and let this thing just roll to some sticky end. Our President is missing, and we do intend to find him, with or without the cooperation of the US government. Forget about the task force, Jim, forget about the CIA or the FBI. We'll find him first. And I mean to have you with us when the time comes.'

He glanced at his watch.

'Before that happens, I've got to get back home and see what my people are up to.'

'You going back to D.C.? It'll be dark before you even get off this mountain.'

Greg shook his head.

'D.C., no. But I can't tell you where I'm based. That's not because I can't trust you, but because my group has strict rules. Everything's done on a need-to-know basis. You understand that, don't you?'

'Sounds to me like you've got a regular army back there.'

Greg looked at him evenly, but neither his eyes nor his mouth betrayed anything.

'Just be patient, Jim. I'll be all right. I reckon I can get back to the Cherokee before it's fully dark. Now, the door's open. Just get inside and make yourself at home. Stay in the living room for now. I don't expect he'll keep you waiting long.'

'Won't you tell me who he is? His name, at least?'

Greg grinned.

'Come on, Jim. You know me better than that. I think he'd prefer to introduce himself. He's a good man, you can trust him. In fact, you can put your life in his hands if it ever comes to that. Now, I've got to start back or I'll be here all night.'

They shook hands, and Greg started off back down the invisible trail that had led them to the cabin. Jim watched him go down the slope until he was out of sight, then he turned and headed for the door.

He'd half-expected something Spartan, a real backwoodsman's log cabin, hung with pelts and muskets, and furnished with bearskins. Instead, it was one of the best-appointed rooms he'd ever set eyes on. The wooden walls and ceiling had been waxed and burnished over a period of many years to achieve a deep shining patina that made the wood sing. He ran his hand over its surface, and found it warm and without irregularities.

Scattered as if at random round the circular room were chairs and sofas upholstered in expensive-looking fabrics. Jim had seen so many hunting lodges done out in chintz that he'd fancied himself in for another variation on the time-honoured theme; instead he was met with bold colours and simple designs. There were sturdy handmade tables and a variety of cabinets constructed by the same hand. Some were carved with intricate designs which on close examination appeared to be made up of motifs from American Indian mythology.

Walking in a slow circle round the walls, he examined the various paintings and framed photographs that hung there. Most of the paintings showed battles from the Civil War. Examining these more closely, Jim discovered they were all engagements that had taken place in this part of West Virginia (after it became West Virginia). One painting depicted the almost bloodless battle of Philippi, the first land battle of the entire war, another the Battle of Droop Mountain, West Virginia's largest Civil War engagement, and a third the conditions for Federal troops at Cheat Summit Fort during the harsh winter of 1861–62.

Each of these and several other paintings bore the artist's signature in the bottom right-hand corner: R. L. Mygate. The name tugged at something in Jim's memory, but the harder he tried to retrieve it, the less tangible it became. He'd ask the owner when he turned up.

Alongside the paintings hung a series of framed photographs, portraits of a man who, Jim reckoned, must be the lodge's owner, alongside a mixture of people, all smiling and hugging one another by the shoulder. Friends and family members, obviously; one appeared in several photographs next to the owner: Jim took her to be his wife.

He found the bathroom by the sign on the door. Obviously, his host was used to having guests who didn't know their way around. There was hot water, and for a moment Jim was tempted to take a shower; but the owner might return at any moment, and it would have been embarrassing to be caught naked and wet. He just freshened himself up a little, then went back out to see what the main room had to offer.

There were books on shelves at several spots around the walls. Jim browsed along the spines and was intrigued by what he found. Not surprisingly, whole shelves were devoted to the Civil War. Several more had books on the Vietnam War, including a couple of dozen in Vietnamese. Jim took a number of these down and opened them: they had been well thumbed, and page after page carried pencilled annotations. Other shelves held more pacific titles. An entire section was devoted to Zen Buddhism, another to meditation techniques. Some were written in what looked to Jim like Japanese – he didn't need to take any of these down to know that they must have been read.

In a section towards the rear of the room (at least, that part of it furthest from the entrance), he found shelf after shelf filled with works of fiction. Several editions of Tolstoy's *War and Peace* sat next to a single, beautifully bound copy of *Anna Karenina*. These were followed by Russian editions of Tolstoy, Dostoyevsky, Solzhenitsyn, and others. There followed whole shelves of classics translated from a variety of languages, from French and Italian, German and Spanish. A great line of handsome eighteenth- and nineteenth-century renditions of the *Thousand and One Nights*, some plain but for the binding, others packed with the most exquisite illustrations. He took down a version illustrated by Detmold, and opened it. Rocs and elephants, sultans and turrets of light dazzled him.

'Beautiful, isn't it?'

Jim nearly dropped the volume, so startled was he by the voice coming out of nowhere just behind him.

He spun on his heels and caught sight of a man in winter clothes smiling and extending his hand.

34

'My name's Russell Mygate. Needless to say, I'm Russ to just about everybody, including my dog. You must be Jim Crawford.'

Jim looked down at the labrador lying flat on the floor next to his master, then back up at Mygate. He seemed about sixty, but healthier than a jack rabbit. His cheeks were red from exposure to the rain and wind outside, and his white hair looked as though it was about to win first prize in a modern art exhibition. Jim put his own hand out and took Mygate's. The older man's grip was firm, almost brutal. He held Jim's hand just long enough for it to start hurting, then let it go with a smile. His left hand went down to catch the dog's wide collar.

'You must be hungry, son,' he said.

'Yes, sir, I do feel a mite peckish.'

'You eat a good breakfast, son?'

'Yes, sir. Hot sausages, and I don't know what else.'

'Will you stop calling me "sir"? I just told you, most everybody calls me Russ. You included.'

'If you'll stop calling me "son".'

'That's a deal. Now, let's find the kitchen and see what I can cook up. Glad to hear you eat a good breakfast. I reckon that's the secret. You think that's the secret, Jim?'

'Secret of what . . . Russ?'

'Secret of getting through the day. Physically, I mean. A soldier never knows when he's going to eat his next meal. Isn't that right?'

'At times, yes.' He'd guessed Mygate must be a military man.

Mygate smiled and went ahead to a plain door on the left. It led them into a shining, well-appointed kitchen.

'Tyrant, you aren't allowed to come in here. Go and lie down somewhere.'

The dog was thus dismissed to its own quarters. It ambled off, tired from its exertions and ready for a long drink, a bone to worry, and a long sleep.

Jim followed Mygate inside. Just then the penny dropped.

'Russ,' he said. 'Did you paint those Civil War pictures on the wall outside?'

'You saw the name?'

'Yes, but it took a few seconds to click. They're very good. Is that what you do?'

'You mean, for a living?'

'Well, yes, I guess that's what I do mean. I've seen paintings like those in galleries.'

'Sorry to disappoint you, but I've never sold a painting in my life. I paint for my own enjoyment, and sometimes for a friend, if they have a real interest. I started back in college, but most of these I did after I retired. Now, let's get dinner started. You must be starving. Did Greg leave you here?'

Jim nodded, but mentally he was straining to work out what it was Mygate reminded him of, apart from the signature at the bottom of his paintings.

Mygate steered the conversation nimbly away from himself and on to Jim, and within minutes they were talking like old friends. The older man had a skill in bringing people out, and by the time they sat down to eat, he was able to persuade Jim to talk openly about Laura, Tina, and what had been happening since. Jim saw no reason to hold back.

They ate a substantial dinner of chargrilled grouse followed by jugged snowshoe hare and roast potatoes.

'Shot the grouse up by Sugar Creek Mountain last week. The hare was passing the front door a couple of days ago.'

'Where'd you shoot the potatoes?'

'Red Cross flies them in once a fortnight. Now try the ice cream, and let me do some talking.'

258

Jim took a spoonful and nodded approvingly.

'Don't tell me the Red Cross parachutes this in as well.'

'I get it in a little place not far from Cass, the Green Bank Country. Surprising what you can find in these sleepy hollows.'

After the last spoonful of ice cream had been put away, Russell made some coffee and led the way to his study on the other side of the central room. It was only when his host asked him to find the light switch and press it down that Jim realized the anomaly: they were in the middle of a vast mountain wilderness designed and managed expressly to keep the twentieth century out. He thought of the meal, of the electric oven in which items had been cooked, of the refrigerator and the freezer, the coffee maker, and he wondered how it was done. Surely not even the most desperate electricity company would run lines out this far. And he doubted whether the Forest Service was in the habit of laying on creature comforts in designated wilderness areas.

'How do you manage this?' he asked.

'This?'

'The electricity, running water, everything. By rights, this lodge shouldn't be here at all, much less kept like a five-star hotel.'

Mygate laughed.

'You obviously haven't spent very much time in five-star hotels, son. I'm sorry – Jim. I'd call this three-star at a pinch.'

'Not where I come from.'

'Maybe not.'

'But even three-star, there's still electricity, double glazing . . .'

The older man grinned.

'I know. It is pretty damn peculiar, but don't ask me why. Not yet. You'll be shown in due course. Maybe tomorrow. For the moment, we still have more important things to talk about. Close the door and come on in.'

Jim found himself in a wedge-shaped room lined with books. He remembered he had never asked his host about the volumes he'd discovered earlier, and now he was confronted with further evidence of a keen and roving mind. The rear wall contained a large stone-built fireplace that looked as though it had been there since

259

pioneer days. A fire had been left to smoulder behind a metal guard. Mygate removed the guard and started to poke the fire, adding logs from a stack on his left.

Jim joined him. On either side of the fireplace, framed photographs had been hung in neat order. These were not family portraits like the ones outside, but shots of Mygate with a variety of military, Navy, and Air Force men and women. Jim recognized a senior USAF officer as Lieutenant General Kurt Lawrence, a former head of the Air Intelligence Agency. He saw one or two other faces that seemed vaguely familiar. Then he looked more closely at Mygate and the uniform he was wearing. That was when he realized what a dumb fool he'd been.

'You're General Mygate, aren't you, sir?'

Russell grabbed a nearby chair arm and pulled himself upright.

'That's right, Jim. Does that cause you a problem?'

'No, not a problem. But at least I know who you are now.'

'Well, you think you do. But you've only just met me, and I promise you I won't come crying my heart out when I've had a whiskey sour too many. I'm a lot harder to get to know than I seem. Don't let yourself be misled by my manner. I'm friendly, especially when it comes to a man I respect, and I have to tell you I respect you immensely. But I play my cards close to my chest, and I let nobody past my defences. A bit like yourself.'

But for the moment, it was enough for Jim to know. Mygate had been a successful and ambitious army colonel of forty back in 1977, when Colonel Charles Beckwith set up a new-style special operations unit in the US. This was Delta Force, which Beckwith modelled on the British 22 SAS, with whom he'd spent a year in the early sixties.

The two men had worked together to build the new unit into something viable. Mygate had gained a reputation for radical, even downright insubordinate, thinking, and as a result he'd got things done, and shown his men how to get similar results. Many of his ideas had spread to other branches of the service, notably to Navy SEALs, and he'd been personally decorated for his involvement in actions that were not officially supposed to have taken place. He'd resigned a couple of years ago under mysterious circumstances.

They sat and sipped their coffees in heavy leather chairs while the fire took, sending long tongues of flame into the chimney. Tyrant had slipped in from somewhere, and was lying on a black bear rug in front of the fireplace. After a bit, Russell got to his feet and crossed to a little cabinet on which a variety of drinks were standing.

'Scotch or bourbon, Jim?'

'Bourbon will suit me fine. And just a drop of ginger ale, if you have any.'

'You're having it neat. This is Cranberry Wilderness, and bottles of soda don't grow on the trees round here. Though I don't doubt that the great Coca-Cola organization would paint each and every tree red and white, and sell Coke to the foxes.'

He handed Jim his drink, and took his own seat again, a rare Scotch in hand.

'OK, Jim. I'm feeling settled. Suppose you tell me what happened up there on Forrest Island. See you don't leave anything out.'

35

Darkness dogged their every movement, as though the fabric of this cold country was woven from it, as if the clay beneath their feet had been compounded with it. They were not very far past the winter solstice, and there was no day now, only perpetual and ubiquitous night. Sometimes, an hour or so after noon, the sky would faintly lighten while the sun rose and set again beyond the horizon. But not today, not for three or four days now, for a dense cloud cover went with them however far they travelled, blotting out both sun and moon as though it were a shroud.

Tina was sinking rapidly. Her breathing was causing the young doctor the gravest concern. There were times when it seemed to fade so completely that death seemed stark minutes away. Then she would rally, and her breathing, though remaining stertorous, would pick up again, and sighs of relief would pass round the truck.

The pace at which they travelled seldom varied. If their driver – there were three of them in all, squeezed into the cab like astronauts in a rocket nosecone – tried to push his vehicle much over forty miles an hour, the bumping and rattling would in a flash become unbearable for everyone on board, forcing him to drop back down again. On the one hand, the truck was on its last legs; on the other, the terrain across which they were moving was rough, hard, and speckled with potholes. When a thin stretch of tarmac did emerge, indicating the presence of an old farm track, or a hastily-constructed military road, it would turn out a deception, offering a few yards of smooth going in return for

262

half a mile of lurching and swaying, punctuated by bangs as they hit the ever-present bumps and craters.

Sometimes they would succeed in finding a small river or large stream, and the driver would drop down several gears and gingerly work his way down onto the thick ice, then drive forward without hesitation, using the frozen waterway as a highway.

There were no towns or villages along their route, which seemed surprising, given the presence of the short strips of road. Joel surmised that there had been townships, farms, and villages in this region, but that they stood abandoned now. Twice they saw bright lights flashing on the horizon, like the Aurora Borealis.

'That's not a natural phenomenon,' said the doctor the first time. 'It's gunfire.'

'Gunfire?' Joel was bemused. 'What's going on?'

'Rebels are fighting government troops in several provinces. That's all I'm allowed to say. It's more or less all I know.'

'Is that why we were moved out of the last place without warning?'

The doctor nodded.

'The convoy we're with – which side is it on?'

The doctor looked at him blankly.

'I don't really know,' she said.

'Don't know or can't tell me?'

She hesitated.

'A bit of both,' she said. 'Now, I'm sorry, but I must get back to Tina.'

'Just a moment. Doctor, can you just tell me . . . Do you know who I am?'

'Who you are?' She shrugged. 'No, why should I know that? You're a foreigner, an American by your accent. This is your wife, who is also an American, and this is your little girl. Why? Is there something else you think I need to know?'

'No,' he murmured, more confused than ever. 'Get back to Tina.'

Rebecca had been sleeping, or dozing off between rude awakenings, when she felt someone shake her shoulder. She came properly awake

263

at once to find the doctor bending over her, and her first thought was that Tina had died while she was asleep.

'Tina . . . ?'

The doctor shook her head.

'She's all right. No better, but no worse.'

'Why did you . . . ?'

'Look.'

The doctor wiped some condensation from a side window, and pointed away into the blackness. Rebecca squinted, trying to make out what it could be. At first she thought it was some sort of mistake on the doctor's part, or inability on hers to see whatever was out there. Then she saw a small cluster of lights low down. It was impossible to tell how far away they were. A second cluster revealed itself quite close to the first.

'What are they?'

'I think they're the lights of a village. I want us to stop. They may have a doctor there, someone with drugs, a few basic facilities.'

'But they're refusing to stop for anything.'

'If we don't stop, Tina will certainly die. I don't know who you are, but I think they will listen to you.'

'Don't you have any influence?'

'No, they grabbed me and made me join this convoy. They won't listen to anything I say.'

'Very well, help me speak to the driver. You'll have to translate for me.'

It took some time, and then the driver had to speak to someone superior via a hand-held radio set. He spoke earnestly into the handset for some time, then switched it off and shook his head.

'No,' he said. 'They say is more important reach now our destination.'

'Let me speak to him.'

'He not listen for you.'

'He'll listen. Tell him this is Rebecca Waterstone. The wife of the President of the United States.'

The doctor's eyes bulged wide, and her jaw dropped. Rebecca smiled and nodded. Reluctantly, the driver handed Rebecca the handset.

The voice that reached her belonged to Varvara.

'This is Rebecca Waterstone. You already know that the little girl, Tina Crawford, is very ill. I have a doctor here who says she is dying. She must not be allowed to die. We have seen lights which suggest there is a village or town near here. I insist we turn and go there in the hope of obtaining medical help for Tina. There is no other choice.'

'I don't have the authority to order such a change.'

'Then radio for permission. And do it now, because we can't afford to waste a second.'

Varvara waited a moment or two longer, then disconnected. When she came back on, her tone had changed.

'Very well, we've been told we can make a stop. They want to look for food and drink.'

They slowed, then made a long, sweeping turn. Rebecca watched through the windscreen as the huge truck slewed round. Its headlights picked out a frosted landscape, then found their tracks. They picked up speed again, then turned gently to the right.

In the distance, the lights swam like small luminescent fish in a sea of darkness. On their slender jewelled points, Tina's life hung shaking in its balance.

36

Monongahela Forest

Mygate had Jim up at 6.00 a.m., in order to go hunting. They ate a quick breakfast of bacon, eggs, and black coffee, then headed out into the freezing cold. It was half dark: in the morning sky stars danced among slow-moving banks of cloud, and from time to time, a moon like ice shimmered against the blackness of space.

Before leaving, the General took Jim down to the basement, where he kept his weapons. One wall was taken up with a large gun cabinet. The doors were locked, there was a separate alarm, and each gun was chained in place. Mygate selected a rifle, unlocked it, and handed it to Jim.

'Here. This should suit you.'

It was a Winchester 94 Timber Carbine, fitted with a high-precision sight. The moment Jim took it in his hands, he felt at ease with it: it was well balanced, compact, and a good weight.

'It's chambered for 444 Marlin ammo. Take what you need out of that box.'

Once Jim had his ammunition, Mygate closed and locked the cabinet.

'Aren't you taking a rifle?' Jim asked.

'Haven't hunted with a rifle in years. The hunting bow's my weapon now. If we get time, I'll show you how to shoot one. You'll need a lot of practice, though.'

He went to a wooden cupboard set against a further wall, next to the wine racks. From it he took a huge compound bow, a Jennings Buckmaster, painted in camouflage colours.

'What do you think?'

Jim looked the bow up and down. It was just over three feet from axle to axle, and was fitted with stabilizers, a game sight, and a quiver into which Mygate started to fit a row of twenty-eight-inch arrows. With pulleys at either end, and a complex system of strings, the whole rig seemed centuries removed from the simple recurve bows of the Indians who had hunted in these regions before the coming of the white man.

'I've never seen anything like it before,' Jim said. 'I wouldn't know where to hold it, let alone fire it.'

'Like I said, I'll give you some lessons. This bow has an eighty-pound draw-weight, so it's heavy for a beginner. I'll start you tomorrow on a recurve, then find a lighter compound to suit you. Now, let's get on the road.'

'What are we looking for?' asked Jim, who had only hunted before as a boy, in the mountains surrounding Wickensburg. He'd never shot anything very big, being restricted to a light .22 rimfire. His father hadn't been much of a hunter, and his trips into the wild had mostly been with his Uncle Pete, who was a good shot half of the day, and a drunken sot the other half.

'This time of year, we might run into some white-tailed deer, wild turkeys, some ruffed grouse, and bobcats. There's plenty of squirrel around, mostly black and albino up here. Some fox too. I bagged me a pair last week. Cottontail rabbits are in season, and snowshoe hare, like the one you had last night.'

'Are you sure all those are still in season? I thought the deer season was just a short time in December. We're well into January . . .'

'Jim, this is a wilderness area. Truth is, almost everything is out of bounds. But the only hunter up here is me, so they just put up with me and let me do pretty much what I want. That doesn't mean I have to do it, of course. I'm respectful of the creatures I hunt, and it doesn't always seem right to shoot them. We can't just up and open fire on all of them, specially the bears.

'Some days it gets so cold up here, you won't see hide nor

hair of another living creature, unless it's some environmentalist congressman come in from D.C., or a New Age type come up into the mountains to walk the old Indian trails and commune with her shamanic nature. I tend to shoot first and ask questions later in those cases. Come on, we've got some climbing to do.'

They climbed up to the forest, and started to walk along a steep gully. Just above them, the trees were dark and pungent. White pine and red spruce closed their horizon on all sides.

'I'm sorry you had to witness that thing up by Vancouver Island,' said Mygate. 'Maybe those New Agers are right, maybe we could all do with thinking more about our lives. A man who just lost his wife the way you did, and found her body the way you found hers, such a man should not have been put through that charade.

'I think Greg has already told you about Jurgensen's unit, that they aren't regular SEALs. Jurgensen himself was responsible for putting them together about ten years ago. I believe it all happened someplace in Washington State. Jurgensen hand-picked about twenty men for Top Secret missions. Nobody got to volunteer, because nobody knew this thing was going on.'

In the branches above them, a winter bird let out a cry of alarm.

'They were mostly SEALs, but he recruited Marines, Delta Force, and ordinary soldiers he thought could be trained up to his standards. Jurgensen had access to the records of any soldier, whether in active service or retired. He was only a major, and a lot of the information he was looking at was way above confidential or even Top Secret. He could pull down files, not just on personnel, but on missions they'd taken part in, on entire units, on the families of possible recruits. Nobody knows who authorized all that, or who gave the go-ahead for the unit in the first place.

'What we do know is that Jurgensen had the backing of a shadowy group that operates out of Washington. Have you ever heard of Respice Finem?'

Jim shook his head.

'It's made up of about twenty members, whose identities remain a dark secret. Over the years, I've tried to uncover their faces, but I never get even remotely close. I think they meet in the Cosmos

268

Club, and in each other's houses. They are all immensely rich and immensely powerful, and they appear to consider themselves the true government of the United States. They're impatient of democracy, you see.

'Jurgensen and his secret unit are one of the many tools they use to bring their influence to bear. The unit members are pledged to do whatever Respice Finem asks them to do, regardless of whether it contravenes ordinary morals, or military ethics, or even the US Constitution.'

'How do you know all this?'

'Shhhh!'

Mygate knelt down suddenly, pulling Jim down with him. He pointed ahead to where a white-tailed deer was standing. Its antlers had just begun to form. The animal seemed oblivious of the two men stalking it.

The General offered the shot to Jim, but he shook his head.

'I'm out of practice. You'd better do it.'

Mygate took an arrow from the quiver and slotted it against the back string. Slowly, he drew back, pulling hard while sighting the prey. Jim held his breath involuntarily. There was no sound except the wind sawing through the trees. The deer stood silhouetted in the growing morning light, proud and enigmatic in its mountain world.

Mygate let the arrow fly. Jim blinked, and when he next looked, it had embedded its broad blade in the deer's chest. The beast tottered, at a loss to understand what it was that had destroyed its world and its life so finally, and as it tried to take a step, it stumbled, and stumbling, its legs went out from under it, and it died as it reached the earth, and shook three times, and a fourth time, and lay still, with its unseeing eyes focusing on the wind.

They started walking towards the fallen deer.

'As a general with responsibilities for Delta Force, I was necessarily briefed regularly about SEALs and Marine activities.' The General started up a steep slope that would bring them more quickly to their target. 'Sometimes, I found myself coming up against mysteries I couldn't explain, or I was blocked in finding out more about this or that. I decided to investigate further, and

269

found a few colleagues who had been equally disturbed. We found ways of making ourselves and our investigations invisible. And in the end what we discovered frightened us. It was never a conspiracy in the normal sense. I think we could have brought that out into broad daylight and watched it wither away.

'This isn't that sort of thing. It's not just a cabal of Supreme Court judges and oil barons making themselves a government within the government. There's a network of power and influence that stretches all round the country, and which is manipulated daily by the cabal. SEAL Force 9 is only one of the tools they have at their disposal.'

They reached the deer. Surprisingly little blood had come from its chest. Its dead nostrils were flared, its eyes were wide with fear. Mygate placed a marker near its head, a wand with a small flag.

'Let's leave it here,' he said. 'Nobody's going to disturb it. We'll pick it up on our way back. You can have venison when it's been hung.'

They headed on into the forest. Once among the trees, it was dark, and the air was filled with the fragrance of pine.

'My friends and I decided something had to be done, but we knew we couldn't go directly up against our opponents. However senior we might have been in military terms, we were small fry compared to the members of Respice Finem and their accomplices.

'We set up a loose organization of our own. It has two arms, as it were. One is for information gathering. The other is for action. Mostly covert. Your friend Greg is in charge of that. He's put together a bunch of ex-soldiers who train harder than SEALs and fight tougher than the SAS.'

Their feet were soft on the deep moss of the forest floor. Both men took great care not to stand directly on any twigs as they walked, or stumble, or make sudden movements. Mygate spoke softly while Jim listened.

'When the President was kidnapped, plus his wife and your little girl – what's her name again?'

'Tina.'

'Right, Tina. I won't forget again. When they were all abducted, we started to put out feelers. We have our own networks, and some of them feed pretty deep into government and government agencies.

At that point, we didn't suspect anyone of anything. Why should we? All we wanted was to know if there was anything we could do. After all, we had men, resources, know-how. It wasn't impossible we'd hear something on our grapevine that the task force had no idea about. Or we might be in a position to do something they couldn't.

'At first, there was so much going on, we gave up even trying to keep abreast of things. Everybody and his uncle knew where the President was, or thought he knew somebody who knew somebody. It was impossible to get any sense out of our usual sources. Then, one of our people in New Jersey got lucky. Guy called D'Annunzio, third-generation Italian, his grandparents owned a pizza parlour in downtown Newark, his father had some involvement with the Mob. Joey D'Annunzio, the son, became a cop and joined the New Jersey State SWAT unit. He won a lot of awards, medals, you name it. He got one of our invitations.

'So, when D'Annunzio says he has a Mafia connection who has a mouth, and this mafioso says he knows where to find the President, says if he had enough money he could buy himself into something big, we pay attention. The mobster is an asshole called Al Marinetti, a small-time loser who somehow or other manages to insinuate himself into every level of organized crime in New Jersey. What this prick tells D'Annunzio is that some Russian Godfather, what he calls a *pakhan*, has arrived in New York for talks with certain Mr Big types. This *pakhan*, according to Marinetti, knows where the President is, and is in this country to set up some sort of deal through his friends in New York.

'It's a far-fetched story, and we came close to ignoring it. But D'Annunzio says his source, for all the guy's a loser and everything, is actually a mostly accurate informant, and tells us to look into it a little. I sent one of our investigators down to Newark. We set up a little meeting for Marinetti, D'Annunzio, and my man, an ex-FBI agent called Baker. They were due to meet at noon in D'Annunzio's pizza joint, now run by D'Annunzio's father. None of them turns up. Later that day, the police find D'Annunzio with a sock stuffed down his throat. Marinetti is in a car park on the east side of town with his cock in his mouth and seven nine-millimetre bullet holes through his chest. My man, Baker, is found in his hotel room with a screwdriver in his mouth, coming out the back of his neck. It's like somebody is telling us, shut the fuck up, or this will happen to you.'

The forest was growing loud. As they climbed, winds came fast across the mountain, screaming like banshees, and shaking the highest branches like grass.

'It was a stupid move. We got onto this Russian creep straight away. His name was Grigory Remizov, and he'd flown in a couple of days earlier from Moscow. We discovered that he was the head honcho, the *avtoritet*, in one of the big Moscow crime syndicates, the Podolskaya. He'd come over with a few of his henchmen, and gone straight into hush-hush meetings with some of our Italian brethren, first in New York, then in Chicago.

'That was all we could find out at first. To tell you the truth, we still weren't that much interested. The schmuck Marinetti was very probably just indulging in some stupid gossip, to make himself look good. The rest was just some criminal business as usual. That's how it looked. Then we got another lead. Mr Remizov wasn't just meeting with a bunch of *baklani*. They had all been holding undercover conferences with Adam Sorokin, a Russian-speaking analyst working with the Presidential Task Force. That's when we sat up and took notice.

'We were pretty sure we'd cracked the secret behind President Waterstone's disappearance. From what we could see, the Russian Mafia, or elements of it, had abducted him. Now, they were negotiating his release, through the intermediary of our local Cosa Nostra. So, we breathed a sigh of relief, and sat back to wait for the public announcement which would tell us a deal had been struck. But nothing happened. No government spokespeople on TV, no reassuring noises from the Vice President or anybody else. Remizov returned to Russia three days later, just hopped on the first Aeroflot departure and sailed off into some smartass sunset. He's the original Untouchable, Jim. The plane lands in Moscow, our man gets out, and next thing anybody knows, he's stepped off the face of the planet.

'We were going frantic. Our best lead had gone, and we had no easy way of picking him up again. Then Greg told us what happened up beyond Puget Sound. Which brings me more or less up to date, and tells you why Greg brought you here.'

'You think the President's in Moscow?'

Mygate shrugged.

'Maybe not Moscow. But Russia, yes, we think it's possible. Beats me how they got him there, though. There's a strong chance they may still be in England. The Moscow and New Mafias may just be the organizing geniuses behind this. Somebody used that church, the . . . ?'

'The Watch.'

'Somebody made use of them. Made them promises in return for their help. But some kind of crime syndicate is behind the whole thing. Somebody big enough to negotiate with the US government.'

'You think this was all done for money?'

'Sure, why not? That's what kidnapping's usually about.'

Jim shook his head. It was growing light inside the wood.

'I don't think so. A simple demand for money would have been worked out by now. The raid on Forrest Island wouldn't have been necessary.'

'I'm not sure about that.' The General stopped and pointed ahead. They had come to the end of the trees. In a different light, the two men stepped out into a cold, white world. A high wind bayed around them, turning their breath to ice.

'Come on, Jim,' Mygate shouted, lifting his voice above the screaming of the white wind. 'It's time we did some serious hunting.'

37

Mogochin Village

They might have missed the village entirely had they driven past even fifteen minutes later or an hour earlier. The lights that had drawn their attention had been lit in the tiny church for the duration of an evening service of prayers for peace. Even as they arrived, the worshippers were trickling out of the little wooden building, and the priest had started to extinguish the oil lamps within the sanctuary.

The truck pulled up outside the church door, screeching to a halt with such ferocity that the inhabitants of the village, always expecting the worst, thought their end had come. They expected soldiers to pour out of the truck, and were astonished when a young woman appeared instead.

The priest, a heavily bearded man in his twenties, not long out of the seminary, was already waiting for them. He knew that a good half of his flock would by now have made themselves scarce, slipping off into the night. He also knew that they would be back by morning, driven home by a combination of the extreme cold, lack of food, and the knowledge, so much a part of the fabric of their narrow lives, that there was no other habitation in any direction for two hundred miles or more. The road was all that connected them to the outside world, and the present unrest made even that unsafe.

'I am Father Grigory. Welcome to Mogochin. Are you in need of help?'

The doctor put out her hand, then withdrew it again, being unsure how to address a priest, for she had never spoken to one before in her life.

'I am Dr Yulia Zaslavskaya,' she said. 'I have a sick child on board. She will die if she does not have medical treatment.'

'I thought you said you were a doctor.'

In the unclear light of the lamps, the priest's headgear made him seem like a creature from a science-fiction film. His face was unreadable behind the beard.

'I don't have the medicine I need inside the truck. Have you medical supplies of any kind?'

'What is wrong with the child?'

'She has septicaemia. Blood poisoning. It's very advanced. I've done everything I can for her, but I can't save her life without drugs.'

'My child, there's nothing we can do for you here. These are simple people, Dolgans, they know nothing but superstition. When they fall ill, they take to their beds, and if they do not recover, they die. That is life in these parts. Now, you must be on your way. It would go badly for the village if you were found here.'

'But . . . surely you keep some basic medicines. Some antibiotics. What do you use yourself? You don't take to your bed when you're ill, surely.'

'I take myself to the Lord, and He cures me. You had better leave, all of you. You aren't wanted here. No-one wants strangers at a time like this.'

Suddenly, from behind the doctor, a man's voice cut into the priest's.

'He is lying. He is trying to save his own skin, because that's all he ever thinks about. I can help you. Bring the child with me.'

Dr Zaslavskaya turned round.

'I'm sorry,' she said. 'Who are you?'

'My name is Lavrentiev. Dr Lavrentiev. My house has a small clinic attached to it. What medicine I have here is limited, but it will be enough for what we need. Now, if Father Grigory will permit us, I think we should get your little girl and hurry. There may not be much time to lose.'

275

38

It was late afternoon, and almost dark before they got back to the cabin. The only substantial kill of the day had been Mygate's deer. On the way back, they cut the body into small pieces, which they dragged home on a transom made by the General out of fallen branches and twine. What they could not carry was left on a rock for carrion birds and winter-hungry animals.

They were surer of one another now. The forest and the mountain had brought them close, taught them it was possible to rely on one another. Without his being aware, Jim had been tested by Mygate, and had passed each time.

'Let's get washed and changed, then we'll eat. After that, I've got something to show you. And there's someone I'd like you to meet.'

'Here, in the lodge?'

Mygate smiled enigmatically.

'Sort of. You'll find a second bathroom upstairs. It has a separate boiler, so there should be no shortage of hot water. You can't miss it – there's a sign on the door.'

Over dinner, the conversation was limited to Army and Air Force reminiscences, the plot lines of several TV shows, and chat about books they'd both read, films they'd seen, and music they'd liked. It was inconsequential talk, and the more welcome for that reason. Hunting had both exhilarated and tired them, and neither man wanted to talk further about their real reason for being together in the first place. Then Jim asked some questions which, on later reflection, he realized he should not have asked.

'Russ, how come you spend so much time up here? Doesn't your wife complain? Doesn't she come out here with you sometimes?'

They were finishing the main course, a dish of brook trout that Mygate had fly-fished two days earlier, with rice and a pepper sauce. Mygate finished clearing his plate, and laid his knife and fork down carefully. There was a look on his face that Jim could not properly interpret, but it was enough to tell him he'd asked the wrong question.

'I'm sorry, Jim,' he said. 'There was no way you could have known. Not many people do know.'

'I'm sorry, I just assumed . . .'

'You saw the photographs in the big room?'

'Yes, I automatically assumed . . .'

'She's not dead, if that's what you're thinking. And we're not divorced either. Millie has Alzheimer's. It started about ten years back. She'd just turned sixty. To begin with, she started forgetting simple things, people's names, telephone numbers, what she'd bought for dinner. Her doctor just put it down to age, or maybe he just didn't want to frighten her at that point. It's been downhill since then. Now, she doesn't know who I am ninety per cent of the time, she doesn't recognize our daughter Jill, she thinks Tyrant is a dog we owned twenty years ago, she doesn't even know her own name.'

'I'm sorry. And I'm sorry I asked. I didn't know.'

'Like I said, almost nobody knows, and I'd appreciate it if you kept it to yourself.'

'Do you see her much?'

'See her? Who's to see? I know that sounds hard, but I had to make a hard choice. There's no telling when she'll get a lucid moment and recognize her nearest and dearest. Could be tomorrow, could be a year's time, maybe she'll never say my name again. I don't want those memories of her, Jim, just like you probably wish you could wipe out those last images of Laura. About a year ago I decided I could make more use of my life getting my little army together. And looking at what we're getting into now, I think I was right. I hope that isn't pride speaking. But I believe I have good men, and a cause worth anything to fight for.'

He stood up and took the plates from the table. As he put

277

them straight into the dishwasher, he straightened and looked at Jim.

'Jim, I don't feel much like dessert. To tell you the truth, it only puts weight on. What if I were to show you what I said I would? We can have coffee or whiskey or whatever you like afterwards.'

'Why not?'

Jim pushed his chair back and joined the General. There were tears in the old man's eyes, and shadows deep inside them that had been there a long time.

Mygate led the way out into the central room, and from there down into the cellar. The walls were lined with wine racks, the racks filled with dusty bottles. Thousands of bottles, far more than even a medium-sized family could ever drink.

'You must love wine,' Jim said.

'Never drink it.'

'Then why . . . ?'

Jim stopped and looked up and down the nearest rack. Laura had tried to develop an expertise in wine, had introduced him to her better purchases.

'May I?' he asked.

'Sure, go on. Why not?'

A smile had somehow spread itself across Mygate's face.

Jim lifted down a bottle at chest height. As it came clear of the rack, he knew something was wrong, and when he lifted it upright, he knew what it was: the bottle was empty.

'You keep your empties in the same place?'

Mygate shook his head.

'They're all empty, son – all but the ones at the foot of the steps. It's just a façade.'

'You shouldn't call me son.'

It was as though a door had slammed shut.

'Don't get sassy with me, kid. From here in, you call me "sir" or "General", and I call you "Crawford" or "Major". Understand?'

'No, sir, I don't.'

'You will in a minute.'

The General went to the wall on his right and pulled a lever. There

278

was a shunting sound, and suddenly the wine racks began to pull back together. As Jim watched in astonishment, he could see the rails they were travelling on become exposed.

It took a full minute for the racks to roll back into the walls. In front of them stood a blank stone wall. Jim remembered the sets of the *Thousand and One Nights* upstairs, and half expected Mygate to pronounce the words 'Open Sesame', to see the wall split open and admit them to a dark cavern filled with jewels.

Instead, the General marched up to the wall and rapped it hard with his bare knuckles. It gave off a slightly hollow thunk.

'This is all a sham too, Major. It's theatrical canvas painted to looked like stone.'

He took a small remote control from his pocket and pointed it at the fake wall. At once, it began to rise, until it had all vanished into the ceiling.

In front of them now was what appeared to be a huge door of steel, rather like a bank vault, only considerably bigger.

'This, however,' said Mygate, knocking once more, 'is the real thing.' His knuckles produced a metallic sound. Jim went up to the door and tried himself. The general had not lied. This was solid steel.

'It's two feet thick. Fortunately, I have a key.'

'Key' was, perhaps, a misnomer. Mygate produced from somewhere an electronic device about one foot long and four inches wide, and inserted it into a tube near the wall on the right-hand side. The key went in about halfway, then was pulled flush with the door by some corresponding mechanism inside. Within seconds, it lit up, then a panel appeared on which a numerical keyboard had been etched.

The general keyed in a sequence of numbers, in response to which a long code appeared. He did a rapid calculation, then keyed in more numbers, and received another code. When his third set of numbers had been keyed in, a second panel appeared, bearing the outline of a hand. He pressed his palm against this, and ten seconds later a message flashed, telling him he had been allowed entry.

'Good thing I didn't come down here just to change a bulb,' he joked. 'I'll see you're fitted up with a key and codes later on. Right

279

now, Major, let's get you inside before it gets wind of a stranger in our midst.'

There was a loud click, and the steel doors began to slide apart. When a ten-foot gap had been created, a second click marked a halt to the process. Jim looked down a concrete corridor, with bare walls on either side.

They walked down the corridor together.

'What is this place?' asked Jim.

'It's a government facility, or at least, it used to be. It was built during the Eisenhower administration as the base for the US government in the event of a nuclear war. They needed to build it in a wilderness not too far from Washington. The idea was to use choppers to fly in the President and other members of the administration, along with a handful of Congressmen. It was built between 1958 and 1961, and once it was finished it was kept in constant readiness by a cover company by the name of Forsythe Associates. They called it the Monongahela Government Relocation Facility.'

They reached a second door. This had a much simpler opening mechanism, and this time, when they stepped through, it was as though they'd entered a suite of offices. Glass doors opened off the corridor on both sides, windows allowed light to pass from room to room, the ceilings hummed with bright fluorescent lights.

'This is amazing,' Jim exclaimed. It seemed to go on for ever, corridor branching off corridor, one room leading to the next. In several offices, men and women were working at desks, bent over computer consoles, or on their feet, searching through tall filing cabinets.

'It looks like nobody left.'

Mygate shook his head.

'Quite the opposite. Nobody ever came, apart from a skeleton staff sent in by Forsythe Associates to keep things ticking over. Bulbs were changed, filters were renewed, the heating and air conditioning and other systems were put through their paces. But the facility was never needed, as you know. When the Cold War ended, it was just run down and abandoned. I'd been here on inspections, since I was one of a handful of military men listed to head here in the event of a war.'

'You aren't going to tell me the government just sold it to you.'

The General laughed.

'It was a lot simpler than that. Strictly speaking, I guess this place still belongs to the taxpayer. But the present administration just wrote it off. It was disused, keeping it running cost so much a year, they'd never need it again, and it was out of date anyway, so they called it a write-off and sealed the doors. I was inside a week later. My friends and I have liberated it in the name of the American people. I'll give you a proper tour later. First of all, I'd like you to talk with our most recent recruit.'

'Apart from me?'

'You haven't been inducted yet. The person I want you to meet joined us about a week ago. We decided that finding the President was getting too complex using the facilities available. Our computer staff advised us that we need to get inside ECHELON. You know what ECHELON is, don't you?'

Jim shook his head.

'I've heard it spoken about. It's some sort of state-of-the-art computer system, isn't it?'

'It is and it isn't. I'll get somebody to explain it to you, to keep you in the picture. They tell me that, if any system has the information we're looking for, it's ECHELON. But ECHELON is the most closely guarded of all computer networks. That's why we needed a hacker, a world-class hacker who could get inside without leaving any traces of someone's having been there. And last week, lo and behold, one became available.'

He stopped outside a plain white door marked CL 19. Mygate knocked, then turned the handle.

They stepped inside. A solitary figure was bent over a computer, one hand extended towards a keyboard on which letters and figures were being typed in bewildering profusion.

The figure turned at the sound of their footsteps.

'Jim, let me introduce . . .'

'It's all right, General. We already know one another.'

He took a step forward and stopped.

'Hello, Holly,' he said. 'I was wondering when I'd see you again.'

281

39

Mogochin Village

'Put her down there.' Dr Lavrentiev pointed to a small pallet bed in a corner of his consulting room. The bed, like everything in the little clinic, was spotless.

'That priest,' muttered Lavrentiev, crossing to a cupboard and taking out the equipment he would need to test Tina. 'One day he'll drive me too far. He encourages the villagers in the rankest forms of superstition, tells them to pray when they're ill or even dying, and warns them away from this clinic, saying it's a nest of Satanic influences. At least under Communism we could make him and his ilk shut up, but now they've got carte blanche to do and say what they want.'

'Whom do the people actually prefer?' Yulia Zaslavskaya asked, helping him carry trays and instruments to his one and only working surface, a long metal table.

'Me or the priest? You'll have to ask them. When they're sick, they come to me for pills, when they're dying and they know there's nothing more I can do for them, off they trot to the altar and the sacred host. In the end, I suppose they like him best. I'm just a doctor. What do I know about man's immortal soul?'

'I'm hoping we can do more for this child than save her soul.'

'We'll see. Have you done this before?' he asked.

'For septicaemia? No. I only graduated four months ago.'

'But you understand the basic principles?'

'Yes, of course.'

'Let's get her onto a glucose and saline drip first of all. While I'm doing that, maybe you can take some swabs and prepare to do a culture. Have you any idea where the site of infection might be?'

She showed him the stump.

'Who did this?'

'I don't know. I don't know what's going on. I was forced to go with the girl and some other people. They're still in the truck.'

'Take the swabs. We can find out about that later.'

She started work, taking swabs of pus from the wound, and sputum. Tina was still flickering between consciousness and delirium.

'It's all right,' Yulia soothed her. 'You're in safe hands now. The doctor will take care of you.'

'I want my mother. Where is she? Why can't I see her?'

Yulia mopped her forehead.

'Why does she speak in English?' asked Lavrentiev, flicking a finger against the drip tube to start the glucose/saline mixture running.

'Two of the people with her are Americans. She's American as well. I don't know what they're doing here.' Something told her it was best to pretend ignorance of the Waterstones' identity.

'I think we should find out. Under present circumstances, anything out of the ordinary needs closer scrutiny. But let's get her treatment moving first. Can you do the Gram staining?'

She nodded and went back to the table, where primitive equipment had been laid out. Lavrentiev proceeded to an overall examination of Tina, taking her temperature, checking her pupils, and listening to her chest with an old stethoscope.

'How do you come to be in a place like this?' Yulia asked.

'In Mogochin? I was sent here fifteen years ago, under the old government. It was part of a laudable effort to send health professionals into remote areas. They'd paid for my medical training, they said, so they had the right to post me anywhere they wanted. So I wound up here. For several years I hated it. I wrote letters almost every week, asking for a transfer. No-one ever answered me. Then the government changed. It made not the slightest difference here, of course. But it did to me. I was free to leave, you see. I knew I could pack my bags and waltz away without giving a moment's notice. That was when I realized that I was actually doing a little good. That my little clinic saved lives and made things better for the Dolgan population. I found I'd accommodated myself to the state of things. So I stayed. Lucky for this little girl that I did.'

Yulia stained the first specimen with gentian violet, then with a solution of Gram's stain, and then treated it with acetone. That done, she counter-stained it with a red dye. She put the slide under a microscope. The bacteria had retained the dark violet stain.

'They're gram positive,' she said.

'Right. We don't have time for a blood culture. I'm guessing we're dealing with β-haemolytic streptococcus. There's penicillin in the cupboard, on the top shelf.'

'Do you have any flucloxacillin?'

'Why? In case there's any staphylococcus?'

'Yes.'

He shook his head.

'I'm extremely limited. Supplies arrive twice a year, if I'm lucky. Penicillin is the most appropriate drug. I want her to have it intravenously. Could you prepare it while I set up another drip?'

It took some time for the drug to begin to show even a tiny effect.

'Do you ever leave the village?' Yulia asked.

'To go where?'

'Moscow. St Petersburg. Things are very different to what you remember.'

'I know. More crime, more poverty, more desperation.'

'But freedom too,' she said. She was young, and idealistic, and he envied her almost as much as he pitied her.

'I go to other villages sometimes,' he said. 'But any one of them is more than a day's journey. During the winter, it's impossible, even with a sled. Now, let's see how our patient is doing.'

'She seems less febrile.'

'It's too early to tell,' Lavrentiev said. 'We may not know till morning. She's a long way from being out of the woods, but we may have caught it just in time. Whether she'll suffer long-term damage, I can't say. Now, will you keep an eye on her? I want to go see what's happening to the people who were with her.'

They'd been kept in the truck. When Lavrentiev asked to be let in, the woman called Varvara came to the rear door. She was carrying a heavy pistol in one hand.

'You can't come in, *dolboy'eb*,' she bellowed, waving him away with the gun.

'I want to speak with the parents of the little girl. I'm Dr Lavrentiev. I've been treating her. But I need to know how her accident happened.'

'Just mind your own business. Get on with treating her, so she can be put back on this truck. You have half an hour, then we leave.'

Just then someone appeared behind Varvara, a man.

'It's all right, I'll speak to the doctor,' the man said. He spoke in English. 'Let him come in.'

Reluctantly, Varvara let the doctor come on board. Lavrentiev pulled himself up the steps and into the truck. It was not as crowded as he had expected. He turned to speak to the girl's father. And, as he looked at him in proper light, he saw just how great a mistake he had made.

40

Monongahela Forest
14 January

There was a little stream, Laurelly Brook, that ran down between two mountains on the very edge of Pocahontas County, coming within the space of two miles into Middle Fork Williams River. Jim brought Holly there early that morning, not caring for appearances. Since leaving Washington for Puget Sound, he'd been sure he'd never see her again. His heart had leapt so wildly when she'd turned and looked at him the night before that he had no more doubts or fears, only infinite regret that he had come to this through the death of a wife and the abduction of a child.

It was icy cold, as though snow was on the way, and up on the mountains dense fog shrouded everything, creating an illusion of a simple world without great heights or depths. On every side, the forest spiralled upwards into the fog, a dark place full of ghosts. He dared not venture there with her, for fear of the darkness and the shades.

They sat on rocks and watched where a hawk dived to break an unsuspecting rabbit's back, and soar back up to disappear in swirling fog.

'It's cold,' he said, unable to get past the banal. There had been little time to talk last night: Mygate had wanted to show Jim round the underground facility. Nobody in the Pentagon had wanted it, and the General had exploited all sorts of loopholes to acquire it for a peppercorn rent, no questions asked, and with a free hand to use it for whatever purpose he had in mind.

Its numerous rooms were used to store arms and ammunition, explosives, canned foods, clothing, even reading matter. At weekends and on public holidays, a group of hikers would stray from the trails and byways of Cranberry Wilderness, and turn up here for intensive training sessions. At other times, they would sail or row or swim in the Atlantic, or climb mountains in the highest stretches of the Appalachians, or go HALO parachuting out of propeller planes taken up past their limits above eastern Virginia. Most of the time, the Cranberry Nuclear Facility served as offices for the organization. Full-time staff worked with computers, building databases relating to US Special Forces, HRT units, and the national security agencies.

Funding was a problem. Secrecy meant that Mygate and his associates could seldom make approaches to potential backers. Even if they had done, the money raised would still have been a tiny fraction of the budgets available to the military and civilian organizations with which they sought to compete.

Fortunately, Mygate had an insider's knowledge of Pentagon expenditure. He knew that, over the years, numerous projects were initiated which never came to anything or were called off for technical or political reasons. If you knew the right codes, it was possible to access the original budgeting centres and simply order further funds to be paid into this or that bank account. Whether this was stealing or liberation depended on your standpoint. But Mygate never tired of explaining exactly what some of those projects would have entailed, had they ever got off the ground. American soldiers sent mad by experimental drugs, sailors exposed to the raw material of biological warfare, airmen deprived of oxygen. Mygate had no scruples about using the monies he rescued from such purposes.

'Kiss me,' she said.

He looked at her with such astonishment that she burst out laughing.

'Did I say something wrong?' she asked, knowing perfectly well what she had asked.

'It's just . . .'

She took off her mittens and reached for him, taking his reddened cheeks between her hands and drawing him to her. And so she kissed him. The moment their lips touched, everything fell away but his need for her, and the knowledge that this was the fruit of grief, that his love for her, and his sense of being in her, and his sudden, unimagined joy were no betrayal, but completion.

For a long time they kissed, but it was too cold to go further, and in time they drew apart and looked at one another.

'When did you know?' he asked.

'More or less the minute I walked through your door, that day we came to put a tap on your line. I hadn't expected you. I didn't know what I thought I'd find, but whatever it was, you weren't it. I loved you the second I set eyes on you. It was hard, because I thought you would never open. I thought Laura was still fresh for you, that it was far too soon for you to love anyone else.'

'She is still fresh. I see her all the time. I love her desperately.'

'Then, why . . . ?'

He shook his head.

'There's no need for questions. I don't think I can answer them. It was the same for me, the moment you came into my room, I knew. I never doubted we'd be lovers.'

'We aren't lovers yet.'

He smiled.

'We never will be if we stay out here. Come on, it's time we headed back.'

By the time they reached the lodge, flakes of snow the size of rose petals had started to fall. Already the countryside was blurring, taking on a new, rounded outline that would soon cancel out all differences of plant and rock, trail and boundary.

He led her silently to his bedroom. His thoughts were racing faster than his pulse, his eyes could not take in enough of her face. They were wearing heavy parkas, like Eskimos. He pulled back her hood and smoothed her hair.

'I've never felt this way before, with a man,' she said.

'What way is that?'

'The way I feel with you. I'm nervous. As if I'd never made love

to a man before. I feel like a little girl, a teenager on her first date.'
She laughed nervously and ran her fingers along the stubble on his
cheeks. He pulled back his own hood.

'You're not a little girl,' he said, unzipping her padded outer
garment. 'And you're not a teenager,' he said, as he helped her
slip out of it. Her figure was clearly visible beneath the tight jumper
she was wearing underneath. 'I'm twice as nervous as you are. This
isn't a one-night stand. You understand that?'

She nodded, and her head dipped. Her hair fell down like a curtain
round her pale face.

'I don't mean to let you go, Holly. I can't walk away from
something like this. Can you?'

She lifted her head and smiled.

'What do you think?'

He brought her to him, his padded arms struggling to embrace
her. They kissed again, and his right hand went to her breast and
held it, and she kissed him harder.

They removed their clothes and moved to the bed, and he wanted
this to go on for ever, simply looking at her, and touching her. This
time when they kissed, their bodies touched. He kissed her breasts
in turn, and she brought his hand between her legs.

'I love you,' she said.

After that, words became unnecessary.

Afterwards, they lay in bed in silence. He would look at her from
time to time, and she would do the same. After a little while, he sat
upright.

'Tell me about ECHELON,' he said.

41

Mogochin Village

Joel Waterstone and Rebecca insisted on being shown to the village clinic. After frantic consultation with Tolbuzin, Varvara acceded to their request, and sent them there under heavy guard.

'She looks better,' Rebecca ventured.

Dr Lavrentiev shrugged.

'I don't want to hold out false hope. She has a long way to go. These antibiotics may deal with the infection, but if they don't, I have no others.'

'She has a better colour. Her sleep is calmer. You must have done something right.'

'I hope so, but it's much too early to tell. Ideally, I'd like to keep her here through tomorrow. How much further do you have to go?'

'I've no idea. You'll have to ask her.' She indicated Varvara.

Lavrentiev put the question to Varvara in Russian.

Varvara shrugged.

'You don't need to know.'

'When will you need to leave?'

'In an hour. That's all I can give you. As it is, we're taking risks. Rebel troops could be along here any time.'

'You could leave the child. Nobody would think to find her here.'

'I'm sorry, but that's out of the question. Now, do what

290

you can with her. We mean to leave as soon as the deadline passes.'

With Dr Zaslavskaya's help, Lavrentiev went back to his patient. The Waterstones returned to the truck, still under guard.

In the church, Father Grigory and his flock resumed their prayers. The smell of incense floated into the shivering air and crept between the cracks in the truck, filling it with a strange, floral smell. Time passed, Godly time and secular time. In the clinic, Tina's life flickered in and out like a tiny flame that has been blown too often.

But when an hour had passed, it was clear some progress had been made. Tina was far from out of danger, but she had taken the first tentative steps towards safety.

Varvara arrived at exactly the time she had stated, accompanied by two tall men carrying guns. She nodded to Yulia Zaslavskaya.

'You, take the child to the truck. Make it quick.'

'What about Dr Lavrentiev? Perhaps he can come with us?'

'I'd be happy to accompany the child.'

'Just pack up whatever medicines she'll need.'

'I've already done that.'

He handed over a leather bag packed with dressings, drips, and antibiotics.

'Thank you,' said Varvara. Her full name was Varvara Mochanova, she was twenty-five years old, and she came from a village just like this one, more than a thousand miles away. She hated villages, and poverty, and the many men who found her ugly. Without the least display of emotion, she raised the pistol she always carried and shot Lavrentiev in the throat. Blood spurted from an artery, the doctor coughed and choked and tried to breathe, then fell to the ground with a crash. Yulia cried out and made to bend down, but the two men took her by the arms and dragged her screaming from the room.

Outside, the sound of gunfire came suddenly through the night. Yulia saw to her horror that the church was already in flames, the doors barred, the congregation prevented from leaving. Elsewhere, men with guns were passing round the village, entering houses and shooting the inhabitants.

291

It took ten minutes all told to render Mogochin a village of the dead and damned. Even as the flames took hold of building after building, the little convoy of trucks headed back to the road on which they had been travelling. Inside, nobody spoke. The darkness did not change.

42

'ECHELON started in the early eighties – are you paying attention?'

His hand was stroking her thigh, and he seemed a lot more interested in her body than what she was saying.

'Sorry.' He took his hand away. 'Go on.'

'Back then, the National Security Agency at Fort Meade introduced a new computer system called PLATFORM.'

'And now it's called ECHELON.'

'You wish.'

'I wish. I'm not a computer buff, you know.'

She kissed him on the forehead and retreated.

'Jim, you really have to listen. ECHELON is important. It's hard to believe that any government with access to a system like this could have failed to track President Waterstone down. It's just a matter of technique and luck. I think somebody *does* know where he is, and where Tina is, but they aren't saying.'

'Why not?'

'Think about what General Mygate told you. There are some very serious people involved in this thing, and I think they are all involved in some tough negotiations.'

'To secure the President's release?'

'That, or leave him where he is. Or have him killed.'

'You think he's in Russia?'

'Maybe. It would help to narrow the search down. The big problem is sorting out how he got there. Every plane, every ship, every

293

train and car crossing Europe has been tracked and investigated. It's the first thing I looked into, and it's a blank.'

He looked at her, wondered at how matter-of-fact she had become.

'Did you know you have beautiful eyes?' he asked.

'Yes. Two of them.'

'What about helicopters? They could do that journey in a series of hops, depending on the size of craft.'

'Not that day. The more hops, the more likelihood of being tracked. They'd have known not to risk that.'

'Then what?'

'A submarine. I think they were taken on a submarine.'

'But wouldn't that mean a government was involved?'

'Not necessarily. There are some very large private subs nowadays. If you've got enough money, there's no problem finding one.'

'I need to know about ECHELON.'

'ECHELON is a result of a secret listening agreement made in the late eighties, between this country and Britain. It's known as UKUSA, and it divides electronic espionage between the two national eavesdropping agencies: the GCHQ in Britain, and the National Security Agency over here. What that means in practice is that the GCHQ coordinates snooping on Europe, Africa, and Russia west of the Urals, while the NSA covers the rest of Russia, most of the Americas, Australia, the South Pacific, and South East Asia. It's the world, Jim, it's the entire fucking world, and ECHELON knows all its dirty little secrets.'

'But it's just an agreement.'

'No, the agreement is UKUSA. ECHELON is what they set up. It joins together a string of listening posts round the globe, it takes their raw material, and it analyses it. The system covers mainly non-military targets: governments, organizations like Greenpeace, businesses of all sizes. It intercepts everything, whether it goes through satellites, oceanic cables, or radio transmitters. Telephone calls, e-mails, faxes – if it's out there, ECHELON can read it.'

'There must be millions of the things going back and forwards at any moment.'

'ECHELON can handle that. Look, the listening station at Menwith Hill in England – you must know about it.'

'Of course I do. It's down in Yorkshire. Not too far from our base, in fact.'

'Well, Menwith Hill is the biggest spy station in the world. It has radomes that can listen in to the communications spectrum through Europe, western Russia, and Africa. Last I knew, there were twenty-three satellite terminals and three satellite dishes. The station can make two million intercepts an hour.'

'But nobody could read them all.'

'Nobody has to. ECHELON couldn't care less about ninety-nine per cent of those communications, what little Johnny said to his Great Aunt Hortense. It's the one per cent or less that gets read.'

'Who decides?'

She smiled.

'If I'd known you ask so many questions . . .'

'What?'

'Oh, come here. I can think of better things to do with my mouth than answer everything you come up with.'

When she had come to his navel and was still moving down, he held her shoulders.

'I do . . . want to know . . . about . . . ECHELON.'

'Not just now, Major Crawford. ECHELON isn't going anywhere.'

It was four in the morning. Holly had brought Jim down into the underground facility, to the computer room. Though they were in a world of perpetual artificial light, at this early hour it seemed more fragile than ever. Dawn was still a couple of hours away. On every side consoles displayed coloured screens. Lights flashed intermittently, and from time to time an alert would beep or ding. Holly was sitting in front of a laptop through which she had direct access to a Univac supercomputer. Jim was on her left, Greg on her right. He'd joined them a few hours earlier, eaten, and gone into a lengthy one-to-one with the General. He'd brought two new recruits with him, a couple of data analysts from MIT. They sat behind, while Holly tried to explain about ECHELON.

'OK,' she said, an edge of excitement in her voice. 'He's logging on now.'

A row of letters and digits raced across her screen. They origi-
nated at a computer terminal in Cheltenham, England, where it
was 9.00 a.m. This was the home for GCHQ, one of several
intelligence-processing stations working on ECHELON material
round the globe. The log-in was being made by one of a group of
specially indoctrinated signals intelligence analysts, putting him into
the system of Dictionary computers that ran ECHELON's keyword
recognition operation.

ZHQβλ2653948ALPHA-ALPHA GAMMA STEEPLEBUSH
MAGNUM RUNWAY VORTEX

'Right, those are his security passwords.' She scribbled them down
on a paper pad next to her monitor.

'Do they mean anything?' Jim asked.

'Of course not. He just makes them up every day as he goes
along. What do you think? The first lot are his personal numbers.
Or hers, quite a few of the cryptanalysts in England are women.
ALPHA-ALPHA is the station sign for GCHQ. GAMMA is a code
used on reports and gists to signify Russian intercepts. STEEPLE-
BUSH is a control centre at Menwith Hill which is connected to
the latest and biggest overhead listening satellites, the code-name
for which is . . .'

'MAGNUM.'

'How observant of you. RUNWAY is the control network for
an eavesdropping satellite code-named VORTEX. VORTEX is
geostationary, which means it always stays over the same spot,
in this case Russia, which is, of course, our chief area of interest
at present.'

More letters streamed across the screen.

'OK, watch this. He's now in a directory that lists the different
categories of intercept available in different databases. They all have
four-digit codes set by Univac-powered encryption devices. There's
1911, for example: it links to intercepts of Japanese diplomatic
cables out of Latin America; lower down, there's 3848, which is
any kind of political communication out of some African country,
Nigeria possibly.

'Right – our man has just selected a code for western Russia. His
search result is coming on screen.'

'This is a bit like using a search engine, right?' Greg asked. Until getting mixed up with Mygate, he'd scarcely looked a computer in the face.

'More or less, except that this is far more selective. In a minute, he'll start downloading faxes, e-mails, whatever. But it's all been pre-screened for him by the Dictionary computers.'

'And this goes on round the clock and across the globe?' Jim asked.

'Like clockwork.'

'And the Presidential Task Force has access to all this information?'

'So we're told. The whole thing's effectively run by the US anyway, so setting new coordinates and getting supplies of data or borrowing personnel wouldn't have posed a problem.'

'What do they cover?'

'For communications intercepts? Everything, Jim. They start with the twenty Intelsat satellites, the Inmarsats, the CIA-controlled SIGINT satellites like Mercury, Mentor and Trumpet. Telecom surveillance is carried through the Orion and Vortex systems, Trumpet handles cellular phones, Advanced KH-11 and La Crosse Radar Imaging provide five-inch to ten-foot resolution photographs. And there are three Parsae satellites that carry out ocean surveillance.

'Some of those are out of date now, and are being replaced. A new system called GT-6 was installed at Menwith Hill towards the end of 1996. It's a receiver for the third-generation geosynchronous satellites like Advanced Orion or Advanced Vortex. There's also a new polar orbit satellite called Advanced Jumpseat, which handles some Russian traffic. It goes through Menwith Hill as well.'

'Does anybody make sense of all this?' asked Greg.

'It depends what you mean by sense. There are so many filters, none of the analysts or Dictionary Managers or even station chiefs ever know more than a fragment of what's going on. Back at Fort Meade, and probably at the National Security Council and the CIA, there will be a handful of people who receive this information in summarized form, designed to allow them to form a broad picture. The President receives gists too, of course, but I suspect nobody ever paints him a picture of the true state of things.'

'What are you able to get through here?' Jim asked. 'I mean, can you get ahead of them somehow?'

Holly shook her head.

'Not with this computer. Or, to be honest, any other computer commercially available. This is a state-of-the-art supercomputer, but the ones these guys are using are beyond state-of-the-art. They use super-giants like MAGISTRAND, which is part of the Menwith Hill SILKWORTH supercomputer system that drives the keyword search program. I can't begin to compete with that. There's no software available that can do what a new system called VOICECAST can do. It can target an individual's voice patterns, monitor every call they make, whether it's cellular, cable, or satellite, and produce a transcription for later analysis.'

'So what's the point of even trying?'

'You don't need me to tell you the answer to that. We try because your daughter's life is at stake. Because the lives of two other good people are at stake. If we don't try, they may die. The longer this goes on, the more likely this becomes.'

Jim stared at the screen. Screeds of Cyrillic letters rolled down it, as alien to him as Greek or Arabic. Dawn was still a while away.

'I need to get some shut-eye,' said Greg. 'I'll leave you young-sters to it.'

He went out, closing the door behind him. The two recruits went with him.

Holly leaned back in her chair. She shut her eyes and ground her knuckles into them. When she opened them, the room had filled with tiny points of light.

'What is it, Holly? You look all done.'

'I feel all done. Let's go to bed.'

'We can't sleep together. You understand that?'

She nodded and found his hand, holding it tightly in her own.

'You don't have to explain. If I didn't love you, I wouldn't understand or sympathize, I'd just say, "How come he's dating that cute young thing from computing when his wife's a month dead?" I'm sorry, I didn't mean for that to come out so flippant.'

'It's not an easy thing to say. And you're right. People wouldn't understand. It would harm morale.'

'More than that, love. Mygate would have us off the team so quickly our moccasins wouldn't touch the trail.'

He brought her to her feet, and kissed her with a slow and intricate and maddening kiss, and she took his tongue in her mouth and gave herself to him. When they pulled apart, he looked at her, and something in her eyes alerted him that something more than their loving each other was wrong.

'What is it, precious? Something's wrong, isn't it? You said, the longer this goes on, the more likely it is they'll all die. Is there something you know?'

She didn't answer at once. Then she seemed to reach some sort of decision.

'Sit back down again, Jim. There's something you need to see. Mygate didn't want me to show it you, but I think it's better you know.'

'Tina's dead, isn't she?'

'I hope not. But I found this earlier today. I think the General told you about a secret cabal called Respice Finem. They meet in the Cosmos Club mostly, or in one another's homes, and, as far as we know, they have no actual offices or headquarters. But they obviously have to have access to information, and nowadays that means a good mainframe computer. It took some time to find it online, but I did find it.

'Back in 1995, they put some money together and donated it to George Washington University to build some computer labs. Like all good universities, GWU wasn't fussy about where the money came from, and even though it doesn't actually teach computing sciences, it had a large supercomputer installed, way above requirements. It's used by staff, undergraduates, and postgraduates, to take pressure off their existing mainframe, which should be good for another year or two.

'The supercomputer is actually much bigger than anyone at George Washington realizes. They have no specialist staff, and the nearest they come to anyone with profound computing knowledge and skills will be the occasional postgraduate or staff member with a serious interest. Even then, the other part of the computer has been so skilfully built into the wider system that you would really have to know what you were looking for to find it. Communications in and out of the Respice Finem computer are labelled as though they originate in or are addressed to the GWU staff and student computer. Meanwhile, all members of Respice Finem have easy access via their desktops.

'And they can get into ECHELON?'

'Some of them created ECHELON. This afternoon, I found a file that had come through the ECHELON system, via Fort Meade, which is code-named OSCAR-OSCAR. The file was marked GAMMA UMBRA, meaning a Russian intercept carrying Top Secret classification. It's very short, and gives no clues as to who wrote it or where it was written. All I know is that it was written at 7.45 this morning, somewhere within the Russian Federation. Here, I've made a copy.'

She clicked a few times, and at last a page sprang onto the screen. Jim bent down and read it, and as he straightened, the room was spinning round him. Holly reached out and read the text quickly before closing the file.

'CHILD IS SICK AND POSSIBLY DYING. PLEASE ADVISE AT ONCE.'

43

Yulia sat in the rear of the truck with Tina, holding her drip steady, checking her temperature and other signs from time to time. The child's temperature had already dropped by one degree, and for the first time Yulia let herself entertain some small hope that Tina might pull through. And yet, that little hope notwithstanding, beneath her breath Yulia cursed the malign god who had brought her country into being, and put such creatures into it as her fellow-citizens.

Then she thought of Lavrentiev, and revised her opinion. And, thinking again, she remembered that there had always been Lavrentievs, in fact as much as in fiction, and no shortage of men and women like Varvara. The holy fools and the commissars, the poets and the men with guns. They had gone through a revolution, and then undone their brave new world, and here they were again, dodging and weaving just to survive. And in the midst of the chaos and carnage, someone was playing a deadly game, a game that involved the President of the United States and a little girl whose life hung by a thread.

The road had been smooth for a while. Suddenly, they were back on bad ground, bumping and swaying to get through. Tina moaned in her sleep, and Yulia swore, conscious of the desperate need to give the child some respite.

Joel Waterstone came over.

'How's she doing?'

'Her temperature's down a little. But she's not out of danger yet.'

'How long has it been?'

'Since Mogochin?'

He nodded.

'About ten hours.'

'If we don't eat soon, some of us will fall ill.'

'I've told Varvara. She just shrugs and shakes her head, or says there's nothing she can do.'

'Do you know what's going on?' he asked.

'I'm not really sure. There were some radio broadcasts before this convoy left. There's been an attempted coup. President Garanin has retained control of the armed forces, but some Mafia elements are coordinating widespread strikes and acts of violence against those loyal to the Kremlin. That's practically all I know.'

'You haven't heard who's behind this, have you?'

She shook her head.

'It's been predicted for some time now. But, then, you'd know that better than I, wouldn't you?'

'You're right. The truth is, it's a scenario that's been scaring us all shitless for years. If the Russian Federation goes into meltdown, the global effects will be catastrophic. I need to be back in Washington, I need to get a handle on this. My Vice President is a capable politician, but he's not the man to cope with a crisis of this order.'

'Not to mention the crisis he already has, with you missing. Do you think there could be any connection between the two events?'

Waterstone's face froze, as though someone unseen had thrown a bucket of ice-cold water on it.

'I hadn't given it any thought,' he said. 'But it's not impossible, I suppose. I would need more information.'

'I'll do what I can.'

He reached out and took her hand.

'I'm concerned for you,' he said. 'I don't think you should be around me and Rebecca any more than is strictly necessary. You saw what happened back in Mogochin.'

'You mean Lavrentiev?'

'Was that his name? The doctor?'

She nodded.

'If I ever get out of this, he's going to have a plaque the size of

302

Vermont over his grave. And when I've done with that I intend to bring to book every last one of his killers. They won't get the chance of a trial: it won't be like that.'

Tina moaned, then muttered something. Yulia bent down.

'What is it, sweetheart?'

'Thir . . . thirsty.'

She gave her some water through an improvised straw, and Tina managed to take three or four sips before falling back onto her pillows. Her eyes fluttered open.

'Wh . . . who . . . are . . . you?' she asked.

'My name's Yulia. I'm a doctor. Are you feeling any better?'

Tina took some deep breaths, and her eyes started to close. Yulia thought she was about to lose consciousness again. But she rallied and opened her eyes again.

'A . . . little.'

'Let's take your temperature.'

Yulia placed the thermometer between Tina's lips. The mercury moved up to 38°C and stopped.

'Is it still high?' asked the President.

Yulia shook her head.

'It's no longer critical. One degree down will get her to normal body temperature. I think she's over the worst.'

'Thank God.'

'Do you believe in God?'

'I'm a Jew. God is part of the furnishings, like chicken soup.'

She frowned.

'I don't understand. How can chicken soup . . . ?'

'I inherited God,' he said, 'I didn't choose Him. It's supposed to be the other way round.'

'You mean, that you're the Chosen People?'

'That's right. But I'm President of the United States, and I think the American people are chosen, that they have a destiny, and I'm not sure that God didn't have a hand in that. I don't think I could go on being president if I didn't believe that.'

'I was brought up to believe there is no God. And when I meet men like Father Grigory, I'm convinced there's no-one. It would be too grotesque.'

'Yes, that's always troubled me too, that God has the most dreadful supporters. Lavrentiev was an atheist, was he?'

She nodded.

'He was. Goodness and godliness don't always go together.'

Tina was still drifting in and out of a fitful sleep.

'Doctor?' she asked, her voice weak. 'Am I going to die?'

'Not if I can help it.'

'Where are we going now?'

'We don't know. No-one will tell us. Perhaps they don't know themselves.'

'Are they going to kill us?'

Yulia bent and wiped her forehead with a soft cloth.

'You should try to sleep, darling. We're all here, there's nothing to be afraid of. Go back to sleep.'

44

The Cosmos Club
Washington

Dinner had been excellent, much to their surprise. The new chef, a twenty-eight-year-old Frenchman called Patrick Vanier, whose father had been *chef de cuisine* in the household of the late King Idris of Libya, had been appointed over their heads, and they had greeted his arrival in the club kitchens with mutterings and shakes of the head. Tonight's offering – which they had requested with many reservations – had been a triumph worthy of the great cook in *Babette's Feast*, a film none of them had ever seen. They had started with a croustade d'oeufs de caille Maintenon, followed by a small plate of sole meunière, a red wine sorbet, and then pintadeau en cocotte grand-mère, with an extraordinarily dense dark chocolate mousse to end. The guinea fowl had come in for particular praise. Henry Bremahide had remarked on the general absence of garlic, a substance he could not abide, as though he was some sort of vampire. Things had gone well. Spirits had been lifted. Which was just as well, because outward affairs were not particularly likely to sharpen anyone's appetite.

'If you've all finished digesting,' Thomas Ellison prompted, 'I'd like to begin, because it's getting late, and I'd like to get home to my wife.'

What he meant was, he'd like to get back to his new mistress – if that was the word – a nubile nineteen-year-old whom he'd rescued from anorexia and the attentions of younger men, and who, he naively

305

believed, was at this moment waiting, naked and libidinous, in his bed. He was seventy-five years old, and had as little excuse as she had.

'We'd all like to get home. What's the latest?'

Ellison paused.

'Somebody's watching,' he said. 'I don't mean literally. On a computer, perhaps on several computers. Fort Meade have picked up traces of a snooper, but whoever it is is covering their footsteps. The NSA can't get a hold on them.'

'Surely that shouldn't be too difficult?' Warren Patrick asked.

'That's what I asked. Actually, the answer is, it can be next to impossible. But it shouldn't matter. Our concern is to find the President, and it shouldn't matter who knows about it, provided we get in ahead of anyone else when the time comes.'

'Any guesses when that will be? Some of my people are getting real impatient.' Henry Bremahide disliked being fobbed off, and he sensed that was what was happening tonight, and had been happening for some time.

'Very soon. Trust me, Henry, trust me.'

'But Russia's coming apart at the seams.'

'I know, I know. But in many ways that will make our position easier. When nobody knows who's in charge, anything can happen. Now, if only . . .'

There was a firm knock on the door, and a man in club uniform entered.

'Mr Ellison, I have Mr Kropotkin outside for you. Shall I let him in?'

'Thank you, Stephens. Is he alone?'

'Yes, sir.'

'Has he been searched for wires?'

'I searched him myself, sir. He was clean, sir.'

'In that case, I see no reason not to show him in. Maybe we'll get some sense this time.'

Stephens went out, returning seconds later with a stocky man with pock-marked face and sweaty hands.

'Gentlemen,' he said. 'The Russian Ambassador.'

45

Monongahela

Jim moved into a room inside the bunker. Originally conceived as a bolt hole for the entire US government should nuclear attack have been imminent, the complex included a lot of well-appointed bedrooms, all situated on Level Two, beneath the operational facilities on Level One. He prayed he would not be there for long. Since receiving the news that Tina was sick, he'd scarcely slept. The facility doctor, a woman called Quinn – they all called her the Medicine Woman – prescribed Amitriptyline Hydrochloride. When he read the leaflet that came with the drug, Jim found that, among its many potential side effects, he could look forward to a dry mouth, blurred vision, nausea, and drowsiness. When he read a little lower and found he might also enjoy a life of sexual dysfunction, he took the box and threw it in the bin.

'I've got to get some action,' he said to Holly, who was red-eyed from sitting long hours at her monitor.

'Not while we're down here, kid.' She summoned up a smile and stroked the back of his hand.

'I don't mean that. I've got to do something. This sitting around is driving me insane.'

'Jim, we've got nothing to go on. I'm narrowing things down, but it takes time.'

'Tina doesn't have time.'

'I understand that. But I can't change the way computers work,

307

I can just do what I can to improve the odds of getting a real hit. Remember that Waterstone's location is probably the most closely guarded secret since the German Enigma codes. Why don't you do something useful? Get yourself into shape. If I find what I'm looking for, you could be moving out inside the hour.'

Jim kissed her on the cheek, then went out and reported for duty to Greg.

'I want to be on the team, Greg. Waiting around like this is wasting me.'

'You sure you're up to it? It's been a few years.'

'I used to work out back at the base. It pays to be tough when you're fighting all those Gs at altitude. A jet cockpit isn't some sort of armchair.'

'OK. You can start training. But if you don't shape up, I can't let you come with us. One weak link, and the whole team goes down.'

'I'll be there. Don't worry.'

By that night, he was ready for sleep. Greg woke him at 5.00 a.m. He ate breakfast with the rest of the team, had some short conversations, and spent the rest of the morning in the gym with them. The afternoon was spent on weapons and explosives training. That evening, they were back in the gym. Jim was finding it hard to keep up with the others. He was in good shape, but his new companions were hot. The next day or two would see him crash or fly. One good thing, he thought: he was glad he'd thrown the tablets away.

The next day, during afternoon training, they received a message from Holly. 'Come at once' was all it said. Jim and Greg made their apologies and hurried to the computer room. Mygate was already there.

'What's wrong?' asked Jim. 'Is there fresh news?'

Holly shook her head.

'Not in the sense you mean, no. But I think I have something. I've managed to get into part of the task force's computer. It wasn't easy, and even when I hacked in, all the files were encrypted. They used a K-7 cryptographic machine on a Univac computer. It's taken me several hours to decode it.'

308

'And . . . ?'

'Very early on, they started looking for a submarine. It was a good line to follow, and they had access to all the right equipment. They had to do it without alerting the US Navy, which isn't easy. I think they must have pulled in some very sophisticated intelligence raiders from Fort Meade.

'They made an interesting calculation. Just looking at the map, a submarine could head in several directions away from the British Isles. Down through the Channel, along the French and Spanish coasts, into the Mediterranean or further on down to Africa. Or a sub could head west past Ireland and cross the Atlantic, maybe steer on down to Latin America. Plenty of rainforest out there, lots of places you could lose a president.

'Only none of those options makes much sense. You could probably get him out to those places just as effectively by ship. There's less concealment, but it could be done. Subs are slow, so you'd have to have a good reason for using one.'

'Such as?' He didn't say so, but Greg had a bad thing about subs. He'd always avoided being shipped in one, and he was still terrified that one day he might be forced to make a journey like that. It was simple claustrophobia, but it felt like a dread of being buried alive.

'Such as going places a ship couldn't get to. Maybe somewhere that couldn't be easily reached overland or even by air. There could be several reasons for that. Political factors could make air travel unwise. A ship can be tracked on the surface by satellites. Overland from Britain means crossing too many international borders.

'But there's something else. What if you want to go somewhere that just can't be reached by boat? Say, the Arctic circle. What if it's winter and you want to travel north? What if you want to go to Russia?'

'Tina's in Russia?'

Holly nodded.

'I think so. Until I decrypted these files, I thought they might be anywhere. But now, I think maybe Russia is where we should be looking. Unfortunately, the Russian Federation covers the largest land mass of any country. We need to get more precise than "Russia".'

'What makes you so sure it's Russia?' asked Mygate.

'I told you, the task force files. I don't know how many lines of investigation they opened up. Maybe they were going by instinct, maybe they had inside knowledge we don't know about. But they started looking for Russian submarine movements in and around Britain at the time of the President's kidnapping.

'There are two major submarine bases for Russia. One's at Polyarny, north of Murmansk on the Kola Peninsula. That's eighty miles from the Norwegian border.'

'And the other one?' Greg had been brought up on tales of the Soviet empire. He still had not adjusted to the concept of a non-belligerent Russian Federation. Eighty miles sounded dangerously close.

'We can ignore it. It's at Petropavlovsk, right on the other side of the Federation, on the Kamchatka Peninsula, where it borders the Pacific. That would be a very long journey from Britain, in fact they'd probably still be on their way, and I don't think that's the case.'

'You think they're at – where did you say? – Polio . . .'

'Polyarny. No, I didn't say that. But the route between Polyarny and the Atlantic is vital. It's kept under heavy surveillance by this country. Russian subs have to pass through the Barents Sea, along quite a narrow channel between Nordkapp in Norway and a tiny island near Spitzbergen, called Bjørnøya. Bjørnøya marks the southern limit of the winter pack ice.

'We have a string of listening satellites which relay data round the clock to the Current Operations Department of the Navy Operational Intelligence Center outside Washington. Remember that a lot of the Russian subs, even now, are carrying intercontinental ballistic missiles.'

'Hell, you're not saying the President was on some leaky Russian nuclear submarine, are you?'

Greg had gone red in the face. All this talk of subs was making him feel queasy anyway.

'Let her finish, Greg,' said Mygate soothingly.

'Look, all I'm trying to do here is go over the basics of submarine surveillance, so you know how reliable these fresh data are. Our satellites are mainly listening to sounds picked up by a line-up of highly sensitive hydrophones which were placed on the sea bed in strategic places. This is the Sound Surveillance System, better known as SOSUS. The bit that concerns us is an array called Barrier. It comes in two parts, one moored across the channel I just mentioned, the other linking northern Scotland, Iceland, and Greenland. When a sub goes over Barrier, its engine and other sounds are picked up and relayed to a base on the Norwegian coast, then sent up to one of the five satellites which make up the Fleet Satellite Communications System. The satellites instantly beam this back to the States, where they're sorted out by Illiac 4 computers. The computers have databanks of all the possible sounds.

'Now, let's go back to last month, to the third – the day the President was hustled off somewhere. Our satellites were monitoring Russian submarine traffic pretty much as usual. They've got a record for that day at the NOIC, but I don't think it will contain anything of real interest.

'What *is* interesting is this.'

She tapped some keys and her computers started flashing new screens at them before settling at last on one that had numbers from top to bottom.

'That's the encrypted version,' she said. 'Here's what it looks like in real life.'

She pressed another key and the screen began to download as a photograph of some kind. About halfway along, they all burst out laughing. The 'photograph' seemed to show nothing but a blue-green expanse with very little variation.

'That's the most boring photograph I've ever seen. You get off on that stuff, miss?'

She glowered back at Greg, then put up her hands for calm.

'OK, I know it looks stupid. I thought it was stupid myself, until I wondered how come someone had taken the trouble to have this encrypted and stored in a file directly related to the day of the President's kidnapping.'

311

'It's a KH-11 reconnaissance satellite picture, isn't it?' Mygate asked. Except that it didn't sound much like a question.

'That's right, sir. It was relayed by one of the Satellite Data System networks. The signal was picked up by the satellite ground station at Vetan. I'll come back to the photograph in a moment. When I found it, I ran a cross check on transmissions from Vetan. There were several. No photographs, all text. I discovered that Vetan's antennae also intercept transmissions from Russian Molniya communications satellites, as well as listening to the Russian ferret platforms as they pass over Murmansk and dump their data.'

'Holly, my head's in a spin. Can you please at least tell us what's in the photograph?'

'It's a submarine vortex,' said the General. The excitement in his voice was unmistakeable.

Holly nodded.

'A satellite photographed it about forty miles east of the Scottish coast.'

'A vortex?' Greg asked.

Jim remembered some of the reconnaissance work he'd helped with.

'It's the wake left by a submarine's propellers,' he said. 'Sooner or later, the vortex they create comes to the surface. You can't see it from a boat, you can't see it from a plane, however high up. But you can see it from three hundred miles away, from a satellite. It shows up against the water round it.'

He pointed at the screen, tracing the faint line of the vortex. A computer had found it first, now the human eye could track it. Just.

'There were two electronic notes attached to the photo,' Holly went on. 'The first was a question directed at the picture interpretation office. The operator simply pointed out that the vortex pattern did not correspond to that of any known Russian or US or British or French submarine, so what the hell was it?

'The answer didn't come till the following day. They must have known that the President had been snatched by then, but nobody seems to have put two and two together.'

'Perhaps they were instructed not to,' Greg suggested.

'Yes, perhaps something like that happened.'

'What was the answer?' Jim asked.

'A photograph analyst code-named JENNIFER said the vortex may have belonged to a private submarine. She recommended obtaining better SIGINT material in order to identify the class of submarine, its speed and so on. Later that day, a P-3 Orion antisubmarine plane from Simonsford AFB flew across the North Sea and dropped a series of sound-sensitive sonobuoys. These began to give feedback that evening. First impressions suggested a Phoenix 1000 luxury submarine, over two hundred feet long, with a fifteen-hundred-ton displacement, travelling at eighteen knots at a depth of just over three hundred metres.

'NOIC contacted the manufacturers, who said the vessel had been sold to a private client, who was using it for luxury tours in the North Sea and sub-Arctic waters. That was the last anybody in the Navy thought to ask about this sub. The tourist explanation was taken at face value. The manufacturer would not disclose the name of their client, but they did supply details of the sub. Believe me, this thing is an underwater hotel.'

'So, we stopped tracking it?'

'Not exactly. It showed up automatically on routine photographic surveillance. Then it vanished for a while. Three weeks later, we got this.'

She keyed in a command that brought another photograph to the screen. This seemed more like a conventional aerial photograph taken at night. Jim identified it immediately as a shot of a port from above.

46

'To save you all guessing, this is the port of Dikson in the Arctic sector of Western Siberia. Here, let me bring up a map. OK, this is one from the Defense Mapping Agency's Aerospace Center. It was updated about a week ago. Now, let's just . . .'

She scrolled up several degrees.

'Right, that's Dikson. You can see it's on the northern end of the Taymyr Peninsula, where the Yenisey estuary enters the Kara Sea.

'My first thought was that this was just a routine shot taken by a reconnaissance satellite that had made its tenth or eleventh pass over Noril'sk to the east. The region is photographed a dozen or more times a day. Noril'sk is a massive industrial city, and the most polluted place on the entire planet, so it's always worth a few passes for its own sake. And if the satellite happens to be going over Dikson a few moments later, it's no skin off anyone's nose to take a few extra snaps. This is one of them, and for some reason it got noticed and sent to the National Photographic Interpretation Center in Washington. Inside twenty-four hours, it had been analysed, reported on, and archived. Which is why I took a second look. Unfortunately, I wasn't able to get hold of the report, which was made available to only a tiny number of people on a need-to-know basis. I've tried to access it electronically, but I think it only exists now on paper.

'Anyway, take a good look. You'll see that where the sea should have been is now ice. It's a mixture of sea ice and frozen river water. At this time of the year, most of the Arctic Ocean is frozen over, and the Yenisel is frozen the whole way down. Our submarine will have been in normal seas all the way past Norway to the north of the White Sea. From then on, he'd be diving deep to stay under the pack ice. Dikson is a tiny port, and not one where a submarine would normally make a landfall unless it had to. It's not equipped for subs, and it couldn't be adapted.

'Nevertheless, if we can go back to the photograph for just a few moments ... The first thing you'll notice is that it's pitch-dark. But the picture was taken around 2.00 p.m. Dikson is in the Arctic Circle, and this photograph was taken about a week after the shortest day. Northern Siberia gets five months of total darkness. Naturally, the intelligence satellites that pass through this orbit are equipped to take photographs in the dark, and the NPIC analysts who work on the results undergo special training first. On some runs they use infrared film, on others ordinary film so as to pick up light sources. Which is what happened in this case.

'I was never given that sort of training, but I do know a bit about photographic interpretation. This presents very few problems, but for one thing. Fortunately, there's something else about this photograph that's very easy to spot.'

'The fact that this is a port in December on the edge of the Arctic Ocean, and it's lit up like Las Vegas.' Jim understood why she'd singled the picture out.

'That's more or less it,' Holly answered. 'They do a little work at the ports in winter, moving stuff out of the warehouses for shipment inland, and sometimes putting shipments in. But they don't load or offload ships for the simple reason that ships can't get through the ice.

'What you're looking at is at four-metre resolution, giving sharp images, but very little detail. I had the photograph blown up to one-metre resolution and enhanced.' She clicked a mouse and a slightly blurry but more detailed picture appeared on her screen.

'Any bigger than this and its loses all focus. I've cropped away the edges and left the central section. Now, what do you see?'

Mygate bent close, slipping on a pair of reading glasses in order to see better.

315

'Couple of gantries here, little bit of railway siding, some ware-houses back here. And these must be wharves.'

Holly nodded. Then she pointed with her finger at some tiny details.

'These took me a while to work out. In fact, they are two fork-lift trucks. If you look very carefully indeed, you'll see that the one headed towards the dockside is carrying a load, while the one moving away is empty. Which means they are loading only. Now, look more closely at this area. This is our problem.'

She pointed at a grey stretch that had to be the frozen river.

'Jim?'

Jim, whose eyes were best accustomed to picking out objects from the air, saw it at once. He pressed his finger on it. A dark area in the centre of the ice. Holly continued.

'I think they were putting supplies on board a vessel somewhere under the water, in other words, a submarine. If you look at this photograph, which is an infrared taken exactly twenty-four hours later, you'll see that the hole in the ice has gone. The port is quiet, and it stays quiet for the next four days, until some trucks arrive from Noril'sk and start offloading nickel into warehouse number two. There is no further activity around the wharves.

'But someone had caught hold of the submarine's tail and guessed which direction he was headed in. In summer, the Yenisei is navigable as far as Sayanogorsk. The depth varies a great deal, but in the northern section we're looking at a valley ninety-odd miles wide, and a depth of about eighty feet in places. The submarine commander would have had to negotiate his way down the delta, then past the Brekhov islands north of Ust-Port. A bit further, he'd encounter some bigger islands, maybe ten or twelve miles long. It would be a scrape, but he could get through. Of course, his worry all the time would be coming up against a block somewhere upstream, then finding he had no room in which to turn, or, if he was able to swing round, that the river downstream was icing up to trap him. Underwater ice is a common problem on the Yenisei.'

Mygate, who was sitting next to her on a swivel chair, smiled, then seemed to slump.

'I'm sorry,' he said. 'I'm growing tired. It's one of the many curses of old age. Actually, my eyes are strained looking at this screen. Can you print out some more of your photographs, and maybe we can just sit round that table and study them in comfort.'

'Don't you think perhaps you should go to bed?' asked Greg. 'We can go on with this later this morning.'

Mygate cast him a look that made it more than clear sitting round the table was the only option on offer. Greg squirmed and went off to find chairs to put round the table. It took a few minutes for Holly to find and print off the material she wanted. She took up where she'd left off.

'Somebody at Fort Meade gave orders to move several of the SDS platforms into new orbits, and to keep a Jumpseat ferret in a hanging orbit over Western Siberia for eight hours every day. Whatever they picked up was relayed to the ground station on the Vetan Peninsula. Several days later, they were drooling over these at NPIC.'

She pushed several photographs across the table.

'According to the overprint, these were all taken at different times on the second of January. The location is 68°N, 86°E, which puts us several miles upstream from the river port of Dudinka, just west of Noril'sk.'

'But all this is is cloud. I can't make out anything.' Jim, who knew a lot about cloud, felt out of his depth.

'That's right. The cloud is sulphur dioxide belching out of chimneys in Noril'sk. Anything could be happening down on the river, and we wouldn't know. I think that's why the submarine was brought to this spot.'

'Hell, this is just guesswork,' protested Greg. 'We don't even know that hole in the ice had anything to do with a submarine. The good folk of Dikson might have been putting in some winter fishing. Like Eskimos dangling little rods outside their igloos.'

'Come on, Greg. Did you see anybody fishing in the photograph? Just some fork-lifts taking supplies to the river,' Jim countered. He wanted it to be true, he wanted them to find a submarine, he wanted the submarine to be true the way a believer wants the Sacred Heart of Jesus to be true. Above all, he wanted the submarine to lead him to his missing daughter.

'Be patient, Major,' said Holly, and neither Greg nor Jim knew

317

which of them she meant. 'They were concentrating on the river, and on the ocean beyond Dikson. After all, the sub, if there was one, could only have gone in three directions.'

'Or stayed put.'

'Or stayed where it was and got iced up till May. Anyway, we have three days of photographs showing a heavy pall of sulphur dioxide over the entire Noril'sk *raion* and beyond. Then an Arctic hurricane comes along. There are several photographs of its progress, if you're interested. The main thing, it was moving southeast, at about one hundred and ten miles an hour. The sulphur dioxide got blown right away for a period of seventeen hours.

'When the hurricane blew itself out, there was a satellite hanging in orbit, ready to take these photographs.'

Saying nothing more, she laid three photographs in line like cards on a gambler's table. Jim looked down. He saw a river, and the banks on either side. The river was ice, but there was something in the ice. In one of the photographs, tiny dots appeared on the east bank, that might have been people. He noticed a large truck standing near the shore.

Holly took another photograph from the pile in front of her.

'This is the one-metre resolution.'

As before, the ice had been breached. But this time the hole was larger, and something rose visibly above the surface. All along one side, a row of lights appeared.

Jim whistled.

'I take it that is a Phoenix-class submarine.'

'That,' smiled Holly, 'is indeed a Phoenix. And that's a Kamaz truck waiting on shore.'

'You think the President is in this place? Does it have a name?'

She shook her head.

'Not as far as I know. As for the President and your daughter, it's my opinion that they were disembarked shortly after this photograph was taken. The next photograph in the sequence shows nothing but a hole in the river and tracks where the truck was.'

'Any clues where they were taken?'

In answer to Jim's question, Holly produced a map and unrolled it flat across the table.

'This is Siberia,' she said. 'One-third larger than the United States. A quarter bigger than Canada. The state of Maine is nearer Moscow than is the Kamchatka Oblast' in Eastern Siberia. I'm sorry, but this is what we're faced with. Siberia isn't the whole world, so we have a focus for a change. But if somebody wants to lose the President there, he'll stay hidden unless we are very, very lucky indeed.'

47

Anabar River
Due South of Saskylakh
Central Siberian Lowland

The Kamaz groaned loudly as it ground its way down from eighth gear to fifth, then a notch further to fourth. The driver let up on the gas until he felt the tyres take purchase on the sudden incline, then let a little back in as he pressed ahead at a steady fifteen miles an hour. Speed was not an option here. He could feel the torque converters straining as he moved forward on the river ice. He kept his right foot firmly off the brake, proceeding by the use of gears alone. Ahead of him, powerful headlights revealed a long ribbon of frozen water, in places as bright as crushed diamonds, shining off into the darkness like a white highway.

The rig was a 6350, a 360-horsepower sixteen-wheeled monster that had been built in Tatarstan and modified for Siberian conditions. This was an old military juggernaut that had seen better days and was now dicing with death in the middle of what was rapidly turning into the worst Arctic winter anyone had seen. It was colder, darker, stormier, and grimmer than a dozen winters put together. You might have expected that grunting old monster of the North, Grendel, to come stalking from the surrounding forest, munching on bones and spitting out splinters. And every day, when they thought it could not get worse, it got worse.

The driver, an ex-Alpha marksman called Sasha Shalamov, held his breath and prayed the ice beneath his wheels did not cave in. He had seen river ice crack beneath a lighter truck than his Kamaz, splitting, barking, bursting along a thousand cracks at once, sucking the vehicle, nibbling it with icy teeth, then swallowing it down whole, like a wolf devouring a reindeer that has strayed from the herd. And he remembered the cries of the men on board, brief frantic cries that bellowed in the air like a reindeer's death cries, then were silenced by icy water that killed his friends the second it reached their lungs.

Perhaps it was cold enough today to freeze the river along its entire course, and as far down as its sunless bed. It was minus sixty degrees Centigrade, but on a day like today, with thirty-mile-an-hour winds coming in from the sea, the wind-chill factor could bring the temperature down to minus seventy or eighty. He'd driven in these parts before, escorting trucks to the secret military base to which they were now headed. He knew the dangers of driving here in winter, above all the risk of being exposed on the open expanse of a river like this, where you could be caught by a *burany*, a vicious blizzard capable of destroying everything in its path.

Several days earlier, they had crossed the border into Yakutia, the Sakha Republic. Not long after that, the truck had jolted its way onto the Anabar just below Yuryung-Khaya, at a spot about one hundred miles south of the river delta. There, in spring, the little river would throw its suddenly thawed waters into the Laptev Sea. But spring was many months away, and water was not even trickling towards the north. They'd turned south at that point, making strenuous efforts to avoid even the smallest settlements, and to steer clear of roads where their lights might be seen at a distance.

As with the roads and settlements, so they maintained strict radio silence. This meant they could not call ahead to establish whether all was well at their destination. Conversely, no-one at either end knew their position or their radio wavelength. For all anyone knew, they had vanished into the Siberian night, never to return. They depended on public radio broadcasts for news, but found that one report was contradicted by another, and that, as far as Yakutia was concerned, only a tense uncertainty prevailed. Some said that the Republic still considered itself part of the wider Federation, others that it had swung firmly behind the nationalist cause, and yet others declared that the Yakuts and their fellow-Siberians had expelled the Russians and declared full independence.

Between Yuryung-Khaya and Saskylakh there lay nothing but wind-blasted tundra. On both sides of the river, a vast emptiness stretched away from them. Passing through it, the Kamaz was exposed and vulnerable. At any moment, they expected spotter planes equipped with infrared scopes to report their presence to the nearest Army or Air Force base. Or they thought to see the lights of Jeeps or motorcycles stabbing through the dark as they drove towards them across the frozen tundra. But darkness and the time of year, combined with the unusual cold, conspired to lend them a sort of invisibility that kept them safe from capture.

They'd travelled southwards without interruption, the ice smooth beneath their wheels, the sky lighting at times above them to reveal a growing moon, pale and curious, looking down at them briefly before dark clouds removed it from the heavens.

Just before they reached Saskylakh, there was a marked increase in the traffic, and they knew they had to get off the river. The little town and its airstrip were situated on the east bank of the Anabar, and all along the west bank straggled the beginnings of a forest that rapidly thickened into real taiga about ten miles further south. On the west, if they'd been able to cut a track for themselves through the trees, they would have come into steep hills without any sort of cover, with neither roads nor streams on which to travel further.

Just before Saskylakh, however, a short road bypasses the town, to merge before long with a vastly longer track that travels east about fifty miles, then meanders south, and finally makes its way back west. It was too roundabout a way in itself, but Tolbuzin's military map showed a small river about ten miles out of Saskylakh. They followed this narrow track of ice all the way down to the Udya, and then back until they were on the Anabar and travelling south again.

Their goal was a secret military base in a clearing south and west of where they now found themselves. Manned entirely by Russian troops, and marooned among Evenks and other minority peoples,

322

the base would have remained loyal, if only in the hope of being taken out by helicopter.

Sasha drove slowly, without headlights, picking out the river ahead of him as best he could, watching all the time for lights that might warn of another vehicle. In winter, all but the smallest rivers served here as routes for all manner of vehicles: trucks carrying sand and gravel extracted from the diamond placers along the Ebelyakh; small lorries driven from village to village by Russian middlemen from as far away as Yakutsk, stuffed with the meagre supplies of canned foods, tobacco, and medicine that would see the villagers through the rest of the long winter; pony sleds manned by Yakut traders, piled high with the pelts of foxes, ermine, and sable destined for Moscow, St Petersburg, or New York; and little covered wagons to carry contraband: mammoth ivory for shipment to China, Chinese aphrodisiacs destined for the bags of local shaman-healers.

Most of the roads that showed up on the map were little more than sled trails, their surfaces covered with a light coating of snow that betrayed no hint of the 1,000-foot-deep permafrost underneath. There were mammoths buried deep beneath the ice, frozen for ever next to the fur-clad bodies of deer-headed shamans and sacrificial ice-maidens. Ancient things, their memories frozen in absolute darkness. Sasha shivered as he thought of it. He shifted down to third.

The day before, they had come down through a twenty-mile defile on the eastern edge of the Syuryakh-Dzhangy Ridge. Now, with the ridge behind them, the river had entered true forest at last. On either side, tall trees encroached upon the river's fragile banks. There were no signs of human habitation here, no passing vehicles from which to hide.

In the rear, the guard Varvara shook Tolbuzin awake. He lifted his head from sleep with an almost electrical reactivity, as though he'd been pretending all along. One moment, he was fast asleep, the next fully alert. He was a man for whom grey meant nothing, for whom half measures were no measures at all.

Varvara slipped behind the thin screen that provided the only privacy in the truck. The hastily-erected chemical toilet was struggling to cope with the pressures five adults and a child could place on it. The stench inside the vehicle was terrible, but no-one thought for a moment of throwing open a panel to let in fresh air. They hoarded every fragment of warm air, however foul.

At Mogochin, one of the drivers had found chains and padlocks in a house that had belonged to the village blacksmith. Varvara and Tolbuzin had attached them to the floor of the truck with nails that they'd hammered in place and bent like staples, then fastened the Waterstones and Dr Zaslavskaya by their ankles, giving them very little room in which to move. They hadn't spoken for days. In part, it was shock at the events of Mogochin, a revulsion against everything their captors had inflicted on the village. Beyond that, it was the very heavy numbness all this had created in them, and the impossibility of responding to it by any means other than introspection. There was, moreover, the impossibility of real thought. They ate if food was offered, they used the toilet with as much dignity as they could muster, and they helped Tina when Varvara or Tolbuzin allowed them. But what could they possibly think? Too deep, and the thoughts would penetrate minds that had ceased to function. Too shallow, and they would stir up emotions best left untouched.

The bed of the truck was constructed of wood and metal, and made a very uncomfortable place on which to lie or sit. Stretched over it, across a framework of metal rods, was a large canvas tent or awning. Someone had done their best to improve the insulation this provided by erecting sheepskins along the 'walls', but it was still hopelessly inadequate to their needs. At Mogochin, Tolobuzin had taken on board a medium-sized paraffin stove, together with several jerry cans of paraffin. This now smoked unhealthily in one corner, giving out a little heat and a singular amount of fumes. By a combination of tightly-roped canvas, the stove, heavy clothing, and the body heat exuded by five adults and one sick child, they managed to avoid freezing.

The President had given up asking where they were headed, and at times he thought this was all random now, and that they might

324

end up like the Flying Dutchman or the Wandering Jew, chugging across the endless permafrost, neither living nor dead.

Later that day, Sasha handed over the wheel to his companion, an old Alpha buddy called Stepan, and huddled on the other side of the cab to eat his ration of cold potato and salted *muksun*.

Stepan had piles, and driving had become a torment to him. He shifted uncomfortably into the driving position, snatching the gas pedal from Sasha and pressing it down. The truck shuddered momentarily, then continued forward, weaving a little as Stepan fought to straighten the wheel. As his eyes adjusted to the snow-sprinkled surface ahead, the Kamaz came back on course again.

They stopped as seldom as possible, fearing that they might not get the engine to start again once it was turned off. Even when refuelling, they kept the engine running. Whenever they caught sight of the lights of other vehicles coming towards them, or detected them in the wing mirror, picking up speed in their direction, they would pull off to one side, extinguishing their sidelights (the headlights and rear lights being switched off permanently) and wait for the truck or *kibitka* or *bobik* to pass. The engine stayed on even then, since no-one cocooned in a motor vehicle would be able to hear it, and anyone driving a sled was unlikely to pose a threat.

About one hour into his shift, Stepan, who had been kept awake for several hours now by his physical discomfort, found himself falling asleep. It was gentle at first, and he would wake within seconds, make a minor correction to the steering, and carry on until the next slip. Each slip took him deeper into real sleep, and it might have been the eighth or ninth time that he did not come awake.

At first, his hands retained their grip, and the truck, travelling slowly, stayed on a more or less straight line, held there, as much as anything, by its own weight. But as yard succeeded yard and furlong stretched to furlong, the distortion in the Kamaz's forward movement grew slowly greater until it fell at last on a collision course with a stand of Dahurian larches that bordered the river on its eastern bank.

Though an external observer might have thought the truck merely coasted into the trees, coming to an immediate halt against their cushioned trunks, inside things were a great deal less comfortable. Stepan's arms, rigid against the huge steering wheel, snapped on impact, and his forehead was badly gashed as he was flung forward against the windscreen.

In the rear, fire broke out as the stove spilled paraffin in every direction. The Waterstones and Yulia were thrown hard forward and painfully, pulled up short by the chains that held their ankles. Joel looked round desperately, knowing they had only moments before the flames reached them.

Tina was tossed forward into a pool of snarling paraffin, and snatched out again as quickly by Varvara, who had been leaning up against the bulkhead and merely jolted by the impact. Tolbuzin reacted almost as quickly. Seeing the flames, he grabbed hold of the jerrycan that held the rear compartment's water: it had been replenished several hours earlier, filled with snow while the truck stood idling nearby. Tolbuzin soaked a blanket with the contents, and hurried to damp down the flames, pressing them out on all sides.

'*Dermo!*' shouted Varvara, visibly frightened. As the shock of the crash began to recede, it sank in on her that any real damage to the truck could prove fatal to them and their mission.

By the time she and Tolbuzin had lowered the rear gate and stepped out onto the ice, the reserve drivers had taken Stepan out and laid him just inside the treeline, where he was wide awake and moaning ceaselessly.

Surveying the scene, Tolbuzin swore beneath his breath. '*Cho eto za piz'dyulina?*' He strode up to where Stepan lay in a heap on the snow. '*Mudilo! Sukin syn!* Imbecile! What the hell do you think you were doing?'

The only reply he had was a series of moans from the injured man.

'*Bardak!*' the Colonel swore again. He hadn't even planned to be in this situation, had been forced aboard the Kamaz in order to avoid arrest by a gang of rebels on their way to overrun the camp where they'd been holding the President. Now, here he was, running from capture and almost certain execution, stranded in the middle of Siberia with a bunch of no-brain special operations types who couldn't even steer a straight line along a river course.

'I don't think it's too bad, sir,' said Sasha, who'd been looking at the point of impact. 'I'll get the engine started again before it gets cold, and we'll try to back out. We'll be on our way again in five minutes.'

'And if the engine doesn't start?'

'It fucking better start,' broke in Varvara. 'It's cold enough out here to freeze a polar bear. I can scarcely breathe.'

'Don't joke about that, ma'am.' Sasha was glad she could not see his face. 'If we don't get moving soon, we *will* die.'

He and the third driver, a mechanic from the base they had been in before their flight, set about getting the truck out of its bed of snow and branches. The third driver, whose name was Ivan Valentinovich Stul'nev, was a Don Cossack from Rostov. His grandparents and great-grandparents had suffered severely under the Soviet regime, and he carried a grudge about that and the treatment of the Cossacks that FSB types like Tolbuzin and his female companion only exacerbated. He had already decided to hand himself over to the first rebel company that happened along, and to make sure that the little girl got out of this alive. Of the rebels, he was sure; but the girl's escape was more a faint hope than anything.

Varvara went into the rear section of the truck and released the doctor.

'We need help out here,' she said.

Tolbuzin had found some torches and was handing them round. They wouldn't last long, and there were no batteries to replace those now in use, but at least they would be able to see what they were doing.

The white light revealed pale and haggard faces from which all animation had departed.

While Yulia made to do what she could for Stepan, Varvara pulled her away to where Tolbuzin was breaking off the thin lower branches of the larches and occasional birches.

'It's vital we get a fire going,' he said. 'We could be here for hours.'

The silence was appalling, it seemed to stretch through forest and tundra, out through the vast blackness to the white ocean and beyond, to the heart of the whiteness and silence of everything.

They hurried to follow Tolbuzin's instructions, some collecting wood, others setting it alight. The repair of the truck, not to mention Stepan's injuries, could wait till later. For the moment, fire was their first essential.

Yulia bent to disentangle a long branch of birchwood, then straightened, listening. She could feel the silence in her bones, and, more violently, something like glass. A storm was coming, a storm that would make this cold seem tropical. She threw the branch onto the growing pile. Stepan moaned nearby. Yulia went across and examined him with the help of Sasha's torch. She wanted to get him inside – he was already falling into a severe chill, and his arms would suffer if he got any colder.

She went over to Tolbuzin.

'When the *turany!* comes,' she said, 'we must be in shelter, not out in the woods like this. The fire will just spread among the trees once the wind comes.'

She glanced round at where Varvara had got a fire going on the ice. How wise was that? she wondered.

Tolbuzin looked up at her. He was out of his depth, but he would not lose face by admitting it to anyone, let alone a shrimp of a doctor like her.

'Surely the trees will block the wind.'

She looked at him. She knew these things because of her grand-parents, because they had talked to her when she was a little girl. They had been in the camps, somewhere in the vast territory of Kolyma, east of the Lena, where they had been put to mining gold and cheating ever-present death by what slender means they had. They'd spoken of their despair, of the despair of tens of thousands sentenced to suffer and die by one man's whim. She had never forgotten.

'It will grow cold,' she said. 'Much colder than this. The steel on the lorry will split, its tyres will explode, its glass will shatter – even the larches will go mad. When you breathe, your breath will freeze and turn into little crystals. Literally. Little ice crystals that drop to the ground with a tinkling sound. The Yakuts call it

328

"the whisper of the stars". Some say that when that happens, even words freeze between men and fall dead to earth, and that when the spring comes they will be resurrected, and the air will be filled with curses. In Kolyma, in the camps, spring was a torment.'

At that moment, they became aware of a faint sound. Softly, they listened as it approached them out of the darkness. Yulia strained to make it out. It seemed to approach them, then back off, then venture forward again, growing louder all the time. She felt sick, thinking it was a natural phenomenon rushing towards them, the expected hurricane perhaps, coming with thunder. Worst of all, she imagined the ice cracking all the way down the river, as though a hand was tearing it up like paper. And then, all at once, she heard it properly.

Horses. She could hear their hoofbeats a mile or more away, loud enough now to be unmistakeable, the hooves of scores of horses, or perhaps more, far more than that, she had no way of telling. The tree silence of the woods had given way to their drumbeat, and the ice silence of the river had cracked and become loud water, as though a great waterfall had suddenly opened in the sky.

'Quickly!' shouted Tolbuzin. 'Put the fire out! You, Shalamov. Stul'nev. Extinguish your torches. We've got to get everyone inside the cover of the trees.'

But it was too late. The pounding of hooves no longer came from the river alone. Men on horseback were weaving their way through the forest, picking paths through the larches as though such manoeuvres came to them without effort. It was the horses who picked their way between trunks, while their riders warded off low branches with their arms.

Shalamov and Stul'nev hurried to the Kamaz's cab and hauled out two heavy-duty machine guns, which they set up facing down the river. Their practised movements made it all seem quite simple, but their hands were shaking from fear and cold.

Out of the forest appeared a phalanx of men and horses. Some the unextinguished fire lit from below, bearded men carrying weapons. And the sound of thundering hooves continued to approach from downriver. Only at the last moment did they make out the indistinct pattern of horses, some grey, some white, others undoubtedly black,

329

as they were reined back and came to a halt several yards away. Down the line, a horse whinnied. Everywhere, the air was filled with the white, frozen breath of its companions. There was a clanking of metal upon metal, and the sound of bolts drawn back on rifles. Then silence that no-one dared to break.

48

An untrained observer would have noticed nothing out of the ordinary had he flown low over Vadsø that morning. Tucked in – just – from the frozen waste of the Barents Sea, the little settlement lies perched on the southern coast of the Varanger Peninsula. Its forest of antennae faces out across the Varanger fjord, down towards Severomorsk, north of Murmansk, and only one hundred miles or so away.

The mythical untrained onlooker might, of course, have worked out for himself the broad meaning of what he saw. Geodesic domes perched on top of sixty-foot-high concrete towers, as bleak as the surrounding landscape, and dripping ice. Tall radio aerials, pylons, radar-type dishes, antennae bristling with rods and wires. With Russia so close, it was obvious what this was all about.

The trained eye would have seen something slightly different. One glance at the long period arrays, closer scrutiny of the chain of vertical wire dipoles set out along the edge of the facility, and due attention given to a group of broadband dipoles with corner reflectors would have suggested not so much power as sensitivity. The same eye would have guessed accurately enough at the contents of the domes, and understood that the sophisticated VHF antennae inside them would have served to intercept telemetry from Russian submarine-launched ballistic missile tests out in the Barents Sea.

That morning, the trained and observant eye would have noticed one more thing, had it been in the right position at the right moment, and had it – given that it was pitch-dark at the time – been using infrared glasses. Shortly after 8.00 a.m., the antennae inside the domes swung inland, while all the external aerials and dishes shifted two degrees to the east.

'Heathrow, this is BA one oh one, request descent.'

'Bravo Alpha one oh one, this is Heathrow control, receiving you. Descend and maintain flight level two four zero, report reaching.'

'OK, we're leaving five three zero. Descend and maintain two four zero, twenty-four. Thank you, miss. BA one oh one.'

'That's correct.'

'Twenty-four set. Can you give us the weather down there?'

'Yes, sir. Temperature is ten degrees. The altimeter is two nine point eight, conversion to two six point seven one.'

'Gentlemen, this is Captain Matthews. We have begun our descent for landing at London, Heathrow. It's a bit overcast, as we predicted, and at Heathrow right now the temperature is one zero, that's ten degrees Celsius, and if you prefer Fahrenheit, that's fifty degrees on the Fahrenheit scale. The winds are ten miles an hour from the northwest.

'Congratulations on making your first supersonic flight. You will be pleased to know that our flight time from New York to London this afternoon was three hours thirty minutes. I wish you all a successful expedition in the frozen wastes of Scotland, and I hope you get better weather than this. Thank you and goodbye.'

As if to punctuate the captain's farewell, the undercarriage came down with a series of alarming thumps. Jim took hold of Holly's hand.

'We've gained a few hours,' he said.

She nodded, but he could see she was tense. London was to be no more than a staging post. As fast as the runway was coming up to meet them, they were busy planning how to get off the ground again in the shortest time possible. Mygate's original plan had been to refuel the Concorde (which they had chartered) at London, and fly on supersonically to Moscow, ready to rock and roll (a phrase he enjoyed using, much to the embarrassment of his junior officers).

Under ordinary circumstances, they might have got away with a trick like that, posing as a baseball team or ice hockey superstars, complete with coaches, managers, and sundry hangers-on. But the circumstances were neither ordinary nor kind, and they all knew that the arrival at Sheremetievo airport of thirty battle-scarred men and a woman weighed down with computer hardware on board a British Airways Concorde would hardly have gone unnoticed by the FSB or any other intelligence operation with a pair of opera glasses and a friend in airport administration.

Mygate had pulled silken strings to charter the Concorde mere hours before its scheduled departure carrying a party of rich Irish Catholic pilgrims en route for the Marian shrine at Knock in the West of Ireland, the world's only religious site to boast its own custom-built airport capable of taking wide-bodied jets.

So fine and expensive were Mygate's strings that when the flight crew arrived for work, they hadn't turned a hair to find that Knock was off the menu and they were now chartered to carry a US mountaineering expedition to the Scottish highlands.

The Concorde was no extravagance. While the pilgrims were sorting out freely-offered flights on board an Aer Lingus 747, and counting up the cash payments that had been handed to them in unmarked envelopes, Greg and his men were supervising the loading and storage of equipment that would have been more useful for an expedition to the North Pole than halfway up the Cairngorms. By the time they'd finished, the Concorde's baggage hold was filled with enough to kit out a small regiment of Arctic commandos.

The only thing they lacked was weapons. But even as the Concorde lifted from the tarmac at JFK, and raised its drooping beak as it levelled itself for flight, Mygate and a small team of assistants were taking care of that problem.

The General had stayed in West Virginia, masterminding the operation from the depths of his bunker in the heart of the Monongahela Forest. They still had no idea where the President was being kept, or whether he was alive or dead; but Mygate wanted his Hostage Rescue Unit to be on the ground and in position, ready to move once he had confirmation of a possible location.

Thirty men made up an oversized unit, but Mygate had been advised that, in this instance, small might not be beautiful. There existed a not inconsiderable possibility that the group might have to split up if intelligence pinpointed two or more potential sites. More seriously, they'd be moving as an armed force through hostile territory, and Mygate wanted them big enough to fight back.

He'd let Holly go with the greatest reluctance. She told him she needed to be on the spot, and that, provided she was equipped with a powerful laptop and a high-speed modem that could operate directly through a communications satellite, she could function so well he'd think he still had her in a back room somewhere.

'And what about Jim?' he'd asked.

'Jim?' she'd replied, all innocence, as though she never thought of Jim.

'Will he notice the difference?'

She caught his eye and realized he knew their secret. Had they been that careless? Or was the old man particularly observant?

'He needs me,' she said. 'With his wife and . . .' Her voice had fallen away suddenly, and she felt her cheeks turn red.

'It's all right, Holly. We don't ask for these things, but they happen. You should think it over very carefully. Are you in love with him, or just feeling sorry for a man in his position?'

'Who wouldn't feel sorry? Practically everyone in this country feels sorry for Jim Crawford.'

'But you don't?'

She shook her head.

'I did. Then he told me about his wife, and I felt jealous as hell.'

'You were glad she was dead?'

Again that sad shake of the head, her black hair framing an angel's face. Mygate felt sorry for himself, for his loneliness, for the useless attachment he had started to feel for a woman almost fifty years his junior.

'No, not glad. It's just . . .'

'What would you do if he cheated on you?'

'Cheated? We've hardly had time to . . .'

'I don't mean having sex with other women. I mean inside. If he goes inside himself along with his dead wife and lets her take up residence?'

'I suppose . . . I'd have to put up with it. If he needed to do that. I'd be jealous as hell, but I wouldn't leave unless he asked me to.'

'Just so you could be with him?'

'That's right. So I could be with him. The thing is, I love him. Didn't I tell you that?'

'You didn't have to.'

After clearing customs, Greg headed for the Diners' Club lounge, where he collected new passports and new identities for the whole unit. They'd been left there less than an hour earlier by a motorcycle courier. The seals were intact and Greg's signature checked with that on the release form.

Greg's first port of call was the lounge toilet, where he sat inside a cubicle and defused the incendiary device that would have taken the entire parcel and a hand with it had anyone tried to force their way in without permission. It took him three minutes to render the parcel safe, and another two to calm down.

By the time this had all been taken care of, the unit had broken up into little groups of one, two, or, at the most, three. Greg found them one by one, and handed them their papers, and when that was done, they went off to a series of check-in desks, where tickets were handed to them.

In the next few hours, most of them flew to a variety of destinations, including Stockholm, Helsinki, Warsaw, Vilnius, Minsk, Tallinn, Riga, Oslo, Kiev, and Malmö, where tickets would be awaiting them to fly on to Russia throughout the next twenty-four hours. Jim and Holly – who discovered they had been granted the status of a married couple by Mygate – took the next Aeroflot flight to Moscow, and found themselves sharing the journey with half a planeload of British journalists. Holly wanted to get to Russia as quickly as possible, in order to set up her computers and establish satellite links with the States. Jim, meanwhile, had been given a mission of his own to fulfil.

Even as they flew, the situation in Russia was deteriorating. Outside the central areas still in control of the government, it was every man for himself. It was not civil war. Civil war gives everyone an almost even chance. There are killers and slain, winners and losers: but it all happens on two sides. This struggle had no sides, and when it ended there would be no winners or losers – perhaps no survivors. The largest country in the world was bludgeoning itself to death.

Getting hard information out was difficult. Television crews stayed in the southern half of the country, where there were plenty of hours of daylight in which to film. This meant that important cities and regional capitals were left to get on with things. Murmansk, Archangel, Vorkuta, and the whole of Northern Siberia were all dark holes as far as the world's media were concerned.

Since all communications with these and dozens of other places were controlled by the Kremlin, and the Kremlin's spin doctors had no desire to admit to even the slightest setback unless absolutely forced to spit it out, foreign journalists found themselves making up stories that changed from day to day. A sliver of gossip here, a fragment of innuendo somewhere else, was often sufficient to make a headline in the *New York Times* or a column in the *Daily Mail*.

Some intrepid souls headed down to Volgogradskiy Prospekt, where they hired a succession of little cars before setting off in every conceivable direction. Fourteen Japanese reporters combined their resources and rented Alexel Tsyganov's famous Ford van, complete with driver. And a columnist for the *Irish Times* was said to have hired or bought a horse sled and headed north. He was the only one to get through. It was later whispered that he'd trotted gamely as far as the Yaroslavskaya Oblast', where he'd been shot as a spy while trying to circle a rebel checkpoint outside Rostov.

As for the rest, they were stopped while trying to leave Moscow, and returned ignominiously to their hotels. An order was passed, forbidding the hire of cars or transport services to foreigners.

Moscow and the main Russian centres were still in the hands of government forces, as were the nuclear arsenals, most military and Air Force bases, and the Navy, most of whose fleet was ice-bound at this time of year. But even within the central regions, there were pockets of anti-government activity. In the south, Volgograd, Rostov, and Krasnodar were in the hands of a rebel coalition made up of far-right nationalists, neo-Nazis belonging to the RNE, and Barkashovtsi fascist paramilitaries.

In several places, there had been attacks on synagogues, and there were rumours that Jews were being rounded up and sent to detention centres. It made no difference whether the rebels were right-wing nationalists or hard-left Communists, since both sides fell back on a Jewish-American conspiracy as the source of Russia's many ills.

The Chechenskaya Republic had declared its independence within minutes of hearing that rebel forces had taken the military base at Murom east of the capital. Seven other republics had followed, including the Chuvaskaya, Ingushkaya, and Mordoviya, and at least five *oblast's* were teetering on the brink. Siberia was in a state of near anarchy, and the further one went from the Russian heartland, the more tenuous grew any sense of loyalty.

Things might have been easier to interpret and decide had there been two sides of this after all, but it soon became apparent that there were at least three. There was the government to start with. Then, a collection of right-wing forces under the overall command of an Orthodox priest, Metropolitan Filaret of Omsk, were growing in numbers every day. Filaret claimed to possess the Mandylion, a cloth bearing the true face of the Saviour, and to have a divine warrant passed to him by St Nicholas, the sanctified persona of the last of the Tsars. Wherever Filaret went, the Mandylion went with him, and wherever the Mandylion was shown, people flocked for the blessing of Christ and the prayers of St Nicholas. The worst atrocities of the war had been committed by Filaret's special troops, the Soldiers of Nicholas, who carried the emblem of the Mandylion pinned to their breasts.

On the other hand, the government found itself having to deal with a surprisingly large body of old Communists and neo-Communists. It seemed that the KGB, during the last days of the Soviet Union, recognizing what the future held in store, stockpiled weapons in every major city and scores of smaller towns. Secret committees, styling themselves *soviets* in the old fashion, had been working for years among the military, and now the moment had come, they called their followers to arms. Their leader was a former Soviet General, Varlam Sumarokov, a one-handed veteran of several coups, and a formidable military strategist. What his followers lacked in numbers, they made up for in their ruthless efficiency.

* * *

337

Coming through passport control had not been easy, and several times Jim had been sure they would be turned back, or discovered to be bearing forged documents. But he hadn't reckoned with Mygate or the attention the General gave to detail. The Canadian passports on which he and Holly were travelling were impeccable. Holly's computer hardware had caused raised eyebrows at customs, but she had finely printed letters indicating that she had come to work for a Canadian IT company that was currently advising the Russian government. A telephone call to the number on her letter of introduction gave the customs officer a high-ranking official in the Ministry of Telecommunications. Holly was waved through.

'What now?' she asked as they headed for the taxi rank.

'Stay here,' said Jim. 'I have to make a phone call.'

He found some phones, then went down the row until he found one that worked. Putting his flight bag on a shelf, he reached into his trouser pocket and fished out enough small coins to see him through a dozen calls. He dialled and heard a phone start to ring somewhere far away. A voice came on the line.

'Vronskiy.'

'This is Stewart Campbell. I believe you have some things belonging to me.'

There was a brief hesitation, then the man called Vronskiy replied in English.

'Be here in one hour. I'll be waiting for you.'

In an unmanned computer room in Vadsø, with white walls and a low ceiling, a series of chirrups burst from a terminal, followed by the flashing of a row of lights, and finally the sound of a printer chattering to itself while it disgorged a series of white paper sheets. Outside, the first flakes of a fresh snowfall fell like gossamer on land and sea. A radar dish tilted in the darkness. A screen inside showed something huge crawling inland across the Laptev Sea. Not a blizzard, not a hurricane. Something worse.

49

Riders approached, bearing torches. The flames burned in the soli-
tude with the intensity of knives. Stul'nev recognized the uniforms
straight away. Yenisey Cossack, he thought, noting the tall fur
hats, the coats, and the long *shasqua* sabres across their saddles.
It was as if the mysterious horsemen had emerged from the past,
dressed as they were in clothes that had been last worn under Tsar
Nicholas II. Mist drifted upwards from the horses' nostrils and was
lost in moments. The clinking of bridles and the stamping of hooves
comforted the silence.

One rider came forward and stopped in front of Tolbuzin. The
Colonel lifted the torch he had been holding. Behind him, the
fires they had just lit picked him and his companions out from
the night.

'*Mjinja zavut* Sapozhnik,' said the horseman. Though the torchlight
played around him, his features remained obscure. One hand held
his horse's reins, the other a long *nagayka*, the traditional Cossack
whip, weighted with lead. The voice was confident, marked by a
certain coolness and correctness in the intonation. 'Count Rostislav
Sapozhnik. I am the commanding officer of the first Yenisey Cossack
Brigade, currently chief of the Pugachev Regiment, of which this is
the sixth *sotnya*.'

A *sotnya*, Tolbuzin thought. That meant Sapozhnik was leading
one hundred men. The Colonel stepped up to him and lifted his hand
to take the horse's bridle.

'I am Colonel Gennady Tolbuzin, formerly head of the Taymyrskiy

Okrug FSB, currently the officer responsible for a federal mission in this region.'

Sapozhnik stood in his stirrups, then sat back down. His horse ducked its head, blew out hard through its nostrils, and settled, pawing the ice with its front left hoof.

'In that case, Colonel,' the Count said, 'I regret I must inform you that, as you are no longer in a region under Federal control, you and your men are under arrest. Assuming, that is, that you still owe allegiance to the Russian Federation.'

Tolbuzin noticed Sapozhnik's use of literary speech. The Count had evidently adopted a curious manner of speaking, using a formal vocabulary and diction that he'd probably picked up from a grandfather or grandmother old enough to remember the days when an aristocrat spoke better Russian than anyone else. Or so it must have seemed.

'I'm sorry, Mr Sapozhnik' – Tolbuzin was an old Communist, and if not now a believer in his lost faith, he still could not bring himself to address another man by a title he had done nothing to deserve – 'but things are not that simple. The mission I am on poses no threat whatsoever to you or your men. Go on with your rebellion, if it suits you. Kill whomever you like. I won't try to stop you or inform on you. But my mission is one of the utmost importance. To Russia and to the Russian people.

'If you attempt in any way to interfere, neither you nor your men will leave here alive. That's not an idle threat. If you could see into the shadows behind me, you'd see that two of my men are aiming machine guns straight at your detachment.'

On either side of the Kamaz, Shalamov and Stul'nev had set up their guns. They were general-purpose machine guns, Kalashnikov PKBs set on Stepanov mounts, and either one could have wiped out Sapozhnik's force.

'That's a pretty *shasqua* round your waist,' Tolbuzin went on, 'but it won't prove a match for machine-gun bullets.'

The Count shifted in his saddle. Snow had started to fall, driven by the bitter wind.

'Colonel, I think you are under a misapprehension. Don't be misled by our old-fashioned uniforms and our horses. We are all trained soldiers. This particular *sotnya* is made up of veterans, men who have seen service in Afghanistan and Chechneya. They have gone up against machine guns many times. Don't be over-confident. Our sabres are for decoration. Our real weapons are bullets and grenades, and my men are heavily armed. Now, please make things easy on yourself and your unit.'

Tolbuzin shook his head. He would not let himself be suborned so easily, and by a man calling himself Count.

'Our allegiance is to the Duma and the legitimately elected government of Russia. Perhaps you have lost faith with them. That doesn't concern me. What matters to me is that my mission is one of life and death.'

'All missions in Russia these days involve life or death. Why is yours different? My own mission is life and death to Russia herself. We are spinning a web, Colonel. A web of monarchists and nationalists, large enough to encircle the entire Federation. Grand Duke Georgiy has been proclaimed Tsar in Kostroma, at the Ipatyevskiy Monastery, and will be crowned there in ten days' time. My men and I have been sent to the Sakha Republic in order to secure it for the crown.'

Tolbuzin was not surprised. The first city to secede from the Federation had been Kiev, where a combination of monarchists, right-wing nationalists, Orthodox clergy, and assorted militants of all persuasions had stormed the city hall, arrested local councillors, and taken over the assembly. They had ordered immediate action against the local Mafia, arresting and then executing dozens of local gang bosses, and rounding up every drug dealer, pimp, and *fartsovchik* on or off the street.

Tolbuzin remembered that Grand Duke Georgiy Mikhailovich had for some years now been recognized as a threat. His mother was the Grand Duchess Maria Vladimirovna Romanova, a formidable woman who had celebrated her fiftieth birthday a year or two ago by promoting her eldest son as the legitimate heir to the Romanov throne.

Boris Yeltsin had signed a decree reinstating the family, but had pulled back from implementing it at the last minute. Georgiy's grandfather Vladimir had been a cousin of the martyred Tsar

Nicholas. Now in his early twenties, the boy had just graduated from Moscow's Suvorovsky military academy, and it looked as though his moment had come. How long it might last would depend, as much as anything, on what happened in the next few minutes, here in the depths of the *taiga*.

'And President Garanin?'

The Count shrugged. All the time, he was keeping a close eye on the two men shivering behind the machine guns.

'I can't be sure. He can't be allowed to remain, that's certain. Russia will not stay a republic much longer. We are living in a historic moment, when the holy kingdom is restored. The moment Grand Duke Georgiy mounts the throne, there will be no further need for a president or a *duma*.'

Tolbuzin took several steps back towards the Kamaz. The snow was falling heavily now, blown straight into the Count's face. But he stood his ground, awaiting some sort of outcome.

'For the second time, Comrade Sapozhnik' – Tolbuzin chose the old Communist title and shouted, raising his voice to make it heard above the wind – 'I'm warning you. My men will open fire the moment I give the order. I'm entitled to do that, because you are all in open rebellion against what is still the lawfully constituted government of this country; but I would prefer not to. All you have to do is proceed on your way downriver, and let us get on with our business.'

Count Sapozhnik, visibly stung by Tolbuzin's mode of address, was about to answer when a horse cantered up to him, and one of his officers leaned over to shout in his ear.

'Sir, we have to do something to get the men and horses under cover. Captain Kaltakhchan says this blizzard is likely to turn into a hurricane within the next half hour. It could kill us and the horses if we don't get under wraps in time. Kaltakhchan thinks the tents will be enough if we get well inside the trees.'

Without taking his eyes off Tolbuzin, Sapozhnik nodded.

'Go ahead, Luganskiy. Unload the ahkios and get as many ten-man tents erected as possible. If you come across a clearing big enough to allow you to join some tents together, do so, but don't waste time searching. For God's sake, make sure the snow-cloths are attached to the side walls, and use anything you can find to pin them down. While you're at it, ask Father Maxim to step this way.'

'Sir, one of the ahkio sleds has gone missing.'

'How the hell did that happen?'

'I'm not sure, sir. I think the leading rope broke and the pony got lost in the dark. These aren't the best conditions.'

Without warning, Sapozhnik's whip lifted and snapped across Luganskiy's face, the lead weights cutting deep into his cheek.

'Never make an excuse like that again. It is precisely when conditions are bad that extra care should be taken. You of all my officers should know that.'

'I'm sorry, sir, I . . .'

'Don't whine. See to the tents, and when you're done take yourself off to the MO and have that stitched up.'

Without apology, he turned back to Tolbuzin.

'Your business, Colonel, is now my business. I want a full explanation of who is in your company, what you are doing travelling through this region, and under whose orders you are acting. Since the storm is about to worsen, I regret that you and your men will have to be chained and guarded. Your truck will be the best place for that. When the storm finishes, we will talk. If I were you, I'd think hard about what you have to tell me.'

'Stul'nev, Shalamov – shoot him if he comes any closer.'

In the background, they could hear the jingling of spurs and bridles as the horsemen hurried to pitch their tents.

A rider approached Sapozhnik from the rear. There was less light now that most of the Cossacks had gone, but Tolbuzin could see the tall hat and beard of an Orthodox priest bobbing back and forwards as he came towards him on a fat pony. He halted side by side with the Count, and the two men began to speak together in loud whispers, their speech hidden beneath the howling of the wind. Eventually, the priest nodded and, pulling harder than was strictly necessary on the reins, turned his mount and trotted back the way he had come.

As he vanished from sight, a voice rang out from behind Tolbuzin.

'Your Excellency! I would like to join you. My name is Ivan Valentinovich Stul'nev, and I belong to the Don Horde.'

A silence filled with the wind and the voices of men as though a long way off.

'Step forward, boy. Let me look at you.'

Stul'nev came out of the shadows. He was cradling the machine gun in both arms.

'Where did you say, boy? Where are you from?'

'Cherkessk.'

'And you say your father is Valentin Stul'nev?'

'Yes. The son of Konstantin.'

'And your mother's name?'

'Vera Nikitichna.'

A longer silence. Horses neighed. From the forest, a wolf howled in anticipation of the storm.

'I have read your father's articles. He is a great man. I trust he is well.'

'When I last had news, sir.'

'I am pleased to hear it. And your brother Yuri?'

'I have no brothers, sir. Only one sister.'

'Why, of course, that's perfectly true. I'm pleased to find you here, Ivan Valentinovich. We must talk about this further. For the moment, you have my permission to join my troop. One of my aides will find a tent for you, and tomorrow a horse.'

Stul'nev started towards the Count.

'Stul'nev!' came a stern voice. 'You did not ask my permission to go, and I did not give it. You are still a soldier in Russian uniform, and I am still your commanding officer. If you join this troop, it will be an act of desertion, and I will treat it as such.'

'I've no quarrel with you, Colonel. I believe the Count when he says we are no longer on Federal territory, and I believe I have the right to choose to serve my country and my king.'

'Don't flatter yourself, Stul'nev. You know what brings you here. You're in possession of state secrets, there's no way you can be allowed to defect with them.'

'They'll find out anyway, Colonel. Don't you see when you're outnumbered? If you try to fight back, they'll cut us down. God knows what will happen then.'

What happened next could scarcely have been avoided. Tolbuzin's

344

hand went to his hip and came back up holding something small and shiny – a snub-nosed Makarov pistol. He held it at arm's length and fired two quick shots, *tap-tap,* into the base of Stul'nev's skull. The young recruit jerked once and fell forwards between the hooves of Sapozhnik's horse. No-one moved. Slowly, Tolbuzin's hand was lowered, but he did not return the pistol to its holster.

No-one could have warned Tolbuzin. He had never been around horses or Cossacks very much, could not possibly have anticipated Sapozhnik's response. One moment, the Count was deadly still. The next, he had unsheathed his sabre, and suddenly he urged his horse forward almost onto Tolbuzin. The Colonel tried to raise his weapon again, but he never made it. The sabre was lifted high and brought down on Tolbuzin's skull with such strength that the blow split him in half, from scalp to crotch.

At that same instant, another shot rang out, the bullet taking Shalamov in the back of the head and sending him to slump across his GPMG.

Varvara, who had seen some of what was coming, had managed to slink away into the shadows and under the Kamaz, where she was lying when Sapozhnik killed Tolbuzin. It was her plan to stay there as long as she could bear the cold, then creep aboard the truck, either into the cabin or the rear. She'd just crawled behind one of the truck's giant wheels and was settling down, her Grach pistol in one hand, when a man's voice whispered near her.

'The game's over. Hand me your weapon, and you won't be harmed. I promise.'

She'd thought she had the strength for a fight, but after so many days of cold, discomfort, and sleeplessness, she was in no mood to throw her life away. She tossed the gun towards the voice, then started to crawl back into the open, howling night.

50

Moscow

The words used by Vronskiy – 'Be here in one hour. I'll be waiting for you' – had been part of a pre-arranged code. As far as Jim was concerned, Vronskiy (which was not, of course, his real name) had no address and would never be at this telephone number again.

'Here' meant a stall selling bootleg CDs in the Vernisazh weekend market at Izmailovskiy Park, out towards the northeastern edge of the city. Jim left Holly at Sheremetevo to make her way to their hotel by taxi, while he picked up a hire car that had been reserved from Hertz. The girl at the desk spoke excellent English, and showed him how to find his way to the Pushkin Institute in Belyaevo-Bogorodskoye, south of the city, while keeping as far as possible on the MKAD highway. While she traced a path through Moscow for him, Jim flirted with her, and before leaving, he made an unmistakeable pass at her. She gave him the brushoff; but if anybody came looking for him later, she'd remember, and she'd swear that Professor Bryson had headed for the Institute, anxious to be at his conference.

He drove as far as Planernaya metro, where he dumped the car in a side street, and started on a journey through the complexities of the Moscow underground system. Nine stops got him to a transfer onto the circle line. Six stations later, and he was heading back out of the city in the direction of Schelkovsksaya.

He got out with about one hundred other people at Izmailovskiy

346

Park into weak sunshine. Some of his fellow-commuters were tourists, American and Australian kids mostly, who'd escaped for the day from the dim, over-heated rooms of their backpack hostels and come out here to be curious and cool, and to be ripped off by some of the world's sharpest street traders.

Semi-legal booths clustered like unkempt children around the entrance to the Metro, straggling up along the street that led to the park entrance. Izmailovskiy Park was one of the stadiums that had been built for the boycotted 1980 Olympics. It was surrounded on all sides by the concrete stalks of sports hotels that had never seen any serious business or put up drunken athletes staggering home from a victory against the rest of the world. Whatever promise the Izmailovskiy stadium and its children had once held was long gone.

He followed the crowds past the Izmailovskiy Tourist Complex and down to the park gates, where a gnarled old woman with a face like frozen dough was selling entrance tickets for five thousand roubles apiece. Jim paid her and went inside. He was already feeling bewildered by the noise and bustle, and reckoned this wasn't going to be as easy as it had sounded back in Monongahela.

The stalls sold everything a human being could possibly need: matrioshka dolls painted in lurid colours, old Soviet medals and uniforms, books in about a million languages, reproduction icons passing for holy relics, cameras, radios, *papirosa* cigarettes and something like toasted pot pourri that no doubt passed as tobacco to go into them. The same stall sold fake American cigarettes, with names like Kennedy, Clinton, and even Johnson. Jim looked in vain for some Nixons or Tricky Dickys, and was disappointed to see the great man passed over.

He found the right stall after several dry runs and the purchase of a black fur hat that was definitely not sable. A Russian flag crossed the stars and stripes on a varnished board nailed to two posts. A quick glance told Jim that the stall sold the same hundred or so CDs that all the other music stalls had for sale. The stallholder was a girl of eighteen or nineteen, shabbily dressed, but startlingly lovely. He'd noticed it on the metro, that, whatever had happened to Russia, and whatever horrors still threatened to engulf it, the women were the most beautiful in the world, and could look good in clothes a wino would have turned up his nose at. And he thought of Holly and her lonely taxi journey, of the dangers that hung about her and which he could do nothing to avert.

'Have you got a copy of Bob Dylan's *Desire*?' he asked.

The girl looked him up and down, not sure whether to laugh or nod seriously.

'Is that the one with "Sad-Eyed Lady of the Lowlands"?'

He shook his head.

'This is the one with "One More Cup of Coffee" and "Romance in Durango".'

'Just a moment. I think I may have one here.'

She bent down and scrabbled for a few moments underneath the table that made up most of the stall, then came up clutching a CD jewel-case.

'Here,' she said. 'That's fifteen thousand roubles.'

He took the case and peeled off a small wad of banknotes. It looked like a fortune, but it amounted to no more than three dollars. The CD, if there had been one inside the box, would have been pirated.

'Thank you,' he said. As he turned to go, he looked back at her.

'What's your name?' he asked.

'Anna,' she said, looking straight at him. Another strand in an elaborate joke? he wondered. He smiled and left, wishing he'd had the courage to offer her the money for a really good dress.

The map that took the place of the CD was neatly drawn, and he had no trouble tracing his way past the flea market to the quieter environs of the neighbouring food market. There were no tourists here. People looked at him suspiciously as he walked by, some noticing his use of the map. Under present circumstances, strangers were not welcome.

The shop could not have been more ordinary. It was a *bulochnaya*, one of the little bakeries you find every block or so in Moscow. The name above the door read Bulochnaya/Konditerskaya Karenina, and the smell that hit Jim in the face as he prepared to go in was like nothing he'd known. In the window were two or three shelves packed with the latest delivery: round white and dark loaves

348

labelled *belviy krugliy* and *cherbiy krugliy*, some *bulochki*, and enough submarine-shaped *batons* to feed an apartment building.

The woman serving took one look at him and shouted to someone in the back. A man's voice shouted in reply, then the curtain that separated the two parts of the tiny shop parted to reveal Vronskiy. He jerked his head at the woman, and she disappeared into the back room.

The man who called himself Vronskiy could have stepped from the Russian Middle Ages. He looked like a wild-haired Ivan the Terrible, unbalanced by the death of Anastasia and about to institute his reign of terror. His grey shoulder-length hair was infiltrated by strands of white, and a little beard grown wholly the colour of steel circled a thin-lipped mouth. Jim guessed him to be somewhere between forty and a million years old. He was as thin as a Chalayan model, and his clothes were almost as strange.

'It's all right,' the grey-haired man said, 'she only speaks Russian. With me, however, you may speak little English. Do you have map?'

Jim handed him the jewel-case with its poor-quality reproduction of a photograph showing Bob Dylan in a grey felt hat and a heavy fur-collared coat, looking a lot as though he'd just been snapped in the streets outside.

'I return later,' smiled Vronskiy, reaching into his pocket and pulling out a wad of grubby rouble notes. He counted out fifteen thousand and made to hand it to Jim.

'Keep it.'

Jim opened the travel wallet fastened round his waist and retrieved one hundred dollars. He passed them to Vronskiy.

'Give these to your daughter,' he said. 'Tell her it's for a new dress.'

'Not my daughter,' the man said, and when Jim looked carefully, he saw no resemblance.

'Nevertheless.'

'She's my lover. Do you find objectionable?'

'Only if it's against her will.'

'Why you think that? Perhaps it against mine.'

'She's very beautiful.'

'You are right. That is why men have no will when they looks at her. No thought. Just wants to sleeps with her.'

'I just want to buy her a dress, something pretty for her to wear.'

'You American. Don't worry, old boy, I give money to her.'

He pocketed the hundred dollars and kept the pile of roubles to himself. One hundred dollars would buy a lot of Russian currency, and part of a good dress in one of the new designer shops on the Arbat. But Jim knew that more than that would have been a marriage proposal.

'Time to go,' Vronskiy said.

He led the way outside, ducking round an elderly woman in a headscarf come to buy bread for her family's evening meal. The street outside was half deserted. Jim followed his new companion down one street and along another until he was completely lost. He realized the enormity of the risk he was taking. All that prevented him from being mugged or killed was Mygate's skill in making a deal that released very little money to his Moscow contacts until the goods had been secured. Without so much as a knife on him, he was in no position to defend himself should something go wrong, or should they be attacked by a rival gang of *razboiniki*.

Vronskiy, he knew, was a middleman, a broker who took the heat off both sides in any negotiation. His reputation depended on successful deals and satisfied customers. For that reason alone, Jim knew he could trust him. Up to a point, anyway.

They arrived at a narrow alley lined on either side by Communist-era warehouses built with poor-quality concrete out of Karaganda and badly-forged steel from Tula. There were cracks everywhere, down walls, across roofs, on almost every window. It was hard to believe that sheds like these were still used to house valuable goods.

'Not much security round here,' Jim said, sweeping a hand round the warehouses.

'You think not?'

'I can see not. Those open windows, for example – anyone could crawl in through them. And look at that door – that little padlock would snap in two if I took a wire cutter to it. There's no sign of alarms.'

Vronskiy nodded, then turned to Jim and shook his head sorrowfully.

'Mister No-Name American, you make me want I laugh or maybe I throw up. Be my guest, you open any door you like, take anything you want, go back to hotel. Some time in morning, there will be knock on door. Won't be room service. They kill you very slow, what they call *zamochit*, to piss on you. If you have woman, they kill her too. It is what they call *posadit' na piku*, I think in English it mean put someone on a speek.'

'Spike.'

'OK. Except they use knife. If you Russian, they kill mother, father, brothers, sisters, children. So everybody know nobody touch them. Believe me, all this much cheaper than pay for alarm, lights, big dog.'

It passed through Jim's head that the people who owned the warehouse they were heading for could be the same ones who had carried out the kidnapping. Had Mygate checked on that possibility? he wondered.

They came to a red door that had last seen paint sometime around the time when the colour had real meaning in Moscow. A more recent splash of paint announced that this was the home of Sevastopolskaya-Art: *Neon-Vi'veski: Izgotovleniye, Montazh, Registratsiya.*

Jim looked at his companion.

'Neon signs?'

Vronskiy nodded.

'Until is three years. Now is no more.'

He deployed a large brass key to open the padlock which held a small door in place. Stepping inside, he fumbled on the wall and found a light switch. All over the walls, in strict order, an array of neon signs lit up, their bright colours transforming the dingy interior of this little backwater lockup into a place of rainbows and northern lights. The ambitions of Sevastopolskaya-Art were illuminated and displayed high up for all to see: a giant Coca-Cola bottle inscribed *Koka-Kola*, a red-and-white shopfront sign carrying the ubiquitous arched 'M' of McDonald's, the torso of a half-naked woman with the words 'Kosmos Nightklub' flickering frantically above her head, a roulette wheel whose numbers spun round and round in a never-ending paean to chance, and a big red taxicab that was constantly on the move to nowhere.

'Good thing I'm not given to migraines,' murmured Jim.

'Migraines?'

'Bad headaches. You ever get one of those? As if one of these things went off in your head?'

Vronskiy looked at him as if to say he had just proved the hypothesis that all Americans are crazy. Reaching into his pocket, he drew out a packet of cigarettes. Opening it, he held it out to Jim. Jim took it and looked at it out of curiosity. It was yet another indication of the growing vogue for monarchy among ordinary Russians. The pack was black with a gold double-headed eagle, and the brand name was Pyotr I, the name of Tsar Peter the Great.

'Good,' said Vronskiy. He smiled and mimed the act of smoking, an expression of feigned ecstasy on his lips.

'No, thanks. I don't smoke.' Jim handed the packet back.

Misunderstanding, Vronskiy frowned.

'Need hash? You wait, later I find. Best hash, from Afghanistan.'

'No, I don't smoke anything. *Niet sigareta, niet anasha.*'

Again that look suggesting insanity on Jim's part.

'*Vi' nekuryashchiy?*'

Jim looked at him blankly and shrugged.

'He wants to know if you are a non-smoker.'

Jim spun round. The voice had come from behind him. He noticed that a door had opened in the wall of a little office at the rear. Someone stepped out into the light show. Jim sensed Vronskiy grow stiff alongside him. There was a constant buzzing from the lights. Here and there, a letter or part of an image had expired, or was flickering on the point of extinction. A man started walking towards them. When he was about ten feet away, he stopped. His skin looked red in the neon light, his eyes were invisible behind dark glasses, and he wore a dark suit that hadn't been tailored here in Moscow, or anywhere in the Russian Federation.

'*Da,*' he said to Vronskiy. '*On nekuryashchiy.*'

The middleman nodded sagely, confirmed in his assumptions about the state of Jim's mind. He drew a cigarette from the pack and placed it between his lips. The instant it appeared there, the other man snapped at him.

'*Zdes' nel'zya kurit'.*'

Vronskiy spat out the cigarette and returned the pack to his pocket. Jim noticed that his hand, quite calm before, had started shaking like a rubber toy.

'You must be Professor Bryson.'

Jim nodded.

'Welcome to Russia. This will not take long.'

'Not if you have what I need.'

The nameless newcomer straightened his tie. Jim noticed he was running a small chain of worry beads through the fingers of his right hand.

'I have everything you need. Once I have confirmation that half of my payment has arrived, you may bring your transportation and take it away. It's up to you.'

Jim prayed that Mygate had done his bit.

He watched as the dealer took a mobile phone from his pocket and keyed in a long number. Someone at the other end picked up right away.

'*Todor? . . . Da . . . Parite mi pristignakha li veche?*'

Jim felt uneasy. The language was Slavic, but not Russian. He could not follow a word of it.

'*Kolko vreme zak'snenie ima vlakat? . . . Da . . . Da . . . Bankov prevodzapis? Da, razbira se . . . Dnes. Sledobed.*'

The dealer hung up. Jim noticed a fine scar that ran down his face from forehead to chin. In a different light, it would have been invisible.

'There's been a delay. Your boss back home wants to speak with you, wants to know his baby is safe.'

He handed the phone to Jim, told him the code, and stepped back.

A chattering across continents, then someone picked up the phone. Jim had to be careful. However secure the line at Monongahela, this call was passing through a satellite to be picked up by ECHELON. At the moment, he thought, any telecommunications material originating in Russia was going to be raided, scanned, decoded, analysed, and baked in a hot oven by every spook agency with the means to do it – which, basically, meant the United States.

'Hi, this is Joey Caldarrosta. Who am I speakin' to?'

The mock Italian accent and the choice of name ('roast chestnut') had been two of several options, each saying something different. Tartufo ('truffle') would have meant 'Hang up right away and don't call back'; Joey Sottaceti ('Joey Pickle') would have warned Jim that he was in danger; and so on. Caldarrosta was good. Caldarrosta meant things were fine at Mygate's end. It also meant that any agency listening would start off on a hunt for a non-existent Mafia boss of that name.

'Hi, Joey,' said Jim. 'This is Johnny Cetriolo. Long time no see.'

Cetriolo ('cucumber') meant 'I'm cool, but I'm having problems'.

'What can I do for you, Johnny?' Mygate almost forgot his accent in his pleasure at hearing Jim's voice.

'My friend here says there's been a delay in your getting to him . . . what you promised.'

'Sure, there's been a delay. What does he expect? Has he shown you the merchandise yet?'

'Not yet.'

'OK,' said Mygate. 'Let me speak to him. And, Johnny – watch out for this fucker. He's a Bulgarian, belongs to a bunch of real hard guys from around Varna. Pretend you think he's Russian, and do nothing to get on his bad side. He has muscle, and he'll cut your throat as soon as dance on his mother's grave. Hand me over.'

Mygate and the Bulgarian talked briefly. Without closing the line, the man from Varna gestured Jim forward to a spot near the rear of the warehouse.

'Your boss wants to know if his merchandise is here and ready to collect. This is it. Take your time.'

Jim looked round. There were boxes everywhere. The Bulgarian tossed him a crowbar and gestured with open hands. Jim picked out a box at random, stuck the crowbar in at one end, and levered the lid off.

Tearing the packing material away, Jim uncovered six smaller wooden boxes, each containing a Heckler & Koch P9S automatic pistol.

'Here.' The Bulgarian broke open a second box to reveal row upon shining row of 9mm ammunition. Jim squeezed a few rounds into the gun's magazine and fired them at a target someone had nailed to the wall. The gun worked beautifully, and the shots landed where he might have expected them to land.

He found M16 assault rifles and M203 grenade launchers to fit under their barrels, MP5 compact machine guns that could use up eight hundred 9mm rounds in a minute, M60 machine guns, grenades, several Lockheed-manufactured Javelin anti-tank weapons fitted with infrared focal plane array seeker technology, a French-built Milan post and missiles, radio sets, compasses, GPS navigation sets, night-vision sights, heavy-duty binoculars, boxes of canned food, and a large box of toilet paper.

It was all top-quality Western equipment, the best a lot of money could buy.

Jim nodded.

'It looks OK. Actually, it's very good.' He didn't dream of asking where the Bulgarian had found this stuff, or how he'd got it all here.

The dealer handed him the phone, and thirty seconds later Mygate was ready to release half the money. Five minutes after that, a call from Switzerland confirmed that it had arrived in the bank.

Jim asked to use the phone again. This time, he rang Holly's hotel. Yes, the lady in question was in her room.

'Holly, I want everybody out here ready to go. I'd like us loaded and out of Moscow by midnight. I'll tell you how to find this place.'

The Bulgarian took the phone from him when he'd finished.

'Your people, they are coming soon?'

Jim nodded.

'A few are still on their way to Moscow. But they'll be here.'

'Professor . . . I think I should tell you that you are not the only mercenaries in Russia.'

Jim felt a prickling down his spine.

'You've dealt with others? Other Americans?'

The Bulgarian shrugged. Maybe he was telling the truth, maybe he was winding Jim up. Who could tell for sure?

'I haven't dealt with them. But a friend of mine, yes. He has provided them with some items of equipment.'

'Here in Moscow?'

355

He shook his head.

'Not here. Not in Moscow.'

'These were Americans?'

'I think so, yes.'

'What else do you know? Do you know how many?'

'Twenty. I think they are twenty. The man in charge of them – what is it worth to know his name?'

Jim's first impulse was to choke the name out of him, but he realized it would put paid to everything.

'Dollars?'

'Of course.'

'How much?'

'I can also tell you where they have gone.'

'How much?'

'One hundred thousand. Dollars.'

'That's a lot of money for a name and a place.'

'Not if it's important to you.'

'All right. I can authorize that much. You have my word. One hundred thousand. Dollars.'

A huge smile spread across the Bulgarian's face. Behind him, a Slavic Father Christmas downed a flagon of beer.

'Jurgensen,' he said. 'The leader's name is Jurgensen.'

A deep chill settled in Jim's heart. Jurgensen meant trouble. Jurgensen meant death. They had been sent to kill the President. Jim knew it as surely as if it had been written on the wall in flashing neon letters.

'You said you knew where he is.'

The Bulgarian took a small silver box from his pocket and opened it. White powder lay inside like snowdust. He took a tiny silver spoon and scooped a little up and snorted it, first in the right nostril, then in the left.

'They landed at an air base just outside Dudinka, beside the Yenisey River. This is in Western Siberia. Have you heard of it?'

Jim did not answer. All he knew was that they had come too late. By the time they found Waterstone and his wife, they would be dead. And Tina too. Jurgensen would spare no-one. Not Waterstone, not his wife, not Tina.

51

They got the Kamaz off the ice and into a little clearing created by felling half a dozen trees. Within minutes, the gusts were topping seventy miles an hour and rising. One by one, the torches were snuffed out, and darkness took hold of the forest and the river. By then, something had started happening to the snow.

Before getting the Kamaz moved, Count Sapozhnik had inspected the interior himself. What he found he took at face value. Two women and a man, all chained, and a child who appeared to be quite ill, lying on a makeshift bed in one corner. Tolbuzin and his party must have been transporting rebel prisoners to . . . But his mind froze, unable to think of anywhere in this white wilderness they might want to take them. He decided to leave the matter of their identity until the storm had blown itself out. In the meantime, he made the woman called Varvara hand over the key, and had the prisoners freed.

'Will you let some of my men stay here in the lorry with you?' he asked, and the younger woman answered, nodding, and saying they were welcome.

'As long as they don't interfere with my patient,' she said.

'You are a doctor?' The Count looked at her more narrowly than before, with more than passing interest.

'Yes. I'm a doctor, and I forbid you to move her or disturb her.'

'That goes without saying. You aren't dealing with barbarians any longer. Speaking of which, I want to put the woman called Varvara in here with you. Don't worry, we'll make sure she's firmly chained. I'll speak with you later.'

Just as he made to go through the door, he turned back to Yulia.

'What is your name, Doctor?'

'Yulia. Yulia Zaslavskaya. I graduated from medical college a few months ago.'

'Which university?'

'Chelyabinsk State Medical Academy.'

'A good school. My son studied there.'

'Sapozhnik? Piotr? I know him. He was in the year ahead of me.'

'I'm glad to hear it. We must talk about this later. Now, see to your patient.'

The moment the Count stepped out of the truck, he was sent reeling by the force of the wind, which had almost reached ninety miles an hour. To make things worse, the snow had turned to freezing sleet that slashed everything in sight, tearing branches from the trees and raking the side of the Kamaz as if with a metal brush. And the snow had not stopped changing.

One by one, Sapozhnik's officers made their way to the Kamaz and threw themselves inside, bruised and breathless after a short walk from the forest. Outside, the enlisted men hung on inside their tents for dear life. Torches were lit and hung from the central pole in each tent. From inside, the men could see the canvas pitch and warp and buckle, lifting at times so violently upwards that it was all anyone could do to prevent it flying off with them in it. Any heavy equipment had been placed along the walls in an attempt to add ballast. The men clung to the tents, and to one another, while the wind grew in strength and dragged and pulled at them like a giant boy playing with fighting mice.

As far as possible, the horses had been gathered into one place and hobbled, then made to lie down, screaming with fear as the wind and sleet thrashed them to the edge of their endurance. The horse-handler tied himself to them by means of ropes passed through their saddles, and as he lay there, he called to them, trying to soothe them, but his voice was snatched hard by the wind, and the cries of the horses went with it.

They had managed to get the Kamaz wedged against two trees, where it would be safe unless the trees themselves were uprooted. The Count was the last to enter, gasping for breath and shivering.

'It's turning to hailstones outside,' he said, and they could see tiny blobs of ice clinging to his skin and clothing.

Someone had managed to get the little paraffin stove working again, and this time a close eye was kept on it lest a heavy gust set the truck rocking and upset the whole thing, setting them all alight. A gradual warmth was stealing through the interior of the lorry, and everything might have been cosy but for the inescapable sound of the wind, howling and battering and growing louder every moment.

Things were a lot less cosy outside, where men and horses were struggling to stay alive. The hailstones were scarcely hailstones any longer, but increasingly large lumps of ice that had been whipped off the frozen surface of the Arctic Ocean and hurled across hundreds of miles by the growing force of a hurricane now moving at over one hundred miles an hour and still accumulating speed.

Just how bad things were – and an indication of how much worse they were going to get – came when a jagged sphere of wind-thrown ice ripped its way through one of the tents and struck Private Sergei Sterligov in the back of the head, smashing a hole in his skull and mashing his brains to a blood-soaked porridge. The whole tent hurried to get their heads as low down as possible, and in surrounding tents the message got through quickly.

Inside the Kamaz, people tried to erect barricades against the wind and the missiles it had started hurling through the canvas. They used what they could – pieces of equipment, some of the truck flooring, the backboard.

But the wind had not finished with them. It had started to come in gusts now, mammoth gusts of one hundred and sixty miles an hour that snapped trees in half and sent them hurtling like lances through the air. One of the horses, driven mad by the roaring and cackling of the wind, struggled to get to its feet, only to be caught by the hurricane and spun up towards the treetops, where it was driven forwards screaming through the darkness. It met its end finally when the wind deposited it on some low branches, where it rested momentarily before plunging twenty feet or more to the ground, breaking its neck on impact.

Inside the Kamaz, Sapozhnik's adjutant, Captain Yuri Moiseyev, had bent himself across Tina so that his body would protect her in the event an ice-stone should come flying in her direction. He held her hand, and smiled as best he could in the dim light, then leaned down and whispered in her ear.

'*Tebe nechego budet boyat'sya. T'I dolzhna budes'.*'

Yulia pushed her way across.

'It's no use,' she shouted. 'She can't understand you.'

'What's wrong with her?'

'There's nothing wrong, but . . . She isn't Russian. She can't understand a word you say.'

He looked at the doctor, puzzled.

'She doesn't look like any of the nationalities. Unless maybe Jewish. And her parents, they look Jewish.'

'Yes, but not Russian Jews.'

'What then? Lithuanian? Serbian?'

'None of those. She's not . . . She's American.'

The adjutant's eyes lit up with curiosity.

'And her parents?'

Yulia judged it best to pretend that Tina was the Waterstones' daughter.

'American. Just tourists caught up in this thing. In the killing.'

'Tourists? At this time of year?'

The Count, who had been crouching nearby, pulled himself across.

'They're not tourists,' he said.

'What else can they be?' asked Yulia. 'With a little girl. Not spies, surely. Business people, perhaps?'

Sapozhnik shook his head. The wind howled terribly outside. The truck shook as though stricken, tilted, then righted itself.

'I think you know, Doctor. I think you know very well who our distinguished guests are. In the morning, I shall speak to them. When the storm is over, we shall see. But the truth is very simple. God has sent them to me.'

*   *   *

360

The wind continued in its destructive path for over two hours, then sheared suddenly westwards, cutting a new swathe through the Taymyr Peninsula. Silence returned to the forest.

In Moscow, a single aircraft lifted into the night sky and headed east.

52

The Ilyushin banked steeply as it came down through thick cloud in the general direction of Noril'sk airport. For a moment, Jim thought he'd cracked. There was as much cloud underneath him as there was above. Then he realized that the storm clouds surging beneath him were nothing more than pollution belching upwards from the myriad brick and steel chimneys of the city. He reorientated himself. Beside him, Peter Vitebsky, his co-pilot and a fluent Russian speaker, was talking them down via the airport control tower.

'Noril'sk, we need a lower altitude.'

'Roger. Moscow Airways seven niner five is cleared to VOR DME approach Runway One.'

The Moscow Airways routine served as their cover, for what it was worth. There hadn't been an airline of that name for several years, but the Ilyushin IL-76 that Mygate had chartered for them still carried the little airline's distinctive markings, so they'd used that as the basis for their subterfuge. The Ilyushin had been discovered in a hangar on the northern edge of Vnukovo airport, to the southeast of Moscow.

To be precise, Mygate's Russian agent – a former Norwegian shipping agent whose Moscow-born wife had encouraged him to start up an airline business after the collapse of the Soviet Union – had secured them a rare stretched version of the aircraft, the IL-76-MF. In this model, the plane's four Soloviev D-30 engines had been replaced by more powerful Perm PS-90s, which had the strength to give them the speed and range that this stage of their mission required.

It was really a much larger plane than they needed, but it was still the only medium-sized Russian jet they could find that served military requirements and did not have to be stolen from a military air base. With high wings and strong landing gear, it could operate out of practically any airfield or landing strip, it had a rear loading ramp from which paratroops could jump, or supplies loaded or unloaded. The Russian military had used it and its prototype, the Soloviev-powered IL-76, for a variety of purposes.

Jim had had about a day in which to familiarize himself with the cockpit and controls, using diagrams and photographs downloaded by one of the Monongahela computers. Mygate had suggested hiring a civilian pilot who'd actually flown one of these machines, but Jim knew they could be flying into a war zone, with more to come if the President wasn't in or near Noril'sk.

Back in the rear of the plane, Holly had cleared an area for herself, and was working hard just to find a reference to Dudinka, Noril'sk, or anywhere else in the region they were flying over.

'Holly.' Jim's voice came to her through the headphones that had been fitted to provide a link between her and the cockpit. 'Is there anything we can use to pinpoint this better? I have to commit to landing in about four minutes.'

'Nothing. They just disappeared into a hole somewhere.'

'Keep trying.'

Vitebsky renewed contact with ground control.

'Noril'sk, MA seven niner five, request descent.'

There was no answer.

'Noril'sk, MA seven niner five, do you read me?'

Still the silence. Beneath them a thick smog that did not move. They would have to make the landing practically blind.

'Noril'sk, MA seven niner five, please confirm VOR DME and runway.'

There was a burst of static, then a different voice came through.

'MA seven niner five, please hold descent and return to ten thousand feet. You do not have permission to land.'

'What's this about? We need to land now. Our fuel is low, and there's nowhere else for us to land that we can reach on this fuel level.'

'Just a moment, MA seven niner five.'

Vitebsky kept shouting into his microphone without raising anyone. Jim, meanwhile, had started to climb back towards ten thousand feet, working upwards in a spiral so they could remain positioned above Noril'sk field.

'MA seven niner five, this is Noril'sk tower. Your new destination is Kureyka Military Air Base, coordinates eighty-seven east, sixty-six thirty north. That's just a fraction south of the Arctic Circle.'

OK,' said Jim, struggling to keep his temper under control. 'We're just entering ten thousand feet. Where the fuck is Kureyka, anyway?'

Vitebsky was already studying a pilotage chart.

'It's about two twenty, thirty miles from here, sir.'

'Like hell it is. We can't do that. Tell them there's no way we can do that. I think we should just head back down, take our chances with the landing. Once we're down, there's nothing they can do.'

'Sir, I don't think it's going to be that simple.'

'Why the hell not?'

'If you'd care to take a look out to port, sir . . .'

Jim followed Vitebsky's finger. In the dark, just out of reach of their port wing, a jet aircraft was keeping pace with them. Wing and fuselage lights had been illuminated to enable other aircraft to pick it out of the darkness. A glance to starboard identified a second.

Jim wondered what the hell was going on. To stall for time, he flipped a switch on the console in front of him.

'Gentlemen,' he announced, 'we seem to have company up here. I'll do what I can to shake them, but I'm not holding out any guarantees. In the meantime, perhaps some of you might care to equip yourselves for a landing at a friendly Air Force base near you.'

He switched off again. Vitebsky turned.

'What are they? Can you see, sir?'

The younger man could fly a little and spoke his grandmother's Russian, but those were his only qualifications for being in the co-pilot seat.

'You bet.' Jim looked out again. 'That's a Sukhoi S-37 Berkut. A golden eagle, the latest Russian fighter, the most manoeuvrable

364

bastard in the world. The NATO code-name is Terminator. This is the first one I've seen in the flesh. No way we can outfly it. Look at those engines – D-30F6s with vectored thrust. You can take it into a spin, stall it, do what you like, and those babies will pull you out every time. And, believe me, whoever they've put in the cockpits will know how to fly.'

'Want me to try speaking to them?'

'It won't do any good, but why not give it a try? Spin them some sob story. Say we're all orphans travelling to see our parents' graves.'

As soon as he'd made the joke, he regretted it.

Reading the bort number on the nearest jet's fuselage, Vitebsky put out a call on all bands.

'S-37 Victor Alpha Charlie, please come in. This is MA seven niner five circling Noril'sk. Please come in, S-37 Victor Alpha Charlie.'

'This is S-37 Victor Alpha Charlie. You are instructed to follow me and my companion to Kureyka Air Base, at the coordinates you were given. Any attempt to deploy evasionary tactics will result in your aircraft being shot down. There will be no second warnings.'

Verbitsky interpreted for Jim.

'Looks like we don't have much choice.'

Slowly, Jim began to turn the Ilyushin.

Greg appeared in the doorway joining the cockpit to the cabin.

'What the fuck is going on?'

'Take it easy, Greg. We're in big trouble. Take the jump seat and let me explain.'

With a cruising speed of over five hundred miles an hour, the Ilyushin was within striking distance of Kureyka base in less than half an hour. Fuel was practically exhausted.

'Tell ground control we can't stay up here much longer.'

Vitebsky relayed the message. In the cabin behind him, the rescue unit was armed to the teeth and ready to go. Holly was battering her keyboard past exhaustion in an effort to find out who was in control at Kureyka.

'You may proceed to land. Advance to runway oh two in your own time.'

Jim brought her down slowly. No need to pop anyone's eardrums when they might need to hear orders. On either side, the golden eagles kept pace until they were almost on the ground. At the last moment, they powered themselves upwards, banking sharply to make their own approach.

The Ilyushin landed, bumping along a runway that had known better times. As they slowed, Jim could see lights up ahead, mounted on a little motorized cart. He began to taxi after them.

As he made his first turn down the unfamiliar runway, the door behind him opened and Holly stormed in.

'Jim! I've got something. Kureyka is still in government hands. There was an attempted mutiny yesterday afternoon, but it seems to have been put down brutally. The base is now back under control of the six hundred and eighty-seventh Air Defence Fighter Squadron.'

Jim shook his head.

'Then, why pick on us?'

Holly ran a hand through her hair. 'Rebel aircraft have already carried out sorties against government-controlled installations between here and Noril'sk. They must think this is a rebel troop transport.'

'Maybe.'

The follow-me cart stopped at the end of the taxiing lane, and Jim brought the Ilyushin to a halt. The moment he did so, floodlights snapped on, lighting up the plane and its surroundings as though they were in bright daylight. Jim glanced to starboard, but as quickly snatched his eyes away, dazzled by the lights. Opening them a few moments later, he looked through the port window. The light picked out a ring of armed soldiers. The camp guard detachment? Troops brought in from outside?

Jim switched off the engines, and, as they died, sounds of silence came in from outside. His next move was out of his hands, so he sat and waited. Someone would come.

He'd scarcely waited a minute when the radio crackled.

'Major Crawford. Welcome to Kureyka. I'm sorry we don't have better weather for you.'

Jim leaned forward. Just what the hell was going on? They knew his name, and whoever had just spoken was speaking English with an American accent. What was worse, he was sure he recognized the voice.

'Who the hell is this?' Jim demanded. 'And just what the extreme fuck is going on?'

'Nothing for you to worry yourself about, Major. Just you and your men get yourselves down the steps and over here where we can see you. Leave your weapons inside. Anyone carrying so much as a penknife will be shot. Do I make myself clear?'

Interference made it difficult to tell the identity of the speaker.

'And if we refuse?'

'Come on, Major, don't fuck about with me. You've got a responsibility to the men under your command, you've got a responsibility to yourself. What do you want? You want me to get Mygate, patch him through to you, so he can tell you it's over? Hell, I'll do that if that's what you want. But I reckon since you're an all-American hero, you'll obey orders and get your ass off that plane and onto the tarmac.'

'Who are you? You don't sound like a Russian to me. Being where I am, an American voice is kinda odd. I have a feeling I know you from somewhere.'

'I'm an old friend of yours, Major. Don't tell me you've forgotten Carl Jurgensen. I'm alive and I'm here on a mission on behalf of the US government.'

53

Anabar River

The hurricane ran out of strength two hours after it began. It had been intense, but, like all Arctic storms, it was restricted in size, and, in gaining so much power, had worn itself out. Not, however, before wreaking immense damage across a huge swathe of *taiga*. The silence that succeeded it was a silence of death, not resurrection. New life would come here in the spring, if at all.

Seventeen horses died, and six were badly wounded and had to be put down. The horse-master went among them with a flaming torch in one hand, a pistol in the other. Twenty-three riders succumbed to death in several forms, some quickly, some by slow degrees. They were left beside the horses in a mound that had frozen hard by the time the last body had been laid on it. There was no point in even trying to bury them, for the ground was frozen solid, and the permafrost was harder than steel.

Fourteen men were wounded, three seriously. Yulia Zaslavskaya went round the whole *sotnya*, inspecting broken heads and tying splints on broken legs, binding great gashes that had been staunched until now only by means of tourniquets. It fell to her to say who was fit to ride and who had to be squeezed into the truck.

Father Yefraim followed her, administering the last rites to the dying, providing what spiritual comfort he could to the wounded.

'They find it hard to accept death like this,' the priest said, in an attempt to win Yulia over.

'No-one accepts death easily.'

'That's where you're mistaken. A believing Christian can look death in the eye. A Jew or a Muslim or a Communist cannot. True faith gives the heart strength in times of grief.'

'Then why do you say your men find it hard to accept their deaths? Aren't you all Christians?'

She bent to clean a wound in a soldier's back, a long gash that threatened to turn septic if left.

'Of course, but we are also men. These are soldiers, and they have steeled themselves to accept wounding and death in the pursuit of their profession. Death at the hands of an enemy is what they have come to expect, and on a mission like this it seems very close. But a natural event! That seems more as if God Himself has turned against them, as if He has struck them down, perhaps as punishment for something they have done or left undone. It's more difficult to come to terms with that, to comprehend why God has singled this one out and spared the man sitting next to him.'

'Perhaps it's not God. If you insist on having a God, He's much too arbitrary, much too whimsical. I cope very well without Him, I contrive my own explanations for natural disasters and human hatreds.'

Father Yefraim grew agitated at her suggestion.

'But there has to be God; I can't look a dying man in the face and tell him there is no God. When your patients die, surely you don't deprive them of that last hope.'

'I do nothing to reinforce them in a false belief. Men can die without God as easily as with. But we're going to argue if we go on this way. I think we both have more important priorities.'

Work had already begun on getting the Kamaz back into working order. It had sustained some damage at the front, but when the unit's motor mechanic examined it, he found nothing wrong that could not wait until they reached a garage or blacksmith's shop.

When all had been done that could be done for the dead and wounded, when the last horse had been resaddled and soothed by its rider, and what remained of the tents stowed away, Sapozhnik instructed Father Yefraim to conduct a funeral service for the dead.

* * *

369

St Petersburg had fallen. The flag of Holy Russia flew once more from every public building, the two-headed eagle and triple crowns of the old Empire elevated above the masses to pronounce their subjection to a new Tsar and Emperor. The coat of arms of the dying Federation, with a red background and golden eagle, had been replaced by the old imperial arms, showing a black eagle against a golden shield. In the new flag's centre, St George had turned round, but his lance still pierced the writhing dragon at his horse's feet.

Everything had been meticulously planned beforehand: nowhere was immune. The Winter Palace, reclaimed for the personal use of the royal family, had already blocked its doors to tourists. On top of each façade, flags of the Tsar rustled in the sharp wind next to icons of the Virgin portrayed as Theotokos. On the roof of the Mariinsky Palace, on the triple pinnacles of the Admiralty, and on the ravelin of the Peter and Paul Fortress, banners bearing the Mandylion lay taut against a stiff Baltic breeze. On either side of each one of the city's four hundred bridges hung pennants on which there had been lithographed copies of the miraculous icon of Tsar (or, as he was now proclaimed, Saint) Nicholas II. The original was kept at the Church of All Saints at Krasnoye Selo, where it exuded ointment and an exquisite fragrance.

In St Isaac's Cathedral, Metropolitan Filaret, freshly arrived from Omsk, and splendidly dressed in newly-sanctified vestments, preached to a congregation that spilled out onto the streets. His words were relayed to the lesser cathedrals of the city, to the Spasanakrovi, the Spaso-Preobrazhenskiy, and Svjato-Troitskiy, where thousands more had gathered. Among the crowds, many believed the young Tsar Georgiy would arrive in St Petersburg at any moment.

Behind the Metropolitan stood a tall, beamed flagstaff on which hung the true Mandylion, the image of Christ blessed by the late Tsar and carried to Russian soldiers before they set off for the front in 1914. Throughout the congregation stood bearded men in white uniforms, the Soldiers of Nicholas, the miniature emblem of the Mandylion pinned to their breasts.

At exactly ten o'clock, Filaret began to read Stolypin's *akathist* to the Tsar, Saint, and Great Martyr Nicholas Emperor of All Russia, commencing with the first *kontakion*.

'*O passion bearer chosen from birth and incarnation of the love of Christ, we sing thy praises as one who loved all the Fatherland. As thou hast boldness before the Lord, enlighten our darkened minds and hearts that we may cry to thee.*

'*Rejoice, O Nicholas, God-crowned Tsar and great passion bearer . . .*'

On the banks of the Fomich, a different ceremony was taking place. Everywhere, torches blazed among trees, some standing, some broken. At the centre was a mound of the dead, their faces covered with squares of white cloth weighed down by heavy wreaths bearing the words of the Trisagion.

Reading by the light of an oil lamp, Father Yefraim intoned the refrains of the Parastasa, the general requiem service. He had reached a Kathisma sung in the sixth tone.

'*Truly all things are vanity, life is but a shadow and a dream, and vainly do humans trouble themselves. Scripture says: when we have gained the world, then we shall dwell in the grave, where kings and beggars are the same; therefore, O Christ God, give rest to those who have passed over, as you love mankind.*'

Sapozhnik had ordered everyone, with the exception of Tina and the three or four men whose injuries were severe, to attend the service. Neither of the Waterstones made any issue of their being Jews, convinced that that would not go down too well with the Count. But since the President did not understand a word of the service, his mind wandered, and he found himself reciting the words of the Kaddish, and though he did not know at the beginning the name of the person he was reciting it for, by the time he ended he knew he had been praying for himself and his wife.

In the Cathedral of St Isaac, the Venerable Filaret reached the end of the *akathist* and recited a *tropar* of the Royal Martyrs in the first tone.

'*Most noble and sublime were your life and death, O Sovereigns; wise Nicholas and blessed Alexandra, we praise you, acclaiming your piety, meekness, faith, and humility, whereby ye attained to crowns of Glory in Christ our God, with your five renowned and godly children of blest fame. Martyrs decked in purple, intercede for us.'*

Scarcely had his words faded upwards into the church's great dome, than the congregation became aware of a buzzing of voices and some sort of commotion at the entrance to the building. Heads turned, and necks were craned as the vast congregation, all standing, and dressed in thick overcoats and fur hats, tried to see what was happening.

The commotion seemed to die down and form itself into a small procession. Near the altar, voices of the clergy began to rise in a solemn hymn. And like quicksilver word went round. The Tsar had come to be crowned. All eyes burned for a glimpse of the young man who was walking down the central aisle, dressed in ceremonial robes, censed by white-clad acolytes, drenched with holy oil and chrism, wreathed in perfumed smoke. And soon voices were crying out on every side, hailing the new king until the church filled with his name, proclaiming his coming that would reunite Mother Russia and Mother Church.

Watching him come towards him through the door of the iconastasis, Filaret congratulated himself on a job well done, and looked forward to his eventual appointment as Patriarch of all Russia.

The dead had been left to winter and the promise of spring. Frost would cover their flesh and hair, and in a day or two, fresh winds would come and tear away the handkerchiefs from their faces. Tolbuzin's severed corpse lay a little way apart, with Varvara's and the remains of their staff, except for Ivan Valentinovich Stul'nev, who lay with his Cossack brothers.

Before they started, the Count took Joel Waterstone to one side. They spoke in English, in low voices, so no-one else could hear.

'Mr President, I think you know that I'm aware of your identity. So far, I've told no-one else, but when I get a chance I'll make radio contact with my headquarters. They'll tell me what to do. However, that may not happen for some time, given the present

372

weather conditions, so I've had to do some thinking of my own. We have a new destination, Mr President. Not far from here, not far from here at all. No-one will ever find you there, no-one will even think of it.

'I would like to say, you have your freedom, return to the United States, take up the reins of government again. But I think it's too late for that to happen now, don't you? I think you may turn out to be the best thing that has happened for the nationalist movement in this country. Whether that will prove to be the best thing for you or your fellow-Americans, I really can't say.

'Now, it's too cold to keep my men waiting any longer. You have a place within the truck as before. Please climb aboard.'

While a congregation of social climbers and simple bigots crowned their king in bliss and rapture, the Soldiers of Nicholas were already busy in the streets outside. One detachment had visited a local military barracks and commandeered twenty covered trucks. These were driven in several directions, and behind each one came a covered Jeep carrying four armed men. The leader of each patrol carried in his breast pocket a short list. They knew whom they were looking for. It had all been planned out long beforehand.

'Is your name Izrail Moiseivich Rosenbardt?'

'Yes.'

'Profession, surgeon.'

'Professor of Surgery at . . .'

'Yes, yes. I have all that.'

'But . . .'

'And is this your family residence?'

'Yes, but . . .'

'You live here with a wife and four daughters?'

'Obviously, you are well informed. Can you please tell me what's going on? I can only get music on the radio. My next-door neighbour says . . .'

'Forget what your neighbour says. For now, think about yourself and your Yid family. You're going on a journey. You have ten minutes in which to pack a small travelling case each. One of my

373

men will accompany you to ensure that you do not try to make any phone calls.'

'I don't understand. Where are you taking us?'

'You're the Jew. You work it out.'

54

Kureyka Air Force Base

Jurgensen was not alone. He and his entire team had flown in the day before courtesy of the Russian Air Force, on board a Yakovlev 40 transport supplied and piloted by the Dal'naya Aviatsiya, the Long-Range Aviation unit outside Moscow.

They were lined up now on the tarmac alongside the Ilyushin, dressed in winter combat gear and heavily armed. As Jim and the others descended the steps from their plane, the bright lights made it impossible to make out anyone, much less consider fighting back. In any case, fighting was out of the question: Jurgensen's order to leave their weapons on board had been strictly adhered to.

The moment Jim set foot on the ground, someone came out of the light and snatched him by the upper arm.

'Which of you's in charge? I want to speak with your team leader.'

It was Jurgensen, and from the sound of his voice, he was impatient to get this part of the business over.

None of the Monongahela detachment was wearing uniform, no-one carried any form of insignia, and no-one was singling out their commanding officer for special attention.

'I'm just flying this heap of junk. We're here on the same mission as yourselves, so I suggest we just get down to finding out how we can work together.'

'We sure as fuck are not on the same mission, Major. You and the

375

men with you are an illegal raiding party that has no permission to be in Russia, and even less to bring weapons onto Russian soil.'

'Don't let's talk about legal and illegal, Jurgensen. You know as well as I do just how legal your raid on Forrest Island was.'

'Fuck Forrest Island. Tell me the name of your officer in command.'

Jim said nothing. Suddenly, Jurgensen grabbed the man next in line, a young ex-SWAT team lieutenant from Denver, called Peters. Holding him by one arm, Jurgensen pulled him from the line and kicked him hard in the shins, making him buckle at the knees and go down hard onto the tarmac. Jim made to pull Jurgensen away, but was caught by one of Jurgensen's men and punched hard in the midriff. All he could see as he went down was Jurgensen's right hand coming up from his hip holding an automatic pistol, then a quick movement as he brought the pistol to Peters's head. There was a report that sang through the night air, and Jim felt himself drenched in blood.

'Take that away,' ordered Jurgensen, and someone dragged the body off the tarmac.

'I don't want to hear it,' said Jurgensen to Jim. 'You piss me off, you and your fucking morals. You know shit about morals. Me, I knew all I needed to know the day I killed my first enemy soldier. And at the moment, you are all enemy soldiers. So, what I want to know is, do I have to work my way all down the line here before your leader does the decent thing?'

'Major, you just committed a war crime, and if you ever turn up where I can have you arrested, you'll pay for it. Otherwise, I'll hunt you down myself, and I'll treat you like the piece of shit you are. My name's Major Greg Hopper, ex-Marine Corps. I'm in charge of this operation. And what I would like to know is, if you aren't on the same mission as ourselves, just what the hell do you think you're doing here in Siberia?'

'You want a simple answer? Then I'll tell you. Why the fuck not? You aren't leaving this hole anyway. We are here to see that President Waterstone does not return to the United States. His Jewish ass is no longer welcome there. But if he goes on the loose in the middle of all this mess, a lot of people are in the deepest shit imaginable. We are acting on the direct orders of the Vice President, and our operation, though deniable, is entirely legal. Unlike yours.'

'Since when does an operation to rescue the President of the United States from illegal confinement become criminal?'

'When I say so, fuckface. Come on, I want you and Crawford off the plane and in the briefing room. The rest can stay in the guardroom till I've finished beating the shit out of you both.'

Two of Jurgensen's underlings hauled Greg and Jim off to a small concrete building about five hundred yards away. The rest of the mission filed down the steps and were taken in groups of three or four to a two-storey shed built from breeze blocks and glass window tiles.

Holly was the last to leave. She'd spent the last ten minutes wiping any useful information off her computers. Enough remained to make it look tempting, but the deeper anyone got into the files, the more nonsensical they would become. It was a game she'd amused herself with back in Washington, and now it might serve to gain a little time. But before that she made sure the computer looked useless anyway. Taking out the battery, she replaced it with an old one that had given up the ghost hours ago.

Jurgensen was surprised to see her. No-one had told him there might be a woman on board, and even if they had, he would never have expected her to look like this.

'And what, exactly, are you doing here?' he asked. 'You sure as hell don't look like GI Jane. Maybe you're just along for the ride, maybe you can provide what the American fighting man needs to relieve that old tension down below.'

She stepped up to him. She couldn't see his face, but she knew exactly what he looked like, like a thousand other sex-starved geeks who'd crowded in on her since she was fifteen. It was hard to smile, but she smiled.

'Get me out of this,' she said, 'and you'll never need to buy another copy of *Playboy* as long as you live.'

Just how long that was likely to be, she did not say. He told one of his men to take her to his quarters and lock her in.

The so-called briefing room was in a sorry state. Several windows were cracked, the ceiling had split in two places, through which rainwater had made its way over a period of many months, and the various maps that decked its walls were peeling away. Only a handful of the fluorescent lights worked, and only a few of the chairs were fit to sit on. This was the Russian Air Force in a time of national crisis.

'Leave us.'

Jurgensen nodded to the two men guarding Jim and Greg. They went into the corridor outside.

'To think we were ever afraid of these guys,' said Jurgensen. 'We could have beaten them off with a fly whisk. Whipped them good and proper, never had no more trouble from them. Fucking commies.'

'You've come a long way, Jurgensen. Jews, commies . . .'

'Don't forget blacks. I hate blacks, I hate Japs, I even hate my own mother. What does that make me? Crazy or sane? Which one of you is fucking the kid with the big eyes?'

Jim half rose from his seat.

'If you so much as lay a hand . . .'

'Sit down. Her looks keep her alive a few days longer. You won't be around no more, so my buddies and I get to shag her till it's time to get out of here and on the road again. On the other hand, you could make things easy for yourselves, and save the little lady the embarrassment of a gang rape. All I need to know, where is the President?'

The Navy SEAL who'd taken her to Jurgensen's room had asked her what she was carrying in her little black case. 'Shucks,' she'd said, 'it's just my little ol' computer. I've got some stuff on here ol' Golden Boy back there is going to love. It'll maybe get us all out of this shit we're in.' She'd seen Sissy Spacek play Loretta Lynn in *Coal Miner's Daughter*, and did her best with an Appalachian drawl. The SEAL, a mere drone of a creature, responded well to 'all', took a look at the laptop she displayed for him, and escorted her to his chief's quarters.

Not much comfort here either, she thought. Kureyka must have been a bleak posting for any young officer who'd not been brought up in Siberia. The quarters consisted of two rooms, a small living room, and a bedroom with a shower and toilet in one corner.

Here, as elsewhere, the one concession to human need was the over-efficient central heating. Warmth belched out of three or four fat radiators, and the first thing Holly did was throw off her bulky outer garments and toss them on the bed. If Jurgensen came back to find her half undressed, he could huff and puff as much as he liked at the sight of her in a sleeveless vest, it wouldn't get him anywhere. In any case, she did not expect to see him again, here or anywhere else.

Inwardly, she was shaking, as though blasts of cold air were blowing through the room. She knew Jurgensen's reputation, and she guessed why he and his men were here. Once they'd interrogated Jim, Greg, and a few others, and found that the newcomers knew no more than themselves as to the President's whereabouts, they'd shoot them or have them shot. That could happen in the next hour or so, maybe a lot less. All it would take was for Jurgensen to put his brain in gear for him to see that, if the Monongahela outfit had been headed for Noril'sk, they knew no more than the SEALs, possibly a lot less.

She went into the living room and opened her case. From it, she took out her laptop, setting it down on a low table scorched with cigarette marks. She unreeled the cable as far as the wall, and plugged it into a double adapter that clicked softly into the electricity socket. She prayed fervently that the electricity supply down here wasn't too hit or miss.

Going back to her case, she now retrieved a smaller case that opened to reveal what looked like a second laptop. In fact, this was a Nera WorldCommunicator, a souped-up mobile telephone that operated through Inmarsat's M4 system. By accessing one of four Inmarsat-3-generation satellites, Holly could obtain coverage of the entire globe, except for a thin band across the two poles – a band that, unknown to her, included the tiny area of Siberia across which President Waterstone was being driven.

M4 allowed the transmission of high-speed data applications such as Internet and e-mail, G3 and G4 faxes, large file transfers, and even video conferencing and high-resolution image transfers. It could handle encryption systems like STU III/STE and data streaming, and with a bit of luck, it was going to get them all out of one hell of a mess.

She unfolded the communicator base and plugged it in next to the laptop, then linked them with a short cable, and finally took a telephone handset from her case. One by one, she switched them on. There was no time to lose.

Taking a deep breath, she keyed in a number. Several moments passed. Nothing. Then a series of clicks. More nothing. And at last a ringing sound. She hoped to God it wasn't a wrong number.

'What the fuck sort of time is this? Do you have any idea what . . . ?'

'Calm down, Sergei. This is Holly, and I have absolutely no idea what time it is. Now, I want you to listen . . .'

'What do you mean, you don't know? Like fuck, you don't know. Nobody puts together a mission like yours and sends it this distance without they fucking *know* what they're doing and where they're going.'

Greg sighed. With a bloody nose and split lips, he found it hard to speak. And he doubted it was worth it. Nevertheless, he tried again.

'I've already told you: we know he was landed just north of here, west of Noril'sk, which is why we were flying there in the first place. If we knew he was somewhere else, we'd be somewhere else. We know what you know, that's all.'

'Like fuck you do, like fuck you do. Noril'sk is pretty well at the extreme range of what that Ilyushin can fly, right? You were going to Noril'sk to refuel.'

'We were going to Noril'sk to find out where he is.' Jim nursed a sore jaw and some bad bruising round the eyes. 'We were using satellite photos, and we guessed he had to be somewhere in this region.'

'The hell you did. Even I know better than that. Waterstone was driven from the river to a spot about one hundred miles east of Noril'sk, to a military base called Novaya Kezhma, home to the Twenty-first Mechanized Infantry Division. You're telling me you didn't know that? You didn't know he was kept there under guard until the eleventh? You didn't know Novaya Khezma was taken by rebel forces on that day, and its garrison wiped out? Just what the fuck did you know?'

'You're forgetting that we had no direct access to your intelligence sources. We depended on what we could scrounge from your computers, with the result that we didn't know any of this. Given time, perhaps we'd have found it. And perhaps not.'

'Mister, it's obvious to me that you know diddly-squat, and that it ain't going to get better.'

Jurgensen turned to a burly SEAL next to him.

'Take them out. Put them with the others until I come. You'd better tie their hands behind them and keep good hold of the cord, otherwise they'll be running off in the dark.'

He came round and faced Greg.

'Actually, it doesn't make a fuckworth of difference if you do run off. All there is out there is dark and cold, and after that, a lot more of the same. Make a break for it if you like, but don't say I didn't warn you.'

She replaced the receiver and unplugged both computer and communications module. So far, she'd been able to make good use of the electricity supply, but she realized that, if she stayed in Jurgensen's room much longer, there was a better than even chance that he'd send for her and make her join the others. She had to remain free for as long as she could. The Lithium Ion batteries that powered both units were fully charged, and would provide her with several hours of power. That was more than she needed at present, but she was conscious that it might not be enough later on.

She packed and shut her case, then put on the clothes she'd removed. Here, in an overheated room, it seemed almost crazy to surround herself with so much padding; but she knew how flimsy it would all seem the moment she stepped back into the night.

She'd taken a long Maglite from her case, and held it now ready to use as a club. She took a position out of sight, breathed in deeply, then hammered on the door.

'Help!' she shouted. 'Help, the room's on fire! For God's sake, hurry up!'

Moments later, the door burst open, and the Navy SEAL who'd escorted her there was running in. He had his back to her, and she went in without hesitation, hitting him hard three times in quick succession. He fell to a crouching position, and this time she reached for his rifle, and hit him hard with the butt so he collapsed and started crawling across the floor, and she bent down and hit him again hard, but he was still crawling, and one hand was reaching for his pistol, so she got down on one knee this time, and tossed the assault rifle she'd been holding to one side, and took his pistol from its holster.

Maybe her doing that made him realize just what sort of danger he was in, because he chose that moment to come alive, and let out an almighty yell, a trapped animal yell, and he started coming up, coming up fast, and she knew he would be too strong for her, despite her training, and too skilful for her, on account of his training, and she knew that, if he reached her, if his hands caught in her jacket, she was dead. So she lifted the pistol, and flipped off the safety, and fired into his face, a double tap, two bullets tearing his brain to shreds, and when she sat back on the floor and breathed out, she remembered he was the first person she'd ever killed.

She didn't let the thought hold her back. Next moment, she was on her feet, picking up her case, and making her way through the door.

There was a little yard, a bleak yard at the back of the cookhouse, with grainy concrete walls and a concrete floor choked with weeds, dead but held in place by the freezing temperatures. Jurgensen marched them out there, tied to one another by thick rope, and surrounded by his men, all carrying sub-machine guns.

Jim turned to Greg, who was sucking his gums where he'd lost several teeth.

'Doesn't look too good.'

Greg nodded, and said something that sounded like '*Syu syu syu syu slurrr.*' Jim took that for agreement and supposed they'd serve as last words.

Jurgensen barked out orders, lining them against the wall. When he had them in place, lit by a couple of bare bulbs at either end of the wall, he snapped his own men into place facing them. He stood at one end and made ready to give the order to fire.

55

Jurgensen had opened his mouth to shout 'Fire', when he realized something was missing.

'Where's the woman?'

'In your rooms, sir. Van der Beek's keeping an eye on her.'

'Let's get her over here. Go and find her, and get Van der Beek over at the same time.'

Lieutenant-Colonel Talgat Ramazanov was feeling exhausted. The strain of the past few weeks was telling on him. So far, his squadron had gone into action only twice, engaging rebel fighters converging on Noril'sk, and he knew it was only a matter of time before they were drawn into something bigger than they could handle. There were bigger centres of conflict and more important bases everywhere. But control of the northern end of the Yenisey would be vital at this time of year, and he knew that if rebel forces gained Dudinka and Noril'sk, the only barrier between them and the south would be his men and their planes. He had asked several times for reinforcements, without success. Two days ago, he'd written to his wife and children in Moscow, saying how much he loved them, asking them to pray for him, and bidding them farewell.

He knew what was going on downstairs. His instructions concerning the Americans had been clear, and he'd formed the impression that the US government was sending military units to Russia in order to prevent the CIS falling back into Communist hands. But now they were preparing to kill one another. Jurgensen, who described himself as a Navy SEAL commander but behaved more like some Mafia *avtoritet*, had said the new arrivals were mercenaries working for the rebels, and Ramazanov was willing to let it go at that. But he worried all the same. A firing squad was a squalid thing, after all.

Suddenly, his phone rang, the bell bursting into his reveries quite mercilessly. He picked it up and listened for some ten seconds. When he put the receiver down again, his hand was shaking and the inside of his mouth was dry.

'She's gone, sir. But it's worse than that. She's killed Van der Beek. At least, somebody has.'

'What the fuck are you talking about? She was just some stupid woman Crawford brought along for the ride.'

'She shot him in the head, sir. He didn't have a chance.'

'OK, fuck her. I'm not freezing my balls off out here waiting till she turns up. We'll deal with her later. Let's just get this over with.'

The firing squad detail – which was everyone but Van der Beek – shuffled back into position and raised their weapons.

As they did so, a siren began to wail, picking up strength until it was howling full-voiced through the night. A second joined it, and a third. Lights were being switched on throughout the base. Jurgensen's second-in-command, a man called Squires, ran round to the other side of the wall. Each of the runways was being illuminated. There was a sound of motor engines being started. The squadron was being scrambled, and from the sound of it this wasn't a rehearsal.

'Sir, they're lighting the runways. Looks like they're going on a mission, either that or we're being attacked.'

There was a sound of sprinting feet. Jurgensen flashed a light into the face of a young fighter captain, a man who'd acted previously as their interpreter.

'Major Jurgensen? May I have a word with you?'

'Get on with it.'

'We've just received a warning from regional command that a flight of bombers and attack aircraft is on its way here from Sidorovsk in Yamalo-Nenetskiy Okrug. MiG-29s and Su-27s from the seventeenth fighter regiment, and over a dozen Tu-160 strategic bombers, some Mi-28 attack helicopters, and some old Yak-28 light tactical bombers. They'll be here any minute. The commander wants everything off the runways and in the air. Our instructions are to head for Noril'sk and avoid an engagement. Please get your men back on board your aircraft.'

'What the fuck . . . ?'

'Those are direct orders, Major.'

'What about the Ilyushin that these guys came in? Has it been refuelled yet?'

'Look, you can take it, or you can use the plane you came in. Just don't waste time.'

Jurgensen made up his mind quickly.

'Perkins! Get your sorry ass over here.'

'Yessir.'

'Think you can fly one of those Ilyushins? The one that came in just now?'

'Yessir. No problem, sir.'

'Then lead the way.'

At double pace, the SEALs hurried from the yard. But Jurgensen held his ground. He wasn't being chased off so easily. His victims were still standing with their backs to the wall, tied and powerless.

'Don't you fuckers think, just because the firing squad's not here, you're safe from harm. I brought you here to shoot you, and that's exactly what I mean to do.'

He raised his machine gun and levelled it at the right-hand end of the line. His finger found the trigger. But as he prepared to fire he felt something hard and cold touch his temple.

'I said those were direct orders, Major. I know of nothing that makes you exempt. If you don't want me to put a bullet in your brain, I advise you to join your men on board the Ilyushin. The sooner you get on your way, the better.'

The only plane left standing on the tarmac was Jurgensen & Co's Yakovlev-40. The Yak-40 – code-named Codling by NATO – is older, slower, and smaller than the IL-76, and it carries only thirty-two passengers. It was not surprising that Jurgensen had chosen the better plane to escape in.

Holly was already waiting near the Yakovlev. Jim found her trying to wheel a set of boarding steps up to its flank on her own. When he first approached her, she went on pushing, ignoring everything but the task in hand.

'Holly, it's too heavy for you. Leave it. The guys will handle this.'

She didn't answer, but continued to throw all her weight behind the steps.

'Holly, you're slowing us down. We have to get off the ground fast. Another base is sending in bombers to take this place out. Let's get out of here while we can.'

Suddenly, she stopped pushing, and turned and threw herself at him, beating his face and chest with her bare hands, and finally subsiding into tears.

'You could've been killed. You could've been killed . . .'

'We very nearly were. Jurgensen was planning to execute us. And then this news came through about the raid.'

Just as suddenly as she'd started crying, her whole body rocked with suppressed laughter, and the next thing he knew she was bent over and laughing uncontrollably. He waited until the laughter wore itself out, then took her by the shoulders.

'I thought . . . I thought Jurgensen might have taken you with him. But you can tell me about it later. The bombers are already on their way.'

She reached out and stroked his cheek with her gloved hand.

'There is no raid,' she said.

'No raid? I don't understand.'

'The warning that was transmitted to this base was relayed through the Moscow Headquarters of the Voyska Protivovoz-dushnoy Oborony, the Air Defence Troops High Command. I patched it through my communicator. The voice they heard belonged to a Russian-speaking friend of mine, Sergei Valentinov. An old boyfriend, actually, a dancer with the Washington Ballet. He's in rehearsals at the moment for the February season at the Eisenhower. He's been compared to Nureyev, you know.'

'I don't want you to tell me about this guy.'

'You're jealous?'

'Why the hell should I be jealous? If this joker is anything like Nureyev, you're safe as houses.'

'Baby, no woman was safe from Nureyev, and very few wanted to be. Apart from which, you owe Sergei your life. I think a little gratitude might be in order – and if we ever get back to Washington in one piece, I'm sure he'd appreciate a big hug.'

'So, Sergei told them a bomber wing was headed this way . . .'

'With fighter escorts.'

'Right. And they believed him.'

'You saw for yourself. I patched him through High Command. When they did a codeword check, the computer in Moscow told them just what they wanted to hear.'

'But they'll find out.'

'And head back here. Which is why we have to get this Porsche of the airways up and away from here.'

Five minutes later, they were all aboard. By a ridiculous oversight, the runways were still lit. Jim powered up the plane while the unit medic saw to Greg, and Holly sat on a jumpseat, playing with her laptop.

As they gained height, Jim inclined his head to Holly.

'Wasting your batteries on games again? What is it this time? A flight simulator or something?'

'Pretty well. You play your games, kiddo, and I'll play mine.'

She pressed a key, and her screen came to life. On the floor beside her, a light came on on the communicator.

'What the fuck do you mean, there's nothing out there?'

Jurgensen was becoming irritable. Aeroplanes made him uncomfortable. It was having to rely on other people that put him out of joint. He liked to be in control, liked to call the tunes as they came ready to play.

'I mean that our radar screen shows nothing but the aircraft from Kureyka. Including the Yakovlev we left behind, which is just moving out of the base's airspace. Nothing else is coming in.' The pilot, a New Englander whose grandfather had flown a B-17 in World War Two, and whose father had piloted a Hustler during the Cold War, sensed that something was wrong, but knew there was little point in picking an argument with Jurgensen.

'They're down below your radar, Bryant.'

'That's unlikely, sir.'

'Well, to hell with them anyway. Let's hope it stays this way. How much fuel have we got?'

'Enough to get us to Noril'sk, sir.'

'That's where we're headed, then.'

'*As if I had to think that one over*,' thought Bryant. He hated anyone in his cockpit besides himself and his co-pilot.

They headed on towards Noril'sk. On his radar screen, Bryant could see the blips for the planes that had left Kureyka with them.

They had just come within range of Noril'sk control when a light flashed on the annunciator panel. Bryant tapped it, but it would not go away.

'We have a fire in number-three engine. I repeat, fire in engine three.'

He turned to his co-pilot, who spoke Russian.

'Anderson, please declare an emergency to Noril'sk control.'

'Affirmative. Noril'sk, this is MA seven niner five. Mayday, mayday. We have an emergency.'

On the panel, a second light had come on. Engine four had caught fire too.

'What's your problem, MA seven niner five?'

'We have fires on engines three and four. Request clearance for immediate landing.'

'Roger, MA seven niner five. Heading two seven zero for downwind.'

'Noril'sk, we have lost engines three and four. Which runway can we use?'

'Please use Runway Four.'

'Runway Four, copy.'

Jurgensen was on his feet, swaying as the plane started its descent. He went into the cabin to explain the situation to the men in back.

'MA seven niner five, please call Approach. Tune to radio frequency one twenty-one point two for your line-up.'

A third light went on.

Bryant shook his head in disbelief.

'This can't be happening. It just can't be happening.'

388

Jurgensen reappeared. He looked angry.

'Will you please tell me what the fuck is supposed to be happening? I've looked out on both sides, and none of the engines is on fire. Forget about your fucking lights, there's nothing wrong with this plane.'

A fourth light went on. According to the panel, all four engines were now blazing away.

'MA seven niner five, what is happening? Please contact Approach. You should be making your turn for Runway Four.'

Bryant looked at Jurgensen, then at his co-pilot.

'The annunciator lights must be malfunctioning.'

As he said it, every single light came on. Each one represented a different on-board system. According to the panel, none of the equipment on the Ilyushin was working.

'Just get us on the ground,' ordered Jurgensen.

The panel lights went out. Bryant clapped his hands.

'Maybe the problem has cleared.'

'Just get us down. I'd rather be down there than up here at the moment.'

Suddenly, the Ilyushin jolted as its nose dipped and it started to dive.

Bryant and his co-pilot wrestled with the controls, but they would not respond.

'Noril'sk, we have a controlling problem.'

This time, something bad really was happening.

'Copy that, MA seven niner five.'

'Raise all the flaps, raise all the flaps. Lower landing gear.'

'What's happening?'

'We're going down. I can't get back control of the plane. The flight director's taken over. We're going down straight.'

The air that night was filled with aeroplanes, as though they had come for a performance. Looking down from their cockpits, their crews saw the fireball lift into the darkness like a small atomic bomb. Hitting the frozen ground at over five hundred miles an hour, the Ilyushin dug a shallow grave for itself and its occupants.

* * *

Holly switched off her computer and closed the lid. Jim looked round.

'Good game?'

'Oh, yes,' she said. 'Best fun I've had in ages. I'll tell you all about it later.'

56

Malaya Kuonamka River
North of Zhilinda

The days that followed were as dark as ever, and as cold. The cold acted like a feverish intelligence in everything, transforming warm breath to ice. In the wake of the storm, the skies were clear, and they could see stars, and sometimes the moon, changing before their eyes each night. The riders passed on in a silence broken by few words, and their hearts were curiously painful, and tired. Bowed by the storm and by the loss of their comrades, the Cossacks rallied only slowly. Yulia soothed their wounds and rationed out painkillers and set broken bones, but she found herself helpless before their despair.

She was in awe of them, of their uncanny sense of the sacred. It was not that she hoped for a new king on the throne, or new bones alongside older relics. She did not look forward to a Russia subject to the Church, or even for new songs and new poems to glorify an epoch steeped in blood and servitude. That old world and its inequalities frightened and outraged her as much as the world of commissars and the Gulag. But, for all that, she envied these men their unself-conscious sense of pride in themselves and their unyielding confidence in their future. She was not the first in Russia to feel that deep temptation for order and holy authority.

On the first day, they passed further along the Anabar until it reached a confluence with the Staraya Kuonamka.

'That,' said Sapozhnik, pointing to the spot where the junction with the other river grew visible among the trees, 'is the road to Staraya II military base. It's occupied by the thirty-third infantry. The poor devils must be terrified, wondering which way the tide will turn.'

'Who would build an army camp out here in the *taiga*?' asked Yulia.

Sapozhnik laughed.

'The Russian government,' he said. 'This is diamond country. This is where ninety-nine per cent of Russia's diamonds are mined, ready to be shipped out of Yakutia and back to Moscow. The chief mines are worth millions to the central economy. But now the fear is that Sakha will hold on to what it produces, and go onto the world markets for itself. Hence a discreet army base tucked away where everybody can forget it until there's a strike or a takeover, and it's time to send in the troops.'

Slowly, they refashioned themselves into a working and fighting unit, redistributing tasks and helping anyone who could not cope. Their saddlebags contained meal for the horses, and a supply wagon carried food for the entire unit. The brief periods of rest, when they would tether and feed the horses before seeing to their own needs, were constantly in their minds. That was when they would let slip a little their self-imposed image of hardened soldiers fighting a war for civilization, and become ordinary men again for a little while.

Yulia often joined them, taking these opportunities to monitor their injuries, dress wounds, and murmur words of comfort. She sensed that they were decent men, though proud and extreme in their political opinions, something from which she instinctively steered clear. They sat in small groups, eating and drinking, or snatching five minutes in which to write a letter, or to take an old letter out and read it. They showed her photographs carried in thin wallets beneath their uniforms, photographs of wives, parents, girlfriends, children, even cats and dogs.

In spite of all this domesticity and mother love, she knew she was their prisoner, and that a serious attempt at escape by her or her companions would be ended by a bullet. As often as not, when they were not eating or passing mementoes round the fire, she would find them cleaning their guns. However quaint their uniforms, however evocative their whips, they carried modern weapons and could inflict modern damage. Sapozhnik had disciplined them well, and they in turn showed him total, unreserved obedience.

She and the Waterstones travelled in a single, discrete group halfway down the line, with a contingent of twelve riders who watched them closely in pairs through a rota of four-hour shifts. They were never unwatched, or left in total darkness, and their horses were roped to those of their watchers. Not that any of them thought for a moment of escaping. Where would they escape to? Not even Yulia had a clue as to their whereabouts, other than to say she had heard Saskylakh mentioned, and that they must certainly have crossed the border of the Sakha Republic.

'Not what you're used to, is it?' said the Count, dining with them on their second night. 'Nor myself. But I am a soldier on a mission from God, and you are a politician from a corrupt and degenerate nation.'

Yulia had eaten quickly and gone to tend to her patients. Tina had deteriorated a little during the storm, and Yulia wanted to keep a close eye on her whenever she was able. Because they were deep within the forest, there was little risk involved in lighting campfires to keep warm.

'I've been used to many things in my life,' said the President. 'This doesn't trouble me.'

'You have served in the Army. But your gracious wife . . .'

'I can look after myself, thank you.' Rebecca glared at him. For some reason, she had taken an acute personal dislike to Sapozhnik, which was only partly due to his decision to keep them captive.

They were speaking in English, a language which the Count had evidently mastered in a British charm school in Brighton or Cambridge, under the tutelage of young men and women whose own tenuous knowledge of their mother tongue had proved no match for the detailed imperfections of their students. He spoke flawlessly, yet in an accent that owed more to Ealing films than the modern world.

'Why don't you let us go?' said Waterstone. 'There's bound to be a huge reward, and if there isn't, I can quickly make one available. I can do a lot for your political and military advancement. If you want to come to the States . . .'

'You are trying to bribe me?'

'What makes you say that? I would simply be rewarding you. You've saved our lives. My wife and I owe you a lot. The American people owe you.'

'Do you really think it matters to the American people who their president is? It's all the same to them if it's Kennedy or Reagan or Clinton. Look – here in Russia, we have an established government, mostly created by Yeltsin and Putin: not very conservative, but not very liberal either. We also have Communists, about whom I need say nothing. And, there are the folk like me, nationalists, believers in Mother Church. These are all very different. For Russians, it makes a big difference what they choose. In America, Republican is the same as Democrat, and third party is . . .' His shoulders rose and fell. A red and yellow light shimmered eerily across his uniform. The President felt uneasy, as though he had come to these woods with dead men, horsemen of a dead century.

'Out of the question.' Rebecca sniffed. 'Yes. We know all this, Count Sapozhnik. We don't need you or anyone else to lecture us on American politics.'

'I simply point out why you should not expect such rapture from American people if you turn up again. Maybe by now they already have a new president.'

'Then what use is it to you to keep me alive?'

Sapozhnik's eyebrows lifted. He seemed really surprised that Waterstone had not guessed what was going on.

'You really don't understand, do you?' The Count felt almost disappointed. Yet, in some way, Waterstone's innocence – if it truly was that – absolved him from guilt. 'I thought you would know more, would have a better grasp . . .'

'A grasp? Of what?'

'Of world politics. Of Jewish politics.'

'Jewish . . . ? Sir, I just don't know what you're talking about.'

'You do not know about your own politics? You're President

of the United States, but you do not know how everything is run by Jews?'

Waterstone felt a shudder pass through him. He looked at Rebecca and read the fear and disgust on her face.

'Come on, you can't be serious. *The Protocols of the Elders of Zion*, that hoary old stuff, is that what you mean?'

'Perhaps it is old. But *The Protocols* make things clear, help people see what is beneath the surface of political and economic reality.'

'*The Protocols of the Elders of Zion* is an out-and-out forgery written by the old Tsarist police. No-one has taken it seriously since the collapse of the Third Reich.'

'In Russia, it is taken very seriously indeed. In Arab countries, it is widely available. Who seeks to ban it? The Jews. Shall I name for you all the Jews who run this country? Did you know that six of the seven big names in Russian banking, what we call the *semibankishchina*, are from Jewish ancestors? Kiriyenko, Yeltsin's old prime minister, was a Jew. Boris Nemtsov, the deputy prime minister, also a Jew. Who is the richest man in Russia? Boris Berezovskiy, a Jewish billionaire who exercised the greatest influence over Yeltsin. Who is richer than Berezovskiy? Soros, a Hungarian Jew. Soros was the first to suggest that this country must devalue the rouble. Who . . . ?'

'Count, I honestly have to say that I know nothing about any of these people, except Soros. When I met Soros a few months ago, neither of us said anything in connection with our being Jews.'

'But you have met.'

'Presidents meet men like Soros as a matter of course. I agree, he is tremendously influential, I'd be a fool to think otherwise. But his influence comes from his wealth, nothing else.'

'You are delusioned. But I have other things to attend to. Perhaps we shall talk later about this. It is a matter that has great implications for your life and that of your wife.'

The night swallowed him up, like a globule of quicksilver hurrying to be one with quicksilver like itself.

When, around twenty-four hours later, they had travelled about fifty miles south in all, their guide, a cocky young Evenk herder called Innokent, found what he had been looking for all day. He

395

pointed out excitedly the confluence of the Anabar with a little river called the Malaya, that plunged deep into the *taiga* like a narrow roadway down a dark tunnel. On both sides, the trees bent towards one another. They must have barely touched at first, but with the years their embrace had grown closer and tighter, until now, their branches twisted around one another. They had created a low, curved ceiling and sloping walls that pressed down on anyone who set foot on the ice in winter, or rowed a boat there in summer.

The truck came to a halt, and Yulia got down to see what was going on.

'What is it?' she said. Moonlight was shining on the ice all round her, but the entrance to the tunnel seemed dark and uninviting.

'The Road of Bones,' said Sapozhnik. 'Or part of it at least.'

'You're frightening me.'

'There's nothing to be frightened of in there. Unless you're afraid of ghosts.'

'I don't believe in ghosts.'

'Then you've nothing to be afraid of.'

'Where does it lead?'

'To our destination.'

'The Road of Bones?'

'You'll find out. Don't be afraid – the bones won't hurt you.'

He said no more of what this meant, but Yulia could sense a strange emotion in his voice, and wondered what significance this place held for him.

The Kamaz could go no further. Only a small car would have been able to pick its way between the hanging branches and sudden defiles. Those who could ride were given heavier clothes and spare horses. Tina and the wounded men with whom she'd been sharing the shelter of the lorry had to wait until the unit carpenter, assisted by numerous willing hands, built a rough little covered wagon for them with wooden wheels and a tiny swinging light.

He even succeeded in cannibalizing the springs and some other items from the Kamaz. The headlights and the battery were brought along for use in an emergency. Like the other recruits, the carpenter had no idea who their distinguished guest was, but he had a little girl of his own whom he longed to see again, and, like all the rest of the company, he would have done anything to make Tina more comfortable.

When they were ready to move, the Count led them into the tunnel. On either side of him, two riders carried torches. The long white flame seemed to stretch out for the ceiling, as though to scorch it, or set it on fire. But they did neither, and instead cast flickering lights and shadows up and down the passage.

Filing thus into the narrow entrance to their river-road, it took at least twenty minutes before the last horseman reached the entrance. He stood in his stirrups and looked back on the pools of moonlight glistening on the surface of the Anabar, then turned and persuaded his horse to enter the tunnel.

They were contained now in a realm of echoes, straining their ears to hear any sounds beyond the dull clatter of their horses' hooves. Every third pair of riders carried a flaming torch. At intervals, they would stop to refresh the lights from a barrel of tar and a box of rags. A watcher come from Yakutsk, or from the frozen wastes to the far north, might have thought them figures from the Middle Ages, their sabres catching the reflected torchlight, their spurs ringing, their leather boots gleaming as though newly polished. But a closer eye would have noticed the automatic pistols, the AK-47s, the pouches of ammunition hanging from each saddle.

That night – as calculated by the clock, for there was neither sun nor moon in the tunnel – they were forced to bivouac on the ice. No-one slept for long. The cold would gradually seep through whatever protection a man might place between himself and the surface of the river. A blissful sleep would turn before very long into a struggle against a deep, bone-chilling ache, a profound, life-threatening cold that no-one could fight for very long.

The horses slept tethered and on their feet, their saddle blankets providing only the thinnest comfort against the night air. This was a different cold to anything they were used to, a penetrating monstrosity that felt older than pain.

Yulia woke regularly and made her rounds. Each time she did so, she saw Sapozhnik a little way off, under a torch that had been planted in the ice. He seemed wrapped in thought each time, and she made no attempt to disturb him. Earlier, she had asked him if it was possible for the men to break through the trees and make camp on dry land, but he had only looked sadly at her and shaken his head.

'I told you,' he said. 'This is the Road of Bones. I don't know what they will find out there in the forest. But I prefer them not to go, in case it undermines their morale. You should back me in this. Ask no more questions. All will become clear.'

About the middle of the night, she visited Tina. In spite of the comparative comfort the child enjoyed inside her covered wagon, she still suffered from the cold. Yulia sat with her and told her stories, not so much fiction as tales about herself and her life. The child was still on her way to recovery, and Yulia prayed there would be nothing further to distress her.

'I think my father must be dead,' she said that night.

'Why do you say that? Surely not. Surely he's alive.'

'No, if he was alive, he'd have found me by now, he'd have come to take us all back to America.'

'He's only a man, Tina. He's doing all he can.'

There was a long silence, then a sigh.

'If he comes, Yulia, promise me you'll marry him. Now my mother's dead, he'll need a new wife. Poor man, he won't be able to cope on his own.'

Yulia laughed.

'I'm sure he'll find someone wonderful. But I think we should leave that up to him. Just give him time. He has to find you first.'

There was a suppressed cough at the tightly-strapped entrance to the wagon.

'Doctor? Could you come, please?'

One of the men, Vitaliy Butov, a lieutenant, had been badly crushed by a falling branch on the night of the storm. Yulia had done her best for him, but she had known only surgery could save him. Now, as she bent to him, he was only moments from death. Father Yefraim was already beside him, murmuring the last rites, drawing down God's blessing on a man who had scarcely known life.

'Help me lift him,' said Yulia to the man who had come for her. 'It may relieve some of the pressure.'

The priest looked at her. A nearby torch cast a red glow on his face.

'He belongs to me, Doctor. There is nothing more you can do but trouble him. Let him go. Let God have his soul, then do whatever you wish with his body.'

Yulia took her hand away. Moments later, red blood frothed to Butov's lips, and with three quick convulsions he was dead. Yulia reached out and closed his eyes. The priest continued his prayers, then stopped. He raised his eyes and looked directly at Yulia.

'Your Jews are bringing us bad luck, Doctor. But God does not forget. Tell them to take care. Too much bad luck, and God may have to act.'

She said nothing in reply, but rose and went to where Sapozhnik was standing, still deep in thought. She informed him of Butov's death, and promised to deal with his remains.

'Sir, I feel obliged to tell you that Father Yefraim has just made what I consider to be a threat to the Waterstones, and possibly Tina. May I ask if you will have a word with him? He will listen to you. I want to know that, as long as they are in your custody, the usual military code will apply, as regards their personal safety.'

He looked at her blankly, as though he had not understood her request, then turned to look into the trees.

'Very well, I shall speak to him. But you should take nothing on trust. I have a use for them, just as I have a use for you. But should you or they imperil my mission or the greater mission of my people, I will abandon you to Yefraim or anyone with him. Take great care. There are eyes all around you here. They will watch your every movement, and judge your every action.'

'Eyes?' She looked around uneasily. 'Whose eyes? Who is watching?'

'The dead,' Sapozhnik said. 'The dead are watching you.'

57

The Vice President's House
Washington, D.C.

'Mr Heller, I understand your reluctance, but the fact is that this country cannot continue much longer without a president at the helm.'

Heller squirmed. He wanted the presidency after all, he'd taken steps to ensure it was his, but he was terrified of seeming importunate, of showing undue haste in burying his predecessor as a preamble to snatching his crown. He felt sick with inner conflict.

'You mean big business can't function without somebody to sign the treaties and ensure the right legislation goes through?'

'Put it that way if you like. The truth is, the administration can't handle everything, Congress can't handle everything. There are big issues that need to be ironed out. Russia, for one thing. If Russia goes under . . .'

'I know perfectly well how serious that would be.'

'Then you should have no problems about accepting the presidency.'

'I don't have problems. I want to be sure the people are behind me.'

'They'll be behind you. You'll be the commander-in-chief. You're white, Protestant, wealthy, you have a good-looking wife who doesn't stick her nose in the wrong places, you have good-looking children who've never taken drugs or experimented with sex or listened to rap music. And you have us. We're behind you all the way. Once you're sworn in, you'll have a seat at our table.'

'And a second term?'

'We guarantee it.'

'And after that?'

His interlocutor shrugged.

'It's up to you. Being President of the United States isn't the biggest thing in the world. When there's time, I'll introduce you to some of the possibilities. But you need to take that first step. I can't do it for you.'

Heller stepped across to the window. He didn't really know this house, had made no emotional investments in it. All his memories were of other places. He'd known Joel Waterstone since they were college friends, had admired his honesty and common sense, his devotion to an America without barriers, the time it had taken to persuade him to stand for president. In his mind, he rehearsed all Waterstone's old arguments against standing. But it took only moments for him to recognize that he was neither so principled nor so lacking in worldly ambition.

'Yes,' he said, turning quickly to his three visitors. 'I'll be sworn in. When would be a good time, do you think?'

That had already been decided.

'In three days' time. Does that meet with your approval?'

He nodded.

'Good. See it's announced today. A press conference has been pencilled in for noon. You shouldn't be there. A White House spokesman will take care of everything. Now, if you don't mind, we have to talk about this with our colleagues.'

He showed his visitors out personally. Returning to his study, he was intercepted by his private secretary, an old White House staffer called Peter Latimer.

'Sir, if you don't mind, you have a meeting now with Rabbi Chaim Singer of the United Synagogue, Dr Benjamin Morris of B'nai B'rith, and a woman whose name I've forgotten from the Anti-Defamation League.'

'God, Peter, I'm really busy. I've decided to let them swear me in as president.'

'Congratulations, sir. It's a wise move. I hope you'll take me with you to the White House.'

'Well, of course. There'd be no sense training somebody else to do your job.'

'No, sir. Now, what shall I do with this Jewish delegation? I remember now – her name's Novack, sir. Dr Helen Novack – you've met her before, bossy, feminist type, PhD in something clueless. Feminist Studies, Jewish Feminism, I don't know.'

'Can't they wait till after the inauguration?'

'I don't think they will. This will be their third cancellation if I call off the interview. That wouldn't bother me, but they say they'll go public with this if you don't see them. They seem impatient. I'd be inclined to give them five minutes, then say you have another meeting. I'll come in, create a sense of urgency.'

'You think that's how I should go?'

'Absolutely. Go back to your study, I'll send them in.'

The Presidential Office
The Kremlin
Moscow

'Sir, Colonel Demidov has arrived. Shall I send him in?'

President Garanin looked up from his desk. He looked haggard. The past few weeks had taken their toll, and he knew that, if things continued as they were, he could face an endless succession of sleepless nights and anxiety-filled mornings. In order to make the decisions that were demanded of him every few minutes, he had to try to keep on top of events, something that was getting harder from day to day. Information that would previously have taken minutes to reach the capital, as often as not took days, by which time it was generally out of date.

Demidov was an FSB colonel, intensely loyal to Garanin and to the concept of a Russian Federation. He was one of the few people the President felt he could still trust, which was why he'd been entrusted with more than one highly delicate mission over the past few months.

'Come in, Anatoliy. Sit down. I'll have some tea brought in. Or perhaps . . . ?'

Demidov shook his head. He was older than Garanin, and had about him a perpetually pensive air, as of one who takes life too seriously. Yet Garanin knew he was capable of humour, albeit of the mordant variety.

'You'll have to excuse me,' he said, conscious of what he took to be Demidov's disapproving stare – though it was, in reality, no more than the Colonel's way of looking through his new varifocal lenses. 'I haven't had a chance to shave in over a day. I feel grubby.'

'I hadn't noticed. Don't worry, you look fine. You'd suit a beard.'

The President glanced past his visitor to the row of clocks that indicated the hour across the vast stretch of the Federation.

'We'd better get started, Anatoliy. I've another meeting any minute. Let's get this over with. What have you got to report?'

Demidov handed over a thin envelope.

'Glance through that when you get a moment. This thing is getting messier by the day. We received a report from one of our informants in Moscow, a small-time *makler* who works out of Izmailovskiy Park. Apparently, a second American team has arrived in Russia, this time without our knowledge.'

'What the hell is going on? Was this second team sent by our friends in Washington? Are there other teams?'

'I can't answer any of those questions. But this *makler* – his name's Vronskiy, by the way – told me something more disturbing. All the time we thought we were keeping Jurgensen's unit on a string, pretending to cooperate while feeding them false information . . .'

'Yes? It can't be that bad.'

'Well, the thing is, sir, they were doing the same with us. Somehow or other, they got a real lead and almost got to the base where we were keeping Waterstone. They flew to Kureyka Air Base. Only . . .'

'Only what? I just don't have time to wait for you to pluck up your courage.'

'They weren't on a mission to locate and rescue the President. Jurgensen left with sealed orders. Their mission was to find Waterstone and kill him. And his wife, of course.'

'And they're out there now, looking for him?'

Demidov managed a smile.

'Well, the good news is, no. I haven't been able to get a clear picture of what happened, but it seems there was some sort of air accident out at Kureyka. Jurgensen and his team are dead.'

'You're sure of that?'

'I'm still waiting for confirmation. But my source is reliable. I'm not expecting a contradiction.'

'And this second American team . . . They have, I presume, been given the same orders. Do you know where they are?'

'That's just the problem, sir . . .'

'Jim? I've got what we've been looking for.'

Holly came into the cockpit without knocking. Jim was stretched out in his seat, feet up on the instrument panel, shoes off, mouth open, snoring blissfully. In the co-pilot's chair, Peter Vitebsky had curled himself into a ball and was sucking his thumb vigorously while he slept.

She glanced through the windscreen. In whichever direction she looked, a thin coat of snow covered the Arctic ice in patches. Elsewhere, the ice itself formed patterns, feather-like fronds that grew like colourless ferns across the expanse of the river. They'd landed on the ice strip just below Saskylakh, flying in blind under cover of Jurgensen's set-up. Their plane had a series of code-letters that meant it had clearance to land at any airstrip still under government control, including military and Air Force bases.

They'd flown from Kureyka to Noril'sk, where it was assumed the Yakovlev and its passengers were the same ones who'd passed the day before. Money passed hands, and suddenly there was more aviation fuel on Noril'sk field than there was oil in Saudi Arabia. While Peter went about the task of refuelling, Jim made a search of the cockpit charts, and found one that showed a red circle round Saskylakh.

At Saskylakh, they'd been given permission to land on the Olenëk – and there they'd come to a halt.

She looked at him sleeping. With his open mouth and loud snores, he seemed almost comical. It pleased her more than anything to find him so off guard. Watching him like this felt more intimate than even making love had been. As long as this mission lasted, their relationship would remain suspended: not just making love or snatching guilty kisses when no-one was looking, but much more. They had neither time nor space in which to talk, to find out one another's secrets, to struggle with each other's griefs and disappointments.

It would be like that until the mission ended, whatever way it ended. If they died, then nothing would matter. But if he died and she was left, what then? She scarcely dared think of such an eventuality. It would destroy her, she knew that at least. More than that, the simple thought of their returning home terrified her. He would have his daughter again, and opportunity to examine his life in the mirror of Laura's death. Back home, she would become a shadow and, in time, a ghost. Thinking that, she scarcely dared wake him.

He sat bolt-upright.

'You've found them?'

'I've found where Jurgensen was headed. It meant tracking old radio communications between this plane and Kureyka Base.

'They needed clearance to travel by sled to a secret Army base west of here. It's called Staraya II, and as far as I know, it's occupied by the thirty-third infantry. That's where we have to go, Jim. That's where they must be keeping him.'

'Mr Vice President, you must understand that we need you to take action on this at the earliest opportunity. There's no time to lose.'

Rabbi Singer discovered to his embarrassment that he'd been leaning across the Vice President's desk, as if to harangue him, which was something he had definitely decided not to do.

'Forgive me, Rabbi, but I really don't see the urgency here at all. The State Department has assured me that, one or two isolated incidents apart, there are no signs of anti-Jewish pogroms breaking out in Russia.'

'On the contrary, Mr Vice President, I have to tell you that our reports indicate a very serious situation.' Ben Morris was a veteran of dozens of campaigns on behalf of persecuted Jews, but today was putting his patience to the test. 'Disorganized pogroms have been witnessed in several towns with sizeable Jewish populations. But in the main centres where nationalist and church forces have taken control, we hear of mass arrests, deportations, the confiscation of property.'

'Well, I'm sorry, but that sounds way too exaggerated. A handful of your people getting roughed up doesn't amount to pogroms. I'm sorry if that sounds harsh, but that's the way it is. I can't go interfering in Russia's internal affairs, especially at a time like this, just because of a few alarmist reports. If I go in too hard, it's just going to backfire. If and when the time comes, I'll make a personal approach to President Garanin myself.'

'By then it will be too late.' Dr Helen Novack was sick of being given the run-around. Heller already had a whiff of anti-Semitism about him, and a lot of people in the Jewish community had been surprised that Joel Waterstone had accepted him as his running mate. 'This happened back in the nineteen forties, or don't you read history?'

'There's no need to get hysterical, ma'am.'

'I'm not hysterical. I'm simply trying to get through to you the enormity of this situation. Russia has a Jewish population of around one and a half million. We think over half of that population has already been placed under arrest of some kind. There are rumours of camps being built in Siberia. It's only a matter of time before the nationalists gain control of the whole ex-Federation. When that happens, the trains will start running. Now, I want to know what you're planning to do about it.'

Heller shut the folder that had been lying open on his desk. His hands were shaking, but his voice was perfectly steady when he found his voice.

'The answer is very simple, madam. Nothing. I do not intend to weaken this country's influence by tilting at windmills, nor do I intend to let the Jewish lobby force my hand. No doubt what is happening in Russia is very serious. But when an entire country is at war with itself, the people in it may have to fend for themselves. Even if they have special friends overseas.'

'Mr Heller,' Ben Morris broke in. 'It isn't just the Jews. According to some sources, the Orthodox Church is targeting Protestants,

Catholics, Muslims, Buddhists – anyone who is not an Orthodox Christian. You can't just stand aside . . .'

'I have to stand aside. If we become embroiled in Russia's problems . . .'

'Joel Waterstone would not have stood aside,' shouted Helen Novack.

'Joel Waterstone was a Jew. He'd have backed you to the hilt, to this country's detriment.'

'Was?' The rabbi took a step forward, his face creased in concern. 'You said he *was* a Jew. Was that just a slip of the tongue, or . . .'

The door opened, and Peter Latimer came in.

'Excuse me, sir, but your next guests are waiting.'

Heller nodded and watched without interest as the Jewish delegation was ushered from the room.

58

Solur-Khaya Mines
Malaya Kuonamka River

Sometimes the ice appeared green, and when Joel looked he saw encased beneath its surface strange fronds of water weeds, their movement frozen until spring. Willow moss and featherfoil had tangled with plumes of milfoil and water thyme. In spring, the water would be as clear as crystal, and he fancied that birds would come down from above the trees and bathe in it, or steal moss to line their nests. But he wondered if any birds would come here at all, in spring or in summer.

Once, he thought he saw a face staring upwards at him, and started back. But it was old vegetation turned brown and crumpled, and what he had thought were eyes turned out to be two water beetles trapped there as though beneath glass.

'Have you been here before?' he asked Sapozhnik, who often walked beside him.

'Yes, once,' the Count replied. 'Many years ago.'

'I don't understand why you should want to bury us in the forest like this.'

'You know your own importance. You see how much care your kidnappers took to keep you hidden from others. If I were to let you go, you'd fall into their hands again, and they'd use you to obtain whatever it was they thought they could gain by abducting you in the first place. They were government agents, FBS in all likelihood, as I'm sure you've guessed by now. It isn't in the interests of my side in this war to have you become their pawn again.'

'Instead, I'm to be your pawn.'

'Precisely. Once we get to our destination, I can find out what's to be done with you.'

'You don't know?'

The Count shook his head.

'It's not for me to decide.'

'And what is our destination?'

'You'll see.' And he rode off to the head of the line, watching for what only he knew was there.

They came upon it a few hours later, a wooden wharf that jutted out into a bend in the river. It was old and rotten, and Sapozhnik gave strict orders that none of the horses be ridden up onto it, lest it collapse and break the animal's leg or neck, and throw his rider. But it was recognizably a wharf, with poles and stanchions, corroded metal rings, and heaps of rusty chains that no amount of oil or grease would ever free again.

They entered the forest on either side of it, and regrouped in pairs behind. The trees still crowded in on them, though they were no longer forced to ride through a tunnel. It was not hard to make out a rough path among the trees, a narrow road leading between the wharf and their destination. Sapozhnik urged his men on, though he sensed that he was losing his absolute control of them. Unless he took sharp action, he might have a mutiny on his hands.

They had scarcely started when one of the lead riders spotted the first bones. Broken and covered in lichen, a human ribcage rose out of the earth about a yard from the path. The rider stopped to investigate: a few feet from the ribcage lay a skull, green and mouldy, and missing its lower jaw, but unmistakeably human.

'It's an old labour camp,' said the Count. 'Solur-Khaya. This track became known as the Road of Bones. The bones here belong to the last winter, when no-one could be buried. When the camp was shut down, no-one came back in the following spring, so the bones were just left to rot here.'

'How long ago was this?

409

Sapozhnik directed a look of disgust at him.

'How long ago? You Jews only think of yourselves. If I asked you the dates of Auschwitz or Belsen, you'd know immediately. There are Holocaust memorials and Holocaust museums and Holocaust libraries in half the cities of the world. You've even got a Holocaust Memorial Museum in the heart of Washington. But who remembers the camps under Stalin? Who remembers the tens of thousands who died in his road projects? This happened from the 1930s until the late 1950s. The camp here went on into the 1960s. They mined for diamonds, and every diamond dug out of the ground cost a dozen lives. The Communists only closed the camp when the diamonds ran out, when there was nothing more to extract.'

Up ahead, the lights of the front riders revealed what looked like log cabins.

'I'm sorry,' said the President. 'What you say is right. My people were no more innocent than Stalin's victims. And your losses in the war . . . When I get back, you'll have your museum. And not just in Washington.'

The Count looked at him disdainfully.

'What makes you think I want a museum? And what makes you think you're going back?'

Nothing had been touched since the mine was abandoned in 1963. There were still metal dishes on some of the tables, rusted spoons, boxes of biscuits, the contents turned rotten long ago.

'These cabins weren't for the prisoners,' said Sapozhnik. 'The guards ate and slept here. When the camp was closed, they just shut everything down and went home. None of the prisoners had the strength to attack their keepers. All they wanted to do was get back to Moscow or wherever it was they'd come from. Others just wanted to be left in peace to die.'

'Where did the prisoners live?' asked Yulia.

Sapozhnik shrugged.

'Outside. In tents. In rough huts. Some were forced to sleep on the open ground, and died where they lay. Their daily diet consisted of eight hundred grams of bread. Sometimes they were fed salt cabbage with it, most times not. If they found moss, they

410

ate it. If they overcame their disgust, they ate the grease from their barrows. A working day lasted fourteen hours. Most of them were given sentences of twenty-five years. None of them survived to even a quarter of that. They didn't even let them keep their names. Just numbers, that's all they had as their identity.'

'Didn't . . .' Yulia looked at the Count, stunned by this information, by facts she should have known long ago. 'Didn't the people in charge realize that their prisoners would have worked better if they'd been treated less harshly? It seems so obvious.'

'My dear young doctor, why must you be so naïve? That was not the real purpose of the camps. What if it cost a dozen lives to mine a single diamond? The camps did not exist to recover diamonds or gold, they were built to kill. If Stalin had lived, there would have been no survivors. That was what he wanted, what the system wanted. That is why we had to destroy Communism, why we must never let it return to power.'

'And what will you replace it with?' asked Rebecca.

'With a new order,' said a voice behind her. She turned to find Father Yefraim standing nearby. 'An order based on the Word of God, and the authority of the Church, and the wisdom of an anointed ruler.'

'Like Iran?' she asked. 'Or Saudi Arabia, perhaps?'

He shook his head.

'They worship false gods – much like yourself. No comparison is possible.'

'Why do you call my God false? The God of Abraham, of Isaac, of Moses? And, dare I say it, the God of Jesus?'

'I would take great care what you say. If you do not believe in Our Lord, if you do not accept Him as God's only Son, then you will never find your way to the God Who sent Him.'

'It's as simple as that, is it?'

'As simple as that.'

'And I will go to heaven?'

'You will go to paradise when you die.'

A little smile crossed her lips, invisible in the darkness.

'A Christian paradise?'

'Of course. What other is there?'

411

'To be honest, I'd rather hoped for a Jewish one. It's what I'm used to. What my parents were used to, and their parents before that. I wouldn't be comfortable in your paradise. Everybody would speak Greek or Russian. Even Jesus would find himself more comfortable with my lot. Now, I have to go. Tina was asking for me.'

Sapozhnik let the President wander where he pleased. After all, where was he about to go? He did not expect to spend long in this place. In the meantime, the cabins, broken and dank though they were, would serve at least half of his force as accommodation. The others would sleep in their tents as usual, and a clearing would be cut for the horses. Men had already been assigned their tasks.

Joel Waterstone had gone off on his own, leaving Rebecca with Tina, and Yulia with her wounded. It was coming to an end: he sensed it. He and Rebecca would die here, and leave their bones among those already here. The only thing that alleviated his sense of despair was Tina's slow recovery. Yulia had declared her out of danger now, and he knew he would fight to stay alive as long as there was a chance of restoring her to her father.

He came to the first of the mineshafts that littered the area. Its great mouth opened before him. Among the trees behind it, the great wheel of a lift apparatus hung on its side, half rusted through. They would have died in rock falls, or crushed under heavy machinery, from silicosis and pneumonia and meningitis and a hundred other curable diseases, coughing their lungs up in small pieces, watching their wives and husbands and friends die before them. He'd meant what he said to Sapozhnik: there would be museums and memorials. It was another reason for holding on to life: to restore to some sort of life the jumbled bones of Stalin's killing fields.

He went inside, holding his torch high against the low ceiling. They must have crawled here, just to get to the diamonds buried for aeons, then dug up just to shore up a system that was already rotting from inside. A skull stared at him, challenging him to go further in. But he'd seen enough. He had to go back and face the music, whatever that was.

59

'Come in, Ural Four. Do you read me? This is Vorkuta Nine. I repeat, code-name Vorkuta Nine. Please come in, Ural Four.'

The radio operator turned to Sapozhnik.

'I can't raise him, sir. Something may have happened. Or reception may be poor – after the hurricane, it's hard to predict conditions.'

'Try Krasnovarsk.'

'Sir? We aren't well situated for that. Too many mountains in the way.'

'All right, then, what about Yakutsk? Sakha Division head-quarters.'

'Yes, sir. I have them here. Kontakion is the code-name.'

He placed the headphones back over his head, found the right wavelength, and began to call.

'Kontakion. This is Vorkuta Nine. Please come in, Kontakion.'

'This is Kontakion. Please give the current password.'

The operator had obtained the most recent password from Company HQ some twelve hours earlier.

'*Loshadka.*' The word meant 'little horse', and was a popular password among the Cossack *sotnyas* and *plastuns*.

'What can we do for you, Vorkuta Nine?'

Sapozhnik snatched the microphone from the radio operator's hand.

'This is Count Sapozhnik. Get me General Soshnikov. I don't care if he's getting married. Just get him to the radio as quickly as possible. And tell him to keep it confidential.'

*   *   *

'Yulia nursed you while you were ill. She's a doctor.' Rebecca brushed Tina's hair back from her forehead. She'd have to find scissors to cut it. To cut all their hair, as a matter of fact. At least there were no mirrors, no way of telling how bad one looked. Rebecca had never been vain, but in a place like this appearances started to matter. It must have destroyed the prisoners' morale as much as anything just to look at one another, to realize that, if my neighbour is skeletal, I must be too. In the Nazi camps, they'd shaved the women's heads: to destroy lice, they'd argued, but everyone knew better than that. She'd visited Auschwitz, seen the stacks of human hair piled high like so much hemp or sisal. And how ironic, she'd thought then, that Orthodox Jewish women were required to shave their heads when they married, and to wear wigs.

'I remember,' said Tina. 'You don't think I do, because I was so ill, but I do remember.'

Yulia smiled at her. From where Tina was lying, it must have seemed almost cosy in here. One of the riders had got the stove going again. The room was full of smoke, but that was a small price to pay. For once they were warm. Perhaps they had only hours to live, she thought, but at least they would not die shivering in the open woods.

'There's absolutely no question about his identity, sir. They were taking him . . . What? No, sir, he's not a Russian impostor. What would be the point of that? Sir, the Americans would want confirmation before they handed over a penny or made a single concession. It would only work with the real thing . . . Sir, he speaks perfect English. What do you mean? My own English is extremely good. One of my men spent ten years in New York. He guarantees the accent, everything. Listen, they were taking them to Staraya Two. Yes. I think it must have been arranged well in advance. According to the doctor, they started out at a military base near Noril'sk. Sir, you have to make your mind up. Yes, I understand that. Given the delicacy of the situation, I was thinking that the fewer people know of this . . . That's exactly my point too. No, you're perfectly right. I couldn't have said it better myself, sir.

414

I have your agreement, then? Excellent. You understand that this will swing the war in our direction, sir? Once you have spoken with Metropolitan Filaret. I'll await your instructions, sir.'

Anabar River

'He isn't at Staraya Two.'

'You're sure?'

Greg looked up.

'You said that's where Jurgensen was headed.'

Holly shook her head. Nerves were getting frayed. Stuck out on the ice like this, they all felt vulnerable.

'The NSA intercepted a series of communications from Staraya Two over the past three days. Russian transmissions are getting top priority at the moment, which means they get translated the moment they turn up. The commander at Staraya is waiting for a package, he says it's overdue. He was still waiting as of yesterday.'

'But . . .'

'Jim, they're out there, I'm sure of it. Or maybe they're dead. Who knows? That's a possibility we have to face. But we can't just stay in this spot for ever, and we can't go off in whichever direction takes our fancy. Jim, whoever is behind this knows we're here, and knows we're after Waterstone. All they have to do is find us, Jim. It's just a matter of time.'

'Yes, Your Holiness, I do understand that . . . More than you think. Evidence won't be a problem. Once we establish contact, I can send out anything you want – photographs, audio recordings. They'll never stumble on our whereabouts. The mines at Solur-Khaya have scarcely been mentioned in the literature about the labour camps. It's the perfect hiding spot. Of course, I have perfect trust in you. Yes, I know they are Jews. That's the point, really. The Americans will go any distance to get their President back, and they'll do anything to keep the Jewish lobby happy. We can use that to our advantage, and to the advantage of Mother Church. What's that? Yes, certainly, I'll speak to him directly. Apparently, his wife was carrying a mobile telephone when they were captured. It was confiscated, but somehow it's been sent along with them. I have it beside me even as I speak. Yes, I'll wait. I'll use the time to pray. Father Yefraim is already holding a service among the trees.'

'We have to call it off, Jim. There's no point in our dying out here as well. This was a crazy mission in the first place.'

'I can't believe you're saying this, Greg.'

'I can't believe it myself, but it's still common sense. Unless we can get a hard lead on the President's whereabouts in the next twenty-four hours, we'll have to take off and try to get back to Moscow. Holly tells me she's running out of batteries, and there's fuck all food on board this plane. We may not even have enough petrol to get us to anywhere useful. With Mygate out of action, we may have to get out of Russia on foot, and, believe me, there aren't that many ways of doing that. Those are good men back there, Jim, and I'm not going to waste them in a lost cause. I'm sorry, but that's how it is. We're going home, Jim.'

'I fully appreciate you saying that, Mr Heller. As I have explained, I am only a humble representative of a greater order. But Metropolitan Filaret will explain that much better than I can. Later, I am sure you and Tsar Georgiy will find much to talk about. For the moment, there is the matter of your lost property. I would be happy to hold on to it a little longer. Unfortunately, events are moving very fast in this country. If you are going to send us help, then it must be soon. You have twenty-four hours in which to think about it. After that, a few more bones won't make the slightest difference to this delightful place. No, sir, I don't think I'm going to tell you that.'

416

60

He watched as grey figures shuffled past, partly obscured by the trees. The women were returning from their long daily march to collect the cold rations on which everyone depended. Above them, a wooden watchtower loomed like a stilted creature from War of the Worlds. Only a tiny light up there indicated the presence of human beings, but everyone knew that an escape attempt would be met instantly by a raking hail of machine-gun fire, the killers as anonymous as their victims.

Walking through the trees, he could hear the sound of digging and cutting as men worked their way with pickaxes and shovels through the nearest mine section. The deeper they dug, the more bodies they brought up, the deepest old as time itself. The oldest Siberians had faces as grey and as lined as the youngest. There was no singing as they dug, no music of any kind. He'd read Conrad, he'd found hearts of darkness beneath every stone he'd ever lifted, but until now he had never come face to face with a darkness that had no heart at all.

He had to be careful not to walk into the barbed wire that had been strung round the different enclosures, the camps within a camp that made a pitiful geography out of the endless forest. On that side was the enclosure for criminals, there the camp for the insane, there the unit for political prisoners. And the women, of course, the grey women, their rags torn as often as not from the bodies of the dead.

He limped to the hill from which the earliest camp builders had

417

stripped away the trees, so they could build a cemetery there. With the passing of the years, tombstone had succeeded tombstone until the forest floor was paved like a city street. No matter that the stones were made of leaves, and the inscriptions carved in water. All distinctions had been wiped out: the graves were covered by a steady sprinkling of snow that never changed, even when the bodies of the newly dead were added to the old. He knew the different parts of the cemetery better than he knew his own changed heart. Here was the Jewish section, the darkest and oldest, and the Armenian, the Cambodian, the Rwandan, the Amerindian, the African – they went on for ever through the forest of bones. The largest were two great outcrops into which the bodies had been crammed like sild: the Russian graves and the Chinese graves.

The prisoners came here at night carrying candles, and tended the graves, and opened new ones into every mound, and they prayed as they did so, in every language, to every god, and never heard a word in reply. Some had been priests or rabbis or shamans, message-bearers from a silent, autumnal world they themselves had never set eyes on. Their followers built crosses as high as the forest, or rams' horns that could rouse the dead, or minarets from which all the world's faithful could be summoned to prayer. But when he looked closely, he saw that the minarets were watchtowers, and the horns were mines, and the crosses struts for the cableways that carried the dead from mineshaft to grave.

He woke confused. Once they'd been unable to waken Richard Nixon, even though there was a nuclear crisis, for which his presence was desperately needed. Unlike Nixon, it wasn't prescription drugs or booze that made him sleepy. It was just the constant darkness, combined with the daily inactivity. He yawned and tried to shake off the dream, but bits of it still clung to him. The wooden hut in which he was sleeping was filled with angry ghosts, the forest outside teemed with them, the ground was peppered with their bones. Out in the woods, when all other things were silent, you could hear the howling of wolves.

He sat on the edge of the bed, shivering. Something was wrong tonight. He sensed it. Hours still remained until it was time to wake.

On the floor beside him, Rebecca was murmuring in her sleep. No doubt she too had dreams.

Bending his head, he began to recite the Kaddish, not knowing for whom. For all the dead, a voice prompted. For all the dead.

'*Yisgadal veyiskadash shmay rabbo, b'olmo divro chirusay v'yamlich malchusay . . .*'

'May the Name of the Lord be exalted and made holy throughout the world that He has created . . .'

Jim looked up to see Holly standing in the cockpit entrance.

'What was that?' she asked.

He folded the sheet of paper and put it back in his trouser pocket.

'The Kaddish,' he said. 'It's a Jewish prayer for the dead. I recited it at Laura's funeral. Her father gave me a copy in English. I've carried it round with me ever since. I read it once a day for her now. It's a bereavement thing, I . . .'

His eyes welled with tears, but he refused to let them get the better of him. Holly watched him till he'd regained control. She did not touch or embrace him. She did not even hold his hand.

'Jim,' she said, when he seemed more himself, 'we have to talk about Laura. When this is over, we need to sit down and talk, and try to reach some sort of decision. I can't do it on my own.'

'What is there to talk about? Laura's dead.'

Holly shook her head pensively.

'What's dead about her? For you, she's as alive as ever. For you, she never died.'

'Of course she did. For me more than anybody. What are you trying to tell me, Holly? That I'm not able to let go? Well, if you don't mind, I think it's way too early to be asking that. I thought . . .'

'That isn't what I'm asking. It's just . . . Listen, Jim . . . Hell, this isn't easy for me to say, but I think we may have to abandon our mission and go home. That has greater implications for you than it does for the American people. They can have a new president in minutes, but you can never replace Tina. Or Laura, even though you can remarry someday. I'm just trying to say that our affair, our fling

419

– whatever you want to call it – it's . . . I think it was premature, before either of us was really ready for it. That's all been covered up by what's been going on around us. We've been able to pretend our emotions are in a normal place, that we have feelings that owe nothing to the past. But I can't go on without some resolution of what went before. That includes Laura.'

'Are you saying you want to end it?'

'I think it's better it should be ended, yes.' There were tears in her eyes, but she refused to lift a finger to wipe them away. 'Now, Jim, before we go home, if we ever get that far. You'll have stuff to deal with when you get back, hard stuff, stuff that could destroy you if it got out of hand. I'm not the person to be round you then. I don't know who would be. Your family, maybe?'

He almost snarled at her.

'My family? Dear God, you've never met my family. You don't have to worry yourself, I'm sure I'll find someone else to hold my hand. I think you're right. This isn't what I need right now. Just do whatever the fuck it is you have to do with your computer, and we'll get this baby in the air. And, yes, it *is* time to go home.'

He got up as if without feeling and walked past her out of the cockpit. Peter, about to enter, looked at him in surprise, then at Holly. He started to wonder, then told himself that was no territory for him to stray into uninvited. He heard the main fuselage door opening. Moments later, it slammed shut again. Hunched over her own misery, Holly winced.

'What was that about?' Peter asked, thinking it would seem stranger if he said nothing.

'I don't know,' replied Holly, running past him.

The more he thought about it, the tidier it grew in his mind. The situation, the contrasts, the theological justifications all combined to make a wholeness. It felt like a deep warmth around his heart, and a constriction in his veins, as though his blood was a different blood. He, Yefraim of Pechora, had become his own God. He had solved the dilemma of a wicked and ungodly age. The problem was no longer one of understanding, but of action.

In a lifetime serving the Church, he had been forced into inactivity time out of mind. Under the Communists, he had been forced into hiding more than once. Whenever he had expressed his longing to preach God's Word openly, his superiors had bidden him hold his peace. It was not time, they said, it was not wise, it was not in the Church's best interest.

Now, like the Church, he had been unleashed upon mankind.

Up and down the country, Metropolitans like Filaret, Abbots like Tikhon, and the Patriarch Alexei III himself had joined hands with forces dedicated to the restoration of a faith-sustained political system, a union of Church and Crown such as had not existed for almost a century. Yet it was out here on the periphery, in a place as remote from the doings of the world as it was possible to find, in a shrine to the dead of ungodly Communism, he, Yefraim, had been called by his Lord to perform the most holy act of all.

It irked him, for all that, that it had to be here, so far from men's ears and eyes, in darkness, among brutes such as these. They were horsemen and soldiers, with neither learning nor a thirst for knowledge. Perhaps they could follow a story from the Old Testament, a parable from the New, no more. He had seen men like them rejoice at the story of Christ's birth, and shed tears at the images of his crucifixion. It was for simple folk like them that the Church had decreed the painting and placing of icons in churches and in homes. He could never hope to explain to them why they had to die, or that they had to give their lives for something as abstract as an antitype.

61

She found him far out on the ice, where he'd gone to stalk away his anger and his grief, and the memories that fuelled both of them. It was too cold for anyone to stay exposed on the river for long, but he was boiling inside and scarcely minded the discomfort. She watched him from a distance for a little while, until she felt the cold in her own bones and started forwards to speak to him. Otherwise, it was anybody's guess how long it might have been before he went back in again. Perhaps not at all, if there'd been someone else to fly the plane home. He felt as if his insides had been removed and hung out to dry. Nothing would ever be the same. He'd given up all hope of seeing Tina alive again, and he'd just lost a woman he knew he loved.

'Jim . . .'

'OK, I'm coming. Tell them not to worry. We can leave any time you like, once we get clearance from the tower.'

She looked at his face, at the pale skin and the dark stubble that marked the jawline. He seemed to blend with the river, to be at one with it, he seemed almost to merge with the ice and loneliness and the aching sense of loss.

'Jim, it may not be too late. I think we've found them. And I think we can get to them.'

Antitype. Once he'd allowed the word into his mind, it had lingered and worked on him. To those who knew how to read the text, the Bible was filled with examples of antitypes, people and things in the

422

latter days prefigured by their parallels in the Old Testament. Jesus was the great antitype, of course, for was not the old scripture from end to end a prefiguration of his coming? As the apostle Paul had put it, 'For as in Adam all die, even so in Christ shall all be made alive. For Adam, who brought us to sin, made necessary Christ, who saved us from it.' Jesus had saved Father Yefraim from his sins, and comforted his heart, and blessed his mind with illumination.

The antitype on which he now proposed to act had been revealed to him a few hours earlier while reciting the Tropar for the Royal Martyrs that begins, 'Most noble and sublime were your lives and deaths, O Sovereigns; wise Nicholas and blessed Alexandra, we praise you . . .' He had started to wonder why it was that, although everything had been restored and a Tsar sat again on the Romanov throne, there had been no visible sign of their martyrdom in modern times. And then the answer had come to him like a sibilant call to wake up.

The Jew President and his Jew wife were the antitypes of Nicholas and Alexandra. After all, it had been a Jewish conspiracy that had engineered the downfall and execution of the blessed couple and their five children. He had asked Sapozhnik if he knew the ages of Waterstone and his wife, and the Count had shrugged and said, 'Fifty, I think. He's exactly fifty, she must be forty-six.' Sapozhnik hadn't guessed, but he, Yefraim, had known. Waterstone and his wife were the exact ages of the Tsar and Tsarina at the time of their deaths.

The child Tina had to represent the antitype of all five martyred Romanov children: Alexei, the Tsarevich, and his sainted sisters, Olga, Tatyana, Anastasia, and Marie. She was not their blood child, he knew that, but they treated her as though she were. As for the young woman doctor, Zaslavskaya, was she not an antitype for the royal doctor, Botkin, who'd been martyred with them? And since that terrible storm, the number of those guarding the President had been reduced by God's hand to seventy-seven, exactly seven times the number of those who shot the royal family and bayoneted them. He smiled to himself, recognizing in Count Sapozhnik the antitype of Yakov Yurovski, the Bolshevik secret policeman who led the firing squad. It all fitted, fitted so perfectly that only God could have designed it.

Only one person in the entire world understood all this, and that was himself. Without him, it would fall apart, the perception and the intense longing that went with it. Without him, the new Tsar would topple from his throne. Without him, the Jews would spew out into every street and every alleyway, like a contagion that would contaminate God's holy Church, and usher in an era of death and unfulfilled desire that would shake the pillars of the earth until God Himself cried out for peace.

He got to his feet silently. On the wall, a taper burned weakly, providing just enough light by which to move. The future of all things lay in his hands. In a few minutes, he would change the course of history. In God's Name.

It was exactly what he'd wanted to hear all along, but now it had come, he found himself unable to believe it, knowing it would hurt too much to have his hopes revive only to be dashed at the final moment.

'I think we should just go, Holly. They're out of reach. You know that. You've tried your best, and God knows I'll never be able to thank you for that. But now it's time to let go.'

Her eyes stared defiance. If he could have felt her heart, it would have been ice, ice ringed with fire.

'No, I'm not letting go. I wouldn't let go earlier, and I'm not doing it now. We have them – or as near as makes no difference. Listen, Jim, and just try to forget any problems there may be between us. I've been tracking back through communications between Jurgensen and the States. It was all handled through a special office in the National Security Agency. They had all Jurgensen's reports transcribed for secure transmission elsewhere, and all the transcriptions were kept on disk.'

'They'll have wiped all that stuff out, now that Jurgensen and his team are dead.'

'They don't know they're dead, Jim. I guess they suspect something's wrong, but they'll have reports of this plane, and they'll conclude that Jurgensen is keeping radio silence. The unit hasn't shut down. Several hours ago, they facilitated a two-way conversation between the States and Russia.'

'A conversation? Between whom?'

'Between Vice President Heller in Washington and a Russian called Sapozhnik here in Siberia. Count Sapozhnik, a Cossack right-winger, to be precise. This is the transcript.'

She held it out to him across the ice. The stiff wind threw itself at it, as if to tear it from her hand.

He hesitated for a moment, then reached out across the gap that separated them and took it from her.

He bit down hard on his resolve, and crossed the room. Cold assailed him, but however hard it bit he meant to go on with this thing. Sapozhnik was snoring gently. He and the priest had taken the best cabin for themselves, as was theirs by right.

'God understands all that I do,' he thought as he detached the Count's sabre from the hook on which it hung. He'd seen Sapozhnik polish and sharpen its blade daily. A bright sabre was something the Count insisted on, for himself and his men alike. They had their guns and grenades, but it was to their swords that they looked for strength and identity.

The sabre slipped from its scabbard without a sound. The moment he felt it naked in his hand, Yefraim fancied he could hear it sing. Its long, high notes stretched through his mind like silver threads. He thought himself the rider on the red horse, to whom a great sword is given, and who is sent to take peace from the earth. Had not God said through Isaiah, 'The Lord has a sword that is sated with blood', and again through Jeremiah 'The sword of the Lord devours from one end of the land to the other, and no flesh has peace'? And was he, Yefraim of Pechora, not the sword of the Lord?

He raised the sabre and heard it sing in his heart. The light glistened all along the blade. The Count moved, troubled by something in his sleep. Yefraim brought the sword down hard across his neck, severing bone and sinew in a single stroke.

He wiped the bloodied blade with a piece of cloth. Tossing the cloth aside, he lit a torch, then set out, sword in hand, to do God's work.

If it was ever possible for a man's face to turn white against a background of snow and ice, then Jim Crawford's face qualified.

There was no mistaking Sapozhnik's meaning, no need to interpret Heller's unambiguous replies.

'Thank God,' he said. 'They're bound to come to some arrangement. I don't know who this guy Sapozhnik is, but if he's part of the circle round the new Tsar, if he knows how to get to him and talk to him . . .'

'It's not that simple. We know Heller sent Jurgensen to kill the President.'

'We can't be sure . . .'

'I'm sure. Open your eyes, Jim: there are plenty of people back in the States who'd as soon as not Waterstone didn't come back. Vice President Heller is number one. We know that. We know some of these people were behind the Forrest Island stunt, and you can bet the same ones were responsible for sending Jurgensen on another mission.

'Heller said all the right things to Sapozhnik. Right after that, he'd have been on the phone to whoever his controllers are. It won't have been an easy shot to call. The Sapozhnik deal could have untold benefits. The US would have more influence in Russia than NAFTA already gives it in Canada or Mexico. Their chief fear would be for Waterstone to come back and renege on everything.'

He shook his head. The motion, in a world without boundaries, made his eyes swim.

'These guys know what they're doing. They'd make sure they had everything in place before Waterstone set foot on American soil again. Treaties, contracts, most favoured nation agreements. Things Waterstone couldn't change without the full backing of Congress, and maybe not even then. They'd probably make him sign some sort of waiver of powers before he came back anyway.'

Holly wanted to shake him.

'You'd better think harder than that if you want to see your daughter alive again. Don't you understand that they don't really care what happens to the President? They don't need Waterstone. Sapozhnik probably thinks he does, or his cause – but that's about it. Think about it. If they want to do a deal with the Russian right, what's to stop them? If they don't, fine. You've just heard Heller say he's to be inaugurated in less than two days' time.

Why the hell should he welcome his old running mate back with open arms?'

'You may be right. But so long as they're with Sapozhnik, we have to assume they're safe. He's not going to give away his big chance to call the tune.'

They started to walk slowly back towards the waiting plane. She didn't know if she should tell him or not. It would worry him, and perhaps to no purpose. And yet, not knowing, he might be too laid back, might put off action until a better moment.

'Jim, it's not Sapozhnik I'm worried about.'

He turned and looked at her uncomprehendingly.

'But there is someone you're worried about?'

She nodded.

'I hacked into the CIA's Russian Desk. After that, it was just a matter of locating the archive for their right-wing surveillance unit, the RRSU. Over the past few years, that collection has grown rather large. They keep files on all national and regional leaders, most local leaders, and individuals close to the Tsar and his circle.

'In addition, they hold a separate archive on the Orthodox Church, especially its more fascist-minded priests. I looked up Sapozhnik. Nothing unusual about him. He comes from an old aristocratic family which has had long-standing contact with White Russians in France, Canada, and other countries, including various claimants to the throne. Sapozhnik's been offered the presidency of the Sakha Republic if and when it raises the royal flag. That doesn't look too likely, which is why Waterstone matters.'

'You said there was somebody else.'

'Sapozhnik employs a priest as the chaplain to his Cossack military unit, a man called Father Yefraim, originally Vadim Semianko. There was an asterisk against Yefraim's name, which means he's considered worth a second look. So I clicked his file open. There's no time for you to look at it now. I'll summarize as well as I can.

'Jim, this crazy could have taught Adolf Hitler lessons. He's written more anti-Semitic tracts than the whole of the Third Reich put together. He was diagnosed several years ago as a violent paranoid schizophrenic, and he spent about eighteen months in the District VII psychiatric hospital at Pechora. That was after he attacked and wounded a group of Jewish schoolchildren, and tried to kill their teacher. According to the file, neither Sapozhnik nor anyone around him knows about this. They think Yefraim spent that time in a monastery in Syktyvkar.

'A looney tune like this is going to be dangerous. If he knows Waterstone and his wife are Jews, if he finds out that . . .'

'How do we find this place?'

'I'm not sure. But it has to be somewhere in this area.'

He started running towards the plane. The Solur-Khaya Mines had to be on his charts. Holly ran after him, but in her heart she knew they were too late.

62

Wickenburg
Arizona

'Mary-Beth!' Bob stuck his head round the door, but there was still no reply. 'Mary-Beth, where the fuck are you?' Still nothing.

He went to the kitchen, where he found his sister with her head in the oven. Since he knew it wasn't a gas oven, he didn't much care how far in her head had gone. But he smelled something very like half-burned cookies and reckoned she must be cooking again. He admired her taut backside with more than brotherly interest, and not for the first time debated the possible advantages of incest. She'd be keen, he thought, if only because it would mean adding another taboo to her stock of life experiences.

'Mary-Beth, I'm calling you here.'

She extracted herself from the oven and straightened.

'What the hell is it now? Can't you see I'm trying to set up a photograph here? I mean, Jesus, you hang around all day doing nothing, then you turn up just as I'm setting this thing up.'

'You're photographing the oven?'

'It's part of a series. I'm getting hold of one of those endoscopes so I can photograph my womb. Then the oven, which is another female interior and a place of fertility, you know, then . . .'

'Something's going on, sis.'

'Of course something's going on. You're just so spaced out, you never notice it.'

429

She'd come home from college a few days earlier, at her mother's request. All this stuff with Laura getting killed and the kid snatched, and now her big brother disappearing was driving her parents mad. They were out now, shopping or praying or something, and Mary-Beth was helping out.

'There's something on TV. Like every channel suddenly has like just this one thing, newscasters everywhere.'

'You think it's got something to do with the kid?'

'How the hell should I know?'

'You haven't listened?'

'I've been asleep. Come on.'

She turned on the kitchen television. A picture swooped onto the screen, a local anchorman looking serious. She found the remote and turned up the volume.

'. . . and prayers in churches throughout the land. I'll be rejoining you with more news as it comes in. Now, for an estimate of the political fallout, we're joining . . . Actually, let's just stay in the studio. We've got . . . Yes, we've just had official confirmation from the White House that President Joel Waterstone and his wife, the First Lady, have been found dead. There are no details as yet as to where this discovery has been made, but rumours suggest a European location. As I said earlier, Vice President Heller is being sworn in just about now, and we hope to have coverage of that event direct from Washington any minute now. Ah, yes, that's affirmative, we have live coverage from inside the White House press room, we'll cut to that now . . .'

Mary-Beth reached up and switched the sound off. The kitchen felt suddenly very small and quiet. They'd said nothing about the kid, but that meant nothing. She guessed something bad was going to happen. There'd be more weeping and wailing and gnashing of teeth.

'Shit,' she said.

Bob looked at her. He hadn't worked it out yet.

'Mary-Beth,' he said, 'are you feeling horny? Like, would you get annoyed or anything if I said, let's go upstairs and get it on? You and me, you know.'

She looked at him as if through a fog. Her brother was a prick.

On the other hand, she was planning to do an extended video diary of her vagina, and incest could get her the sort of attention naked penises had got for Mapplethorpe.

There was the sound of a key in the front door. She braced herself. Maybe she'd be better off heading back to college.

He knew the Lord was with him now. Wherever he went, he would find groups of men fast asleep like innocents, their faces tight with little dreams. Their deaths were instantaneous and soundless, and he walked away each time refreshed and fulfilled. Their pure blood had frozen instantly on contact with the air, leaving the corpses with a curious appearance, as if death had stopped short in them, or life still kept a foothold there.

A few, uncannily snatched from sleep at the last moment by some spiritual or animal apprehension of his presence, sat up as he neared them; but one glimpse of his cassock and his tall hat served to reassure them, and he was able to approach closer to offer religious counsel, and so reassure them further until, with the quickest of divine motions, he would stand, lift the sabre high, and hew their heads from their bodies, while inwardly he cried out 'Hallelujah!'

Jim had watched the Twin Otter landing about five hours earlier, illuminated briefly by the floodlights that had helped it find its way down to the river. It was fitted with ski landing gear that reduced to almost zero the risk of skidding on the ice. He'd watched as the crew had climbed down to the hard-packed river surface, followed a couple of minutes later by four passengers. They'd been met by a large 4X4 and driven off in the direction of Saskylakh.

He watched now as the 4X4 (or possibly a different one, how the hell was anyone supposed to tell them apart in this perpetual darkness?) drove up to the little aircraft and left crew and passengers beside it. A small set of steps were wheeled up and pushed against the fuselage.

'Let's get over there now, before we lose it.'

He was speaking to Peter and the three men he'd picked to come with him on the final leg of their rescue mission. One look at the pilotage chart had shown him there was no way to get to

431

Solur-Khaya without a helicopter or a light plane. He'd started to think of flying back to the airbase at Kureyka, when he'd remembered the Twin Otter parked a quarter of a mile away.

They ran all the way. Jim paused only briefly to flash a message with his torch, warning the pilot not to initiate take-off. The De Haviland's twin engines were already running, and the little plane was slowly turning in order to face back along the main drag.

As they reached the plane, Jim ran in front, still flashing the light. This time, the pilot saw the warning and cut the engine.

Peter already had the steps by the plane. He ran up, followed by the others, opened the door, and shouted in Russian for everyone on board to put their hands behind their heads. Several did so immediately, others looked scared and uncertain.

They piled into the plane, fully armed, their faces blackened, their whole manner intimidating. But it rapidly became apparent that no-one on board the Twin Otter posed a threat to them.

One of the four passengers, his hands tight round his neck, shouted across the tumult.

'You've no right to take this plane. This is a scientific expedition. We have two American scientists on board.'

Peter let his pistol fall.

'Americans?' Then, in English, 'Which of you are Americans?'

The two who had not understood the order about hands bleated their identity.

'OK,' said Jim, coming forward. 'Calm down. Nobody's going to hurt you. Pete, tell them they can all put their hands down. No, sorry, not the pilots. I don't want anybody speaking to the tower.'

He turned back to the Americans.

'What are you doing out here? Don't you know there's a civil war?'

The scientist on the left, a middle-aged man with white hair that swept back from his forehead, answered nervously.

'I'm Dr Rostam Khosravi from the University of Anchorage, this is my colleague, Dr Rob Butler. We're carrying out a joint study with the Archangel Diamond Corporation, assessing the effects of the recent storm on the coastline between the mouth of the Anabar and the Lena delta. That's an ATM-II back there, the red box over the belly camera port.'

'It's a what?'

'It's a scanning LIDAR altimeter. It measures topography. Mixes laser altimeter measurements with readings from onboard GPS receivers. After a storm like the one that just passed over here . . .'

'Yeah, I understand. Problem is, we need this plane a whole lot more than you guys. We're requisitioning it, and we'd like you off and onto the ice as fast as it takes you to skim down those steps.'

'Hell, you can't just . . .' Dr Butler, a thirty-year-old going on ninety, with gold-rimmed glasses and a wispy goatee, had been to the Arctic north of Russia twenty-five times in his short career, but the truth had not really sunk in. He was neither in Alaska, nor his native Iowa, and the Fifth Cavalry did not wait at his elbow to dispense justice and massacre the Indians. As he was expelled from the aircraft, he filled the night air with protests, threats, and curses, leading to carelessness on his part, and a painful fall on the ice. His older colleague knew enough about life to recognize folly and avoid it where possible. The Russians, long accustomed to obedience, went down the steps without a murmur.

It took ten minutes to dismount the altimeter and send it out. Not everyone would have a seat for the journey back, but there were stanchions to hold on to, and the team wore helmets capable of taking the worst of a roll. Peter spoke to the tower, apologizing for the delay. The floodlights came on, and they taxied forward. Next thing, Jim gave the little aircraft full throttle, the runway slipped past under them, and they were airborne.

'Oseh sholom bimromov, hu ya'aseh sholom olaynu, v'al kol yisrael. Vimru Omayn.'

He looked up to see the darkness confronting him. He had recited the Kaddish until his throat was dry and his tongue exhausted. While he'd been praying, Rebecca had come awake, and now she sat beside him, holding his hand. The ghosts were gone, or most of them. On her pallet, Tina tossed and turned through passages of sleep and despair. At her feet, on a handful of rags, Yulia snored.

'Something's wrong,' whispered Rebecca.

'Wrong?'

'Yes, dear. Very wrong. I'm not sure what it is, but I can sense it. I can hear the horses, they know something's not right.'

At that moment, there was a flash of light as a torch was carried past, and then there was darkness as before.

'Go and find Sapozhnik,' she said, whispering still. 'He'll know what's going on.'

'What about the guard?'

'There's been no guard there for half an hour. Go on, hurry. I'll get Yulia and Tina awake.'

He almost tripped over the guard. There was enough light from a nearby torch to see what had been done. By the time he got to Sapozhnik's quarters, he had a fair idea of what was going on, though he could not begin to guess how many were involved, or why they had turned on their fellow-Cossacks in this way. He slipped on the Count's blood and pitched face forwards onto the floor, mere inches from his head. It took all his resources not to scream aloud.

Back outside, he began to stumble back to his own hut. Suddenly, he was caught again by that momentary flash of light as a torch passed between the trunks of trees. But this time, as he looked round, he saw a more stable light several yards away, and captured against it a man's silhouette. He recognized the man right away by his tall headgear: Father Yefraim. Keeping himself back inside the shadow of the hut in which he had just been, he watched as Yefraim approached one of the guards. A murmur of low voices reached him across the clearing, then he started as he saw Yefraim lift his hand with something long in it and bring it down across the guard. A sabre, a sabre with a sharp blade. Horrified, he crept as quickly as he could in the opposite direction.

By the time he returned to his own hut, sticky with blood, Rebecca, Tina, and Yulia were all awake and getting dressed to go outside. He'd overcome his revulsion and stopped at more than one corpse to remove pistols and ammunition.

'Here,' he said, 'take these.' He handed a pistol each to Rebecca and Yulia. They slipped them inside their pockets without a question.

'What's going on?' Yulia asked.

'I don't know. I just saw Father Yefraim kill one of the guards. Sapozhnik's dead. I don't know who's on what side, or what they mean to do with us. We've got to get out of sight until this is over.'

'Out of sight?' Rebecca looked round the little room in terror. She knew there were no real hiding places in this compound.

'In the mineshaft,' the President answered. 'Bring any clothing, blankets, whatever you can find. And some torches: we'll need those. We've got to get down the mineshaft and stay there until this is over.'

Rebecca looked at him. A greyness had settled round her eyes.

'We'll die down there,' she said.

'We'll die if we stay up here. I'm going down there. I want you with me. Yulia and Tina too, that goes without saying. It's our only hope, love.'

She held him briefly, and kissed him. And as she did so, the words of the Kaddish ran through her mind like grey mice.

63

'Mr Vice . . . I'm sorry, Mr *President* – we've lost that radio link with Russia.'

'Damn it. How long before we get it back again?'

'There's no way to say, sir.'

'This is important, James. A lot depends on that link.'

But, when he thought about it, nothing very much depended on it at all. He'd made his mind up, and his decision had nothing in it for Sapozhnik or his soi-disant Tsar or a soi-disant nobility flown in from all corners of Europe and the States. The Heller administration would be putting its weight behind President Garanin. But before that could be communicated, Garanin owed him one final favour.

'James, can you find out for me if Kureyka Air Force Base has bombers?'

'Bombers, sir?'

'Any kind will do, as long as they can find a target and drop bombs on it.'

'Yes, sir. And where exactly will they be bombing, sir?'

'You can have the coordinates later. And, James, will you see that a direct telephone link is reopened with President Garanin?'

'Yes, sir. I'll be right back, sir.'

'James – this is between President Garanin and myself. Is that understood?'

'It won't go any further, sir.'

'Be sure that it doesn't.'

*   *   *

'How much fuel?'

'Enough to get us back to Saskylakh if we land in the next five minutes, sir.' Pete tapped the fuel gauge for luck. The needle stayed firm at about halfway.

The searchlight fitted beneath the Twin Otter's belly moved back and forwards, tracing the line of the Anabar as it snaked through the forest. Jim knew they were near the mines, but without some sort of visual clue on the ground, it would be suicide to land.

'We're outside the coordinates again, sir.'

'Make another pass. And descend to three hundred feet.'

They went even lower and started back up the river again, watching it snake out like a line of silver etched against the night. Beyond the circle carved by the searchlight, everything was as dark as a dead pig's insides.

'Sir, I think we have something.'

He pointed to his right. In one small area, tiny pinpricks of light danced among the trees, like fireflies out of season.

Jim called back into the fuselage.

'I want someone down there now, with flares, on the ice.'

All three volunteered at once. Jim shouted back again.

'OK, Andrews, you've done this more times than is normal. Take all the flares and give me a landing strip.'

The door opened. Andrews strapped on one of the three parachutes, grabbed the bag containing the flares, and jumped.

'Sir, Kureyka Base has two Tupelov Tu-160s, NATO code-name Badger. They also have a Blackjack belonging to the 121st Heavy Bomber Regiment at Machulishchi.'

'Blackjack?'

'The Russian code-name's "Tushka". It's a long-range strategic bomber, a bigger version of the Rockwell Lancer. Carries four Soloviev jet engines. Room for up to thirty-six thousand pounds of bombs.'

'Tushka, you say?'

'That's right, sir. It means "corpse". Don't ask me why they called it that.'

'How's that call coming along?'

'We have an open line, sir. President Garanin's waiting for you now.'

'Thank you. You pronounce it how?'

'*Tushka*, I believe.'

'And this one's ready to go?'

'It arrived with its full complement of weapons, sir. I don't believe it's been unloaded.'

'Thank you. I'll call you when I finish speaking with Mr Garanin.'

The aide sidled out. Heller hesitated, forming the word 'Tushka' on his lips, then picked up the receiver and put it to his ear.

They'd shut down the mines from one day to the next. One day, you were a slave, the next a free man – or, at least, a little more free than you had been. They just dropped their tools where they stood, turned and walked out of the black hell in which they'd been living for a year or two years – nobody ever got further than that, few made it beyond a week or two. For some, it had been too much. Lacking the strength or the will to walk any further, they'd sat down in the mineshafts, hundreds of them, and died of cold and starvation.

They were still there, their pathetic rags rotted away, their flesh burned, their bones catching the light from Joel Waterstone's torch. In some cases, the skeletons were pretty well complete, in others arms or legs or skulls had fallen from the torso and lay scattered in all directions.

They had to walk bent over, stooped like old men or slaves, their backs aching, their necks almost snapping, so far out of position were they. Yulia tried to prevent Tina from seeing too much, but the child was innocent no longer, and stared at the dead with horrified fascination. She asked no questions, and no-one had answers for her. She was a little girl in hell, and her breath froze white in air that had not been breathed in decades.

Far behind them, they could hear the mad priest shouting their names: 'Nikolai! Alexandra! Alexei! Olga! Tatyana! Anastasia! Marie! Where are you, all my dears? It's time to fulfil the scriptures.'

*   *   *

438

The Otter dropped to the ice with inches to spare. Jim let out a long gasp of relief and fought to keep the aircraft under control as it slowed and taxied to a halt. Everyone piled out, weapons at the ready. If the President's captors had heard them coming, they could be out there, waiting for the order to open fire with mortars, heavy machine guns, or grenade launchers. The thought of Middlewick was still in everyone's mind.

'What the fuck is this place?' asked Andrews.

They were using third-generation night sights to see by. Above, the cloud cover had thinned, and enough starlight was getting through to give them good-quality vision.

'There's some sort of camp on the west bank, some distance back,' said Jim. 'I think it was a Stalinist labour camp. God knows if there's anything left of it. But they're being held in there.'

Wallis, a black kid from Queens, New York, let his light run back and forwards over the ice.

'How many people with them?' he asked.

'No way of knowing. We think it's a military unit of some sort, a Cossack unit,' answered Jim.

'Most likely a *sotnya*,' said Peter. 'My folks are Cossacks, Kuban Cossacks. We're part of a community round Lakewood, New Jersey.'

'Hell, I thought you was an American, man,' Wallis protested.

Peter looked him straight in the eye.

'You ever watch *The Deer Hunter*?'

'*The Deer Hunter*? What the fuck is that?'

'Robert De Niro. Christopher Walken. There's a wedding that goes on for ever, and De Niro shoots a deer. Bad things happen in Vietnam.'

'Sure, I saw that. Walken blows his brains out. You tellin' me he was some kinda Cossack?'

Jim broke in. Their banter had eased the tension, but now time was crucial.

'Break it up, you guys. We have to get moving.'

'Sir, I was just askin', how many of these wackos might have come through here.'

Dropping the banter, Peter gave him his answer.

439

'Hundred or so. Maybe not that many if they've been caught up in any of the fighting hereabouts. What's wrong? You think maybe five of us can't go up against a hundred Cossacks?'

'If they're all like you, we could whap them with our hands behind our backs. But, if you wanna know, I'm asking what these marks are on the ice. Those weren't made by soldiers in boots.'

Peter bent down. As a boy, he'd spent time with a local Russian outfit that re-created historical events on horseback.

'Horses,' he said, straightening. 'Lots of them.'

'Going which way?' asked Jim.

Pete pointed.

'OK, let's get back in the plane. We follow this direction, keeping the spotlights on the west bank. Pete, I want you to take the wheel, Wallis, I'd like you to walk in front, away from the light, and Andrews, same thing, follow in the rear, keep your eyes skinned.'

He was driving them deeper inside all the time, and now he had them trapped in a narrow shaft that looked as though it had been disused even when the mine had been abandoned. The struts holding the walls and roof in place were worn and cracked, and it seemed that, at any moment, the shaft and everything on top of it would collapse and bury them. The President had long ago realized that their guns were of no use to them: a shot in here would send reverberations through miles of tunnels, causing props to splinter and collapse, sending millions of tons of raw earth into every shaft and pit.

Tina was growing weaker with every step she took. Rebecca would support her for a while, then Yulia. They went ahead, while the President took the rear, waiting for the inevitable moment when Yefraim would come crawling round the corner, sword in hand.

The priest's voice came to them from time to time, distorted by the strange geometry of the trenches through which they crept.

'Your Majesties, Your Imperial Holinesses, Your Sublime Highnesses, grant me a word. I have come to serve you, and I have come to serve my God. A moment's audience, that is all I want.'

Down here, cut away from every trace of sunshine, every remnant of heat, the mineworkers must have suffered intolerable cold summer and winter alike. This seemed the very end of the world's coldness, the end of light, the end of life itself.

Right up until the last moment, they thought they could choose, find a side-shaft that would lead back up to the light again, or a second seam in which they could hide until their killer went past, then hurry back to the surface. Then Yulia lifted her torch and saw where their efforts had brought them. A skeleton, pick-axe still in hand, lay face-down in front of the diamond face at which he had been working. Who could say whether he'd died before or after the order had come to shut it all down?

'What's wrong?' asked Rebecca.

Yulia looked at her despairingly.

'This is it, Rebecca. We can't go forward, and we can't go back. He has us where he wants us.'

64

'Sir, sir – just ahead. Can you see it? The river branches off to the left. The left-hand section heads on into some kind of tunnel.'

Jim thought back quickly to the image of the river he'd obtained from the air, and placed it side by side with the lights he'd glimpsed.

'OK, that's it. Pete, we'll park the Otter here. The rest of you, double speed. We go down the tunnel on foot. Everybody keep a sharp eye for lights.'

'What are we looking for, sir?'

'Let's see what there is when we find the lights. Pete, I want you to stay on board. No, no "buts". I know you want to be in at the rescue, but if there's no-one ready to get this bird in the air the second we come out of there, we could be trapped on the ground.'

They began to turn the aeroplane manually, sliding it round on its huge skis until it faced back along the straight stretch on which they had landed. If they left the camp under hot pursuit, the plane would be ready for takeoff. Assuming they were alive and fit enough to get it off the ground.

'This is Tushka Bravo to Tushka Charlie. Request Alpha Check.'

'Wilco, Tushka Bravo. Bearing is one one fiver by seven three, range is one twenty miles.'

'Roger that, Tushka Charlie. ETA is five minutes forty seconds.'

'Copy, five forty.'

'Check left seven degrees. No strangers on radar.'

'This is Tushka Bravo to base. Request authorization for ordnance release. Closing on target.'

'Copy that, Tushka Bravo. You are both cleared hot.'

'Copy, cleared hot. Tushka Charlie, you are cleared hot. Please check angels.'

The tunnel in front of her turned from blackness to light. She could not see him on account of the torch, but she knew he was there, on his hands and knees, creeping towards them. Yulia had volunteered to sit there, to be the first to greet him, in Russian. They had not extinguished their own torches: that would have been too much. She would speak to him, remind him of who and what he was.

'What's that noise?' Andrews stopped and grabbed Jim's arm. They all halted.

High above, and a little distance away, was a sound of low-pitched engines.

'Bombers,' said Jim. 'Long-range. Coming this way.'

'The war must be heating up if they're using brutes like that against their own people. Some poor bastards are going to have hell tonight.'

'OK,' shouted Jim. 'They aren't coming for us. Let's keep moving.'

His face was more lined, his eyes redder, his skin more inflamed than she remembered. She noted the sabre in his right hand. He had leaned the torch against the wall.

'Father Yefraim,' she said, 'may God bless you and your family.' She was kneeling in front of him in the pose of a postulant.

He could barely speak. His lips had twisted into an almost permanent grimace.

'Gift ...' he said. 'Grace ... Angels attend ... You are all blessed.'

She recognized the madness in him, saw the blood that stained the sword blade from top to bottom. Behind her, Tina whimpered, scared beyond measure. Rebecca Waterstone comforted her as best she could, in spite of her own terror. She wondered that Yulia could be so calm.

And Yulia wondered she was still alive.

'How can we help you, Father?' she asked.

'By giving me the Jews,' he said. His voice sounded as though it had been thickened by soot, or by the black soil that pressed in on them from all sides.

'They're not mine to give,' she said.

'Give them to me,' he said, 'and I will see you go free. God does not need your death. But they must die. They are God's antitypes.'

'I don't understand.'

'You don't have to.'

He was growing agitated.

'The Tsar cannot reign without . . . Russia cannot . . . You must . . .'

His hand tightened on the sabre, and he made to draw it back, ready to pierce her.

She acted without hesitation or guile. Her hands reached down between the cloth that covered her legs like a skirt. Beneath it was the diamond miner's pick-axe, its wooden handle broken about halfway down. Holding the handle tightly, she thrust upwards with all her strength, and cried out as though in death or orgasm, and the point of the axe entered Yefraim's throat right under his chin, and came out again through the top of his forehead. He did not cry out or call on God, but a great spasm ran through his body, and another, and another, while Yulia held on, leaving nothing to chance or God or a moment of darkness, while he jerked on her hook like a wounded fish. And at last, his eyes, that had burned with the fire of his killing, lost their light and became fish eyes, and not even then would she let go.

'It's over,' said the President. 'Let's take Tina out of this place.'

'Tushka Bravo to Tushka Charlie. Twenty miles to target.'

'Roger that, Tushka Bravo. Request climb to six thousand feet.'

'Check bomb range and bomb trail first. Make that half a mile and one mile. Do you copy?'

'Roger, Flight-Lead. Beamer eight hundred West. No identifiable bandits within range of target.'

'Closing now. Two minutes to first pass.'

'Sir, there's a landing stage over here. Couple of boats, they don't look up to much.'

'There's a light,' said Wallis in a hushed voice. Life in Queens had taught him how to be tough, but it hadn't prepared him for a place like this.

They avoided the stage, knowing the wood must be perished and could crumble beneath a man's weight. One at a time, they crept between the nearest trees. More lights became visible. Jim directed them through his laryngophone, bringing them in slowly towards the huts.

'This is Wu. I have a body here. Decapitated. In this cold, it's hard to tell how long he's been dead.'

Bobby Wu was the patrol's fifth man. He'd left the army a year earlier to become a martial arts instructor in Wisconsin. His military bosses said he was the greatest living exponent of the Shaolin tradition. Right now, he sounded seriously scared.

'OK, Bobby, where are you?'

'Just outside hut number one.'

'I'll join you.'

Jim fixed on the torch flame that burned outside the hut. Bobby was still bent over the still figure. A few yards away, the dead man's head lay face upwards.

'Let's go inside.'

As they made to move, another voice came through Jim's head-piece.

'Sir, two more bodies here.'

In the air, the growl of engines was growing unavoidable.

Jim tapped Wu's shoulder, and they covered one another going in through the broken door. More bodies lay on pallets or the floor, and someone had placed their heads in a line, like footballs ready for practice.

'OK, everybody, we've got some sort of maniac loose. Watch each other's backs.'

445

They went out again. Next thing, they were shaken by a loud explosion, a giant thudding sound followed by thousands of small echoes.

'What the fuck was that?' 'What the hell . . . ?' 'Jesus!' Jim's headpiece filled with oaths and expressions of incomprehension.

The answer came as a second and third bomb ripped the night apart.

'OK, those fuckers are bombing this site. I'd guess they're making their first pass about a mile away. When they finish, they'll have to turn and come back again. Depends how heavy they want to plant their bombs. Let's check out these huts and get out of here.'

His heart had gone out of the thing, all their hearts, all their joy in action had been lost. He knew they were dead by now, one way or another, and the most he hoped was to find his little girl and take her body home and bury her beside her mother. Maybe he'd find and kill her killer, but it didn't really matter. He just wanted to be somewhere where they didn't kill people.

'Guys, use your flashlights if you have to. We need to do this quickly.'

They ran from hut to hut, while bombs dropped. They could make out the flames that were consuming the trees and lighting up the forest.

'Sir. Will you have a look at this, sir?'

Bobby and he were in the last hut, in which no-one had died. On a low pallet towards the back of the cabin, Bobby had found something. He held it up.

Jim felt his heart turn to water. It was a school pin, an enamel badge that bore the word 'Librarian' in gold letters over a green background. It had been presented to Tina two weeks before the kidnap. He took it in his hand and felt himself about to retch.

'Sir! Get out here fast!' Andrews sounded panicky.

Jim and Bobby Wu dashed from their hut. Andrews and Wallis were standing several yards further into the forest. They had their high-power flashlights switched on and trained on a single spot, what seemed to be the entrance to a mineshaft. Crawling from the entrance came four people, a man, two women, and a child.

'Sir, we need your instructions.'

446

Jim could not have spoken if he had been possessed of all the world's voices. The flashlights showed nothing in particular, just shabby Russian outer clothing and four hunched figures cowering in bright light. But he would have known his daughter anywhere.

'Sir, the bombers are circling to make their second pass. We have to get out of here.'

He couldn't move. He couldn't make those extra feet to pick her up, embrace her, carry her home. The second bomb run began, much louder this time, very near at hand. He reckoned that the third run would wipe them out of existence.

And then something acted on the water that had been his heart, and froze it. Emotions were no use to any of them right now. Emotions would kill them. He took a deep breath and stepped forward, and he went to her first, because she was the reason he was there; nothing else and no-one else mattered. In that moment, he'd gladly have taken her up on his shoulders and walked away, leaving the rest behind to the bombs. It was that simple.

She'd changed a lot, he could see that right away, as if he'd sent her to school one fine morning, and welcomed home a grown woman with something unspeakable in her heart.

'Tina,' he said falteringly, and she looked up at him with wide eyes, and he wondered if she could recognize him in his helmet. 'Tina, it's me, I've come to take you home.'

'Home?'

It was as if the word meant nothing to her. Somewhere nearby, the bombers were pounding the *taiga* back to a stone age before Stalin or the first Tsar.

Behind her, a woman he did not know bent down and spoke into her ear. Then she straightened.

'It's all right,' she said. 'She knows her mother's dead. It's just been hard for her to take in.'

Then Tina had her hand in his.

'I knew all along,' she said. 'I knew you'd come to get me.'

He picked her up, high into the air, and brought her down, pressing her to him. She seemed light as a feather, and when he held her out and looked into her face, her features were drawn and wasted, and there were lines under her eyes. She bent forward and kissed him on the cheek, then her courage broke, and she clung to him, crying her heart to oblivion. He held her for a few moments, not knowing what to do next, then felt her taken from him.

'I'll take her from here, Major. You concentrate on getting us out of here.'

'Yes, Mr President. Air Force One's waiting just off the landing stage. You'll have to run. Those bombers plan to hammer this place into the ground.'

Waterstone looked round him, and brought to mind his own short, terrible memories of the place.

'Maybe it's best they do, Major.'

65

Thibodaux, Louisiana

They walked side by side like old friends, even though it had only been weeks since they first met, and a week that they'd been together. Plato Perodeau had been given indefinite leave, for a holiday back home in Louisiana, at his mother's place. He was still one of the few people who knew the President was alive and back in the States. That he was, in fact, only a few inches away, humming a French song he'd learned the night before, 'Jolie, Petite Blonde', which Plato's Uncle Louis had sung for him at a private *fais do-do* they'd held.

It had been the strangest week of Plato's life. The Waterstones had arrived in Simonsford AFB late one night, as if they'd never gone. A lot of people had been formally sworn to secrecy, and Plato had been called in to see the President the following morning.

'Colonel, I hope you remember me. Joel Waterstone.'

'Well, I hardly think I was going to forget you, sir. I can't say what a pleasure it is for me to see you sitting there large as life in front of me. It's just real good.'

And real tears had started to his eyes.

'Colonel, do you mind if I call you Plato?'

'No, sir, you can call me what you please.'

'Well, Plato, I'd like to take you up on that invitation of yours, to spend some days at your mother's house. As long as you understand you couldn't tell your neighbours, or talk about it.'

'I'm a serving officer in the United States Air Force, sir. I know when to speak and when to keep my mouth shut.'

'Good. It's settled, then. We'll leave today. You, Mrs Waterstone, and myself. I want you to make *les bons temps rouler*.'

That was how he and Joel Waterstone had come to be big buddies, and his wife close friends with Mrs Waterstone. They hadn't talked much about their ordeal, just relaxed and drunk beer, and enjoyed his mother's Cajun cooking. It had been the best week of Plato's life. He'd have broken his heart if it hadn't been for Joel's promise to return next year. It was the strangest thing: he hadn't known any Jews before, and always thought them halfway to being devils, and now here he was, walking side by side with one of the biggest Jews in creation. He knew he'd have to do a lot of thinking when he got back to England.

'What's on your mind, Joel? What are you planning when you get back?'

'I can't tell you those plans, Plato. That's why this week has meant so much to me. Tomorrow, I'll be President again. I'm going to have to do some hard things. Being here has helped that. I'd stay here with you till the Angel of Death came looking for me, but that's not the way life is.'

A long black car drew up in front of the Perodeau house late that afternoon. At the airport, an unmarked Learjet was waiting.

As it lifted from the ground, the President picked up a telephone.

'I'd like to speak to Judge Bradley Hyatt. I'm sorry? No, I realize that, but I want him to come to the phone right away. Tell him this is the President.'

Hyatt was a Supreme Court judge, and Waterstone's only appointee to that body. The older man had been a mentor to Joel at university, and the President trusted him implicitly.

'Joel? Is that you?'

'In person.'

'God, it's good to hear your voice.'

'Likewise. Bradley, I need to know that those arrest warrants are all ready.'

'I have them here. They'll require your signature. I'll make sure

450

they're at the airport when you arrive. You do realize this will cause ripples right through US government?'

'I'm fully aware of that. But I am accustomed to consequences. May I ask if you'd oversee the arrest of Mr Heller in person?'

There was the briefest of hesitations.

'I'd be honoured to.'

'Thank you. I look forward to seeing you tomorrow.'

Disneyworld
Florida

The week had flown by as fast as a Tomcat on afterburners. Tina was still way below par, but the doctors who'd examined her at Simonsford had all agreed that a week visiting Disneyworld would do her more good than a month of their treatment. Nobody expected her to rally fast. With Yulia's help, her story was gradually emerging. Jim had not yet been able to raise the subject of her mother's death. It would have to be done, and everything possible done to help the child come to terms with it. But Jim had not yet come to terms with Laura's violent end himself. For the moment, all he cared about was having Tina back again. Someday soon, he'd have to let her out of his sight again, if she was to have a normal life of any sort. But not yet.

Yulia had accompanied them, equipped at last with a bag of proper medicines. She was fighting with her own demons. Florida provided such a contrast to Siberia, indeed to Russia in general, that she found herself shell-shocked by sights any American would have found tame. As for Disneyworld . . .

While Tina played, Jim and Yulia talked.

'I have to go back, Jim. Russia needs doctors. Now especially.'

'America . . .'

'America has more doctors and more hospitals than it knows what to do with. I must go back. Perhaps not immediately. I want to see how Tina gets on. She was my first life-or-death patient. She's important to me.'

'I know. And you're very important to her. Stay till she's well again. Then you can think thoughts of home.'

451

Tina came haring from yet another dizzying ride. Yulia tried to ration her, but it was useless. And the more useless it was, the better Yulia felt about it.

'Come with me, Yulia,' Tina cried. 'You have to see this for yourself.'

Yulia protested, but with only half a heart.

'Are you coming, Jim?'

He shook his head.

'I'll watch you both from here,' he said.

They went off together, and he watched them go. Yulia was so good with Tina, so careful of her, and so tuned to her needs. It was almost as if . . . He smiled wryly to himself. Was that what he wanted? She'd make the best possible mother for his little girl. And Yulia was pretty and fascinating, he could imagine . . . They climbed onto the ride and waited for the next cycle to begin.

He went to a booth where they sold coloured drinks and ordered three. The terrible thing was, he found he couldn't imagine being married to her. Not properly. He could imagine her naked, or making love to him, all the old simplicities of the male imagination. She was attractive; no normal man would find it hard to imagine her in bed. But it went no further than that, he could not see them talking afterwards, or picture them on the back porch laughing. She did not come to him like that, and he feared for the future.

'Got one for an old friend?'

He spun to find her there, not Yulia, not Laura, but Holly. Holly, whom he'd thought gone for ever.

'Jesus, you frightened me. Look, you made me spill my drinks.'

She laughed. 'That's what you get for being greedy.'

'These aren't all for me.'

'I hope not.'

'But, hey, have one – here.' He held a container out to her, but she shook her head.

'You disappeared,' he said.

'In Simonsford? Yes, I'm sorry about that. There were things the President wanted me to do. I got Mygate out of prison, started putting files together . . . Hell, you don't want to know all this.'

'How'd you find me?'

'I was told you were here. I've finished in Washington for the moment. I wanted to see you.'

He remembered that first night, in the restaurant in Washington. He'd known then.

Turning briefly, he put the cardboard cups back on the booth. When he looked again, he saw her straining to make out something on the ride.

'That's her in the lemon dress. She's much better. Yulia's been looking after her.'

'Yes. I never really got to meet Yulia. Tina was still asleep when I left.'

'She needs to put on weight. At night, she needs sedation. She saw some dreadful things.'

'I've heard.'

'Have you spoken to the President?'

She shook her head.

'I've been dealing with other people.'

'What's he planning to do?'

'There's been a lot of pressure on him just to let the people behind this retire gracefully. It's the way it's usually done. But he isn't doing that. They conspired to kidnap and, in the end, to assassinate the President of the United States. There are to be no amnesties. They will be arrested and tried publicly. I don't think any of them will ever come out of prison again. Some may face the death penalty, for all those deaths in England.'

'Don't forget Forrest Island.'

'No, I've not forgotten that. That was when I really knew.'

'Knew?'

'About you, love. My feelings for you. How afraid I was you might not come back.'

'Yes. I was afraid too. That I'd never see you again.'

He paused. There was a flash of bright yellow as the ride swung past.

'It will take time,' he said. 'She has to get over Laura first. As much as she ever will.'

'I understand.'

'But it will be you. No-one else.'

'Come here,' she said. 'Come to me.'

They held each other then against the world. Like a couple first in love, or a couple long years into love. He kissed her face like delicate china, or glass, as though she might break.

When she looked up, she saw Tina standing five feet away, staring at them. Yulia smiled awkwardly.

'Tina, honey,' Holly said, 'this is an old friend of mine. She helped save your life. And the President, and his wife.'

Tina stretched out an uncertain hand.

'What's your name?' she asked as Holly took her fingers.

'Holly.'

'That's nice. Is that like the stuff they have up North at Christmas?'

'You bet.'

'I guess I missed Christmas this year. But I had Purim and Hannuka, so that was OK.'

Holly could sense the very palpable strain that Tina's every word involved.

'Something tells me you'll be celebrating next Christmas in the White House.'

Tina looked at her wide-eyed.

'But . . .'

'They celebrate Christmas. He's the President, remember. He has to celebrate Christmas. It comes with the job.'

Tina considered this for a moment.

'Does kissing my father come with your job?'

'Not really.'

'But you were kissing him anyway?'

'Is that all right?'

Tina took her time to answer.

'I'll have to think about it a bit.'

'Take all the time you want, sweetheart. Take till Christmas. Take till next year.'

'Just what is your job, anyway? And how come you know my Dad?'

'Well, I have a new job. I'm sort of in charge of computer stuff at the CIA.'

Tina looked impressed.

'Cool. You like doing that?'

'Sure. I have a great boss.'

She looked up at Jim.

'Don't tell me you're working for that asshole Cohen?' he said.

'Jim, you've been out of touch. Cohen's going on trial. He sold out, like you thought he'd done. He's history now.'

'So, who's your new boss?'

'You know him, Jim. General Russ Mygate. He asked me to work for him, and that's what I'm doing. Oh, and I nearly forgot. He would like Brigadier General Jim Crawford to join him at Langley.'

'Did you say . . . ?'

'Brigadier General. You'd have to give up flying. Except, maybe, for a hobby.'

'You said, "join him".'

'He wants you to be Assistant Director. The pay's good, or so he says.'

'This is assuming you're not just making all this up as a means of worming your way into my affections.'

'No, but I promise to leave your computer records alone.'

'And no kissing.'

'You're right. It wouldn't do for us to be seen kissing on the job.'

'And no kissing off the job either,' said Tina. 'Hey, the ride's just starting again. Let's go.'

She took their hands and pulled them towards the ride. Just behind her eyes, her vision faded, and she could see nothing but trees, trees that stretched away from her on all sides, and men with torches riding without a sound. On her left, just where the entrance to the ride began, a mineshaft opened in her mind. From deep inside, there came sounds of someone hammering. She held their hands tightly, and smiled, and took them into the ride.